The shining splendor of our Zebra Lovegram logo on the cover of this book reflects the glittering excellence of the story inside. Look for the Zebra Lovegram whenever you buy a historical romance. It's a trademark that guarantees the very best in quality and reading entertainment.

DESIRE'S AWAKENING

"You should trust me, Mark," Anna scolded gently. "I'm not the coward you obviously think I am."

"No. You are not a coward," he said in a low voice. "Far from it. You are the most beautiful and courageous woman I have ever known."

His compliments caught her by surprise, and she couldn't think of a thing to say. But words were no longer needed.

Slowly Mark lowered his lips to hers, and her heart pounded with anticipation. Instinctively she leaned forward to meet him halfway, eager to sample the taste of him.

His kiss was so tender, yet so powerful, that it left her breathless. Anna closed her eyes as an all-consuming warmth invaded her body. Overwhelmed by a desire to be closer to him, she put her arms around his neck and met his kiss hungrily, yearning to explore the passion that swelled inside her . . . .

Taylor—made Romance From Zebra Books

WHISPERED KISSES (2912, $4.95/5.95)
Beautiful Texas heiress Laura Leigh Webster never imagined that her biggest worry on her African safari would be the handsome Jace Elliot, her tour guide. Laura's guardian, Lord Chadwick Hamilton, warns her of Jace's dangerous past; she simply cannot resist the lure of his strong arms and the passion of his *Whispered Kisses*.

KISS OF THE NIGHT WIND (2699, $4.50/$5.50)
Carrie Sue Strover thought she was leaving trouble behind her when she deserted her brother's outlaw gang to live her life as schoolmarm Carolyn Starns. On her journey, her stagecoach was attacked and she was rescued by handsome T.J. Rogue. T.J. plots to have Carrie lead him to her brother's cohorts who murdered his family. T.J., however, soon succumbs to the beautiful runaway's charms and loving caresses.

FORTUNE'S FLAMES (2944, $4.50/$5.50)
Impatient to begin her journey back home to New Orleans, beautiful Maren James was furious when Captain Hawk delayed the voyage by searching for stowaways. Impatience gave way to uncontrollable desire once the handsome captain searched *her* cabin. He was looking for illegal passengers; what he found was wild passion with a woman he knew was unlike all those he had known before!

PASSIONS WILD AND FREE (3017, $4.50/$5.50)
After seeing her family and home destroyed by the cruel and hateful Epson gang, Randee Hollis swore revenge. She knew she found the perfect man to help her—gunslinger Marsh Logan. Not only strong and brave, Marsh had the ebony hair and light blue eyes to make Randee forget her hate and seek the love and passion that only he could give her.

Available wherever paperbacks are sold, or order direct from the Publisher. Send cover price plus 50¢ per copy for mailing and handling to Zebra Books, Dept. 3140, 475 Park Avenue South, New York, N.Y. 10016. Residents of New York, New Jersey and Pennsylvania must include sales tax. DO NOT SEND CASH.

WILD WESTERN BRIDE

ROSALYN ALSOBROOK

ZEBRA BOOKS
KENSINGTON PUBLISHING CORP.

ZEBRA BOOKS

are published by

Kensington Publishing Corp.
475 Park Avenue South
New York, NY 10016

First printing: October, 1990

Printed in the United States of America

This book is dedicated to the Children's Aid Society of New York, now 137 years strong.

Acknowledgments

I have recently come across many "exceptional" people who have proved quite willing to go one step above and beyond when helping total strangers locate needed information. I want those people to know how very much I have appreciated their assistance.

Therefore, special acknowledgments go out to: everyone connected with the National Committee for Adoption in Washington, D.C.; to Winnifred O'Hara with the Texas Department of Human Services in Austin; to Stella Coate Wells, RN, and Dr. Paul E. Weathers, MD, both of Denton, Texas; to Ruby Kilburn of Pittsburg, Texas; to Jeff Wells of Pilot Point, Texas; to Bill Wells, also of Denton; to Tina and Ted Williams of San Antonio; to the American Adoption Congress in New Mexico; to Mark McAck with the Texas Board of Vocational Nurse Examiners in Austin; to Pat Palmer with Searchline in Irving, Texas; to Larry and Katy Vick, also of Denton; to the Texas State Library, Archives Division, in Austin; to the women who work in Judge John Narsutis's and Judge Phillip Vick's office in Denton County; and especially to Judge Phillip Vick.

Also, special thanks to the Texas State Historical Association in Austin; to Margi Bice of Garland, Texas; to Enedina Martinez with the Texas Bureau of Vital Statistics in Austin; to both the Service Rubber Company and the Church of Nazarene in Rock Island, Illinois; to the Upshur County Library in Gilmer, Texas; to Tom Rutledge with the United States Post Office, Gilmer branch; and to Bonnie, a very convincing lady indeed. Also a very, very special thank you goes to Carole Ruth Stickrod Sanford, who gave me what no one else could. Also, to Tom Owens, DC, of Hollywood, Florida, for the part he had in all this. While I'm at it, I'd like to thank Mom, Bobby, and my two sons, who drive me crazy and keep me sane all at the same time.

Chapter One

1890

"Jenny, let me redo your bow," Anna Thomas said, calling the small girl to her side.

She wanted the five-year-old to look her very best when they disembarked from the train. It was important all these children make the very best first impressions possible.

"And let's run a brush through your hair again." Since Jenny was otherwise such a plain child, Anna wanted those beautiful blonde curls to capture the morning sun and shine like expensive silk.

Hurriedly, she worked to tie Jenny's sash, then felt a sharp tug at the back of her tailor-fitted indigo skirt. "Miss Anna, is my shirt tucked in all right in back?" little Johnny wanted to know, twisting in an impossible effort to see behind him.

Anna smiled when she noticed the child's attempt to put his shirt neatly into the waistband of his trousers. The front was magnificently done, but in the back his suspenders were twisted and his shirt puckered out in several places. A wad of cloth bulged below the waistband, where he had failed to smooth the hem. It would crush what little confidence Johnny had mustered if he knew how poorly he had tucked in the back. He so wanted to impress the people waiting outside. They all did. She could see it in their wide eyes and in their afraid-to-hope expressions.

"Almost perfect," she told him. "You do have one place, though, that could use a little straightening. Let me finish with Jenny's hair and I'll help you with your shirt."

"Hurry up, Miss Thomas," Gordon Franklin interrupted in a low, cautionary voice after he walked up the aisle behind her. He spoke as if afraid he might be overheard by the people who might be outside waiting for them, though there was very little chance of that happening over the loud rumble of the train's engine. "We have people waiting."

"I realize there are people waiting, and I am hurrying," Anna informed her supervisor, though she had not actually seen the people outside. Just before they had arrived at the train station, she had instructed the children to pull all the shades down. She'd discovered long ago that they remained much calmer as a group when they could not see whoever waited for them.

Kneeling, she quickly turned Johnny about and straightened first his suspenders, then his shirt, tucking the hem with tidy folds beneath his trousers. She then pulled a comb out of her skirt pocket and ran it through his thick reddish-blond hair. When she spoke again, she did not take time to glance up at Gordon, who tapped his foot impatiently. "Why don't you go on out there and greet everyone who has come to meet the train? I'll have the children ready in a few more minutes."

"You need to do something about Abel's shoes. They aren't buckled, as usual," he told her, then strode toward the front of their privately occupied passenger car. "I'll prepare everyone for the children."

He paused to straighten his coat, derby, and necktie, then pulled the door open and stepped outside.

10

Anna frowned, wondering why he couldn't have offered to buckle the child's shoes for her. She had enough to do. But then again, *he* was the supervisor on this trip, she was merely an aide. It was his job to see to the legalities of the adoptions. And even though she had worked for the Children's Society far longer, her job was to take care of the children's personal welfare while they traveled together on what was rapidly becoming known as the Orphan Train.

It was also her job to make sure the children were well groomed. Sighing, she turned her attention to the ribbon that had come loose from Stacy's long, fat braid. At least the group had dwindled down to only thirteen children. They had been very fortunate to find homes for nine of their orphans at the last stop.

At the end of most trips, there were usually one or two remaining children, children who were not fortunate enough to be adopted, children who would return to the orphanage in New York with hopes of finding parents on their next trip on the Orphan Train. But, after having already placed twenty-seven of this particular group, and with a town this size and one other town still ahead, there was a good chance that on this trip all the children would be placed.

The thought of that sent waves of nervous energy through her. In her four years of working for the New York Children's Aid Society, she had never experienced the joy of having been on an Orphan Train that had found a home for every child aboard.

Holding onto that hope, she hurriedly retied bows, brushed hair, buckled buckles, smoothed out stockings, washed faces, and straightened shirts, skirts, and trousers until she felt the children were finally ready. After cautioning them one last time to be on their best behavior, she stood and smiled proudly at the little troop of five- to twelve-year-olds.

Because the youngest children as well as the very oldest were always the first to be selected, all that remained were those ranging in these age groups.

"Well, this is it. Smiles in place. Let's show them what cheerful little boys and girls you are."

Everyone smiled for her except Jamie and Abel, who both seemed very bothered about something. Although it was not unusual for five-year-old Abel to look pensive, his older brother, Jamie, was usually full of mischievous laughter. But, today, when he took his younger brother's hand in his to make certain they were not separated, Jamie's freckled face had pulled into a solemn frown. Suddenly he looked much older than his eight years.

"Jamie, I said to smile. You've got yours turned upside down," Anna said, hoping to encourage a smile out of him yet. She understood why he was so pensive, and it broke her heart to know he had every reason to be. She glanced then at Abel. "Maybe if Abel would put on a bright, happy smile, you would feel more like smiling, too. How about it, Abel? A sweet little smile for Miss Anna?"

Abel just stared at her as he always did, his big gray-green eyes expressionless.

"He ain't gonna smile," Jamie said, disappointed that Miss Anna had yet to accept the fact that Abel rarely showed any emotion.

"Don't say 'ain't,' Jamie," she corrected him. "If we want these people to get the very best impression of you children, you must use proper grammar."

Jamie sighed heavily and looked down at the scuff marks marring the wooden floor. "Yes, ma'am, I know." Then he slowly lifted his large hazel-color eyes. Tears clung precariously to his lower lashes. "It's just that I heard Mr. Franklin say how this is the next to the last stop. Do you think me and Abel is going to get picked this time? Or are we going to have to go back to the orphanage again? Abel 'specially don't like having to sleep in that room with twelve other boys. They always pick on him and laugh at him."

Anna had opened her mouth to correct his grammar, but decided it was not really the best time for that. Kneeling in front of the small boy, she rested her hands gently on his shoulders and met his gaze. "I honestly can't say. You have to remember that because there are two of you, it will take a little longer to place you. Most people prefer to take in only one child at a time. The thought of suddenly being responsible for two new children can be a little overwhelming."

"But Eddie and Christine found theirselves a home together," he said, his expression a little more hopeful. "So, there is still some folks out there willing to take in two of us at a time."

The sheer desperation in the small boy's voice tugged painfully at Anna's heart.

Knowing he needed reassurance, she gently massaged the bunched muscles that stretched across his shoulders and smiled, blinking back a sudden rush of tears. She wanted to find the right words to comfort him, to take away all his heartbreaking fears and somehow restore his hope. "Of course there are still people out there who are willing to take in more than one child at a time. Why, a few couples have been known to take in three and even four. We just have to find those people is all."

Finally Jamie smiled. "Maybe some of the folks who lives right here in this town are the sort to take on more than one of us. Maybe me and Abel are goin' to find us a real home with a real family this very Tuesday. Do you think that's so?"

"There's always that possibility," she answered in a light, happy voice, silently praying it would happen.

She was relieved to see his expression lift. A smiling, cheerful child had a much better chance of being selected than a sullen, withdrawn child — which was why she had such grave doubts about Jamie and Abel anyway. Although Jamie was usually very cheerful and full of laughter and boyish fun, Abel remained extremely withdrawn.

It broke Anna's heart to know that the sad little five-year-old had not spoken a word in well over two years. Though the doctors had been unable to find anything physically wrong with him, the little boy did not speak. Nor did he laugh. In fact, Abel rarely showed emotion of any kind. It was as if he was afraid to reveal anything about himself. And as long as Abel continued to be silent, it would be almost impossible to place him. Handicapped children were always difficult to place, and the fact that the two boys hoped to be adopted as a pair made finding a home for them that much harder. It might be years before the right people came along. But she didn't want to think such negative thoughts right now.

"Give me your hand, Abel," Anna said, still trying to sound cheerful as she reached out to him. "Let's go out there and see exactly what sort of people *are* waiting for us."

Obediently, Abel slipped his tiny hand out of his brother's grasp and placed it in hers. Together they walked toward the front of the passenger car with Jamie right behind them and the rest of the children directly behind him. No one spoke. No one had the courage. They were all too preoccupied with thoughts of what lay ahead.

One at a time the frightened children stepped off the train and out onto the platform. They looked around curiously for the people who usually crowded around them. The only person at the depot other than

14

Gordon Franklin and the usual station employees was an elderly man dressed in black who looked to be in his sixties. He was very thin, balding, and slightly stooped—hardly the type to adopt a small child. The children whispered to each other, quietly voicing their worst fears, that no one had cared enough to come and meet them. None of them would find a home here.

"Where is everyone?" Anna asked, glancing worriedly at Gordon, able to hear many of the children's pitiful comments.

"Waiting at the church," Gordon told her and pointed off toward the main part of town. "That's where the children will be viewed." He then turned to glower at Johnny and Greg, who had immediately passed this information along to those who stood too far away to hear. Immediately the two boys froze, so still they could have passed for statues.

"Hello, I'm Reverend Cross," the man beside Gordon said to Anna in a warm, friendly voice when it was obvious he was not to be formally introduced.

The reverend displayed a smile so kind and so deeply sincere that she immediately returned it with one of her own.

His smile widened. "I've been asked to escort all of you to the church."

"I'm very pleased to meet you," she responded, offering her hand. "I'm Anna Thomas. And these are the boys and girls who hope to find homes here in your lovely town."

The children shifted nervously when the reverend turned to look at them, all except Johnny and Greg, who had yet to even twitch a muscle. Their gazes were fixed on Mr. Franklin.

"And what a fine group of children they are! Come, let us go on to the church. My wife and several of the ladies in the congregation have prepared fruit punch and cookies for these youngsters. Everyone is so very eager to meet them."

"Come, children," Gordon called out in clipped tones, patting his hands together as if he were herding sheep. "Form a single line. We have to walk down the boardwalk to the end of the block where we will all turn left and cross the street. Follow the person in front of you at all times. I don't want anyone getting out of line."

Anna rolled her eyes heavenward, exasperated. She tried to keep in mind that this was Gordon Franklin's first trip, and he still had a lot to learn about handling children. Even so, the man was almost thirty years old. Didn't he have enough sense to know they, like anyone, resented being treated like mindless geese? Maybe it would be better for all concerned if he stayed in his office and left these train trips to someone else.

"I don't think there is much chance the children will get lost between here and there. It's only a block away," she commented.

Gordon looked at her with a raised brow, warning that she'd come close to overstepping her bounds— again. "Shall we go, then?"

Anna glanced back at the children with a what-are-we-going-to-do-with-this-man expression that caused many of them to burst out in fits of giggles, but she cautioned them to hush by lifting a finger and pressing it firmly against her lips.

Gordon never looked back, but his chin lifted and his shoulders arched visibly the moment he heard the children's laughter. Anna grimaced, aware of the tongue-lashing he would no doubt dispense later that day, when they were alone again. Gordon Franklin always took every little thing that happened far too seriously, and there was no doubt in Anna's mind that he

16

had reached the conclusion he'd been personally insulted by the children's laughter and probably believed she had purposely encouraged them.

But at least the incident had lightened the children's mood. Smiles had returned to their faces—despite the fact that barely a hundred yards away their fate awaited them.

Shortly after the children had had their fill of fruit punch and freshly baked cookies, the initial viewing began. The children were presented either individually or in pairs, until all thirteen had been introduced and a little had been told about the background of each. Then, with no further delay, the couples who had shown any real interest in adopting a child were asked to take the children home and simply get to know them for the remainder of the day.

Everyone was instructed to meet back at the church by six o'clock, when a potluck supper would be provided by the same generous women who had brought the punch and cookies. At that time the formal selection process would begin. By bedtime, Anna and Mr. Franklin would know which of the children had been selected and which would be traveling on to the next town.

Facing several long hours before the children returned, Anna took a leisurely stroll through the busy little East Texas town. She knew only too well that the next few hours, until the formal selection process was finally over, would be the longest of the day.

While browsing in the local shops and getting to know the many people who stopped to talk with her, Anna quickly became comfortable with the thought of leaving some of their children in such a place. Pinefield was nothing like the thriving, bustling city of New York, but it had a church, a school, a bank, a train station, a sheriff's office, a freight company, a ho-

17

tel, two restaurants, two liveries, a large mercantile, and a dozen or so individual shops.

The town even had its own doctor, whose brightly painted office had been built on to the side of his house, which, oddly enough, was just the other side of the undertaker's.

Dozens more houses lined the narrow streets that branched off from the main part of town. The homes in town were for the most part neat, with well-kept yards filled with shade trees and brightly colored flowers. But the best attraction of all was that the people of Pinefield were very friendly.

It was exactly the sort of town where her children could find good, decent homes, and families who would accept them as individuals and love them for what they were. She was eager to see as many children as possible placed here.

Her thoughts quickly turned to Jamie and Abel. Wouldn't it be wonderful if they found a home here? Her heart raced at such a pleasing thought. What if the young couple who had taken them both home decided to keep them? They had certainly seemed like caring people and would make wonderful parents for the two brothers. That thought was so delightful that she held it close to her heart during the rest of her excursion.

Eventually, though, the afternoon shadows lengthened and six o'clock grew near. Anna returned to the church to help the women set out the food they had brought for the evening meal. In groups, the people who had been there earlier reentered the small church through the massive front doors. The children were immediately returned to Anna's care.

Though it hurt to think of never seeing their bright, caring faces again, having grown so terribly fond of the little scamps, Anna hoped with all her heart that

18

tonight would prove to be their last meal together. The children who were chosen that evening would be permitted to go home with their new families and start their new lives. Early Friday afternoon, she would be forced to say good-bye to those children forever. As always, her heart filled with the starkly contrasted feelings of loving hope and utter despair.

During the meal, Anna's attention stayed with the children. Some of them ate heartily, and others were too nervous to eat anything at all. She wondered which of those adorable faces she would never see again and which would suffer yet another bitter disappointment. Finally the reverend stood near the pulpit and clapped his hands loudly to capture everyone's attention. The hour of reckoning had arrived.

"Now that we've all eaten our fill, it is time to let Mr. Franklin and Miss Thomas know your decisions. Mr. Franklin has asked that the children be taken outside to play while those of you who are interested in adopting one or more of the orphans move forward to the front pews. He will speak to the couples one at a time in my chambers." He paused, glancing out over the crowd, and smiled. "It is my hope that by now many of you will have found a warm place in your hearts for these homeless waifs. I truly hope to see several of those bright young faces in my congregation on Sunday."

As soon as Anna had been assured the children were properly supervised by several of the older women from the church, she hurried back inside. She wanted to be present during the final proceedings. She had to know who would be given the responsibility of her children. It was important to her that those not returning to the Orphan Train on Friday would be left behind in good, loving hands.

"So you both feel you can provide Jenny with a

happy home along with proper food and clothing—and, of course, a good education," Gordon was saying to a young couple when she first entered the room.

As was usually the case, both prospective parents sat on the edges of their seats, leaning forward in their eagerness to convince him of their worthiness.

"Oh, yes, sir. I got me a real nice farm just south of here. I grow some of the best corn and raise some of the fattest pigs around these parts. You can ask anybody. They'll tell you," the man said, nervously twisting what was probably his best Sunday hat. Anna was pleased to see such earnestness on his face and on his wife's face. They truly wanted Jenny.

"And, because we lost our own child a few years back, we already have a furnished room waiting for her," the wife added quickly.

Anna felt her body tense. Were they trying to replace their own lost child with Jenny? Many times that meant trouble. No child could ever replace the loss of another and might be unreasonably hurt while trying.

"You've recently lost a child?" Gordon asked, jerking his gaze away from the papers in his hands to look at both of them.

"No, not recently. Our son died several years ago," the husband explained. "We just never saw a need to make any other use of the room, so all the furniture is still in there. There's a half bed, a dresser, shelves, and a small desk with two chairs."

Anna felt some of the apprehension drain out of her. If they were out to replace their son, they'd have chosen a boy. Evidently, Jenny had stolen their hearts all on her own. Anna smiled while she quietly slipped into a nearby chair, not wanting to interrupt the proceedings. She was there solely to listen and to answer any questions the prospective parents might ask about the children themselves, because she knew them far better than Gordon. All Gordon could tell them was what little had been written in his reports.

"Well, Mr. and Mrs. Jackson, since everything seems to be in order here," Gordon said, glancing again at the forms they had just filled out, "and since you both seem so very eager to open your home to Jenny, I see no reason why you can't go right out there and tell her the good news. You may take her home with you tonight. Your two-month trial period begins as of now. Then, if, after the follow-up visit, you and the child have no complaints, Jenny can be yours permanently."

The man and woman hugged each other, then the husband turned and stuck his hand out to Gordon. "Thank you, Mr. Franklin. Thank you so much."

Anna was torn between the urge to go outside and watch while the Jacksons told Jenny the good news and the desire to stay put and find out who was next to be selected. Finally, she chose to stay.

Shortly after the Jacksons had left the small room, the reverend entered with another couple. Her heart froze when she first glanced up. She recognized them immediately — they were the pair who had taken Jamie and Abel. She felt such a surge of hope and joy that she could hardly breathe. At last! Jamie and Abel would have a home — a real home. It was all Anna could do to stay seated and not rush forward to hug them both.

"Mr. Franklin, this is Tom and Jane Porterfield," the reverend said by way of introduction. "They have a small farm north of here and come in to services nearly every Sunday." He then quietly stepped back.

"Any children of your own?" Gordon asked as he reached for the forms they had filled in while waiting to talk with him. He then indicated that they should sit in the two chairs facing the desk.

"No, sir," Tom answered. He waited until his wife had settled onto the edge of her chair before stiffly lowering himself into the chair beside it. He started to place his hat back on his head, then realized that was not the thing to do and put it in his lap. "My wife can't have children."

Anna's heart accelerated to a rapid beat. Childless couples often made the best adoptive parents. She wanted to sing out with jubilation.

"And which of our children interests you?" Gordon asked, already glancing down at the form to make sure everything was in order.

Anna leaned forward in her chair. She wanted to hear the boys' names roll off their tongues—hear if they spoke of them with true affection or with calm reserve.

"Jamie Wilkins," Tom told him with a definite nod of his head.

Anna waited an endless moment for them to speak Abel's name, too. But his name did not come. Her feelings of joy turned immediately into dark pangs of despair.

"Jamie Wilkins," Gordon repeated, reaching next for Jamie's file so he could have it ready in case any questions about the boy's background were asked. "And why have you chosen Jamie?"

"Because he's such a bright and personable young man. My wife took to him right off," Tom said, smiling as he turned to glance at his wife, who stared intently at the polished wooden floor beneath her slippered feet.

Anna knew she was not supposed to interrupt, but she couldn't help it. She could not allow this couple to take Jamie and not at least consider the possibility of accepting Abel as well. "But what about his brother, Abel? Surely you don't intend to take one child and not take the other. They are brothers. They belong together."

"Miss Thomas!" Gordon admonished. His brows drew into a menacing scowl as if to issue a warning. "It is not your place to comment during these proceedings."

"But it's true." Anna knew she was getting into even worse trouble by continuing to speak out, but she didn't care. Those boys' future was at stake. "Jamie and Abel love each other. You can't separate them. You just can't."

"Miss Thomas, that is quite enough." Gordon's grip tightened on the papers until they buckled.

Anna knew she would find no sympathy there. Turning to the Porterfields, she continued her pleas for the boys' happiness. "Mrs. Porterfield, if you truly care for Jamie, as your husband says you do, you will find room in your home for Abel, too. It would be too cruel not to. Jamie loves his younger brother dearly, and Abel adores Jamie."

Jane Porterfield's lips pressed together, but she continued to stare sightlessly at the floor. Anna could tell by the way her hands clutched the knitted handbag in her lap that this decision to separate the boys had not come easily. Hoping there might still be a chance, Anna knelt at the young woman's feet and gazed imploringly into her downturned face only to discover that the woman refused to look at her, refused to meet her gaze straight on. "Please, Mrs. Porterfield, reconsider . . . please don't separate those two boys."

The woman's eyes pressed closed, as if attempting to hide from her own tortured thoughts.

Tom reached over to place a comforting hand over his wife's. He looked pleadingly, first at Anna, then at Gordon. "I am not a wealthy man. We can afford to take in only one child at this time."

23

"Then why did you select both boys to take home with you? Why didn't you pick only one to take home?"

"Because my wife wanted to get to know Jamie and Jamie refused to go home with us unless Abel went too. But we really cannot afford to take care of two little boys right now."

"Are you sure? Are you absolutely sure?" she asked, directing her attention to him. "What if by some divine miracle, your wife became pregnant? Would you then be forced to give Jamie up because you can afford only one child?"

"No, of course not. If that were ever the case, we'd find a way to manage," he insisted. "Once Jamie becomes a part of our family, he will always be a part of our family." His forehead notched. "But what if we took in both boys and she suddenly became pregnant? There'd be no way I could clothe and feed three children. Still, I would find a way to feed two if God suddenly chose to bless us with a child of our own and we already had Jamie. Once I've claimed that boy for my son, he'll always be my son. I'd never send him away."

"Because deep down inside you know that a family and its ties are important," Anna concluded. "Which is why it is so very important for these two boys to remain together. They are already a family."

"I'm sorry," Tom said with finality, and now he, too, refused to meet her gaze. "We only want Jamie."

"Why? Because Abel does not speak?" Anna asked, suddenly wanting to make them admit the truth. Angered to the breaking point, she wanted to hurt them as much as they were hurting her, as much as they were about to hurt Jamie and Abel.

Tom glanced at his wife and again squeezed her hand reassuringly before answering. "Partly."

Anna's eyes widened. "Then you admit it? You admit that the reason you don't want Abel is because he's not quite like the other boys?"

Tom's expression hardened. "Okay, I do admit it. Even if we *could* handle two children financially, we could never cope with a child who cannot speak. It would be too large a burden for my wife, never knowing what was inside the child's head, never knowing what he was feeling. The boy does not respond to anything. To pour our love into him and never have it openly returned would be too painful."

"But he can show love. He *does* show love!"

Tom thrust his angular chin forward, took a deep breath, and looked at Gordon with renewed determination. "We only want Jamie. We believe we can give him a good Christian home with plenty of love. We will feed him, clothe him, and see to it that he gets a proper education."

"We can't ask for more than that," Gordon agreed, then returned his attention to the forms in his hand.

"What?" Anna asked, horrified to have heard the decisive tone in Gordon's voice. She could not believe he would even consider separating the two boys, yet it sounded to her as though he'd already made up his mind to do just that.

Jumping to her feet, she reeled about to face him, her expression a twisted mixture of stark anger and total disbelief. "Those two boys have already been separated from their parents. Don't separate them from each other, too. You will cause irreversible damage if you do, especially to Abel. If Jamie is taken away from him, he will withdraw into himself even more."

Now even Gordon refused to meet her gaze. Instead, he continued his perusal of the forms the Porterfields had handed him. "My job is to see that as many of these children get placed as possible. If I have to split up those two boys in order to find one of them

25

a good home, then I will. The boys will simply have to understand that it is the best thing for both of them."

Anna's mind reeled with disbelief. This could not be happening. Tears burned her eyes while her frustration grew to unbearable proportions. Spinning about to make one last desperate plea, she sank to her knees again and took Mrs. Porterfield's hands into hers. "Please don't do this. Either take them both or pick one of the other boys. Just don't separate those two."

"Miss Thomas, that is quite enough!" Gordon thundered, rising from his chair as if he intended to remove her forcefully from the room. "You have no real say in this matter. The only reason I've allowed you to be in here is because I know how much these children mean to you. But until you learn to keep your opinions to yourself, I must ask you to leave."

The reverend, who had remained quiet through the ordeal, stepped forward and grasped her gently by the arm, pulling her to her feet. "Miss Thomas, why don't we step outside and get some fresh air? I think it would do you a world of good." His voice was firm, yet filled with compassion. He was clearly trying to solve the problem without watching her suffer the embarrassment of being forced to leave the room.

Blinking back her tears in an effort to focus on his kind face, she tried to solicit his help. If she could only get one other person to take her side, maybe she could force these people to listen. "Please, don't let them do this. Don't let them separate those two boys."

"It is not my place to intervene," he said in a calm and soothing manner while he slowly and skillfully led her from the room. "Nor is it yours. I think we must leave this decision entirely to the Porterfields and Mr. Franklin. It really is their decision."

Suddenly, it felt as if her heart had been impaled on sharp spikes. The situation was utterly hopeless.

Nothing she said had dissuaded the Porterfields or Gordon Franklin from their horrible decision. The only thing she could do now was to be close by when the boys were told of their fate and do whatever she could to comfort them, especially Abel. Quietly she allowed the reverend to lead her outside to where the Orphan Train children and several of the town children were busily playing a boisterous game of kick ball in the dim light of the narrow, brick-lined street.

Knowing Abel would be sitting off to the side watching his brother play, she hurried to find him. As expected, he sat on the curbside, his hands folded neatly in his lap. Except for his eyes, which followed his brother's every move, he sat perfectly still.

Afraid her voice might reveal the hard, throbbing ache that filled her heart, thereby alerting him to the fact that something terrible lay just ahead, she said nothing when she sank down onto the sidewalk beside him and waited with her knees tucked under her chin.

All too soon, the Porterfields came outside and walked toward the children. Jamie froze when he glanced up and noticed they were headed in his direction. His hazel eyes widened with such sincere hope that Anna thought she could not endure what was about to happen. Part of her wanted to run away and not return until it was over, but another part of her had to be there for them, had to do what she could to cushion the blow.

"Jamie, come here," Tom Porterfield called out when he neared the end of the sidewalk.

Jamie swallowed hard and did as he was told. The other children stood by, watching silently, eager to hear the good news, that Jamie and Abel had finally found a home.

Tom knelt before the boy so he could watch his reaction. "Jamie, it's settled, son. You are going home

27

with us. We are going to be a family."

Abel watched them intently, but the only indication that he'd overheard what had been said was in the rapid manner in which he blinked. He turned and looked at Anna as if seeking verification. Anna felt a tiny piece of her heart fall away and plunge into the very depth of her soul. She reached over and took his small hand in hers.

"You mean it?" Jamie asked. His mouth dropped open with sudden excitement. Then he turned to look at Abel, his face glowing with sheer joy. "Did you hear that, Abel? We got us a real home. A *real* home. And we got us a real family!" Then, unable to contain his happiness any longer, he threw his arms around his new father and squealed with delight.

"I'm afraid you've misunderstood," Tom said, swallowing hard.

Anna's grip tightened around Abel's tiny hand. She wished she could pull him right into her heart and protect him there. She bit her lower lip. Her stomach curled into a painful knot. How she dreaded Tom Porterfield's next words!

"Abel is not going home with us. We have room at our house for only one child and we've chosen you."

Jamie jerked back as if he'd suddenly been burned. "You can't mean it." He then turned to Anna; his eyes instantly filled with tears. "I won't go. Not without Abel." His voice rose with each word he spoke, straining until his lower lip trembled uncontrollably. "He's my brother."

Having expected complications, Gordon had delayed seeing the next couple and had come outside to assist with Jamie. "I'm afraid you'll have to go. The arrangements have already been made. You now have a new home with the Porterfields."

"No. I'm not living *anywhere* without Abel. You can't

28

make me." His entire body shook. "Please, don't make me."

Gordon showed no emotion whatever. "Son, don't make this more difficult than it already is. Just go quietly. It will be best for everyone in the long run."

"I won't go. You can't make me," he cried, becoming hysterical. Rushing to Anna, he flung his arms around her shoulders and held tight. "Miss Anna, don't let them take me. Please, Miss Anna, don't let them take me."

Anna squeezed her eyes shut, unable to bear the pain spilling out of her heart, filling her with anguish. "I-I'm sorry, Jamie. I've already done all I can. They won't listen to me."

Tom stepped forward and grasped Jamie by the shoulder. When he spoke, his voice was firm, but not without compassion. "Come along, son. I know it will be painful at first, but eventually you'll get over it."

"No!" he shrieked and tried to jerk his shoulder out of the man's strong grasp. "I'm not going with you!"

"Yes, Jamie, you are," Gordon put in firmly.

Jamie twisted from side to side in his attempt to wrench himself free, but his new father had too tight a grip on him. "Let me go!"

Pain swelled in Anna's chest until it pressed hard against her lungs, making it impossible to breathe while she watched Tom Porterfield and Gordon Franklin literally drag the screaming boy away. When she felt Abel's tiny hand tighten around the three fingers he held and then looked down to find tears spilling from his huge gray-green eyes, she quickly gathered him into her arms and held him close. *How much more heartbreak can one little boy take?* she wondered, with a fresh onslaught of pain.

Chapter Two

There was still a chance, however slight, Anna might yet be able to stop Jamie's adoption from taking place. Somehow she had to convince the local judge not to approve it. Although Gordon had already penned his signature to the papers that would set everything into motion, they were worthless until an area judge had also signed the papers. And because Gordon had not scheduled a meeting with the local judge until ten o'clock the following morning, Anna still had the opportunity to try to do *something* to keep the boys together.

But first she needed to find out where the judge stayed whenever he was in Pinefield and then go there to have a talk with him that very night; yet she was not too sure he would appreciate such an intrusion that close to bedtime. He might not listen to her plea with as clear and open a mind as she'd liked. But then again, if she could get to him before Gordon and the Porterfields did, she might be able to convince him not to sign those papers.

With that thought in mind, she vowed to awaken at the crack of dawn, find out where the judge had his breakfast, and be there waiting for him. Or better yet, she would wait until he had finished with his morning meal.

Anna clung to her decision tenaciously while she continued to hold Abel in her arms, allowing his silent tears to soak the front of her blouse. Though he made no audible sound other than ragged gasps and he trembled violently, it was the first real sign of emotion Abel had shown. Her heart ached with the need to comfort him, to take away some of his pain, all the while knowing that was impossible. Abel's pain would be a long time healing.

That night, after several quilt pallets had been prepared for her and the six remaining children, Anna continued to cradle Abel in her arms, aware by the way he continued to clutch at her clothing that he desperately needed to be held. Though generally it was not a good idea to coddle the children like that, she felt this situation called for it, and while Gordon Franklin took advantage of the comfortable room offered by the reverend and his wife, she stayed with the children.

Still angry at the injustice in separating the boys, Anna found it hard to fall asleep. After she had turned out the lamp and the church filled with darkness, she continued to hold Abel close. When he finally fell asleep, she lowered him from her arms to her own pallet, then lay down beside him. She kept one arm around him, holding him protectively, while she tried to figure out exactly what she would say to the judge. It needed to be something powerful, something that would make him understand how serious a mistake it would be to allow this separation.

Hours passed before exhaustion finally overcame her and she slipped off into a deep but fitful sleep full of shadows and faceless children.

When she awoke the next morning, the first thing to

enter her mind was the judge. Glancing at the windows, she saw that the stained glass glowed with dim, cheerful colors. The sun had already risen, but barely. She had to hurry if she wanted to speak to the judge before Gordon or the Porterfields did.

Having slept in her clothes, all she needed to do to make herself presentable was brush out as many of the wrinkles as possible, put her shoes back on, wash her face, and comb her hair. She'd start with her hair.

Not until she had sat up and lifted her hand to check her hair did she realize that Abel was gone. Her heart pounded frantically when she glanced around at the other children, hoping he had snuggled against one of the others in his sleep, thinking it was his brother.

"Abel!" she shouted, bringing the other children awake with a start. There was no response to her call. She quickly shoved her feet into her shoes, buckled only the top buckles, and stood. "Abel? Where are you? Come out where I can see you."

Knowing he would not answer even if he was still somewhere in the building, she searched the pews for him, hoping he had decided to make his bed in one of them.

"What's wrong?" Johnny asked, sitting up on his pallet and rubbing his eyes with the backs of his fists. "Where's Abel?"

"I don't know. Help me find him."

Soon all the children were searching for Abel, first inside the building; then, without bothering to change out of their sleeping gowns, they hurried outside to search the church yard.

Once outside, a brisk, chilling wind tugged at their thin clothing while they scurried about the yard looking in every nook, cranny, and crevice. Anna joined them.

Glancing up, she noticed that dark clouds had gathered in the distance, which only made matters worse. Alarmed to see the late winter storm headed their way, Anna cried out Abel's name louder than ever. The children joined her with high-pitched shouts of their own. The only response was a low, menacing rumble from the ever-darkening sky.

Anna pressed her hand against her mouth to help calm her rising panic. She tried to think where Abel might have gone. The Porterfields. Of course! He'd want to be with his brother. But where did the Porterfields live? Abel may have remembered the way out there from his visit the day before, but all Anna knew was that the young couple lived on a small farm north of town. Realizing Reverend Cross would know where the Porterfields lived, and fully aware they needed to find the child before the storm broke, she hurried through the front gate and turned toward the reverend's house.

She had barely gone ten feet when she noticed a buckboard headed her way at breakneck speed. Immediately she recognized the lone occupant: Tom Porterfield. She pressed her hand against her wildly hammering heart and prayed that he had come to tell her that Abel was with them.

"Have you seen Jamie?" he called out to her even before he had brought the buckboard to a halt. His voice was elevated with panic.

The question struck Anna so hard against the pit of her stomach, it knocked the very breath out of her. Jamie was missing, too. She opened her mouth to speak, but only a whimper came forth. The boys had run away together, but where could they have gone? Who would take them in? The town was filled with strangers.

A loud clap of thunder broke in the distance startling Anna as it sounded a dark, dreary omen for the two lost children.

The approaching storm well suited Mark Gates's dour mood. He rolled his wheelchair to the front door and sat staring glumly at the dark mass of clouds that had rolled in from the northwest. Plucking at the ends of his beard with the tips of his fingers, he wondered if Harry would be fool-headed enough to try to ride over in such miserable weather. Or did the old man actually have enough sense left in that bald old head of his to stay home out of the rain and not take the chance of catching a chill or, worse, be struck down by lightning? With Harry, you just never knew what to expect. Why that old geezer still bothered to visit him at all remained a mystery to Mark. No one else did—not anymore. But then why should they?

Grumbling bitterly, he gripped the wheels of his chair and rolled farther out onto the front veranda. For some reason he wanted to feel the cold, gusting wind against his skin. He wanted to watch the force of the approaching storm plow through his tattered fields and bend the trees toward the ground, showing them just how insignificant they really were. *Insignificant.* Actually, that word better described himself, because a man without the use of both his legs was about as insignificant as they came.

Lolling his head back against the top brace of the chair, he studied the churning clouds with morose fascination. Dim spatterings of glowing light were followed several seconds later by low, mournful rumblings. The storm was still miles away.

Then suddenly there was a brilliant blue-white streak of light almost directly overhead, accompanied by an immediate clap of thunder so loud it shook the windowpanes. Mark was not sure, but he thought he heard a scream. Had it come from his own throat? Surely not. He glanced around, but saw nothing. Not even his cat, Mop. He blinked with startled confusion, for the first time seriously questioning his sanity. He had already lost the use of his left leg and most of the strength in his left hand. Was he losing his mind too?

A second flash of bright light was followed by yet another clap of thunder so powerful it again rattled the windowpanes. This time he was certain he'd heard a high-pitched yelp. He turned to face the direction the noise had come, thinking maybe a dog had taken refuge from the storm on his front porch, which would explain why his long-haired yellow cat was not on her usual perch near the door.

But he saw nothing, and all he heard now was the low, mournful howl of the wind. He shook his head, thinking something had finally come loose inside. Then, just when he turned back to face the storm again, he heard a muffled voice insisting that everything would be all right soon.

"This is only a little thunderstorm. We'll be on our way again just as soon as it blows over," the hushed voice proclaimed, though it did not sound very convincing.

Twisting his bearded face into a dark, cautious frown, Mark turned his wheelchair toward the voice, but still he saw no one. Whoever had spoken was hidden from plain view.

Slowly, he rolled his chair forward, keeping alert to his surroundings while he searched the cluttered porch for intruders. Without glancing down, he lowered his right hand and felt for the small pistol he kept tucked between the cushion and the frame of the wheelchair.

His hand closed around the curved handle when he noticed a movement in the shadows at the far end of the veranda. Something had moved beneath one of the small tables against the wall. He tried to get a better look, but the surrounding chairs and a large empty crate blocked his view. After moving the pistol to his lap, where he could get to it easily, he rolled the chair slowly toward the table. As soon as he was closer, he could see blue and white clothing through the legs of the surrounding chairs, but could not tell anything else about his intruder.

"Who's there?" he called out, bending forward in an effort to see if the person was armed. Though the space beneath the table was not large enough to hide an adult, he felt a strong shiver of apprehension when he reached for the pistol again. He was well aware it would not take a large person to overpower a cripple. Disgusted with himself and his damnable affliction, he gripped the pistol tighter. "I warn you, I'm armed."

"Don't shoot. Don't shoot, mister. We don't mean no harm. We're just lookin' to get out of the storm is all. We'll be on our way. Just, please, don't shoot."

Mark watched with startled amazement while two little boys slowly crawled out from beneath the small table, their eyes as large and round as wagon wheels.

"What are you doing hiding under there?" he asked, sounding angrier than he actually felt. He was too curious to be angry. "You have no business here."

"I know," the older boy answered. Afraid to look into this angry man's face, he peered down at the dead leaves the wind batted against his feet. "And we didn't mean no harm. We only wanted to get out of the storm." Finally, after managing to swallow, he brought his gaze up to meet Mark's eyes. "We'll be on our way."

The older child then turned toward his younger companion, who stood frozen at his side with his gaze locked on the pistol still in Mark's hand. "Come on, Abel. Let's go."

36

"You two are not going anywhere," Mark interrupted, his pale blue eyes narrowing while he studied the boys. He lifted a hand to stroke his whiskers, unaware what a menacing figure he presented with his broad shoulders, dark beard, and long hair.

Both boys turned as pale as corpses.

"Please, mister, don't shoot us. Just let us be on our way. We promise never to come back here again."

There was something in their terrified expressions that touched Mark's heart in a way it had not been touched in quite some time. It was more than their fear . . . . There was a strong sense of forlornness about them, a feeling of utter hopelessness. "Get inside, both of you!"

"But, sir, we haven't done you no harm," the older boy said, his voice filled with panic. He reached up to push his unruly dark brown hair away from his face with the flat of his hand. "Please, let us be on our way. I *promise* we'll never bother you again. Ever!"

Aware the younger boy had yet to take his eyes off his pistol, Mark quickly slipped it back between the cushion and the chair where it could no longer be seen, then softened the harsh tone in his voice. "I'm not going to hurt you. I just want to get you both inside and out of this storm. It's about to become a downpour. And the way that wind is whipping about, you two will both get soaking wet if you try to ride it out here on the front porch."

The boys looked at each other hesitantly, then back at Mark. The younger boy, whom the other had called Abel, stretched up on tiptoe and peered down into the wheelchair as if to make sure the pistol was completely gone.

Mark frowned. Never having had any experience handling children, he wasn't quite sure how to go about convincing these two that he had only the best of intentions. "You'll be much safer in the house," he tried again. "Besides, it's startin' to get downright cold. We could all catch our deaths. I've got a fire already lit in the kitchen stove. It should be pretty warm in there by now."

He could tell they were mentally debating his offer by the way they glanced at each other. Then suddenly a third loud clap of thunder shook the sky, and he had no trouble convincing them to go inside. The two boys lit for the door as if their britches were on fire.

Chuckling to himself, Mark followed them.

"There, now, I won't have to worry about you two getting soaked to the bone," he commented, carefully maneuvering his chair to the side, where he could close the door. "I don't think I could live with myself if I let you stay out there and you both ended up deathly sick." When he twisted in his chair to look back at his unexpected guests, he found them huddled together in the middle of the room. The older boy held his arm protectively around the younger, and both were staring at the awkward angle of his almost useless foot.

Mark felt a cringe at seeing such horror in their eyes, but tried not to let it get to him . . . not this time. "You boys look hungry to me. I'm afraid all I have to offer you at the moment is a little bread and some cheese. I finished off the last of the stew last night."

He noticed the way their eyes widened at the mention of food and felt certain he was about to have two unexpected guests for breakfast. He was somewhat perplexed when, instead of accepting by graciously thanking him, they shook their heads and politely refused his offer. His dark eyebrows pulled together over a pair of stark blue eyes. "Have either of you had any breakfast?"

Again they shook their heads, indicating they had

38

not.

"And are you accustomed to having breakfast?"

This time they nodded in perfect unison.

"Then you'll eat," he insisted, then rolled his wheelchair in the direction of the kitchen. "It's after ten o'clock. You boys should have eaten hours ago. Follow me."

Glancing reluctantly at one another, they followed Mark toward the back of the house, but paused inside the doorway. They watched apprehensively while Mark rolled hurriedly about the kitchen, gathering up the things he needed and carrying them to a long table in the center of the room. The table was meant to have six chairs, but there were only five. The sixth chair sat near the back door, leaving a space at the table for the wheelchair.

"Come on over here," he instructed while he quickly leaned forward in his wheelchair and sliced the two-day-old bread into manageable chunks. "My friend Harry made this bread. He may not be the best cook in these parts, but I promise it won't poison you. It's probably a little dry, since it was made day before yesterday; but with a little cheese on top, it ought to taste pretty good."

"No, sir, we can't take your food," the older boy insisted, though his hazel eyes remained focused on the large chunks of bread Mark had set on dull blue napkins directly in front of two of the empty chairs. By the looks of things, the man barely had enough food for himself. It would be wrong to take that from him.

"I'll bet you boys would like a cool glass of milk to go with this," Mark said with a confirming nod. He pretended not to have heard the boy's refusal when he glanced back at the counter. The only glass within his reach was the one he used every day, that and his stoneware coffee cup. His mouth flattened into a grim line. Damn his useless leg. "Maybe I could get one of you to climb up there and get a couple of clean glasses down while I get the milk and the cheese out of the cooler."

"No, sir, we couldn't take—"

"I suppose you want me to have to eat alone," Mark sighed with a sad shake of his head. "Do you know how many meals I've had to eat alone here lately?"

"Well, no, sir, but—"

"Good, then you'll join me," he concluded cheerfully. "The glasses are in that cabinet next to the sink."

Looking back at Abel, the older boy shrugged, then quickly hopped up onto the counter and pulled open the cabinet door. Choosing two of the largest glasses, he hopped back down and placed them on the table beside the bread.

Mark studied the glasses with a raised brow. "Better rinse them out. Looks like they got a little dusty sitting up on that shelf. And while you're at it, you might as well wash your hands. You may even want to wash your faces. There's a washcloth on that little shelf. And would you get my glass, too? It's there beside the sink," Mark said, then returned to the cooler to get the pitcher of milk Henry had left for him the day before.

He frowned when he looked into the large metal container and saw there would not be enough for all three of them to have a second glassful and wondered if he could possibly make it out to the barn should they want thirds. If he went out the back door, he'd have just that one step to contend with. Then it would only be a matter of making his way around all the debris in the yard and opening the barn doors wide enough to get his wheelchair inside.

Mark's eyes widened with surprise. It was the first time he'd considered going out to the barn since the

40

accident.

"Tell me, what were you two young men doing out there on my porch?" he asked while he quickly drove a sharp knife through the tall block of cheese and distributed the generous slices between them. At that moment, the roaring sound of rain slapping hard against the house caught his attention, but only for a moment. He didn't really care if it was raining or not.

The older boy had to raise his voice to be heard over the rain. "We were just passin' through when we noticed the wind had picked up some and that a bad storm was comin'. We needed a dry place to hole up until the storm blew over, and your house seemed the most likely spot."

"It did?" Mark found it hard to believe.

"We tried to get your barn door open, thinking we could hide—er, wait out the storm in there; but the bar across the front was too heavy," the boy continued while he slid into the chair Mark had indicated and immediately picked up his glass. The smaller boy did the same.

"You were just passing through?" Mark asked, still wondering how they had ever spotted his place. There was a thick patch of woods and two windbreaks between his house and the main road. If they were traveling along that they never would have seen his house or even any of his outbuildings. So they must have cut through the fields, probably because someone was following them. What he had here was a pair of runaways.

He waited until the boys had taken a long drink before asking, "So, where are your things? Did you leave them outside?"

Already having stuffed a large chunk of cheese into his mouth, the older boy merely patted his pockets to indicate that was all they had.

41

"You certainly are traveling light," he commented, and noticed the way the two boys immediately exchanged darting glances. They were definitely runaways, and definitely brothers. Though the older boy had a spattering of freckles where the younger one did not, and the older lad had eyes that were somewhere between blue and green while the younger one had a tint of gray to his, they looked remarkably alike. They were both thin and had the same upturned noses, the same dark, wavy hair, the same long eyelashes, and the same high cheekbones. They even had the same hollow look about them, as if they had nothing to look forward to, nothing to make them lift their faces into youthful smiles.

"Yes, sir, we are traveling pretty light," the older boy admitted, while his brain hurriedly searched his thoughts for a reason why. "We figure we can get a lot farther a lot faster that way."

"I see," Mark said with an understanding nod. Wanting to find out all he could about the boys before he sent Harry into town to tell the sheriff about his unexpected guests—that is, if Harry came over at all—Mark continued to ask questions. "And where is it you two are headed?"

The older boy reached up to wipe the milk off his upper lip with the back of his hand only seconds after he'd set his glass down. He wasted little time picking up the cheese sandwich he had made for himself. "Not sure yet."

"Not-sure-yet? I've heard about that place. But I've never been there myself," Mark commented, grinning at how rapidly the bread and cheese disappeared. It was the first reason he'd had to smile in quite some time. Though it felt good, it made his beard itch. "But I've always had a mind to go there one day."

The older boy laughed while the younger one

looked at him with a cautiously raised eyebrow.

"Maybe we'll send you a picture postcard when we get there so you can see what Not-sure-yet looks like," the older child responded, still laughing.

"I guess you'll be needing my name then. The name's Mark — Mark Gates." He leaned forward and extended his hand for a proper greeting.

The boy glanced at the hand with surprise, but quickly leaned forward to accept the handshake. "My name's Jamie. Jamie Wilkins. I'm right proud to meet you, Mr. Mark Gates."

"I don't go much in for that 'mister' business. Just call me Mark," he said as he relaxed back in his chair, quick to offer the boy another warm smile.

Jamie liked the thought of being on a first-name basis with a grown man. Tossing his shoulders back, he nodded happily. "Okay, Mark it is."

"And what should I call you?" Mark asked, addressing the younger boy. Though he remembered the boy's name was Abel and figured his last name would also be Wilkins, he wanted to get a conversation started between them. He could not recollect the younger boy having said a single word.

Abel's shoulders hunkered. He dropped his gaze immediately to the food in his hands. His entire body tensed.

"That's Abel, my little brother. He don't talk much," Jamie was quick to supply. He glanced momentarily at his brother, but quickly returned his attention to Mark.

"A man of few words, is he?" Mark commented, studying the child's odd reaction with growing concern. Again he felt a sharp tug at his heart. Though he hardly knew anything about them, he had already started to care for the two little boys. He wondered what made the younger boy so withdrawn. He paused

43

to let another loud rumble of thunder pass, then asked, "How long have you two been traveling?"

Jamie thought about that. In truth, they had been traveling all their lives. Before their folks had decided to leave them at the orphanage, they had wandered as a family from town to town. And then, after the orphanage had started sending them out on that Orphan Train, they'd spent at least ten weeks out of the year traveling across different parts of the country, looking for someone to take them in. He frowned when he remembered the Porterfields and their decision to adopt only him. An icy shiver ran through his body. Suddenly he lost his appetite and set the rest of his cheese sandwich back down on his napkin.

"I guess we've been traveling for quite some time," he answered finally. Mark had noticed the sudden change in the boy. He'd been eating ravenously, but now he had completely forgotten his food. "You about full?"

Jamie nodded that he was. "Want us to clean up?" he asked, thinking it might be an easier job for them than it would be for him. Again he glanced down at the man's twisted leg.

"Just put your glasses in the sink," Mark told them, aware of the reason the boy had offered. "Then maybe you'd like to go into the front room and play a little cards with me. Or maybe a game of checkers."

"Don't know how to play checkers," Jamie admitted as he hurriedly carried his glass to the sink and pumped some water into it so the milk would not dry, making it that much harder to wash. Having had to help in the kitchen at the orphanage, like all the children did at one time or another, he knew about such things.

"Checkers isn't all that hard to learn. How about I teach you? By the looks of things, that storm could last for hours yet. Might as well find something to do to pass the time."

As expected, the roiling thunder and high winds lasted only for an hour longer, but the rain fell for the rest of the day. In that time, Mark taught Jamie not only checkers, but two separate card games as well. He'd tried several times to get Abel interested in joining them, but the younger boy wanted only to watch.

Soon it was apparent that the rain would last well into the night. They would have to come up with something for supper. To his surprise, Jamie knew how to make johnnycakes, and the three feasted on tall, steaming stacks of them. Already making sacrifices, Mark let the boys have the last of the milk while he washed his meal down with plain water.

"Looks like you two boys are going to have to stay for the night," he commented after glancing out the window. The rain still came down in thick, steady sheets. He glanced up at the ceiling with a curious expression. "I've got several spare bedrooms upstairs, but I don't know if the beds have sheets on them or not. I haven't been up there in quite some time."

The boys glanced at his twisted foot and nodded. They understood why.

Mark shifted uncomfortably in his chair. "But I do know where you can find plenty of sheets and blankets if there aren't any on the beds. They are stored in a large chest of drawers at the end of the upstairs hall. Think you can manage on your own?"

"Mister?" Jamie asked, hesitant to say whatever he had to say.

"Yes? What is it, Jamie?"

"You mind me askin' you what—what—" he paused to run the tip of his tongue over his lower lip.

"Ask me what? What time breakfast is?" Mark supplied for him, having anticipated what he had on his mind but not yet ready to discuss his accident. His nostrils flared with the resentment that so often accompanied thoughts of his mangled leg. He hated being reminded that he was no longer useful as a human being. Looking away, he answered in a voice that sounded a little more gruff than he had actually intended. "Breakfast will be whenever you two get up. You'll probably have to cook it yourselves. I can stand at the stove to cook, but not for very long at a time."

Jamie swallowed hard, having sensed the sudden tension in his new friend. "I guess we'll see you in the morning then."

Quickly he grabbed Abel by the arm and fled the room.

Chapter Three

Anna lay in darkness, listening to the cheerless song of a distant whippoorwill. How forlorn the lonely bird sounded, like a lost child calling out for someone's attention. She wondered if Jamie and Abel could hear it. Were they, too, lying awake, wondering what the future held for them?

By all logic, Anna should be asleep. After spending most of the day and part of the evening searching for the children, she was exhausted. Every muscle in her body felt heavy. But even so, she could not sleep. Although her pallet was made of thick, soft quilts and the children around her slumbered soundlessly, she lay wide awake, tormented by the terrifying thought of those two precious little boys out there in the cold, facing the late winter storm alone.

Where were they? She envisioned them huddled together, hiding beneath the low branches of a tree or bush somewhere, trembling and rain soaked, their skin blue from the cold. She tried to imagine them in someone's parlor, taken in out of the rain and given dry clothes and warm food, but that vision would not stay with her long before her dark thoughts turned back to the pair huddled together beneath a tree, calling out her name.

Tugging her blanket higher around her, she wondered how the climate could be so sunny and warm one day, yet so miserably cold and wet the next. Winter was not ready to relinquish its hold on them. Not just yet.

Anna rolled over onto her back and stared into the gloomy shadows of the vaulted ceiling while she tried one last time to guess where the boys might have gone after they had left the church. Was there some place the townspeople had overlooked?

Shortly after the boys had been discovered missing, two major search parties had been formed, and despite the inclement weather, they had knocked on practically every door in town and had begun to search barns, sheds, carriage houses, privys, and chicken coops.

Most believed the boys were still in town, or somewhere very close by. The rain had started too soon for two little boys to have traveled far.

Judging by the evidence, Jamie had escaped through his bedroom window during the night. The trip to town had to have taken him hours because the Porterfields lived several miles out. It was probably close to daylight by the time Jamie reached town, and then it had to have taken him a little while to locate the church, even in a town as small as Pinefield.

Once he did find the church, he evidently wasted little time slipping inside and quietly waking Abel, careful not to disturb anyone else. Then the two boys must have left together, hoping to be far away before anyone woke and discovered them missing.

Since Abel had always been afraid to face the dark alone, the theory of Jamie having slipped out and then finding his way to the church was the most logical explanation. It made far more sense than believing Abel had bravely taken off for the Porterfields. Yet no matter how it happened, the end result was the same. The boys were gone and no one knew where.

The thought of those two frightened little boys out there somewhere all alone, and during such a dark, cold rainy night, made her insides ache. Unless they had found shelter somewhere, they were undoubtedly soaked to the skin by now and chilled right to the bone. It had now been over twenty-four hours since their last meal. Soon they would be too weak and too ill to walk—if they weren't already.

Another tiny chill raced down her spine, this time settling in the pit of her stomach. It was so frustrating to have to call off the search because of darkness, afraid they might miss something important if they continued their search through the night.

Tossing over onto her side again, she decided the two boys were intentionally hiding from them and, knowing Jamie, it was somewhere very clever, somewhere no one would think to look. Tomorrow, when she, Gordon, and the townspeople resumed their search shortly after the first glimmer of dawn, she would leave nothing to chance. She would search everywhere until she finally found them. But would they still be alive?

Of course they would be! Jamie was a very resourceful child. He'd find a way to stay warm, and he'd have discovered some source of food. She refused to believe otherwise. Still, there *was* that other possibility. . . .

The sun peeked out from between fat, dappled clouds when Harry Munn stepped outside early the next morning. He was pleased to discover the rain had finally let up.

As soon as he'd finished with his regular chores, he could take a little ride over to Mark's house and see how he had weathered the storm. He could also make up another batch of beef stew. By now, Mark had to be completely out, and with nothing left in the house but bread and cheese, he'd probably be even grumpier than usual.

But, then, Mark's moods didn't really matter much to Harry. Harry saw through his friend's outward display of bitterness. In time, Mark would quit his wallowing in all that self-pity and get on with his life—even if he never regained full use of that left leg. After all, hadn't Harry himself found out life was still worth getting out of bed for, even without Lilly, his beloved wife of forty-eight years? Still, he had to admit, it had never quite been the same after her death.

Admittedly, things sometimes changed for the worse, as they had in Mark's case, but still, Harry firmly believed there was always something that made life worth living, if a person just looked for it. Mark's problem was that he hadn't bothered to look yet.

Even so, Harry had to admit, fate *had* dealt Mark Gates a lousy hand. It was a real pity that such a strong, virile young man had to suffer such a terrible blow, especially in the prime of his life. And it was an even worse pity that he'd become so bitter about that injured leg of his that he'd eventually run off all his employees and most of his friends. The fact was, he and old Jake Simmons were the only two that ever came around anymore, and Jake only stopped by every other Saturday while on his way into town to see if Mark needed anything from the mercantile.

Harry shook his head to clear his mind of such dismal thoughts, then hurried outside to get his own chores done. Since Mark's cow had not been milked in two days now, and his horse and chickens had not been fed, there would be plenty to do over there besides fix a pot of stew. He just hoped he had enough time to visit with Mark awhile. Though Mark usually sat in the kitchen while Harry cooked and baked a couple of fresh loaves of bread, it was hard to do any serious visiting because Harry had to keep his mind on his vegetable chopping or risk doing a little *finger* chopping instead. Most times Harry found time to just sit and chat with his friend after he was through feeding the animals and cooking his meal. At least today he wouldn't have to do any laundry. He'd done enough of that last visit. That should leave them some time to do a little visiting.

Though Mark would never admit it, not even to Harry, the young man desperately needed someone to talk to. He needed someone to encourage him to think about things—all sorts of things—other than the fact he had suddenly been made a cripple. That's why, no matter what Mark said to offend him, or no matter how ugly Mark treated him, Harry would continue visiting regularly and would see to it he had something decent to eat and clean clothes to wear. After all, Mark was his friend. Had been since the first day they'd met nigh on ten years ago, ever since Mark bought the old Turner place and moved in. And friends stuck together no matter what.

By two o clock, Harry had most of his own chores finished. He quickly saddled his horse, ready to make the mile-and-a-half ride to Mark's place. Before he climbed into the saddle, he double-checked his saddlebags to make sure he had remembered to put in the meat and the vegetables he planned to use in the stew. Though Harry knew how to cook other things, stew was something Mark could warm up easily enough on his own. And knowing how hard it was for the man to stand on that good leg of his for very long, Harry had to make something that could be slapped on the stove and reheated in a hurry. He knew Mark had to be getting tired of eating nothing but stew all the time, but at least it was filling, and was a heap sight better than the coffee, beef jerky, and crackers he'd lived on there for a while.

Pushing his battered hat to the back of his balding head, Harry tucked part of his tongue against the long, gaping hole at the right side of his mouth where three teeth were missing and whistled a lively tune. How he loved cold weather, as long as it didn't go and get *too* blamed cold. Though most friends his age hated any sign of cold weather, he still loved the feel of a brisk, cold breeze in his face. It stirred his blood and made him feel as if there was some life left in his old bones. Smiling to himself, he kicked his horse into a trot, eager to see Mark.

As soon as he had the yard in sight, Harry noticed that the barn doors stood wide open. His first thought was that vandals had come during the time he'd been gone and spirited Mark's horse and milk cow away, and probably all his farm equipment, too. But when he remembered how fierce that storm had been, especially when it first broke, he decided that the wind had probably blown them open. He was lucky it hadn't broken them off their hinges.

Since Mark had yet to push himself out onto the veranda to greet him, which he sometimes did, Harry decided to check on the animals first. If Mark was in too bad a mood even to come out the door, it might be best he get the chores done first. Quickly he climbed down from his horse and headed for the barn door.

"Here, move out of the way, I think I can reach it," Harry heard Mark say from somewhere inside the barn.

Harry couldn't have been more surprised. As far as he knew, Mark had never left the house, not since the accident, which had been during planting season a little over a year ago. With a look of pure astonishment on his grizzled face, Harry hurried inside to see if his tired old ears were playing tricks on him again.

Well, if his ears were up to their old tricks, then his eyes were too, because there was Mark, his wheelchair rolled right into the stall with his milk cow. Even harder to believe was Mark bent forward in his chair, trying his best to milk that cow himself. Beside him stood two perplexed-looking little boys.

"I still don't see how you're going to get milk out of that thing," Jamie commented, his head tilted to one side. His hand came up to stroke his chin thoughtfully.

"Well, we'd better try our best to get at least some of the milk out of her, because she's going to continue to wail until we do," Mark commented while he tried to keep his balance in the chair by gripping the side with his left hand, as he leaned forward to get a good grasp on the cow's udder with his right.

"Here, let me do that," Harry said, startling everyone.

Jamie's hazel eyes widened while he reached protectively for his little brother, whose gray-green eyes were just as wide and just as round.

Mark saw the boys' reaction and quickly sought to reassure them. "Don't worry . . . that's just Harry. He's that good friend of mine I was telling you about. He isn't going to harm you. I wouldn't let him even if he wanted to."

Harry looked at Mark questioningly while he reached for the three-legged milk stool, then motioned for Mark to get out of his way.

"That's all right. I think I can handle it," Mark said, which surprised Harry even more. It had been ages since Mark had wanted to do anything for himself. Quickly Harry put the stool back where he'd found it, not about to discourage this first sign of independence.

While Mark strained to reach the teats, Harry turned his attention to the little boys standing just the other side of him.

"Who are your visitors?" he finally asked.

"That's Jamie and Abel Wilkins, a couple of new friends of mine," Mark said, through gritted teeth. Though he had the strength in his hands to pull down on the teats and produce a good, solid stream of milk, the stomach muscles he needed to keep from falling out of the wheelchair were straining so hard he'd begun to tremble. But he was determined to see this simple task through. "They're road travelers—just passing through."

Jamie's huge, round eyes lifted to meet Harry's gaze, as if searching for something.

"I see," Harry said, nodding, though he didn't see; he didn't see at all. Even if they were just passing through, which seemed unlikely enough for a pair so young, how'd they ever come to be there, of all places? Mark's house couldn't even be seen from the road. And, even if it could, why were they still there? It had turned into a right pretty day. If they were traveling, why weren't they making good use of the sunshine?

"Where are they headed?" he finally asked, leaning casually against one of the tall posts that held the ceiling beam in place.

Mark paused only long enough to glance back at Jamie and grin. "They're headed on over to Not-sure-yet. They just stopped by here to get in out of the storm."

Harry pushed his hat back to a precarious angle and scratched at what few hairs still grew on his freckled head. He could tell that remark had been some sort of private joke and decided not to intrude. "And how long they plannin' on stayin'?"

"Long enough to taste some of your world-famous beef stew. That is, if you've a mind to make us some," Mark answered, pausing to catch his breath. "I've told them what a great cook you are. Almost as good as Jamie here." He nodded toward the older boy.

Although Harry didn't fully understand what was going on, he was pleased to see Mark in such a good mood. He decided to go along with whatever game they played. "Jamie's a pretty good cook, is he?" He looked at the boy and watched a wide grin split across his youthful face.

"Sure is. Makes a real fine johnnycake," Mark answered with another nod, then grunted when he reached forward to resume his one-handed attempt at milking.

"Hmm, then maybe we can swap recipes. I'll show him how I go about makin' my world-famous stew if he'll tell me how to make a decent johnnycake. It just so happens I got the fixin's for a big ol' pot of stew right out there in my saddlebags. If the boys aren't afraid of horses, maybe we can talk 'em into gettin' the bags off old Ruby so they can tote 'em inside. I'll be right on in to get that stew started as soon as I'm sure everything has been taken care of out here." He was eager to speak with Mark alone and find out the whole story behind those boys.

"Of course we ain't afraid of no horses," Jamie commented with an insulted scowl. "We'll be glad to carry your saddlebags into the house. Come on, Abel."

Harry chuckled when the two boys immediately disappeared to prove they could handle the task. "Cute little fellers. So, what's the full story on 'em?"

Since he couldn't talk and lean forward far enough to milk at the same time, Mark sat back and explained what he knew about how Jamie and Abel had come to be there, as well as the fact that he felt sure

55

they were a couple of runaways.

"I imagine their folks are pretty worried about them," he commented, glancing in the direction of the door where the boys had disappeared. "I know if they were my boys, I'd be worried sick." He then looked at Harry, concern evident in his heavily lashed, pale blue eyes. "I'd really appreciate it if you would ride into town and tell the sheriff they're here."

"Yeah, that's a good idea." Harry reached up to scratch his whiskered jaw. "If they've been gone a whole day or longer, I imagine their folks are worried by now. Tell you what, I'll pretend I'm out of somethin' I need for that stew and head right on into town to get it. That way they won't suspect what I'm up to. If they did, they might try to run away again. I'd hate to go to all the trouble of tellin' that sheriff that he or the boys' parents can ride out and pick up the boys whenever they've a mind to only to have them discover the boys already gone when they get here."

"I don't think I'll have much problem keeping them here," Mark assured him, all the while trying to think of something Harry could be out of. "You use flour in that stew of yours, don't you?"

"Just enough to thicken up the broth."

"Good, because I'm out. Jamie used the last of it this morning making us another batch of johnny-cakes."

"Then I'm off to get flour," Harry said with a grin. "You just be sure to keep those younguns here while I'm gone, so we don't have to do no tall explainin' later on."

"I'll put them to work chopping up the vegetables," Mark assured him. "But hurry back. If you take too long, they might get a little suspicious of where you've gone and why, and we definitely don't want that."

"I guess I'd better at least go on inside and pretend

56

to discover your flour canister is empty," Harry commented, thinking that might seem more convincing, then turned to leave. He stopped inside the doorway and glanced back at Mark. "You sure you can handle that?"

Mark's expression quickly hardened. "Yes, I'm sure. I've been milking cows since I was eight years old."

Harry ignored the biting tone in Mark's voice. "What about getting back into the house? How you plan on managing that?"

"You remember that old door you took off the woodshed because it had warped and was letting rain in? Well, I had the boys prop it against the back step so I can use it like a ramp," Mark explained, this time with less animosity. He knew the old man had meant no harm. It was just that he hated being reminded of his limitations. "It's a little wobbly, but it works. That's how I got out here to begin with."

Harry marveled at the cleverness in that, then strode on out of the barn to get a look at the contraption himself, and to let Mark finish the milking on his own.

Five minutes later, after he'd remounted his horse and headed her towards town, Harry had plenty of time to consider the situation at Mark's a little better. Secretly, he wished those boys could stay on awhile longer. They certainly had brought about a noticeable change in his friend, and in such a short time. It was nothing short of astounding. But then, it was easy to see why Mark reacted to the boys the way he had, because in the short time Harry had been with them, he too had been cast under their spell. They were the cutest little fellers, especially the younger one, who seemed to keep a keen eye on everything.

Delighted that Mark had finally started to do things for himself again, Harry adjusted his battered old hat to exactly the right angle for whistling, then resumed pushing his favorite tune through the wide gap near the back of his teeth.

Forty-five minutes later, when Harry rode into town, he noticed a small gathering of townfolks near the outskirts. Two women and a man sat in a carriage while several other men walked at a brisk pace beside them. Every now and then a couple of the men branched off from the small group to walk up to a house and talk to whoever was home, but then quickly returned, shaking their heads. Meanwhile, others broke off in small groups and searched the outbuilding and the yards, looking in big places and small places, as if they had lost something but weren't sure what. Thinking it was rather odd behavior, even for town-folks, Harry pulled his horse up beside them and asked of no one in particular, "What's goin' on here?"

"Oh, hello, Harry," the reverend answered, recognizing him. Reaching inside his dark wool coat, he pulled a wadded handkerchief out of his shirt pocket and none too gently blew his nose. He made a pitiful honking noise that caused his wife to grimace. Blinking his watery eyes, he quickly tucked the handkerchief back into his pocket, then turned to look at Harry again.

"We're conducting a house-to-house search," he finally answered, his words dulled by a scratchy voice.

"For what?" Harry asked, then glanced at the reverend's wife, who was busily writing down the different places they had searched. His first thought was that someone had escaped from jail; but then none of these men were armed and they were allowing the women-folk to participate, so that couldn't be it.

The reverend took several short, open-mouthed breaths, as if he might be about to sneeze, but the sneeze never came. Still, he reached for his handkerchief again, in readiness.

"We're searching for a couple of little boys who ran away from the Orphan Train," he explained, as soon as he was certain the need to sneeze had passed.

"The Orphan Train?" Harry felt an odd prickling along his skin, just beneath his shirt collar. He remembered having read something about a batch of New York City orphans being hauled down here to Pinefield, with hopes of finding some of them permanent homes. "Why would they want to go and do that?"

The reverend shook his head, as if he was just too tired to answer, or maybe it was a question he'd answered one too many times. Finally he took a deep breath and forced the explanation out, "I guess they didn't want to be separated. They ran away so they could stay together."

"Separated?" Harry's whiskered face twisted with concern.

"Yes. You see, the two boys who ran away are brothers. They had hoped to be placed into the same home, but it didn't work out that way. Tom Porterfield and his wife decided to take the older one in, but didn't have room for the other. At the agent's suggestion, they took the one they wanted home, leaving the younger one behind at the church with the other children. Then, sometime during the night, they somehow reunited and stole away together. That was night before last." He pulled his jacket closer around his neck and sniffed loudly. "We've been searching for them ever since. Can't really understand why we haven't found them. They can't have gotten far, not in the weather we've had."

"You'd be surprised what a couple of determined children can do," the reverend's wife cautioned him. "As soon as we finish searching Jefferson Street again, and the other group finishes with Oak Street, I think it would be best to break up into even smaller groups and start checking with some of the nearby farmers and ranchers. I still think that those boys were able to get well away from town long before that storm broke. And as determined as those two were to have their freedom, they may not have stopped running even then. Why, they could be halfway to Shreveport by now."

"Now, now, Martha, I keep telling you, someone would have spotted them on the road if they'd left town," the reverend reminded, in a soft, condescending voice. "Those boys don't know enough about this area to travel by anything but the main roads. Those are city boys. They aren't about to cut across fields and pastures where they might be trampled by cows or run off by angry farmers. No, they're hiding out in this town somewhere. I feel sure of that. It's only a matter of time until we find them."

Martha Cross sighed and resumed her writing after a pair of men returned to tell her they had checked the Langfords' stables, their carriage house, and their woodshed and had found no sign of the little boys.

Harry's bushy white brows dipped low over his pale green eyes. "If they find these here boys you been talkin about, they still thinkin' of separatin' 'em? Or have they decided to let 'em stay together after all."

"It's my understanding that the older one will be returned to the Porterfields and the younger one will be returned to the agents in charge of the Orphan Train. Which is why we need to hurry and find them. The children who have not been selected are scheduled to be in Marshall on Saturday. They'll have to leave here sometime tomorrow afternoon, with or without that youngest boy."

Harry rubbed his whiskered jaw with the callused

palm of his weathered hand. "Say the little one will have to be left behind if he's not found in time?"

"I'm afraid so. But don't worry, if it comes to that, we'll transport him to where he belongs as quickly as we can."

"Well, good luck in findin' 'em," Harry said with a polite nod, dipping the brim of his hat toward the two ladies. Then, quickly, he turned his horse back the way he'd come. He was a mile out of town before he realized he'd forgotten all about the flour.

Rather than arouse suspicion, Harry stopped by his own place and picked up an unopened bag of flour. Though he would need it by the end of the week, he felt it would be better to give it up than have the children start asking a lot of questions about why he'd returned without any. He didn't want them to worry about what he might have found out while he was gone. It seemed to him that those two younguns had had more than enough to worry about without him adding to it. He just wished he could get his hands on those two orphan agents. He'd sure do what he could to make them change their minds . . . legal or not.

Within an hour after having spoken with the reverend, Harry was back at Mark's with flour in hand.

Mark glanced curiously at the clock, then at Harry when he heard the back door clatter shut. "That was certainly a quick trip. You've barely been gone two hours. The store must not have been very busy."

Harry could tell by his perplexed expression that Mark wondered how he had ever managed to buy that flour *and* notify the sheriff of their little visitors in such a short time. He tried to think of a way to tell him what had happened without alerting the boys to the fact he was onto them. But he couldn't think of anything not bordering on the obvious. "You're right, there was hardly anyone in the store at all. Most folks were—at the church." He glanced at the boys, who sat at the table chopping the last of the potatoes, carrots, and onions. Though the little one had shown no response to his remark, the older boy's eyes had widened immediately. These were the Orphan Train runaways, all right.

"At the church?" Mark asked, curious. "On a Thursday?" He paused to think about that. "It *is* Thursday, isn't it?" He never was too sure about the days anymore.

"Yep, it's Thursday, all right." Then, realizing the older boy looked extremely uncomfortable, probably worried that he'd found out about them, Harry quickly added, "Probably some big church holiday we don't know about. I never did get the chance to ask nobody. But it wasn't an important enough holiday to close down the stores, and I was in too big a hurry to buy the flour and get back." Then he changed the subject, waving a bony hand toward the table. "I see you already got most of those vegetables chopped. I guess I'd better go ahead and get that meat cut up."

"Already done," Mark told him with a pleased smile, motioning toward the stove. "Already cut up into mouth-sized chunks and already in the kettle. You just do whatever it is you do to make it a stew." Though he was eager to hear what the sheriff had said about the boys, he feared it might look a little odd if he suddenly came out with some excuse for him and Harry to be alone. He thought it would be better to wait until Harry had put the stew on the stove to simmer before sending the boys outside—maybe to the chicken coop to gather a few eggs.

To his chagrin, it took Harry longer than expected to prepare the stew, considering most of the work was already done. It was well past five-thirty before Harry finally put the lid over the large black kettle and declared all they needed to do now was wait. Meanwhile, because time was so short, too short for him to bake a couple of loaves of his usual yeast bread, he decided to make a quick batch of sourdough biscuits.

Finally Mark felt enough time had passed that he could safely mention the eggs. Placing his finger against his beard, he tapped his whiskered chin lightly. "You know, I can't remember if we thought to gather up the eggs or not." Turning to the boys, he twisted his face into a puzzled expression. "Did we?"

Jamie shook his head. "You didn't say nothing about having any eggs."

"It must have slipped my mind. Would you two mind doing that for me? Although I have a small chicken coop on the far side of the barn, my chickens are partial to laying their eggs out in the big feed trough. And since I didn't bother to get them yesterday either, there should probably be five or six eggs out there by now."

"Is that all?" Jamie asked, as if he'd expected much more.

"At the moment, I have only three hens and a rooster," he admitted. "I lost several of my hens last winter and never did get around to replacing them."

Eager to help, the boys hopped down from their chairs and hurried outside to hunt for the eggs, racing to see who would get there first.

"Now, Mark, you know good and well there should only be 'bout four eggs out there, if that," Harry admonished as soon as the boys were out of earshot. "You know as sure as I do that Old Shirley quit laying eggs early last summer." He shook his head as he thought of the ragged-looking little Banty hen that had provided many an egg in her time. "Too old to lay eggs and too scroungy to make into a stew."

"I know, but I figured if the boys thought there were

63

more eggs out there, they'd stay out longer looking for them," he explained. "And I want to hear what that sheriff had to say. Is he on his way out here?"

"I never got the chance to talk with him," Harry admitted, then told him about the search party he'd come across when he first arrived in town. "After hearing what the reverend had to say about them wantin' to separate them two, I decided to wait until that train had left with both them orphan agents aboard before botherin' to tell anyone about those boys bein' here. That way, Abel will have a chance to stay in town a little while longer and maybe, in the meantime, some couple will find it in their hearts to take the boy in. If that was to happen, they might not be sharin' the same home, but at least they could be in the same town and could still see each other from time to time."

"So, no one knows those boys are here?" Mark asked, glad Harry had decided not to go to the sheriff after all. For once, he completely agreed with his friend. Those boys deserved whatever chance he and Harry could give them. He slammed his fist down hard against his thigh when he thought more about what those heartless orphan agents had tried to do. It made him furious that someone could be that cruel. Why, it would be a sin to separate those two boys, especially when it was obvious that they dearly loved each other.

"For now, just you and me know—and of course, them two out there." Harry jerked his bald head in the direction of the back door, where the boys had just clamored out of the house.

"How long until that train leaves with the other children and the two agents on board?"

"Tomorrow afternoon sometime. I didn't catch no 'pecific time."

"Then we'll just let Jamie and Abel continue hiding out here until sometime the day after the others have left," Mark said, his mouth set with determination. Never had he felt such a need to protect anyone as he did those two defenseless little boys.

Harry thought over what Mark had said and puckered his face into a thoughtful frown. "What'll we do if they come out here lookin' for them? If that reverend's wife ever gets her way 'bout things, they'll split up into small groups and go visitin' with all the farmers and ranchers lookin' to find those two." His eyes widened. "What if they come while I'm gone? What if they come while you're here alone?" He wondered how Mark could ever stop them from searching his house.

Mark's eyes glittered with pure devilment. "Let's just say that if they come knocking on my door at any time between now and tomorrow afternoon, they won't get a very warm reception. Everyone already knows what a mean, cantankerous person I've become since the accident." He laughed out loud, unable to believe that his former foul moods would work so well to his advantage. "I think I'll start by giving my shotgun a thorough cleaning. I imagine it could use it."

"You plannin' on shootin' 'em?" Harry wasn't too sure he saw the humor in that. Protecting the boys was one thing, but shooting a person was quite another.

"Of course not. It's just that I figure the thing will look a lot more menacing laying across my lap if it gleams."

Harry's worried expression lifted into a wide grin. Seconds later, he hurried to find everything Mark would need to make that shotgun of his look so shiny, they couldn't help but notice it.

65

Chapter Four

Anna was relieved. The men had finally decided to listen to Mrs. Cross. After having combed the small town twice, leaving no building unsearched, even the reverend admitted that the boys must have left town.

Taking what seemed the next logical course of action, they divided into small groups of twos and threes, then fanned out to check with many of the farmers and ranchers. Anna wished the men had been more willing to listen to the reverend's wife sooner. If they had, those boys might have already been found and would not have had to suffer yet another night out in this unbearable cold.

By Friday morning, time had begun to run out. There were very few hours left before those still with the Orphan Train had to leave. The unselected children were expected to arrive in Marshall, Texas, in plenty of time for the formal presentation Saturday morning at ten. It would not be fair to those children if they arrived late. They would be nervous enough as it was.

Although time had run short and they needed all the help they could find, Gordon had strongly suggested that Anna stay in town with the remaining children while the men continued with their search. But

Anna was far too concerned to sit idly by. She convinced Mrs. Johns, one of the church ladies, to stay with the children while she continued to help with the search for Jamie and Abel.

Feeling somewhat sorry for the reverend, who had latched onto a nasty cold at some point during the height of the storm, she volunteered to be his search partner. She wanted to do all the legwork — all the climbing in and out of the buggy to ask at the different houses if the two boys had been seen. Gordon also chose to ride along with the reverened. He'd come to know the reverend better than the other townspeople as he was a guest in his home.

Because the last train to Marshall was scheduled to leave Pinefield at one o'clock sharp, everyone agreed to be back at the church by noon to report any findings. With time rapidly running out, it was Anna's dearest hope that when they returned to the church, they would find both boys waiting.

Since it was already well after eleven, they had barely enough time to make one last stop before turning back toward town.

"I'b not sure we should eben bother wif dis next house," Reverend Cross said, then sniffed loudly, trying to clear his nose. Blinking rapidly, he reached for his handkerchief with his left hand while keeping the reins securely gripped in his right. Ever so gently, he dabbed at his red and swollen nostrils.

"Why's that?" Gordon asked, curling his lips in disgust while he watched the reverend put the badly soiled handkerchief back into his inside coat pocket.

"Because eben if dose two boys did decide to take refuge at dat next farm, de man who libes dere is de sort who would have run dem right off his place." He paused to snatch a short breath through his mouth before continuing. "He's a bery angry young man. Bitter

67

because he lost the use of his leg in a farming accident about a year ago. Been confined to a wheelchair eber since."

"How bitter is he?" Gordon wanted to know. His face revealed his personal concern.

"Extremely bitter," the reverend assured him. "I know. Ebery time I'be tried to visit with him, hoping to bring him some comfort despite his injury, he's done his bery best to make me feel unwelcome. He's actually ordered me out of his house before. I can imagine how he would treat a couple of vagabond children looking for a handout or a place to stay."

"Then perhaps we shouldn't waste our time with him. Let's go on to the next farm," Gordon suggested. He jerked his watch out of his vest pocket and snapped it open. "After that, we will have to go back. I certainly don't want to miss that train."

Anna shook her head, not convinced they should overlook even one farm, no matter how contrary the owner. "But what if the children are hiding there? The man is in a wheelchair. He obviously can't get around well. The boys could be living in his barn or in one of his other outbuildings without him even knowing it. Or it's possible one of his field hands may have seen them. I really don't think we should overlook any possibility, no matter how unpleasant it is for us."

"Dat man doesn't have any field hands. He has no employees at all dat I know of. It's my understanding dat he ran them all off soon after he hurt his leg," the reverend quickly informed her. "But, you're right. De man neber leaves his house for any reason. Dose boys could be hiding in one of his outbuildings widout him knowing about it. Maybe we should check his place after all." He paused to groan. "That is, if he'll agree to let us."

"I'll check that place out even if he doesn't," Anna

said with a determined toss of her head. "The man will just have to understand how important it is that we find those children."

Besides, how much harm could a crippled man cause?

Several minutes later they arrived at the man's house. Although the exterior had undoubtedly seen better days and had fallen into a shabby state of disrepair, it was not hard to imagine how stately the home had once been. It was a tall, two-story frame painted white with faded blue trim. Large trees heavy with spring foliage loomed high over their heads, shading much of the yard and part of the house. Near the front steps, several purple irises struggled for survival in flowerbeds overgrown with weeds and grass. Dead leaves were scattered everywhere, even across the porch.

"Looks like the place could use some work," Tina commented as she followed Gordon across the unkempt yard to the front steps.

"Looks like it could use a lot of work," he retorted. His nose wrinkled with disgust as he stepped over a rotting limb that had fallen from one of the trees. "Has the man no pride?"

Together Anna and Gordon ascended the steps, then paused outside the door. It was then Anna noticed a fat yellow cat, perched in a nearby window, watching her every move.

"I'll knock," Gordon offered.

Prepared to counter any contrariness the man displayed toward them, Anna stood proudly at Gordon's side with her shoulders rigid and her chin thrust forward. She would not let anyone prevent her from doing her job. Not anyone.

Immediately after Gordon's knock, they heard a soft scramble of noises inside the house, yet no one came to the door.

"He's in there," Gordon grumbled and knocked again, louder this time.

Finally they heard sounds that had to be coming from the other side of the front door, then finally the rattle of the bolt being shoved back. Anna took a deep, fortifying breath and readjusted her dark gray tailored jacket while she waited for the door to open.

"Yeah? What do you want?" the deep voice called to them even before the door had swung open.

The low, unfriendly voice had come from just to the right of the doorway, but when Anna looked down she saw no one, only a well-worn carpet that she supposed had at one time been blue. Then, suddenly, a man in a wheelchair rolled into sight.

She was startled to see a large, gleaming shotgun balanced across the arms of the chair, his hands resting lightly on top. The man was armed!

Slowly she pulled her gaze off the intimidating shotgun, ready to look the man in the eye, only to find herself startled yet again.

Despite the wheelchair, and the obvious fact that his left leg was useless, he struck quite an imposing figure. His shoulders were broad and his expression harsh. Pale blue eyes glared angrily at them, giving sharp contrast to his heavy black beard and the thick crop of dark hair that reached down to his shoulders. Frightened by his anger, Anna felt a definite urge to take a cautious step backward and let Gordon handle this one, but in the end she decided to stand her ground. She would not be intimidated by such a man.

Gordon stood motionless at her side, mesmerized by the frightful expression on the man's face.

"I asked you two what you wanted." His hand traced the smooth lines of his shotgun while he waited for someone to speak.

Finally Gordon cleared his throat and forced his words out. "Sir, my name is Gordon Franklin, and this is Miss Anna Stone. We are dreadfully sorry to impose like this, but we have lost a couple of young boys and are out searching the countryside for them. We wondered if perhaps you had seen them."

Mark's gaze swept the thin, dapper young man and knew immediately that this dandy had to be from some big city up north. Deciding that this fancy slick had to be one of the New York agents Harry had told him about, his eyes then moved to take in the appearance of the young lady who stood rigidly at his side. Mark's eyebrows rose with unexpected interest, because despite her drab clothing and the haughty angle of her chin, she was really very attractive.

Reluctantly he allowed his gaze to drift downward until it settled on the soft curves that the fitted lines of her gray jacket revealed. He was perversely pleased by the way she bristled at his boldness. Too bad she didn't have enough backbone to say something about his obvious display of bad manners. He'd enjoy the banter.

For some reason not quite clear to him, he wanted to cause her even more discomfort and turned in his chair so he could continue to peruse the pleasant shape of her body at his leisure. How very prim and proper she was—almost as prim and proper as the dandy at her side.

"And how, pray tell, did you two manage to *lose* a couple of children?" he asked, ignoring the man entirely while he divided his attention between the high color that had risen in the woman's cheeks and the intriguing way she filled out her clothing.

How unfortunate that a woman that pretty was also void of any real human emotion on the inside. If it wasn't for the fact that she was one of the agents who wanted to separate Jamie and Abel, he might have liked to get to know her a little better, to find out if she looked as appealing without the dark gray jacket and pleated skirt as she did with them on.

But then he remembered his mangled leg and knew that even if she did not have a heart of ice, she would never look twice at a man like him. Why should she? He wasn't the same anymore. Suddenly he resented her even more.

"We didn't exactly lose them," Gordon tried to explain, stepping closer to Anna in an attempt to recapture the man's wandering attention. He was obviously used to having a man look at him when he spoke. "They ran away."

"And why would they do that?" Finally Mark pulled his gaze away from the woman's hardened expression and looked again at the man. What a fop he was, dressed in his fancy three-piece suit, with an immaculately brushed derby perched high on his head. It was easy to see by his cocky manner that Mr. Gordon Franklin was full of himself.

"The boys are with the Orphan Train," Gordon went on to explain, shifting uncomfortably beneath Mark's studious gaze. "They, like the rest of the children, were brought to Pinefield in an effort to find them homes. We were lucky enough to locate one of the boys a very nice home a few miles north of here, but unfortunately we failed to find a suitable place for the other. Because they are brothers, and do not want to be separated, they ran away. They could not quite understand how, in the long run, the separation would be best for both of them."

Anna clenched her jaw to keep from speaking out. She, too, had yet to understand how separating those boys would be best for either of them and wanted to say so, but at the same time she realized it would do little good to argue the point, especially now. Her foremost concern was to find those boys. She'd worry about the other after she had Jamie and Abel safely back in her care.

Mark's pale blue eyes narrowed while he slowly rolled forward, effectively blocking the door. "You mean to tell me that you'd separate a pair of brothers even though they have pleaded with you not to? How cold-hearted can you be?"

Gordon's shoulders tensed and his jaw thrust firmly forward. "Sir, I have neither the time nor the inclination to stand here and discuss the reasons those boys decided to run away. Have you or have you not seen them?"

"I don't think I'd tell you even if I had," Mark told him through gritted teeth, rolling forward again, enough to make Gordon opt to take a tiny step back. "People like you disgust me."

Mark then looked at Anna, who had pressed her eyes closed, as if to show him his insults could never reach her. That made him just that much more determined to see that they did. "So, tell me, how much do you two get paid to destroy young children's lives?"

His words cut through Anna like the cold blade of a jagged knife. She opened her eyes and then her mouth to explain that it had not been her decision, but was cut short by Gordon's angry retort.

"I fail to see how finding a home for an orphaned child is in any way destroying his life." Gordon sniffed loudly and turned briskly away. "Come, Miss Thomas, I cannot see how standing here arguing with this irrational creature is going to help us find Jamie and Abel. It is obvious that the boys are not here. Good-bye, Mr. Gates."

"And good riddance, Mr. Franklin," Mark added, with a disgusted snort. Pumping his jaw muscles back and forth in an effort to contain his anger, he watched while the two returned to the buggy and hurriedly climbed inside. He waited until they had completely disappeared from sight before letting go the breath he'd held with a relieved sigh. That had gone exactly the way he had planned, all except for the part where he'd been called an "irrational creature." That had not set too well with him, any more than the thought of separating those two boys had. Quickly he rolled the wheels of his chair backwards until he was through the door, then closed it. If he never saw those New York agents again, it would be too soon.

"The gall of that man," Gordon said with a huff, shifting in his seat so he could glimpse the house one last time. "How dare he speak to us like that."

"I warned you," Reverend Cross said, clearly not surprised by the outcome of their visit. "He's a mean one."

Anna closed her eyes and tried to push out all memory of the crude way the man had looked at her. It was as if he'd wanted to do everything he could to make her feel uncomfortable. Well, if that had been his intention, he had certainly succeeded. She still felt a desire to grit her teeth and blush, especially when she remembered how his eyebrows had arched with obvious interest when he had raked his gaze over her clothing. Self-consciously she crossed her arms in front of her, as if he might still be able to see her.

"That didn't take long. Do we have time to make one more stop?" she asked, not at all ready to give up yet.

Gordon quickly took out his watch and popped it open. "No, we really must get on back to town now. I still have to meet with the judge and get his signature on the papers for those children who are to remain

74

here. And we do have the other children to think about. We need to get them on their way."

That was true, yet Anna wished they could delay the trip to Marshall at least one more day. They were very close to finding those boys. She could feel it in her bones. "Is there any way we could reschedule Saturday's viewing in Marshall?"

"If we did, we could lose some of the interest our advertisements may have aroused. And if that happened, we could also lose several prospective families," Gordon reminded her. "Besides, we have the reverend's assurance that when the boys are found, he'll keep them both under careful supervision until we can return for Abel on our way back."

"But that will be at least a week," she complained. "Can't I be allowed to stay here in Pinefield during that time and continue to help with the search for the boys? There are only a few children left. Surely you can handle them well enough without me."

"I don't know if it would be wise to leave you here," Gordon said, stroking his chin thoughtfully. "Your place is with the remaining children. They may need you."

"Please—I can't bear the thought of Jamie and Abel being out there all alone. Nor can I bear the thought of them being found by strangers. It is especially heartbreaking when you consider that you and I were responsible for those two when they disappeared. I really do think one of us should stay behind to help with the search. And since you will be needed in Marshall to oversee all the legal aspects of the proceedings, I'm the logical one to stay behind."

"I'll think about it," is all Gordon would say. "Besides, there's still a chance that the boys have already been found by one of the other groups. Let's wait to see what happens at the church before I make any decisions."

Anna agreed. The boys could have been found and her heartfelt request to stay behind may have been for nothing. But when they reached the church less than an hour later, she was again disappointed to learn that the other groups had come away as empty-handed as they had.

None of the farmers or ranchers had admitted to having seen the boys, though several had quickly volunteered to help with the search. Finally, Gordon agreed to take the rest of the children on to Marshall without Anna. He promised to return for her, and hopefully for Abel, too, as soon as he'd completed his business there. He left her with enough money for a modest room at one of the local boardinghouses and daily meals, should the church stop providing her a place to stay or her food.

Anna was so grateful to Gordon for letting her stay that she wanted to throw her arms around him and hug him, but she quickly thought better of it. A man like Gordon Franklin would never understand such an outward display of emotion and would undoubtedly reprimand her for improper behavior. Instead, she opted for a warm handshake and a promise to do all she could to find Jamie and Abel while he was away.

True to her word, Anna returned to the reverend's buggy as soon as the train had pulled out and she had wished the other children good luck finding homes in Marshall. The sad expressions on their faces had tugged painfully at her heart, but in the end even they had agreed that finding Abel and Jamie was far too important. To those who were selected in Marshall, she agreed to get their new addresses and write often. And to any who remained unchosen, she promised to see them within the week. It had been a tearful parting, but she had too much to worry about to dwell on

76

the deep sense of loss she felt. She had to find those boys.

By the time night had fallen Anna was frantic with worry. It had been three days since the boys' disappearance, three days since their last meal. By now, the two youngsters had to be weak from hunger, so weak that they might not be able to tolerate another night out in the cold. Had she had her way, they would have continued the search right through the night, but the others convinced her it would be pointless. There were too many things they could miss in the dark. They would resume their search at first light.

Early that Saturday, Harry made a quick trip into town to see if the Orphan Train agents had indeed left on that Friday afternoon train. To his dismay, he was told that one of them had stayed behind. The woman. He hurried out to Mark's house to tell him the bad news, upset over how that could affect their plans.

"If Abel and Jamie were to turn up while that woman agent is still here, then Abel wouldn't get that chance to stick around and win nobody's hearts after all. He'll be whisked away on the next train out of here." Harry shoved his hands into his pockets. "It ain't fair. It just ain't fair."

"I wonder how long she plans to stay. Did anyone say?" Mark asked, studying the situation as it was now.

"No. And I was afraid to go askin' too many questions. I was afeared that somebody might start to wonder why I was so curious about somethin' that really shouldn't concern me. All I know for certain is that the lady agent is still here and still helpin' 'em look for Jamie and Abel. We're goin' to have to continue keepin' them boys hid out until she finally gives up and leaves."

Mark let out a slow, annoyed breath. "I wonder how long that will take." Though he didn't really mind having the boys there, he'd hoped to start trying to locate a new home for Abel that very afternoon.

"Can't rightly say how long that'll take, but I'll keep my ears open and as soon as I hear she's left, I'll let you know. Meantime, looks like we're stuck with 'em." His grin let Mark know how little that bothered him. Clearly Jamie and Abel had stolen the old man's heart, and if Mark were entirely honest with himself, he'd have to admit they'd laid a sizable claim to his own heart as well.

Early that Saturday morning, Anna, Reverend Cross, and one of the local farmers, a man named Simms, climbed into the reverend's buggy with a map in hand, eager to resume the search. Because the reverend was still not feeling too well, Anna and Mr. Simms took turns knocking at the doors of the different farms and ranches, each time hoping to hear some tidbit of news that might help them locate the boys.

Each time they were disappointed.

As the morning wore on into afternoon, Anna's thoughts returned time and time again to the heated conversation Gordon had had with that arrogant man in the wheelchair. There was something about that exchange that bothered her, but she could not quite figure out what it was.

It was not until late that afternoon, after they had dropped Mr. Simms off at his house and were on their way back into town, that she finally realized what it was. The man had said something about the boys having pleaded with Gordon not to separate them. How could he know that they'd actually pleaded to stay together? Had he merely assumed that, or did he actually know more about the situation than he had admitted?

There was only one way to find out. Confront him face to face. The sooner the better.

"Reverend? Would you mind stopping by Mr. Gates's house again?" she asked, though she hated the thought of putting him out like that. "I'd really like to question him again."

The reverend turned his red-rimmed, watery eyes to her, blinked once, then slowly shook his head as if overwhelmed by the thought. "Dat's several miles on the other side of town. Almost a full hour's ride from here. It would be nearly dark by the time we got dere. Besides, I habe to get my sermon ready for tomorrow. Though I plan to keep it short so we can spend most of our time looking for your children, I would like to bring the congregation together for a comforting prayer and offer a word or two of encouragement."

Anna glanced at him. What he was really saying was that he didn't feel up to another two hours in the buggy. The poor man had endured far more than any human should have to endure.

"I understand," she assured him. "But could you at least loan me your buggy so I can drive out there to ask him a few more questions? There's something he said yesterday that bothers me. I really would like the chance to question him more."

"He's not at all de sort of man a woman like you should face alone," the reverend insisted, then smiled indulgently. "But den maybe you could ride back out to Simms's house and conbince him to go with you."

"Then you'll loan me your buggy?" she asked, unable to believe he would allow it. It was such a fine buggy and he hardly knew her.

"You know how to dribe one?"

"I most certainly do."

"Den I'll loan you my buggy," he said with a shrug. "Just don't stay gone too long. It'll be dark soon. Probably before you get back. I have lanterns, but they don't help much after it gets very dark."

"I'll hurry," she promised, thrilled that she would have another chance to question that man. "Meanwhile, I think you should get some rest. You look terrible."

"Thank you," he said with a brief smile. "But if you continue to flatter me like dat, you'll just end up gibing me de big head. And if my head gets much bigger dan it feels right now, it just might explode."

Within minutes, the reverend was inside his house warming his chilled bones by the stove and Anna was on her way to have a second talk with that horrid man, Mr. Gates. Having discovered it was nearly six o'clock by the time she'd helped the reverend down from the buggy and into his house, she decided against going back for Mr. Simms. His house was almost a mile out of the way. Besides, she wasn't afraid of driving a buggy after dark and she could certainly handle someone like Mr. Gates on her own. After all, he was in a wheelchair, for heaven's sake. How much harm could he really do? She tried not to think about the shotgun that had rested across his lap or the angry gleam she'd seen in his silvery blue eyes.

With only a vague recollection of where to turn once she was on the main road south, she headed straight out of town. To her relief, the terrain was exactly as she'd remembered it and she found Gates's house with no problem at all.

The sky had just turned a dark, murky gray when she pulled the buggy to a jangling halt in the front yard. The house looked far more foreboding in the dark shadows of dusk than it had in the bright sun of early afternoon when it had looked cluttered and in need of several small repairs. But, now, in the approaching darkness, it appeared almost haunted. Suddenly she was not happy with her decision to come alone.

Swallowing back the sudden burst of apprehension, Anna lifted her skirts and stepped carefully around the ragged clumps of weeds that grew in such abundance. Without taking time to rethink her situation, she marched determinedly up the creaking steps and across to his front door. While she knocked sharply at the door, she refused to dwell on any possibility of danger. Instead, she focused her thoughts on finally getting the truth out of Mr. Gates. She had to put the boys' welfare above her own. She would not allow that man to intimidate her in any way. The shotgun, maybe, but the man himself, never.

By the time the door finally opened, Anna had worked herself into quite a state of determination and anger. She was so intent on finding out exactly what this man did know about Jamie and Abel that she did not wait for an invitation. She immediately stepped inside his house, refusing to take the chance he might decide to slam the door in her face.

"What do you think you're doing?" Mark asked, turning his chair so he could watch while she marched angrily into his entry hall, unable to believe this woman's audacity. He then glanced back toward the kitchen to assure himself that the boys had followed his instructions and remained out of sight.

"I'm here to find out exactly what you know about those two missing boys," Anna told him without mincing words.

Mark's stomach knotted with sudden caution. "And what makes you think I know anything about those boys?"

"I'm not sure. It's just a feeling I have," she told him and quickly scanned her surroundings for any indication that the boys may have been there. She was appalled by the unkempt condition of his house. Clearly the man was not married, nor did he have a housekeeper. A woman would never allow a house to become such a mess. Why, there was dust on the furniture so thick someone could take a finger and write in it. Disgusting. Even if the man *was* unable to walk, he could at least pick up a dust rag and give his furniture a good cleaning.

"I'm really surprised to hear that," Mark responded, his expression hard as granite while his steely blue eyes continued to follow her every movement.

"Surprised to hear what?" she asked, having temporarily lost her train of thought. She looked back at him and felt a nerve-tingling chill wash over her. With his thick, dark beard and his shoulder-length brown hair to accentuate his anger, he was one of the most frightening men she'd ever come up against.

"Surprised to hear that you have any feelings at all. It was my understanding that you had none."

Anna crossed her arms angrily, still determined not to be intimidated by this man's hateful words or his frightening appearance. "Sir, if you hoped to dissuade me by throwing a few insults at me, you are in for a grave disappointment," she responded. Her green eyes glowed with a slowly simmering rage as she met his narrow, threatening glare. The more she talked with him, the more convinced she was that he knew something about the boys. "I came here to find out if you have or have not seen those two boys, and I'm not leaving here until I finally know the truth."

"The truth?" he asked, astonished that she'd dare use the word. Quickly he rolled his chair toward her, wanting her to see exactly how angry he'd become.

"The *truth* is that I wouldn't tell you even if I did know where those little boys were. The *truth* is that you are not the all-powerful god you think you are. You have no right whatsoever to separate those two."

"Then you do know where they are," she said, hoping to trick him into admitting the truth.

Mark's heavily lashed eyelids lowered until his eyes were nothing more than icy blue slits in an angry face. Slowly he uncrossed his arms and pointed at the still open door. "I think you'd better leave."

A tiny thud sounded from the back of the house, causing Mark's heart to leap and his eyes to dart fearfully in the direction of the sound. Holding his breath, he glanced back at his uninvited visitor to see if she'd noticed it too. He was relieved to find that her gaze had remained riveted to him. Obviously she was too angry to notice any unusual noises. Still, he needed to get her out of there before something happened that she could not help but notice.

"I refuse to leave your house until you've told me what I want to know," Anna stated, every muscle in her body rigid with determination.

Though it went against Mark's nature, he felt the time had come to flat out lie. For the boys' sake. "Look, Miss . . . he paused long enough for her to supply her name, not wanting her to have the satisfaction of knowing that he'd remembered it.

"Thomas."

"Look, Miss Thomas, I don't have any idea where those boys are. As you can see, I live alone." He gestured to his surroundings with a wide sweep of his hand. "I don't know why you seem to think I should know something about your runaways. But I can assure you I don't." The lie did not set well with Mark, but he had to do something to get rid of her.

"Then how did you know those boys had pleaded

with us to let them stay together?"

Mark paused, realizing his mistake and searching for the best way to rectify it. "Wouldn't you plead if you were them?" he asked, curling his hands into hard fists at the thought of those two little boys pleading their hearts out to someone like her.

Anna considered the question for several seconds. "Yes," she finally admitted, aware it was entirely possible the man had simply guessed at the fact. "Yes, I definitely would plead for any chance to stay together."

Her voice had softened so unexpectedly, it left Mark suddenly confused. "Then why do it? Why separate them?"

Anna had no answer for that. "I don't think that is any of your concern, Mr. Gates."

"Oh, but it does concern me. It concerns me that there are people like you out there, willing to separate brothers in order to fulfill some sort of human quota. Tell me, Miss Thomas, how much do you get paid for each child you place?"

"I don't get paid on a per child basis," she readily informed him. Her arms stiffened at her sides as her anger quickly returned. "And what right do you have to question me? I'm in no way accountable to you for what I do."

Mark studied her for a long moment, wondering how a woman so incredibly beautiful could be so cold and loathsome inside. "You are a cruel, malevolent woman, Miss Thomas. I shudder to think that there could be others in this world like you."

"And I shudder to think that there could be others like you, Mr. Gates. I'd think you'd be *eager* to help those two children."

"And just how do you expect me to help them when I've already told you I don't know where they are?" He studied the rigid lines forming along her jaw and hoped she had not seen through his lies. "Another thing that certainly bears repeating: even if I did know something about those poor little boys, I wouldn't tell you. I think it's downright unnatural to want to split up a pair of brothers like that. I'd rather adopt them myself than give you the chance to separate them again."

"You?" She responded with a short laugh and an indignant toss of her head, as eager to hurt him as he'd been to hurt her. "Adopt those boys?"

"Why not?" He steeled himself against the coming answer, certain she intended to make some cutting remark about his mangled leg, about the fact he wasn't even a whole man anymore.

"Why not?" she repeated, shaking her head with disbelief. "I'll tell you why not. For one thing, you are hardly a suitable prospect for parenthood. Look at you." Her expression let him know that she found his appearance nothing short of appalling. "You haven't bothered to shave or even cut your hair in what has to be months. You look revolting. Almost as revolting as your house."

She uncrossed one of her arms to indicate their surroundings with a careless flick of her hand. "In case you haven't noticed, you live in a pigsty, Mr. Gates. Your house is filthy and your so-called farm is nothing more than a rundown patch of weeds and brush. No judge in his right mind would allow a pair of impressionable young boys to live in a tumbledown place like this. Nor would he allow someone like you to be responsible for them. You are too busy wallowing in your own self-pity to care what happens to anyone else. You have chosen to use that twisted leg as an excuse for your laziness and your incredibly bad manners. You don't even have any visible means of supporting yourself, much less two others. Adopt those two boys? Don't kid yourself."

"Get out of my house," Mark shouted at the top of his voice, stabbing his finger in the direction of the door. "Get out of my house and get off of my land!"

"Oh, I'll gladly leave this place," she retorted. She curled her lips over tightly gritted teeth as she headed directly for the door. Then, before she stepped through the opening and out onto the porch, she glanced back over her shoulder and glared at him. "But if I find out you've lied to me about those two boys, I'll be back."

Every muscle in Mark's body jumped when she then slammed the door as hard as she could. He closed his eyes and tried to figure out what he would do if she did return. His shoulders slumped when he realized there really wasn't much he could do. She was obviously not afraid of him and certainly didn't balk at the thought of speaking her mind, even to a man confined to a wheelchair.

What sort of woman was she, anyway?

Chapter Five

Harry and the boys had heard everything that had been said between Mark and Miss Thomas. They felt awkward from having overheard such spiteful comments — and a little guilty. They may not have intended to listen in on the conversation, but they'd heard it just the same.

Not knowing what to expect, the three remained cautiously quiet when Mark rolled back into the kitchen with a dark, forbidding scowl.

Not bothering to speak to any of them, though he knew they were all watching his every move, Mark rolled over to one of the glass-fronted cabinets near the back door and stared at his own dim reflection for several seconds. His scowl darkened when he tilted his head from one side to the other, then his expression suddenly turned thoughtful.

"Harry, do you happen to remember where I put my razor?" he asked while he continued to study his shaggy appearance. As hard as it was to admit, that prissy-mouthed lady agent had been right about one thing: he looked terrible.

Having tensed in preparation for another tirade, Harry raised his eyebrows. It had been such an unexpected question. "I reckon it's still out there on the back porch, probably layin' on that shelf by the well. Isn't that where you left it last fall?"

"Has it been that long since my last shave?" He pulled at the wiry brown hair until it stretched out several inches from his face, surprised to discover just how long his beard had grown. He definitely had six months' growth there. Six months of face hair that he hadn't even bothered to trim. "I guess it has been nearly half a year."

"I know it has," Harry said, nodding briskly. He well remembered how hard it had been to convince Mark to shave after all those months of having lain in bed recovering from his accident. At the time, Harry had thought a fresh shave and a haircut might finally bring Mark out of his dismal mood, but it hadn't worked. Nothing had. But maybe this time a good shave and a haircut would be just the thing to lift his spirits, or at least change his pitiful attitude about himself—especially since this time it was his own idea and not something forced on him by someone else's constant harping. "Want me to sharpen 'er up for ya? I know right where the strop is. Won't take but a few minutes to make that razor good as new."

"Nō, I can do that. But, maybe you could locate my shaving mug and whip up some soap for me."

Harry chuckled to himself as he pushed himself up out of the chair. He knew darn well that the only reason Mark Gates had finally decided to make a few changes in his appearance was because of all the spiteful things the lady agent had said about him. Too bad someone hadn't thought to confront him with the truth a lot sooner. Finally Mark was starting to see himself as others saw him, and obviously what he saw did not set too well with him. It was about time he realized the deep, senseless hole of self-pity he'd crawled off into. And it was about time he climbed out of there and did something worthwhile with his life.

"I'll get that soap ready," Harry said happily, already heading for the door. "Meanwhile, why don't you two boys put the cheese and the milk back in the cooler. By the time we get through shavin' away that bush, they'll both be as warm as—" He paused, for what he'd almost said was not something that should be said in front of young boys. "They'll be as warm as that stew will be cold. No sense in lettin' that happen."

"Somebody find the scissors, too," Mark said, turning the chair toward the back porch. "Harry, I think I remember seeing them in all that clutter that's on the table near the front door."

Jamie hurried to do what he had been told, and as soon as he and Abel had put the milk and cheese away and had taken the stew off the stove and set it aside so it would not burn, they joined Harry and Mark in the small washroom that had been added on near the back door to allow the laundry chores to be done indoors during the winter.

Sitting cross-legged on the floor, the boys watched with absolute fascination while Harry did the honors of first cutting away large clumps of excess beard with the scissors, then soaped and shaved off the remaining face hair. Afterward, Harry took the scissors to his friend's thick mane of hair, clipping it to a far more manageable length. It took well over an hour to complete the two tasks, but the results were astounding. Mark Gates did not look like the same man.

Jamie was first to comment after lowering his gaze from Mark's ghostly white cheeks to the mounds of dark brown hair piled high at Harry's feet. "Looks like you've got enough cut hair there to stuff a mattress."

Harry chuckled, handing the mirror to Mark so he could see the results. "Me bein' near as bald today as the day I was born, it's hard to imagine anyone bein' able to grow that much hair."

Jamie nodded his agreement. "Hard to imagine anyone wanting to. Seems to me it would itch something awful."

"It did at times," Mark admitted, handing the mirror back to Harry, pleased with what he'd seen. He looked more like his old self—at least from the waist up. Not wanting to dwell on his injured leg, he looked down at Jamie and shrugged his broad shoulders. "What do you think? Is it an improvement? Or did you like me better with the beard and the long hair?"

"I like you the same either way," Jamie said, all the while studying Mark's smooth face with an arched brow, as if trying to get used to such a drastic change. "But I know for a fact that Miss Thomas is going to like you a lot better this way. She's always after us boys to keep our hair cut short and combed back out of our eyes. She won't be able to say you look revolting now."

Absently stroking his now smooth cheek with the curve of his hand, Mark looked from Jamie, to Harry, to Abel, then back to Jamie. He noticed how deeply concerned they all seemed. "I gather you heard some of what Miss Thomas and I had to say to each other."

Reluctant to answer, Jamie glanced back over his shoulder at Abel, who sat cross-legged behind him. Because his brother sat quietly running his fingertip up and down his pant leg seam, he looked as if he was not paying any attention to the conversation around him, but Jamie knew different. Abel had heard what Mark and Miss Thomas had said to each other. And he knew what was being said now. He just didn't want anyone else to know he knew and in a way that made a lot of sense. Abel avoided a lot of trouble that way.

Finally Jamie straightened back around. Again he lifted his blue-green gaze to meet Mark's. His expression was apologetic. "We didn't mean to listen in, but we couldn't really help it. The way you two got to shouting at each other and all, we had no choice but to hear parts of it." He paused for a moment, searching Mark's face, as if trying to read his thoughts. "You knew about us all along, didn't you?"

"I knew you were runaways," he admitted as he continued to stroke the smooth surface of his cheek, finding the skin became a little less sensitive with each gentle stroke. "The fact that you two were on the run was pretty obvious right from the start. But I had no idea who you were or why you were running until later that next day, after Harry came back from getting the flour. He heard all about it while he was in town."

Jamie furrowed his brow showing that he did not understand. "You knew about us, but you didn't tell anyone. Why? Weren't you afraid you'd get into trouble?"

Mark studied the little boy's pensive expression and wished he could go to the boy and comfort him in some way, and for a moment he considered doing just that. Even with the damage done to his leg, he could still crawl, he knew that; but the thought of letting these boys see him groveling on the floor like

91

a wounded animal held him back. Suddenly he remembered that wooden contraption the doctor had given him to help him walk again. He wondered if it still fit. "I didn't tell anyone because I don't happen to agree with what those people are trying to do. You see, when I was your age, I had a brother, too, and I can well remember how important he was to me."

Jamie's eyes widened. *"Was?* What happened to him? Did they take him away from you?" His cheeks paled at the thought.

Mark looked away to hide his pain. "No, they didn't take him away from me. Seth fell into an old abandoned well when he was eleven, and he drowned. I was only nine at the time, but I can remember how much he meant to me, and how very much it hurt to lose him. I don't want you two to have to go through that same sort of hurt. I meant it when I told the woman that I think it is just plain unnatural to want to separate the two of you."

Jamie ran the tip of his tongue nervously across his lower lip. Slowly, he stood, then took a tentative step toward Mark, his arms frozen at his sides, his breath held deep in his throat. "And did you mean the rest of what you said to her?"

"What's that?" Mark tried to remember exactly what he did say. He had thought of so many things he'd wished he'd said but had not. Now he was no longer certain what he had and hadn't actually said to her.

"You told her that you'd adopt us yourself before you'd let them separate us again."

The raw hope shining in Jamie's blue-green eyes struck Mark hard. He could no longer deny the love he felt for this homeless child. In the few days that

Jamie and Abel had been in his home, he'd come to care deeply for them both. Although it would mean making major changes in his life, he was all for adopting the pair.

"Yes, I meant it. I meant every word of it. But I'm afraid your Miss Thomas was dead right about one thing. Unless I do something to change the rundown condition of this place, and do it in a hurry, the judge who has the authority to decide these things is not about to give either of you permission to live here. I'll have to prove I'm a responsible person, one who is capable of providing a proper upbringing for you two, despite my — limitations."

He turned then to Harry. The more he thought about it, the more he wanted these boys. "You think I could borrow that new Washington plow of yours for a few days? I could probably get twice the work done with that new plow than with my old one."

Harry blinked back threatening tears and gruffly cleared his throat. He knew that the real reason Mark wanted him to bring over his new plow was because it had a seat on it. Obviously Mark planned on doing all this work himself. Harry couldn't be more pleased, but he also could not be any more determined to help. "Sure. Won't be no problem. I got finished with my plantin' last week. Got the seeds down in time for that rain we had Wednesday. In fact, if you're plannin' on puttin' in some corn, I still got over half a sack leftover from my own plantin'."

"Corn would do fine," Mark said. His eyes glittered with excitement. It felt good to have a real purpose in life again. "That way, even if it doesn't make a good enough crop to sell in town, I can always use it to feed the cattle."

Harry wondered at the man's sanity. "What cattle?"

Mark had sold all his cattle so he'd have enough money to pay his doctor bills and take care of his living expenses for a year or so. It had been for the best. Mark couldn't have taken care of his stock anyway, not while he was still laid up in bed. But now that he was able to get around in a wheelchair, and judging by that determined look in his blue eyes, Mark could undoubtedly handle a whole herd of cattle. At that moment, he looked as if he could handle anything—even that self-righteous Miss Thomas from the Orphan Train.

"What cattle?" Mark repeated with a wide grin, and for the first time in ages, Harry got a glimpse of those long crescent-shaped dimples that flanked his mouth. "Why, the cattle I plan to run on that back pasture, of course. I figure if I reseed and fertilize right away, I should be able to start running a small herd of cattle on it, probably by midsummer."

"Can we help?" Jamie asked eagerly, having stepped close enough to place his hand on Mark's arm.

Mark studied the boy's bright-eyed expression and knew that it would mean a lot to the child to be able to help. And why shouldn't he if this place was to be his new home? "I don't see any reason why not. It's going to take a lot of hard work to get everything back in shape. I'll need a couple of good, strong helpers. Of course, I'll pay you the going wage for your help."

"You don't need to do that," Jamie answered in earnest. "We'll do it for nothing. Won't we, Abel?"

Abel nodded his consent, his eyes as wide and as hopeful as Jamie's.

Mark looked at the two of them with a serious expression. "I'm a proud man, Jamie. I can't possibly

94

take any charity work from boys as nice as you. Either you accept a dollar a day for your work, or you'll just have to sit in the house and watch."

Jamie put his forefinger to his chin to think about that. "I sure don't want to be stuck in the house all day," he admitted, then finally agreed, though he had no idea what he'd ever do with all that money.

With so many plans to be formulated and lists to be made, Mark, Harry, Jamie, and Abel sat around the kitchen table until well after midnight, eagerly discussing who should do what. Though each of them had certain limitations, they discovered that if they teamed up into pairs, they could compensate for one another and get a lot accomplished. With any luck, by the time anyone realized the boys were there, they would have made enough improvements in Mark's house and to the land itself for Mark to be seriously considered as the legal guardian of the boys.

Because the next morning was Sunday and everything in town would be closed until early Monday morning, they decided the best place to start was with the house itself. Between the supplies Mark had on hand and what Harry brought from his house, they were able to clean and polish, and make most of the necessary repairs. Knowing how important it was for Mark to be able to provide the boys with a decent place to live, they all worked very hard to restore the house to its original state.

While Mark and Jamie worked as one team, cleaning the downstairs from top to bottom and corner to corner, Harry and Abel worked together upstairs. By mid-afternoon, when they stopped for a quick bite to eat, they discovered they had made remarkable progress. Later that afternoon, after they decided the house looked as good as it ever had except for the faded paint, they started on the yard immediately surrounding the house.

By Monday morning, they had the flowerbeds cleared and the yard cropped and were ready to concentrate their efforts on the farmland itself. When Harry left for home late Sunday night, he promised to return bright and early with his plow and the seeds he had left over from his own planting.

The next day, while Mark and the boys started right to work, Harry made a quick trip into town to buy more seeds for both corn and grass, and everything else Mark had written down on his list, including several outfits of new clothes for the boys, though he knew he'd have to be careful how he explained such an odd purchase to the nosy storekeeper.

Knowing how touchy the situation was, Harry paused outside the store long enough to take off his hat and offer a quick prayer. With any luck, he would be able to purchase everything they needed with no questions asked. That way they might have a chance to get at least one of Mark's fields cleared and planted before anyone thought to link his unusual purchases with the missing boys.

Anna awoke ready to head right back out to Mark Gates's place and confront him again.

During the night she'd had plenty of time to go over their conversation in her mind, and the more she'd thought about their angry exchange of words, the more she believed he had lied to her about the boys. He knew something he was not telling.

When she left for church services, she was determined to borrow the reverend's buggy again and go get the truth out of that man if she had to beat it out of him with her buggy whip.

In fact, if it hadn't been for the announcement made during services that the boys had been seen walking along one of the farm roads north of town late the afternoon before, she'd have done just that. But with the boys having been spotted going in the opposite direction, there seemed little reason to return to Mark Gates's farm. Still, she could not shake the feeling that he had lied to her.

Now able to eliminate all areas to the south, west, and east, the townspeople of Pinefield confined their attention to the farms and ranches that lay directly north of town.

But aware the boys could have hitched a ride with some passing traveler, they sent a group of three men to question the people in several of the neighboring towns off to the north. Meanwhile the rest of the group resumed their house-to-house, farm-to-farm search.

Anna chose to remain with Reverend Cross and Robert Simms.

Together, they stopped at all the places they'd been assigned to, asking everyone they met about the boys. No one had seen them. By Monday afternoon, she was so thoroughly disgusted that she wondered if their "eyewitness" had been all that reliable. The man was not from around Pinefield. In fact, he'd come from somewhere in north Louisiana and was just passing through on his way to visit relatives in west Texas. If the boys had really taken to the road as he said, why hadn't anyone else seen them? Others had traveled the same road at about that same time but had seen no one. It did seem a little strange.

It wasn't long before Anna began thinking about

Mark Gates again and the strong feeling she'd had that he'd lied to her.

Though the others had started to give up all hope of ever finding the boys alive, thinking a week was a long time for the pair to have survived without proper food and shelter, Anna refused to believe God could have a reason for taking two such loving children from this earth. While some of the men looked to the sky for any evidence of vultures gathering, Anna kept her eyes trained to the ground, watching for some telltale movement in the brush, searching for some clue that would prove the boys had passed by. She was determined not to give up hope.

"I don't mean to alarm you," Reverend Cross finally said in that soft, consoling voice of his. "But even though the days are finally starting to grow warm again, the nights have continued to be bitterly cold, and for two young boys without food or blankets, those nights could prove quite harmful." He rested a comforting hand on her shoulder. He hadn't said that to hurt her, just to prepare her for the possibility of the worst.

Still, Anna refused to believe the boys were dead, though she worried they might be ill and undoubtedly very frightened—afraid of what waited ahead for them and just as afraid of what lay behind.

The more she and her fellow searchers asked around and discovered that no one besides the one questionable witness had seen the boys, the more Anna believed the group had been led off in the wrong direction. She believed that the boys were quietly moving about from place to place, stealing food to stay alive, and hiding out in different barns where they could burrow in fresh hay or cover up with horse blankets to keep from freezing. Her theory was that they managed to slip in and out of the barns without ever alerting anyone to their presence. Or had they?

Again she thought of Mark Gates and wondered what he knew about those boys. Had they made the mistake of cutting across his land on their frantic trek for freedom? Was he hiding the fact that he'd actually seen them? If so, why? Just to be contrary? Or had he done something so terrible to frighten them that he didn't want anyone else to find out? She had to know.

"Reverend, I realize it's getting late, and I know you're probably going to think I'm being stubborn, but would it be asking too much to have the loan of your buggy once more so I can make another trip out to Mr. Gates's house?"

"But you've already been out there twice," the reverend pointed out. Though he remembered very little about the events of Saturday night, having been so very ill at the time, he did remember that she'd borrowed his buggy so she could question that man a second time and had come back in a most peculiar mood.

"I know. And I also know how far out of the way it is, therefore, I'm not asking that you go with me. Just lend me the buggy so I can go. I'd feel much better if I could question him at least once more. I still think he knows something he is not telling."

"I really believe you'd be wasting your time," he responded, hoping to discourage her, then let his shoulders sag with defeat. "But I can see that you're determined to go. Take my buggy. Robert and I can ride back into town with Dixon Shultz."

"Thank you," she said, sighing with relief, having worried he might refuse her this time. She really did want to have another talk with Mark Gates. "I'll try to be back by dark."

"You do that," the reverend said with a cautionary wag of his finger. "Don't you go worrying me and my missus by coming back late."

Within minutes they'd caught up with Dixon Schultz and the two men riding in his wagon. After assuring their welcome, the reverend and Robert Simms climbed down from the buggy and hurried to join the other group.

Knowing she had at least an hour's drive ahead of her, and less than two hours before dark, Anna wasted no time getting the buggy under way.

Harry had been nothing short of amazed when he returned from town with the purchases and discovered that Mark was actually up and out of his wheelchair, hobbling across the field wearing a brace and using nothing more than a cane for balance. Though he was having a hard time of it, Mark was walking again, and under his own power. Harry beamed a bright smile when he realized that Mark must have gone looking for that wooden contraption the doctor had given him just a couple of months after the accident.

Though the brace was made up of little more than a pair of sturdy curved boards held in place by leather straps, it offered Mark's leg added support so he could move about with the use of a stout cane. But Mark had never given the thing much of a chance before. In fact, he'd thrown it to the back of his closet and refused to bring it back out after his first attempt to walk with it had landed him on his face.

The doctor had tried to tell him it would take some getting used to because he'd have to learn to walk without bending his knee, which was the whole purpose of the brace, to take the strain off his knee and his ankle, both of which had been shattered in the accident and had grown back crooked. The doctor felt Mark would eventually be able to walk without the aid of the bulky brace, but first he had to condition himself to getting around without bending his knee or ankle, and he needed to redevelop the damaged muscles in that leg.

Knowing Mark had gone to the trouble to look for the brace and had then strapped it on all by himself made Harry realize just how serious he was about adopting those two boys. Harry's smile widened, forming weathered wrinkles in his cheeks when he climbed down from the wagon. Wouldn't it be grand if that judge decided in Mark's favor? Then Mark would have those boys calling him pa, and he would have them calling him grandpa. *Grandpa*. He sure liked the sound of that. Grandpa Harry. Yep, that's what he'd have them call him, all right . . . that is, if they had a mind to. There'd be no forcing those two into doing anything that didn't feel right to them.

"I can't believe my lying eyes," Harry said, after hurrying across the field to where Mark had just climbed up into the high-springed plow seat and settled his cane across the rail beneath his outstretched leg. He watched with amazement while Mark bent forward at the waist and took hold of the reins. "You was walking as pretty as you please."

Mark's broad smile carved proud, curving dimples into his cheeks. "I'm afraid I can't stay on my feet for very long at a time because I start to feel weak and wobbly, but I managed to get from my wheelchair to

101

this plow without falling on my face. That's better than I did the first time I put this confounded thing on."

"And I see you managed to get your mule hitched up to my plow on your own, too," Harry stated, his expression full of admiration. "I'll admit it. I thought I'd be havin' to do that for you after I got back. I figured you'd give out long before you got even the harness straightened out."

"I had help," Mark admitted, and nodded toward the boys.

Harry glanced back over his shoulder to where Jamie and Abel stood several yards away, eager to do their part. He smiled when he saw that although it was barely ten o'clock, both boys were sweating steady streams. Hard workers, those two.

"Before you boys get those fancy city clothes of yours any more dirty than they already are, I think you should know that I got you some new clothes there in the back of the wagon. While I was in town, Mark had me buy some cotton shirts and khaki pants for you to work in. Won't be nearly as hot as those wool clothes you got on. Wool may be a fine thing to wear up north, but it'll burn you alive down here, 'specially this time of year. Why don't you get those new clothes and go on into the house and change?"

While Harry helped the boys find the clothes, Mark snapped the reins. The mule responded immediately. After one hard jerk, the plow moved forward, exposing a trail of light brown dirt in the field that lay directly in front of his house. Though the land there was not the best he had for planting, it did have one advantage . . . it could not be seen from the main road nor from any of his neighbors' land. And with the boys so determined to help in any way they could, such seclusion was important.

"They should be back out in a minute," Harry told him, after he'd returned from the wagon. He walked alongside the plow so Mark could hear what he had to say without having to stop. "What do you want me to do now? Get the fire started?"

Mark glanced back over his shoulder at all the weeds, brush, and mangled roots he'd unearthed. "Maybe you'd better. It'll take awhile to get all that gathered and burned. Just be sure those boys don't get too close to the flames when they go to toss in whatever brush they pick up. I sure don't want them to get hurt."

"Don't worry, I'll do all the tossin' in myself. I'll have the boys stack whatever brush they round up into a separate pile, then I'll see that it gets into the fire. You just keep your mind on your plowin'. I don't want you to go dullin' my new blade on a big ol' rock or some oversized tree root."

Then, without giving Mark an opportunity to reply, Harry spun about and, feeling more spry than he had in years, started right to work. He plucked up some of the larger pieces of unearthed roots and brush until, soon, he had enough to start his fire.

Just before Anna arrived at the narrow entrance of the grass-covered drive that cut through the woods to Mark's house, she glanced up and noticed a large pillar of smoke rising high above the treetops. The smoke was too far away to indicate that the woods near the main road had caught on fire. The smoke was off toward Mark Gates's house.

Her heart froze, then beat at a tremendous rate.

Mark's house was on fire. It had to be. That's all

that lay in that direction. The thought of that poor, helpless man trapped inside a burning house caused her to panic. She had no time to stop and wonder how, on some subconscious level, Mark Gates had gone from being an insufferable clod to a poor, helpless man in just a matter of seconds. She had to save him.

With her pulses pounding, she slapped the reins down hard across the horse's back and pleaded for the animal to hurry. By the time she'd reached the turn, the buggy was traveling at such a rapid speed, it almost tipped over. Putting Mark Gates's safety above her own, she didn't attempt to slow the animal's pace until she reached the edge of the woods, where she got her first real glimpse of the house. The smoke was not billowing out of the windows as she'd expected. Instead it was coming from a large pile of rubbish in a nearby field.

Relieved to the point of feeling physically weak, Anna pulled the buggy to a stop. She had to calm her nerves before going on. While she sat leaning limply against the back of the leather seat, taking in several slow, steady breaths, she noticed activity near the fire.

Sitting forward and shading her eyes from the glaring rays of the late afternoon sun, she studied the movement for several seconds. Though she was still several hundred yards from the house, she could make out the shapes well enough to know that Mark Gates was riding on a plow while another man stood near the fire, hurriedly tossing something into the flames. Then, she noticed the children, running along behind the plow gathering up sticks, rocks, and weeds. It was Jamie and Abel. It had to be. Suddenly, she was so overcome by rage that she could hardly breathe. Her arms shook visibly.

So that was why the man had wanted to keep whatever he knew about those boys such a secret! He was forcing them to work for him, using them to clear his fields. He'd lied to her, said he didn't know where they might be, just so he could make personal slaves out of them.

With no thought for her own safety, no thought that the man might be the type to resort to violence when crossed, Anna snapped the reins hard. The buggy lurched forward, causing her head to snap back and loosen the pins that held her hat. But at that moment she was too upset to care.

She had to rescue those children!

Chapter Six

A wide trail of dust billowed high into the air and formed a swirling, choking cloud around the buggy when Anna brought the vehicle to a clattering stop. She was only a few yards from where the older man stood watching her with a stunned expression. He had stopped tossing handfuls of debris into the fire and now stood stock-still, all color gone from his whiskered face.

It was obvious from the man's open-mouthed, wide-eyed reaction that he knew he was doing something he shouldn't, and that made Anna even angrier.

Not about to face the two men unarmed, she snatched the buggy whip from its holder before she hurriedly climbed down the side nearest the field. She headed straight for the boys, who also had stopped working and stood staring at her, dumbfounded. She curled her hands into determined fists while she marched staunchly toward them.

When she was close enough to see the boys' sweaty, dirt-streaked faces, her stomach coiled into a hard, angry knot. Through the filth and sweat coating their skin she could see that they were both badly sunburned and that merely added to her rage.

"Jamie, Abel, come here!" she shouted. Hurrying, she approached the narrow wooden fence that divided the small field from the yard. She snatched her dark gray woolen skirt high enough to enable her to slip through the twenty-inch gap between the unpainted boards.

As she came up on the other side, her hat came off and fell in the dirt behind her, but she did not bother to retrieve it. She didn't dare turn her back on these men, no matter how far away they were. Anyone who would willingly force such small children into slavery could not be trusted — at any distance.

"Boys, I'm here to rescue you," she said, her voice loud enough for them to hear; she hoped it was not loud enough for Mark Gates to make out what she'd said. When neither child braved a response, she realized their legs were frozen with fear. She took several steps toward them, the weeds and brush tugging at her skirt. "Don't be afraid. I won't let them hurt you anymore — I promise."

She shook the buggy whip to indicate exactly how she intended to keep that promise, knowing she would not hesitate to use the narrow leather strap on either man if that's what it took to get those boys out of there. And if, after she stepped closer to the boys, she saw evidence that either of them had been beaten or mistreated in any way, she would gladly do all she could to whip both those men into a bloody pulp. "Hurry children, please. Run to the buggy. I'll protect you."

Jamie and Abel exchanged confused glances, then

107

looked back over their shoulders toward Mark, who had heard the commotion and had already climbed down from the plow. Leaning heavily against his cane for balance, he attempted to hurry across the freshly plowed field, finding it impossible. The wooden brace forced him to swing his leg around to the side, raking dirt as he went because his muscles were not yet strong enough to lift the leg off the ground. It infuriated him that he could not move any faster.

"Come on, Jamie," Anna called out, and took a few more steps toward them, surprised to see that the man could walk, even with a brace and a cane. Fully aware she did not have enough time to run to them, grab them both into her arms, and escape before Mark would be upon them, she called out again, yet the boys still did not respond.

Pushing aside a strand of hair that had come loose and fallen into her face when she'd lost her hat, she started to panic. Why wouldn't the boys come to her? "Jamie, grab Abel's hand and make a run for the buggy. I'll keep them from coming after you."

Again she raised her whip high into the air and glanced from Mark to the older man near the fire, wanting to see which of them presented the greatest danger at the moment.

"They are not going anywhere," Mark shouted, near enough now to hear what was being said, but still not close enough to do anything about it.

"Oh, yes, they are," she responded. She thrust her chin forward to show how determined she was. "Those children are going back to Pinefield with me. And there's nothing you can do to stop me."

Although she could not actually see his face because he had stepped directly into the glaring rays of the late afternoon sun, she could easily imagine Mark Gates's angry expression and tightened her grip on the stout leather handle of the buggy whip. She was relieved to see she had caught him totally unaware — and without his shotgun. As long as he was unarmed, they had a chance.

Tossing her head back, she stared directly into the shadows that covered his face and bravely added, "What's more, after I tell the sheriff how you've been holding these boys prisoners, making them work for you like a couple of animals, I think you can pretty well count on a trip into Pinefield yourself."

"But he ain't making us work for him," Jamie protested.

Instead of going to the buggy as she'd commanded, the older boy then spun about and ran across the field to Mark's side, his feet kicking the loose dirt high into the air. To add to Anna's confusion, he then threw his arms around Mark's waist and held on tight, his sweaty cheek pressed hard against the man's taut stomach.

Mark stopped his struggle to cross the freshly plowed field and placed a protective arm around the small boy's shoulders. He then looked in the direction where Abel stood, about halfway between them and Anna.

"Come here, Abel," he commanded. His tone was not harsh, just firm.

Abel's eyes widened at the mention of his name. He looked at Anna, then at Mark, then at Harry. Then suddenly, he took off running toward Mark and flung himself against Mark's good leg so hard that he almost caused him to topple back into the dirt.

"Atta boy!" Harry shouted, then pushed his battered hat forward before he, too, hurried to join the other three, marching much like a soldier headed for war, eager to show exactly where his loyalties lay.

Holding the boys close, using them for balance instead of his cane, Mark smiled with more pride than he had felt in a long time. "As you can clearly see, Miss Thomas, Jamie and Abel are here because they want to be here. No one is forcing them to do anything against their will."

Anna's green eyes narrowed with caution as she took several more steps in their direction. The closer she was, the more her blood felt like icewater, but she had to see the boys' faces when she spoke to them. She had to see if there was even the slightest evidence of fear in their eyes. "Jamie? Is what this man says true? Are you here because you want to be here?"

Jamie blinked and nodded, unable to speak.

"Don't be afraid to tell me the truth," she coaxed, misunderstanding the reason for his silence, certain Mark Gates had threatened them in some way. Aware of the danger she was placing herself in, she continued to grip the whip handle tightly while she moved ever closer. "No one is going to hurt you for telling the truth."

"That *is* the truth," Harry put in, unable to hold his tongue a minute longer. His weathered face pulled into a hard, determined scowl while he squared his scrawny shoulders and braced his rail-thin legs. "Those boys are here because they want to be. Anybody can tell that by lookin' at 'em."

"Oh?" Anna responded, able to see the older man

better than the others because he stood enough to one side to prevent the sun from shining directly behind him. "And am I supposed to believe that these two boys willingly volunteered to work like a couple of field hands out under this hot, blistering sun?" She rounded further to one side so she could glance from Jamie's grimy face to Abel's without the sun blinding her. She had to see their expressions to know what their feelings were.

When she slowly and cautiously moved to where the sun was no longer behind them, she noticed again how sunburned the boys were. Her rage grew tenfold. "Mr. Gates, are you aware that both those boys are badly sunburned and are probably close to passing out from heat stroke?"

Mark bent forward so he could get a better look at them, then lifted his gaze to look worriedly at Harry.

Anna gave neither man a chance to respond. Instead she continued her tirade of angry questions, directing them mostly at the older man because she could see more of his face, which was somewhat reassuring. It unnerved her to stare into the face of the taller man because it had remained nothing more than a dark shadow beneath a wide-brimmed hat. "Do you really expect me to believe that those boys actually *enjoy* being forced to do hard physical labor out here in this insufferable heat? That they *asked* to be worked like animals until they drop? Sir, are you not aware that slavery is now illegal in this country?" Her anger had reached such a state, she now found it hard to breathe.

"But nobody has forced us to do anything," Jamie put in, ready for the truth to be known. "We asked to help. Honest we did. Mr. Gates—Mark—he told us we could quit whenever we got too hot or too tired, but Abel and me aren't about to quit. This is too important."

"You volunteered to work for this man?" Anna asked, still not ready to believe it. Why would they? Why would anyone?

A stark white smile broke through the thick coating of grime and sweat that covered Jamie's thin face. "Yes, ma'am, we sure did. And he's promised to pay us a dollar a day for our work, even after we told him we didn't want no pay."

For once, Anna was too concerned with what the boy was saying to notice his bad grammar. "This man has promised to pay you a dollar a day?" Again she narrowed her dark green eyes to show her distrust. "But that's a man's wages. Why would he agree to pay you so much?"

"Because they are doing a man's work," Mark put in, squaring his shoulders and standing erect despite the dizzy feeling floating around in the back of his head. He shifted his weight to his good leg while he fought to keep his balance.

Finally, Anna turned her attention to Mark Gates, who still held the boys firmly in his arms. He'd turned enough for her to see part of his face. Her eyes widened when she failed to recognize him.

This was not the same man. This was not Mark Gates—at least not the Mark Gates she had met just a few days earlier. That Mark Gates had looked like some wild, revolting creature who had been shown to have very little in common with the rest of mankind. This man was his exact opposite. This man was actually very handsome—disturbingly so. Anna

112

felt a sharp, confusing leap of her senses when he reached up and yanked off his hat, quick to place it on top of Abel's head. That small action had taken away the last of the lingering shadows from his face, and she could now see him clearly. Bewildered, she stared at him, unable to believe her eyes.

Not only did Mark Gates have the clearest, bluest eyes she'd ever seen on a man, and the longest, thickest eyelashes, his whole face was astonishingly attractive. It was hard to believe that a scraggly beard and a thick head of shoulder length hair had been hiding such remarkably strong features. His cheeks, though flushed from too much sun, were as hard and lean as his arms, waist, and shoulders. A well-shaped nose, far more noticeable now that he'd shaved, lay long and straight beneath his harsh, penetrating gaze. A gentle afternoon breeze tugged at his coffee-brown hair, quickly erasing the wide crease his hatband had left just above his ears. His hair, though much shorter now, was the only soft feature about him. Now that it had been cut to a more appropriate length it looked as though it would feel silky to the touch.

While he waited impatiently for her response, the hardened muscles in his jaw flexed with powerful determination, sending through Anna a shiver of awareness so strong that it made her toes curl. Though she knew him to be a cripple, she was suddenly alert to the sheer strength and the undeniable masculinity that radiated from him. Her heart hammered violently inside her chest as she tried to sort through her confused emotions, emotions that made it hard to decide if what she really wanted was to stand and admire his extraordinary good looks or turn and run from him before he could cause her undeterminable harm.

Just because he now appeared to be more human than he had before didn't mean he would act any more human.

"Then tell me, Mr. Gates, why are you doing this, if not for the work you can get out of these boys?" she finally asked, forcing her wandering thoughts back to the matter at hand. She could not allow herself to be adversely influenced by either his harsh, angry stare or by his unquestionably handsome face.

"Why do you *think* I'm doing it?" Mark asked, still holding the boys close, his arms resting protectively around their shoulders. "I'm doing it because of what you said to me the other night."

"Me? What did I say?"

"You said that no judge in his right mind would ever allow these boys to live in a pigsty like mine. It didn't take me long to realize that you were right. You also said some thing about having to show some means of providing for them. So after you left, I had a chance to think about that and everything else you'd said. I realized that if I truly wanted these boys, I'd have to make some big changes around here. The boys and my good friend Harry Munn have volunteered to help me with some of the work because they want to be sure the judge finds reason enough to let me adopt both of them."

"But why would you want to adopt Jamie and Abel?"

"Why? To keep them together, for one thing. And because they have finally made me see that there are still things in life worth fighting for." He glanced down at the two smiling faces and couldn't help but return their smiles. "Believe me, these boys are well worth fighting for. And fight I will."

"You're serious, aren't you?" She blinked when that revelation sank in. When he looked back up at her, she could see by his expression that he was— deadly serious.

"Damn right, I'm serious," he answered firmly, then glanced cautiously at the boys. "I mean, *darn* right, I'm serious. Would you care to see how serious I really am? How serious we *all* are? Take a look inside that house." He nodded toward the partially open front door. "See for yourself how much work we've already done. You can't call my house a pigsty now."

When she made no move toward the house, his brow notched. "Go on, take a good long look, because when that judge asks if you think I can provide a clean and proper place for these boys to live, I want you to tell him just exactly how clean and proper my house is."

Anna glanced back at the house. She was curious to see these improvements, very curious, but at the same time oddly afraid. She was uncomfortable with the idea that someone could change so drastically in such a short time.

"Go on," he urged again, this time in an easier tone of voice. "Take a look. I want you to be a witness to the fact that I can provide for these boys as well as any man. I may not have two good legs like most men, and I may have a short temper when it comes to people barging into my house asking me a lot of nosy questions, but I'm as capable of taking care of these boys as anyone."

Harry stepped toward her, just as eager for her to

115

see the house. "Come on, missy . . . I'll show it to you." He extended his arm to her.

Anna glanced at the old man's eager face, then at the boys' hopeful expressions and could not deny them this one small favor. She would take a look inside and see if the house was really as nice as they seemed to think. Reluctantly, she accepted the older man's arm and together they headed for the gate, finding unsure footing in the freshly turned earth. Anna was surprised to see that a gate stood only a few yards away. In her earlier haste, she had not noticed any gate and now she felt foolish for not having used it.

Shortly after Harry had escorted her into the house, he pulled away. Waving his arms with wide sweeps, he rushed ahead of her, indicating what he wanted her to notice first. "See how nice the place looks? No dust on the furniture, no spider webs on the light fixtures. No streaks on the mirrors. I hope you know, we all worked real hard to get the place to look this good again."

There was no doubt in Anna's mind that they had indeed worked hard, very hard. Having seen how dirty and cluttered the entryway had been earlier, she was amazed at how well the furniture and the floors gleamed. Even the carpets had been taken out and thoroughly cleaned. It surprised her to see that they were blue.

"I must say, I am impressed," she admitted, following the man as he encouraged her to take a look at the other rooms.

"And the upstairs looks as good as the downstairs. Want to see?" Harry asked eagerly, already headed for the stairway.

"No, I believe you." And she did believe him.

"Then you'll put in a good word for Mark when the time comes?"

Anna hesitated while she considered her answer. Just because the man had finally decided to clean up his house did not mean he would make a suitable parent. But then again, it was a definite step in the right direction. For the first time, she wondered what Mark Gates was really like. Was he the terrible ogre she'd met that first day, or was he actually the sort of person who could take good care of two young boys?

"Please, ma'am, your support would carry a lot of weight with that judge."

Harry's face revealed so much honest concern that Anna's heart went out to him. She decided she must have judged Mark too harshly. Anyone who had earned this much love and respect couldn't be all bad.

"Please, ma'am," Harry continued, not about to give up until she had agreed. "Mark needs those two boys as much as they need him. Until they came stealing their way into his heart, he had pretty well given up on life. Now, suddenly, he has hope again; he has something worth living for. Don't take that away from him." He reached for her hand and held it gently in his own, not realizing how rough and dirty his hands were in comparison to hers. "Please, ma'am. Don't take those boys away from here. Give 'em a chance to be a family."

"But I have to take them with me," she said, wondering how she was ever going to make him understand that it was her job, her duty, to see that these boys were safely returned to Pinefield. "The whole

117

town is out looking for those two. For the past five days they've searched everywhere. Besides, in just a few more days my boss will be back, expecting to see those children safe and sound."

"Bring him out here," Harry suggested. "Then he can see just how safe and sound they really are . . . and how happy. I know they probably didn't look it, but they are happy here, real happy."

Anna thought about that. "To tell you the truth, they did look happy." Even covered with all that dirt and streaked with perspiration, they had looked very happy. "But whether the boys are happy or not really won't matter. My boss has already decided that Jamie is to live with the Porterfields, and he's not the sort of man who changes his mind easily." In fact, he was not the sort of man to change his mind *ever*.

"Don't waste your breath on her, Harry," Mark said, startling them both. "She's too mule-headed to see that all we are asking for is a chance."

Anna drew in a sharp breath and spun about to glower at him. "I've about had it with your insults, Mr. Gates."

"And I've about had it with your condescending attitude, Miss Thomas," he shot back, waving her feathered black hat at her for emphasis. Now that he was in the house, out of the direct rays of the sun, he felt better, stronger. He was ready to take her on again. "If you came here with the intention of taking those boys back to town with you, I'm afraid you wasted the trip. Those boys are staying right here until I can arrange a meeting with the local judge. Here's your hat," he said, tossing it suddenly. "You may as well get on back to town and tell everyone what you've discovered here. Just be sure you also tell them how determined I am to have those boys, and that I will do whatever it takes to keep them."

"I can't go back to Pinefield without Jamie and Abel," she protested as she jumped forward to catch her hat, which had been thrown short. Though she managed to catch it before it hit the floor, several of the decorative feathers came loose and fluttered to the floor. She glared angrily at him, wondering if he'd thrown it short on purpose. "I'm sorry, but I can't leave without those boys."

"Then you are welcome to stay," Mark said with an unconcerned shrug of his wide shoulders. "I've got plenty of room for one more." He paused for a moment to consider the offer he'd just made. What if she said yes? His blood stirred at the mere thought of having to live with her under his roof.

"I can't stay here!" Her hand flew to her throat at the mere suggestion.

Mark tossed up his hands as if tired of trying to figure her out. "I wish you would make up your mind."

"It's not a matter of making up my mind," she tried to explain. "It's a matter of what's right and what's wrong."

"Damn right it is," Mark retorted angrily, then just as suddenly he realized his slip and glanced around to make sure the boys had not followed him inside. He ran the top of his tongue anxiously over his lower lip while he considered how easily that sort of language came out of his mouth. He really needed to do something about that if he was to have two impressionable young children living in his house. "It is indeed a matter of what's right and wrong.

119

What's right is keeping those two boys together. What's wrong is for you to come in here and try to take them away from me."

"It's my job," she tried again to explain. "There are rules I must follow."

"Why? Why do you have to follow these rules?"

Anna was taken momentarily off guard by the directness of his question. "Well, because—because it's my job." She hated to keep coming back to that, but she had no other answer.

Mark snorted with disgust. "That's a pitiful excuse for what you are trying to do."

"Mr. Gates, please try to understand," she said, hoping to make him see her side of the matter.

"No, *you* try to understand," he shot back, his hands curling into massive fists, one at his side, the other on the curved handle of his cane. "Those boys are not leaving here. They finally have a chance to have a home together and you are not taking that from them."

It was then Anna realized she didn't want to take that from them. If there was even the slightest chance that Jamie and Abel could remain together, she was for it. Mark Gates could very well be one of the most infuriating men she'd ever had the misfortune to meet, but it was clear he cared deeply for those two boys, and they cared just as deeply for him. If only there was some way to help them— some way to break the rules without causing any trouble—and without getting fired. . . .

"Even if I did leave them temporarily in your care, I'll have to tell the people in town that the boys are out here. I cannot allow them to continue the search when they have their farms and their busi-

120

nesses to attend to." Already, she knew that when she left there she would be alone, still she had to make him understand what he was up against.

"Then tell them," he said with a defiant shake of his head. "But in that same breath you'd better also tell them that those boys are here because they want to be. And you can also tell them that they are going to stay here either until they ask to leave or until that judge tells me to my face that I don't have a prayer at adopting them." When she failed to respond to his demands, he waved toward the door, which was only a few feet behind him. "Go on, get out of here. Just don't you dare try to take those boys with you."

"I'm going, but don't think I won't be back," she cautioned him, angered by his cruel taunts. "You just see to it that those boys get in out of that sun and stay out of it until their skin heals. I'm afraid that judge won't look very favorably upon the fact that you allowed them to get so sunburned. In fact, you'd better hope they've fully healed and haven't started to peel whenever you get that hearing with the judge."

When she started for the door, her angry expression softened. "You might try putting some lotion on the boys' faces and hands to help keep the skin from becoming so dried out after it starts to heal. If you have any camphor, you might put that on them, too."

"I don't have any camphor," he admitted glumly.

"Then at least put some sort of lotion on them. It can only help." She paused inside the doorway to look up at him. His face and neck were as red as the boys'. "You could use some lotion, too."

121

Mark stared at her, unblinking.

When she stepped out onto the front porch, she saw the two boys sitting together in a large wicker chair at the far end of the porch, desperately holding each other's hands, as if afraid she might try to separate them again. Turning back to Mark, she studied his concerned expression for a long moment. She was taken aback by the deep concern she saw in his eyes. "I'd like to speak with them before I leave."

"Go right ahead, talk all you want." He leaned heavily against the doorjamb, the first real indication that he was feeling a little weak from having stood too long.

Though he did not follow when she walked over to where the boys sat, she knew he carefully watched her every move. Kneeling in front of the chair so she could look easily into their faces and better see their eyes, she took their joined hands into her own.

"Jamie, I'm leaving now," she said softly, reassuringly. "If you'd like to go with me, I'm sure Mr. Gates would understand."

Tears filled Jamie's eyes. His lower lip tightened then trembled, forcing his mouth to turn down at the corners. "We'd rather stay here with Mr. Gates. Please, don't be mad at us."

A sharp pain pierced Anna's heart, and she lifted their hands to her cheek. "I'm not mad at you. I'm just concerned. You two are very special to me and I only want to do what will make you the happiest."

Jamie blinked rapidly, in a wasted effort to stop his tears from spilling, forming sun-pinkened streaks down his dirt-covered cheeks. Suddenly, he leaned forward and hugged her close. Abel did the same, knocking Mark's bulky hat backward onto the floor.

Swallowing back the painful lump that had quickly formed in her throat, Anna tried to keep her voice from collapsing under the pressure of her own emotion while she reached for Mark's hat and placed it back on Abel's head. "I'll be back to check on you. Until then, you two take good care of each other — and Mr. Gates."

Then, before the boys had a chance to see her own tears, she stood and hurried toward the buggy, her mind awhirl with too many feelings, too many conflicting thoughts. Part of her knew she should have insisted the boys return with her, though she really wasn't sure what purpose it would have fulfilled. Still, that was what she should have done. Yet at the same moment, another part of her was glad she'd decided to leave them there. At least for now, they were happy.

During the ride back into town, Anna realized she had more tough decisions to make, all stemming from the one she had already made. By the time she reached the reverend's house, she'd made the first of them. Though she intended to tell the reverend that the boys had finally been found, she also planned to do everything she could to convince him to go along with her decision to leave them there because for the time being, it was really the best thing for the boys. She knew they would have to be brought back into town before Friday, when Gordon was scheduled to return, but she saw no real reason why they couldn't stay with Mark Gates until then. They were in no danger that she could see, and if she brought them back into town too soon, they very well might decide to try and run away again. At least this way she knew where they were.

Having rationalized her decision as best she could, she entered the reverend's house ready to convince him to leave well enough alone. When she found him, he was sitting alone in the front parlor reading a letter from a friend, his feet propped up on a large, cushiony footstool; but he quickly set the letter aside when he learned she wanted to talk with him.

"You say he's shaved off that awful beard and even went so far as to clean up his house?" the reverend asked after she had told him about her visit to Mark Gates's farm. He tilted his head back against the upper rim of the wing-backed chair and stared at the ceiling, unblinking. "Will God's wonders never cease?"

"Not only has he shaved and cleaned his house, he's started to work clearing one of his fields for planting. He's very serious about wanting to adopt those boys."

The reverend ran his hands along his cheeks as if to cool them, his eyes wide with his thoughts. "I never believed I'd see the day." He sat quietly for several minutes before looking at her. "And you say he was walking?"

Anna nodded. "With the help of a wooden brace and a cane. His movements were awkward and jerky, but he was definitely walking."

"I wish I'd gone with you. I'd loved to have seen that for myself."

"Then maybe you'd like to go with me tomorrow. I told the boys I'd come back to visit with them, check to be sure they haven't changed their minds."

"I'm tempted. I am sorely tempted. But I'm afraid I've neglected my regular duties while out helping with the search. I've calls to make and letters to write."

"Calls to make?" she asked, disappointed. "Then I guess you'll be needing your buggy."

"Not necessarily. Tomorrow, most of the people I plan to pay calls on are widows and widowers who live right here in town. If you'd like to use my buggy to ride back out there in the morning, you're more than welcome to it. Meanwhile, I'd better get the word out that the boys have been found so things can get back to normal around here. Best place to do that is the mercantile. There's always at least half a dozen people gathered there." He pulled his feet off the stool one at a time as if they were heavily weighted, then slowly stood. "You be sure and tell my wife where I've gone when she gets back from her visit with Mrs. Lindsey." Then, without further delay, he headed for the door, pausing to snatch up his hat and plop it on his head.

Relieved that the reverend had agreed the boys were safe enough where they were, at least for now, Anna turned toward the kitchen. She felt the man deserved a nice reward for being so understanding. Hurriedly she searched the cabinets and pantry for the ingredients she'd need to bake a nice, fat apple pie. And if she had time, she'd whip up some sweet cream to go with it.

Chapter Seven

The following morning, before Anna left Pinefield, she stopped by the mercantile to buy a bottle of camphorated oil. She remembered Mark had said he did not have any and she also remembered how pink the boys' faces, necks, and hands had been.

Certain they had all spent a very miserable night, their tender skin flaming from overexposure to the hot Texas sun, she purchased two bottles of the cooling liniment and tucked them carefully into her handbag. Although the medicated oil might not help their skin heal any faster, it would at least ease the pain a little until it did. And with two bottles, there might be enough for Mr. Gates, too, though she refused to consider why his discomfort should matter to her one whit.

During the ride to see the boys, Anna felt happier than she'd felt in days. The sun was shining, there was a cool breeze from the northwest, and the boys had been found not only alive and safe, but for the time being, they were happy, too. Even Abel had seemed happy. Before she'd barged in on them, Anna had noticed Abel outside working in the field every bit as hard as his older brother.

It had been the first time she'd seen the smaller child actually pursue any strenuous activity. Though he always did whatever he was told, never was it with any real enthusiasm. But yesterday Abel had displayed a definite enthusiasm for his work. That in itself was a miracle. Anna turned her face toward the warmth of the mid-morning sun and smiled. The reverend was certainly right. God's small wonders never ceased.

Overflowing with joy, Anna was drawn to the undeniable beauty that surrounded her—God's beauty. For the first time since she'd arrived, she noticed all the different wildflowers in bloom. Bright patches of yellow, gold, pink, blue, purple, and brilliant shades of coral dotted the roadside and splashed the dark green fields beyond.

Odd that she had not paid any attention to the brightly colored flowers the day before, considering she had traveled that very same road. But then yesterday she'd been far too concerned about the missing boys to notice much of anything, except how much time was rapidly slipping away, worried that each passing minute could mean the difference between life and death for them.

Today was different. While listening to the gentle clip-clopping of the horses' hooves and the cheerful chirping of the birds overhead, she felt like singing aloud her joy. The boys were alive and safe, and she felt too happy not to give a little of her attention to her unusually beautiful surroundings.

East Texas was not at all what she'd expected. Having been told all her life that Texas was barren and flat—an open wasteland, her teachers had called it—Anna was surprised to learn that it was neither barren nor flat . . . at least not *this* part of Texas. The land was breathtakingly beautiful. If it wasn't for the heat and the fact that all her clothing was made of heavy wool, which allowed very little air to circulate next to her skin, she might consider East Texas a true paradise.

Huge, leafy trees grew abundantly along both sides of the road. Thick, spreading branches stretched high over her head, forming occasional arches that offered a few moments of cool respite from the hot Texas sun. Though pine trees predominated, Anna noticed a variety of other trees sprinkled throughout. Mingled among the tall, dark green pines were oak, elm, sweet gum, walnut, pecan, and persimmon, and several other broadleaf trees that Anna did not recognize.

In the near distance, just beyond the thick groves of trees along the narrow dirt-and-gravel roadway, lay either large, freshly-planted farm fields, reddish-brown in color, or wide, rolling pastures, thick and green with early grass. Beyond the plowed fields or grass-covered pastures lay tall, wooded hills.

An occasional fence appeared along the roadside, usually whenever she passed a large pasture filled with grazing cattle. Occasionally the fences were made of wood planks, much like the ones she was accustomed to seeing up north. But more often than not, the fences were made of sturdy posts cut from stout trees, set into the ground at regular intervals and joined together by stout strands of stretched wire, each strung a foot above the other.

From the road she could not tell if the wire had tiny barbs or not, but she suspected some of it did.

Barbed wire was reported to be very popular in most southern states and in the territories of the mid-west. She wondered why Mark did not have barbed-wire fences surrounding his land, then realized it was probably because he had no cattle to keep in. Unlike most of the locals who combined farming with ranching, Mark had no livestock other than the one mule pulling his plow — or at least none she had seen.

In what seemed like no time, Anna reached the thick, wooded area less than half a mile from Mark's house. Eager to see the boys again and to be reassured of their safety, she watched to her right for the narrow wagon trail that cut through the woods at an awkward angle and eventually came out near the edge of a wide, sloping field. From there she would be able to see Mark's house.

She would also be able to see if he had taken her advice and kept those boys inside, out of the sun, or if he'd set them right back to work, not caring that it could make them extremely ill. Surely the man had enough sense to realize that, having come from the north, the boys were not used to such heat.

Looking anxiously ahead, for the first time doubting her decision to leave the boys there, she finally caught sight of Mark's house and was greatly relieved to discover only Mark and Harry outside working in the field.

As she drove closer, she was immediately impressed with the progress the two had made considering that one of the two men was hampered by a badly disfigured leg and the other was undoubtedly in his late sixties. It seemed unlikely they could get that much work done without a bit of outside help. She wondered then if the boys were simply taking a break. Could they have been sent back outside to help with the work, despite their sunburn? It was entirely possible that clearing that land was more important to Mark Gates than the boys' health.

But for some reason Anna didn't really believe that. Mark seemed to care sincerely about those boys as much as he cared for his friend Harry. The only person he did not care for was her, and he had made that perfectly clear the afternoon before.

The sudden memory of Mark's hostile attitude toward her caused Anna to slow the buggy and enter the dooryard at a more cautious rate. The muscles around her stomach tightened when she glanced out across the field to the area where Mark and Harry were hard at work.

While noticing the amazing width of Mark's shoulders and the masterful way he gripped the reins, Anna wondered what his mood was today. She did not like the thought of causing more trouble by forcing her presence on him yet again, but she did want to see the boys. And she had every right to see them.

Straightening in the seat, Anna decided she would not be intimidated by the man's obvious dislike of her. He was certainly entitled to his opinion no matter how wrong it was, but she did not have to suffer because of it. Besides, why should she care what he thought of her? What mattered was what he thought about the children.

"Hello, there," she called out in an attempt to sound cheerful as soon as she had pulled the buggy to a gradual stop.

Immediately upon hearing her voice above the loud crackling of the fire, Harry turned toward her, pushed his battered hat back off his forehead, and waved. He did not seem at all upset by her visit, but Mark's reaction was a different matter. Turning in the plow seat to glance back over his shoulder, he glared at her as if she was the last person he wanted to see.

"Howdy, Missy," Harry shouted, pulling off his work gloves one at a time and immediately heading in her direction. When he reached the fence, he bent forward and rested one of his elbows on the top rail while he glanced back at the freshly plowed field. "How's it look?"

"It looks like you're almost ready to plant your corn," she responded with a smile, relieved that at least one of them was willing to be cordial.

"Almost." He nodded, then straightened and headed for the gate. "I guess you're wantin' to see the boys."

"Yes, if you don't mind. I've brought some of Dr. Buller's Camphorated Oil to help ease their sunburn. Until my boss returns, I'm responsible for their welfare."

"That's right nice of you, but they're doin' a whole lot better this mornin'. It's really amazin' how quick children are to mend." Harry tucked the cuffs of his work-worn leather gloves into his hip pocket while he stepped through the gate.

"They are better, then?" She was pleased to hear it.

"If you want to see for yourself, they're in the house. They came out for a little while this mornin', determined to help with some of the chores, but as soon as the sun got up higher than the trees, Mark made 'em go back inside. He doesn't want to take any chances lettin' them get burned all over again. He figures you're right — leastwise about that judge. He ain't gonna like it if he sees those boys all blistered and red from too much sun."

"That's true," she agreed. "And the judge's opinion is important."

Though she really would have preferred to ignore Mark Gates and go on into the house, she couldn't resist another quick glimpse in his direction. *A matter of self-preservation,* she convinced herself, aware she felt safer when she knew exactly where he was and what he was doing. Her heart gave a cautionary jump when she saw that he'd already climbed down from the plow and, with the use of his cane, was slowly headed toward the gate. She really had not planned on having words with him just yet.

"You sure got out here awful early," Harry commented. He glanced up at the sun, then back down as he stopped directly in front of her. "Have you had breakfast?"

When she failed to look at him, he glanced back to see what had captured her attention. He grinned when he saw Mark and how hard the man tried to walk without favoring his injured leg, clearly trying to impress Miss Thomas.

"Yes, I've eaten," Anna answered, then forced her gaze away from Mark. She quickly focused on Harry's smiling face, glad to discover he had glanced away, because if he'd been watching her, he surely would have noticed the rise of color in her cheeks. Closing her eyes briefly, she tried to calm the wild pattering of her heart, but couldn't, not with Mark Gates still headed in their direction. If only she hadn't seen the anger flash from his eyes when he'd first noticed her. "Mrs. Cross had breakfast waiting for me when I came downstairs this morning."

"That's too bad," Harry said then he, too, pulled his gaze off Mark and looked first at Anna's flushed face and then at the house. "You missed a real treat. That Jamie makes a fine johnnycake. But then, I guess you already knew that."

"No, I can't say that I did," she admitted, though she was not too surprised. The children at the orphanage were constantly encouraged to become as self-reliant as possible, and that encouragement included assisting in the kitchen from time to time. "Does Abel try to help him any?"

"He's startin' to," Harry said, then frowned, suddenly reminded of the younger boy's odd behavior. "That lil'est one sure is a hard fella to figger out. At times he opens his mouth and acts like he's goin' to talk up a storm, like he's finally thought of somethin' worth sayin', but then nothin' comes out. How' long's he been like that?"

Anna shook her head, trying to concentrate on Harry, and not look back to where Mark had just passed through the gate. She took a deep, cautionary breath. Mark was now only a few yards away. "I don't really know. All I know is the child shows severe signs of withdrawal and has not spoken one word since his parents left him at the orphanage. He doesn't even attempt to make sounds."

"His parents left him?" Harry asked, his brushy eyebrows jerking together into a perplexed frown. He cocked his whiskered jaw at an awkward angle

133

while he thought about this new bit of information. "You mean their folks ain't dead?"

"Not according to the information in their records," Anna said and knew exactly what had gone through Harry's mind. How could anybody give away their own children like that, and to total strangers? "It seems their parents brought them to the orphanage a little over a year ago and asked that proper homes be found for them. As I recall, the boys were both sickly at that time, and the parents were too poor to take care of them."

"How sad," Harry said, shaking his head as he glanced off toward the house again. His eyes turned red and watery, causing him to blink several times.

"Yes, it is." Anna nodded, straightening her shoulders and taking a deep breath when she realized Mark had joined them. She wondered why he made her feel so uncomfortable, so terribly self-conscious. After all, he was only a man. Deciding she was being silly, she turned and looked directly into Mark's startling blue eyes. "Don't you agree, Mr. Gates?"

While waiting for him to reply, Anna noticed his blistery red face and neck. Despite the wide-brimmed hat he'd worn to help protect his skin from the sun's direct rays, his sunburn was much worse. Yet oddly enough, it appeared he'd shaved again, which had to have been painful.

Glancing down, she noticed how rapidly his chest rose and fell, as if he were desperate for air. The short walk from the field had left him out of breath. She frowned when she realized the man had no business taking on as much work as he had. Having been in that wheelchair for so long, his body was not accustomed to such strenuous activity, any more than his face and neck were accustomed to the sun. In fact, with a sunburn that severe, the man should not have been outside at all. Remembering the camphorated oil she'd brought, she wondered how she should go about offering it to him without in some way upsetting that overblown male pride of his.

At the moment Mark was too lost in his own thoughts to pay much attention to his pain or Anna's concerned expression. Nor was he aware that she had just asked him a direct question. He was too puzzled over the conversation he'd overheard. "And you say Abel has not spoken since the day his parents left him at that orphanage?" His words had been spoken more as a comment to himself than a true question.

"Not a word."

"Did he talk before then?"

Anna's green eyes widened. The concern in his voice had caught her by surprise. She had never spoken with him when he was not openly angry with her. "I'm not sure if Abel has ever spoken. I guess only Jamie can answer that. But I do know that the child has been examined by several different doctors and none ever found a physical reason for the boy's inability to speak."

"Then it must be emotional." Mark, too, turned a thoughtful gaze toward the house. His pale blue eyes revealed just how upset he really was. "Those poor kids. They've lived pretty tough lives to be so young."

"Most of our children have had a tough time of it," she agreed. It had touched her heart to hear

135

such a deep, caring tone in his voice. "Life is pretty hard for any child who suddenly loses part of his family, no matter what the reason."

Mark's gaze met hers and for a moment neither spoke.

Harry sensed a sudden awkwardness between them and decided to come to the rescue. "Well, let's quit all this jawin' and git on inside." He indicated the front door with a quick flick of his hand. "I imagine the boys will be right glad to learn that Miss Thomas has come back out to visit with 'em again." He paused in mid-step. "This here *is* just a visit, ain't it?"

Anna did not want to worry them, but at the same time she didn't want to mislead them. "For today, yes, I'm here to visit. But I can't promise that come Friday I won't try to take the children back with me to Pinefield. You have to understand, I could very well lose my job if I don't have both boys back in my care by the time my supervisor returns from Marshall."

Mark didn't say anything, but Anna noticed that the muscles in his sun-reddened jaw had hardened.

"We can worry about Friday when it gits here," Harry insisted, not ready to see these two get into yet another argument. "By then we'll have this field planted and Mark will have seen that judge and convinced him to let those boys live right here with him. Meanwhile, let's go see what those two younguns are up to. I haven't been in to check on them in over an hour, and with those two whipper-snappers you just never know what to expect."

When they entered a few seconds later, they immediately heard odd little sounds coming from the back of the house. Harry glanced back at Mark, puzzled by the low voices and the sloshing noises. He hurriedly led the way through the kitchen into the washroom, where the sounds grew louder.

"What in tarnation are you boys doin'?" He entered the small room to find both boys standing beside a large metal washtub that had been half-filled with hot, steaming water. Within seconds Anna and Mark had joined him.

The boys looked up with a start. In their grip was a long wooden clothes paddle. Working together, they'd been swirling the contents of the huge metal tub with wide, uneven strokes, sloshing hot water out onto the floor. Because of the steam rising from the tub, steady streams of perspiration poured down their faces and soaked their clothing. Yet despite the sweltering heat trapped inside the small room, Abel still wore the wide-brimmed hat Mark had plopped down on his head the day before.

Anna wanted to laugh at the comical sight before her. Because of the hat's size, the wide brim fell low across Abel's forehead and sagged over one ear. He had to constantly release his hold on the paddle to push the front of the oversized work hat back away from his face in order to see. When he finally pushed it back far enough, Anna noticed that his skin was still a little pink from yesterday's exposure to the sun; but Harry was right, the burn did not appear to bother him any.

"Since no one would let us help outside, we decided to find something we could do to help in here," Jamie stated matter-of-factly, then grinned proudly. "So we decided to do the washing and surprise you."

Pulling at the heavy material of her woolen jacket, aware of the unbearable humidity that filled the room, Anna stepped forward and glanced curiously into the steaming tub. There were no suds. "I see you have quite a tub full there, but I don't think you used quite enough soap."

"Soap?" Jamie asked, then looked at Abel, who seemed just as startled by the suggestion. Both boys looked down at the steaming water and frowned.

"You did use soap didn't you?" she asked, glancing back at Harry and Mark, who both raised their hands to hide their grins.

"Of course we used soap," Jamie lied with a firm nod. "It's just that we must not have used enough. How much do you suppose we needed?"

Glancing around until she spotted the small wooden barrel that held the laundry soap, Anna set aside her handbag and quickly unbuttoned her jacket, overwhelmed by the stifling heat. "Here, let me help you."

To everyone's amazement, she quickly tossed her jacket aside then scooped about half a pound of the soft soap into a small bowl and emptied it into the hot water. Grasping the paddle only inches above where the boys still held on to it, she helped them swirl the water back and forth until the soap was thoroughly dissolved and bubbles began to form.

Mark and Harry exchanged surprised glances. Then, without muttering a word—mainly because he had no idea what he would say if he was to speak—Mark crossed the room and pushed open the window to let in a little fresh air. When he turned back, he stood motionless, leaning heavily against his cane while he quietly watched the three work together as a team. If he hadn't seen it for himself, he would never have believed it. There was some good in the woman after all.

Wordlessly, he watched while they carefully worked the large paddle back and forth through the hot, soapy water. He studied the determined expression on Anna's face. Then, ever so slowly, his gaze drifted downward, drawn by the movement of her arms and shoulders. When he noticed how her crispy white linen blouse had wilted from the heat and had molded to her body, his eyebrows arched with immediate interest. There was far more to this Miss Thomas than at first met the eye. Far more. Suddenly he felt the need for fresh air—and lots of it.

"Since it doesn't look like I'm needed here, I guess I'd better go on back outside. I do want to try to have that whole field planted and another one started before Thursday."

Harry followed him as far as the doorway, then turned to look at the trio one last time and broke into a grin so wide it revealed the gap near the back of his mouth where his three teeth were missing. "I guess I'd better get on back to work, too. Thursday's less than two days away. If you need anything, just give a holler."

"We'll be fine," Anna assured him, taking full control of the paddle long enough to lift one of the garments out of the water—a pale blue workshirt. Carefully, she draped it over the side of the tub to cool.

While she listened to Harry's fading footsteps, she wondered what was so significant about Thursday, then realized that must be when Mark planned to see the circuit judge. With Gordon due to return on Friday, it made sense that Mark would try to speak with the judge before then. Suddenly, she wished she could be there when that happened. Though she might not go as far as to declare openly that Mark Gates would make a good parent, she could at least vouch for all the trouble he'd gone through in his effort to prove himself and his home worthy of the boys. That alone might give him a fighting chance.

"So, Jamie, how are you feeling?" she asked, quickly refocusing her thoughts on the matter at hand. As she let go of the paddle, she picked up the blue workshirt and began to work the suds back and forth through the wet material.

"I'm feeling great!" Jamie answered with jubilation. His hazel eyes sparkled with enthusiasm. He so wanted her to believe that.

"But what about that sunburn?" she asked, noticing that, like Abel, he was still a little pink along the tops of his cheeks and the tip of his nose.

"Ah, the back of my neck hurts me a little, but not enough to matter none." He and Abel continued to stir the hot water with the paddle.

"To matter *any*," she corrected him, still working the suds through the shirt with her hands. When she discovered a particularly stubborn stain, she reached for the washboard and rubbed it with short, firm strokes against the rough metal surface. "If you have any pain at all, I think you should know that I brought some medicine with me that's supposed to help."

"Sunburn medicine?" He looked up at her, clearly

140

interested.

"Yes, it's in my handbag. Since your hands are drier than mine, why don't you open my handbag and get the medicine out? I brought two bottles of it."

Quickly, Jamie did. He took the blue-glass bottles out of her handbag one at a time and placed them on a nearby work table.

"If you want, I could smooth some of it on your sunburn now," she suggested, already looking around for a towel to dry her hands.

"No, that's all right. I want to save it for Mark. Although he don't complain about it much, I know that sunburn he has must hurt something awful. It's twice as red as ours was."

Anna started to correct his grammar, then decided against it. She'd let his future teachers worry about things like that. "That's very noble of you, but as you can see, there are two bottles. There should be enough to take care of all three of you."

Still Jamie refused to have any of it for himself. "I'll get by without it," he insisted, then returned to the side of the tub and took hold of the paddle again. All the while he'd been away, Abel had continued to stir the water, though with greater difficulty.

"What about you, Abel?" he asked, again helping to control the movement of the paddle. "You want Miss Thomas to put some of that medicine on you?"

Abel shook his head adamantly.

"He don't want none either," Jamie announced unnecessarily. Then, when Anna started looking around for something, he did, too, though he had no idea for what.

"You lost something?" he finally asked.

"Where's the rinse water?"

Jamie cocked his head to one side and looked at her questioningly. "The rinse water?"

"Yes, the clean water we need to rinse the soap out of the clothes after we're through washing them."

"*Oh,* the rinse water." Jamie and Abel looked at each other for a long moment, then suddenly ran from the room. Several minutes later they reappeared, each carrying a large bucket half-filled with clean water.

Quickly they poured the water into a second tub, then immediately left to get more, until finally Anna assured them they had brought enough.

Though originally she had not planned to stay but a few hours, Anna was there for most of the day. After she and the boys finished washing the clothes, they hung them on the clothesline in the sideyard, then returned to the kitchen to wipe up the water the boys had sloshed while carrying the water through. Then they looked to see what was available for that night's supper. They felt certain Mark and Harry would be half starved by the time they quit work for the day. Although she found a pot half-filled with vegetable stew in the cooler, after hearing Jamie comment that that was about all they ever ate, Anna decided to leave it right where it was.

Finding a slab of beef large enough for roasting wrapped in paper at the back of the cooler, she instructed the boys to peel the vegetables while she hunted for a roasting pan. Soon they had the meal underway, and shortly after they had brought the laundry in from outside, Anna realized it was past time for her to leave.

Reluctantly, she took off the apron she'd found hanging on a nail in the pantry and paused to hug both boys good-bye. At their insistence, she promised to come back the next day if the reverend would allow her to borrow his buggy again.

While the boys walked with her to the front door, she reminded Jamie of when he should take the roast out of the oven and how to apply the camphorated oil to Mark's skin so as not to hurt him.

"Don't forget, wait until after he's had a chance to wash all the dirt off his skin, then gently smooth the oil over the reddened areas," she cautioned while slipping her jacket back on.

"But what if I rub the oil in too hard?" Jamie asked, truly concerned that he might make a mistake that could hurt his new friend. "Can't you stay long enough to put the medicine on for him?"

Anna's insides fluttered wildly at such an absurd thought. She imagined what it would be like to smooth the cool oil onto his heated skin, to touch the handsome lines of his face with her medicated fingertips, and felt the color quickly rise in her cheeks. "No, I have to go. If I don't return to Pinefield before dark, Reverend Cross will worry about me. If you are that afraid of hurting Mark, ask Harry to apply the medicine for you." It felt odd using the men's first names when she hardly knew them, but that was how Jamie referred to them, and she knew she'd feel awkward calling them Mr. Gates and Mr. Munn.

"What time do you think you'll be back tomorrow?" Jamie asked, eager for her to return.

Anna wondered if he had second thoughts about staying. "I can't say for certain. It all depends on what the Reverend Cross's plans are. Why do you ask? Would you like to go with me?"

"No, I don't want to leave Mark. It's just that I want to be sure that you're going to come back to see us again—because I like you," he said with typical childlike honesty.

"And I like you, too," she assured him then hugged him one last time. "And I like Abel." She looked around to offer a similar hug to the younger boy, but found that he'd become too engrossed with whatever was happening outside the front window. Turning back to Jamie, she shrugged, then smiled.

"I'll tell him," Jamie promised, then followed her through the door to the front veranda.

Once outside they both paused to watch Mark and Harry for several minutes, amazed at how tirelessly they worked, then Anna left.

During the ride back to town, Anna did not feel nearly as cheerful as she had on the way out. If anything, she felt a little melancholy. It was then she realized how very tired she was. By the time she reached Pinefield, she wanted nothing more than a long, cool bath and a good night's sleep. It was only because of the reverend's insistence that she stayed awake long enough to eat a bite of supper.

Shortly after nine, Anna climbed into bed and snuggled beneath the soft cotton sheets. Sighing appreciatively, she closed her eyes and let her thoughts drift languidly over the different events of the day, recalling how much fun she and the boys had shared. She was certainly going to miss those two.

Then, while her mind slowly succumbed to drowsiness, she remembered Jamie's suggestion that she stay long enough to apply the medicine to Mark's skin, which again caused an odd, alarming sensation to shoot through her—a sensation that not only stirred her blood to life, but made her tingle all over, right down to the very tips of her toes. Suddenly she was wide awake. Though her body was still tired and her arms felt like leaden weights at her sides, her mind raced with wild thoughts of what might have happened had she stayed.

Chapter Eight

Because Reverend Cross needed his buggy the following morning, Anna had two choices. Either she could stay at the house with Mrs. Cross, who was expecting several women to drop by for their regular Wednesday afternoon charity quilting, or she could spend part of the money Gordon had left for emergency use and hire a buggy, knowing that when Gordon learned of what she'd done, he would become angry and declare the expense unnecessary.

Truth was, Gordon would probably become so upset with such senseless spending that he'd not just reprimand her, he'd demand that the money be paid back out of her meager salary. He would become so distraught with her for what she'd done, he would have to sit down and forcibly calm himself. But then, Gordon Franklin was always having to sit down and calm himself. It was his nature to overact, even over the smallest matter.

Anna hired the buggy anyway.

By nine-thirty, she was dressed in her usual gray woolen skirt and jacket. By ten o'clock, the rented buggy was ready for travel and shortly thereafter she was on her way out of town. Her heart hammered with unexplainable excitement when she finally had Mark's house in sight. Right away she noticed that the small field he and Harry had worked so hard to finish was fully plowed with all the brush cleared out of the way.

At the moment, the two men were out in the middle of the same field planting their corn by hand. Mark had a large burlap pouch tied around his waist. It hung over his right hip at an angle, where he could reach inside easily. Grabbing up the corn in great handfuls, he was busy dropping a narrow trail of the fat yellow seeds into the freshly plowed furrows while Harry came along behind him and gently smoothed the loose dirt over them with a hoe.

Knowing it would soon be time for the men to break for lunch, Anna paused near the fence only long enough to wave, then hurried inside to see if the boys needed any help in the kitchen.

Because it was such an unusually hot day for April, too hot for anyone to want a steaming bowl of Harry's beef stew, Anna convinced the boys their midday meal should consist of cold slices of a baked ham Harry had brought with him and thick slabs of cheddar cheese, which the boys planned to serve with fresh bread and tall glasses of chilled milk.

Although Anna had staunchly refused to eat with them the day before, claiming she was not hungry when indeed she had been very hungry, today she realized it was senseless to starve herself like that. After being assured it was all right with Mark and Harry, she politely accepted the boys' invitation and joined them at the kitchen table for their noonday meal.

When Mark and Harry entered the kitchen through the back door, where they had washed their faces and hands in a small basin near the porch well, Anna and the boys were already seated, ready to fill their plates. Mark looked at Anna with surprise when he casually pulled his chair away from the table. His eyes never left hers the whole time he propped his cane at an angle against the side of his chair, but then, while bracing one arm on the table and the other on the back of the chair, he grimaced painfully before slowly lowering himself into the seat.

"Taking chances aren't you, Miss Thomas?" he asked as soon as he was settled in. His grimace faded when he leaned back in the chair and his muscles slowly relaxed. Still looking at her, he plucked his hat off his head and tossed it into the empty chair to his left, then self-consciously raked his hand through his hair to remove any unsightly dents.

When Abel noticed what Mark had done with his hat, he glanced up at the low-hanging brim of his own hat. Frowning, he reached up, removed it, then carefully placed it in his lap.

Obviously reacting to what the other two had done, Harry pulled his battered old work hat off his head and laid it on the chair beside Mark's. Though he had only a few hairs to worry about, he too lifted his hand and carefully slicked them back.

"Why would you say I'm taking chances, Mr. Gates?" Anna asked, tilting her head slightly while meeting his pale blue gaze straight on. Though she had used his first name many times when he wasn't around, she would not dare call him Mark to his face.

"Aren't you even the slightest bit afraid we might try to poison you?"

"And why would you?"

148

"So you couldn't possibly speak out against me tomorrow," he answered readily. When the boys looked up at him, clearly startled by the comment, he winked playfully, letting them both know he was teasing. His eyes sparkled with honest delight when Jamie rewarded him with a loud burst of laughter.

The high-pitched laughter made Mark want to laugh, too. He struggled to keep a straight face.

Curiously, Anna waited to see if the jerky movements around the corners of his mouth would eventually spread into a full smile, something she had yet to see from him, but the pain-filled grimace returned when he reached for the heavy platter of ham in front of him.

With obvious effort, he lifted the platter and hurriedly selected two large slices with his fork, then passed the platter on to Abel. The harsh grimace that had formed hard lines along his jaw and the outer corners of his mouth disappeared as soon as he'd released the platter. "I'm impressed that you chose to join us at all," he then continued in a teasing voice.

"I've been known to live dangerously," she responded, trying to keep the tone of their conversation light while she watched the slow, jerky movements he made while trying to cut his meat. Judging by his awkwardness and by the grimace that formed again and again near the lower corners of his mouth, Anna realized he was in severe pain.

Aware he'd been an idle recluse for well over a year, accomplishing little more than moving about the lower floor in his wheelchair, Anna understood the reason for his pain. His body was not used to such hard work. It would not surprise her if every muscle hurt him. Odd that a man like Mark Gates would suddenly be so willing to put himself through that much physical torment just to convince a judge he was worthy of caring for two runaway boys. Odd, but touching. "Besides, Mr. Gates, you don't know for certain that I plan to speak out against you."

"Don't you?" he asked and glanced up from his plate, his food temporarily forgotten. Suddenly, his easygoing manner turned very serious. "Exactly what *do* you plan to tell that judge?"

Everyone looked at her then, even Abel, who until that moment had been interested only in his food.

Not wanting to worry them unnecessarily, she smiled and accepted the platter of cheese Harry held out to her. "I think, if I really set my mind to it, I might be able to find *something* nice to tell the judge about you. True, it won't be an easy task, but I'm sure if I tried very, very hard, I could probably find some little tidbit worth telling him."

The corners of Mark's mouth twitched, and a tiny dimple formed in his right cheek. He set his knife down and studied the amusement sparkling in her emerald green eyes. "Like what?"

Aware how very close Mark had come to laughing, Anna had trouble keeping her own expression serious while she quickly transferred a small slice of cheese from the platter to her plate, then passed the platter on to Jamie.

"Let me think for a minute." She pursed her lips as if having to put a lot of effort into the process.

Jamie looked up from his plate, not yet understanding that she, too, was teasing. "You could tell him how hard Mark's been working to get that field planted," he offered, his eyes wide with hope.

"Yes, I suppose he *has* been working pretty hard at that," she said slowly, as if reluctant to admit it.

Mark lifted an eyebrow, but offered nothing in his own defense. He didn't have to; Jamie was only too eager to do that for him.

"He *has* worked hard. Real hard. He even has the blisters to prove it," Jamie added quickly, then looked at Mark. "Show her, Mark. Show her your hands."

"Not now," Mark cautioned him. "It's not the sort of thing a lady likes to see while she's eating."

Anna's gaze fell curiously on the hand gripping his fork. She noticed how awkwardly his fingers grasped the handle, as if it hurt to do even that. "Don't you wear gloves when you're working, Mr. Gates?"

"Sure he does," Jamie answered for him. "But he's been working so hard that he rubbed those blisters right through his gloves."

Mark directed a firm gaze at Jamie, as if to suggest they change the subject to something more appropriate, something that might make him feel a little less inept. "It's been a while since I've handled reins. My hands aren't used to that sort of work anymore," he admitted.

Harry cleared his throat and grinned. "It's been a while since you done much work outside. That's why you're so sunburned and why you walk like your arms and legs are goin' to fall off."

Harry waved his fork in Mark's direction to emphasize his words before turning his attention back to Anna. "Jamie's right. Mark's been working real hard, which even I admit is a little difficult to believe. 'Specially when you consider he's been pretendin' to be a poor helpless invalid for over a year now. But then, you have to understand he's changed a whole heap since these younguns came traipsin'

151

into his life the way they did. He's back to actin' like his old self again."

"But don't you think he's working a little *too* hard?" Anna asked, glancing back at Mark, aware again of his forced, jerky movements. Between the pain from the sunburn and the pain from his over-worked muscles, the man could hardly function. If he didn't slow down, he'd end up very sick, and where would that leave him in his fight for the boys?

"Sure he's workin' a little too hard," Harry admitted. "We both are. But that's only because we got so little time to get everything done. If we're to have any chance at all at gettin' guardianship of those boys, we're goin' to have to go make our plea to that judge before your boss gets back on Friday. And we're goin' to have to be able to show his honor that we can indeed provide a good, decent home for them."

Anna found the fact that Harry kept saying "we" confusing. "Do you live here too, Mr. Munn?"

"Ah, don't you go callin' me Mr. Munn," he complained with a disgusted shake of his head. "The name's Harry, plain and simple."

He looked at Mark, giving him the opportunity to say something similar, hoping they all might become better friends, but Mark ignored the chance to speak. Instead, he plopped a large piece of ham into his mouth and chewed it slowly. Although he had understood the reason Harry had looked at him with his bushy eyebrows lowered in such a meaningful way, Mark wasn't sure he wanted to get too friendly with this woman.

Something about her made him uncomfortable, made him want to shuffle in his seat even then. He wasn't sure if he was reacting to the determined set

152

of her pretty little jaw or the judgmental way she looked at him with those big green eyes of hers, but whatever it was, it made it hard for him to concentrate on anything else.

"Okay, Harry it is," Anna responded after it became apparent that Mark had nothing to add to their conversation. Although it felt as if Mark had personally insulted her yet again, she forced a congenial smile and fixed her gaze on Harry's apologetic expression. "I'll restate my question accordingly. Do you live here, too, *Harry?*"

Harry grinned, pleased to at least have that out of the way. "No, I got my own place off to the west, but I've spent more than enough time over here to consider this my second home."

"Isn't that the truth," Mark muttered, unable to resist a chance to pick at his friend. "Old Harry comes barging in over here almost every day, whether he's invited or not. He's been like that ever since the first day I met him." Mark shook his head as if annoyed, although the twinkle in his eye betrayed his flat expression. "I might as well go ahead and adopt him, too, while I'm at it."

Jamie giggled at such a thought. "Then Harry would be our brother." He giggled louder.

Anna glanced down at him, planning to ask what he thought about having such an "older" brother when she glimpsed Abel seated on the other side of him. Her eyes widened with disbelief and her throat constricted until she could hardly speak. Joy burst from her heart, quickly filling her soul with pleasure.

Abel was smiling, and not just a little smile: his grin stretched from ear to ear.

Astounded by the sight, Anna pressed her hand to

153

her throat and blinked, then directed her question to the younger child. "Abel, what do you think about that? Do you think Harry would make a very good brother?"

She noticed that Mark and Harry had both stopped eating. They waited to see if the boy would actually answer.

And he did. Not with words, but with laughter. Anna had never heard Abel laugh. She could not believe how delightful it sounded. Tears filled her eyes, and her lower lip trembled with true jubilation. Little Abel, who had not made a sound in well over two years, was laughing!

Harry saw that Anna was too overcome with emotion to continue and immediately took over the attempt to get Abel to speak. "I suppose you think I'm too *old* to be your brother?" Harry asked, as if having taken Abel's reaction as a personal affront. "Is that it? You think I'm too old?"

Still laughing, Abel nodded, agreeing that was exactly what he thought.

"Humph! I'll show you who's the old one around here," he said, pushing his chair back and rising from the table. "I'll bet you think I'm too old to take a few steps back, then, with a little runnin' start, hurdle this here chair without my feet ever touchin' it, don't you?"

Again Abel nodded.

Harry crossed his arms, cocked his head to one side with his chin thrust forward, as if he'd been unjustly insulted, and then he, too, nodded. "You're right. I am too old." Quickly he sat back down and returned his chair to the table. "Maybe instead of a brother, I could be more like a grandpa." He watched their reactions carefully. "I've always wanted to be someone's grandpa." Which was very true, but because Lilly had never been able to carry a child a full nine months, the large family they'd both hoped to have never came about. Maybe that was why he cared about Mark so. Mark was like the son he'd always wanted.

"That'd be great," Jamie answered, his blue-green eyes glistening brightly. "We ain't never had no grandpa."

"Well, looks like you got yourself one now," Harry declared with a confirming smile, then reached up to rub the inside corner of his eye with the tip of his finger, as if he had something caught there. After blinking several times to clear the last of whatever it was, he took a deep breath and added, "Now you'll both be stuck with me forever. What do you think about that?"

"I think I like it," Jamie concluded. "What about you, Abel?"

Abel nodded again, this time so hard his hair bounced. Still smiling, he reached into his plate and picked up a small piece of cheese, then plopped it happily into his mouth.

Jamie watched him for a second, then turned to look back at Harry, his expression suddenly very serious. "But what if that judge says me and Abel both can't live here? What if he makes me go live with the Porterfields, like was already planned?"

"We're hopin' that won't happen, but even if it does, I'll still be your grandpa," Harry insisted, though he knew he'd have no legal claim to either child. "And I'd still be Abel's grandpa. That way, even if it does end up that the two of you have to go live in different houses for a while, you could still see each other whenever you came out to visit me.

155

Nobody with any heart at all is going to keep a boy from visitin' his grandpa." He glanced at Mark to see what his reaction was to this nonsense, but Mark's expression revealed nothing. "So, even if it does turn out that Mark can get custody of only Abel, you two boys will still be a family 'cause you'll both still have the same grandpa."

Anna reached for her napkin and touched it to the inner corner of her eye, aware she had the same thing caught there that Harry had dabbed out of his just seconds earlier. She, too, wondered what Mark thought of Harry's little talk. She studied his solemn expression for several seconds before finally coming right out and asking, *"Would* you be willing to adopt Abel if for some reason that judge decided to return Jamie to the Porterfields?"

She hoped he would not prove to be like so many others and decide that a boy who refused to speak would be too much trouble—especially without Jamie there to act as a go-between. But if Mark did feel it would not work out, she wanted Abel to know about it now. She did not want the child to get his hopes set on something that would never happen.

"Of course, I'd take him," Mark answered, looking at her as if that had been a strange question. "But the judge is no fool. He's bound to see how much happier these boys would be living together here with me."

Realizing all this talk about the judge and his eventual decision had caused the boys to shift restlessly in their seats, Anna smiled, eager to reassure them. "And, in case that judge isn't clever enough to see for himself what is obviously best for these boys, I fully intend to point it out to him."

"Then you'll go with Mark to see the judge?" Jamie asked, his eyes wide with hope.

Anna's gaze met Mark's, then turned quickly away, aware of the awkward situation Jamie's question had created.

"H-he hasn't actually asked me to go with him," she pointed out, then pressed her eyes closed, feeling as if she had just invited herself to something she shouldn't have. When she opened her eyes again, she avoided looking at him. Instead, she fixed her gaze on Jamie's hopeful expression. "But I *do* intend to stop by and tell that judge exactly what I think would be best for you two."

"I'm inviting you now," Mark put in. His deep voice quickly drew her attention back to him. "If you are serious about helping us convince that judge to give me custody of these boys, then I definitely want you with me. As a personal employee of the Children's Aid Society, your opinion should hold a lot of weight."

Anna stared at Mark for a long moment. She felt both awkward and pleased by the invitation to join him. "When do you plan to see the judge?"

"Tomorrow morning . . . about ten."

"Would you like for me to meet you there?"

A smile played at the outer corners of Mark's lips. He was aware that by asking such a question she had agreed to help him. "No, I'll stop by to pick you up a few minutes before. That way the two of us can walk in together."

Anna glanced at Harry, puzzled. "Aren't you coming too?"

"I'll be payin' that judge a little visit right after Mark gets back. I'd go with him, but neither one of us cottons much to the notion of leavin' the boys out here all alone. I don't imagine the judge would take too kindly to the idea either."

"Oh, but you should bring them with you," Anna explained, her gaze darting from one to the other, hoping to convince them both. "That way the judge can see for himself how eager they are to live here with Mark." She then focused her attention on Harry's puzzled expression. "The judge also needs to see how willing you are to help in any way you can."

Though Anna was not aware she had slipped into calling Mark by his first name, Harry had noticed it immediately.

With raised brows, he glanced at Mark to see if it had registered with him, too; but to his disappointment, his friend was obviously too concerned with what was being said to notice that she had suddenly stopped calling him "Mr. Gates."

"What do you think, Mark? Is Anna right?" He purposely used her first name, hoping Mark would too. He'd get those two on better terms yet. "Should me and the boys go with you tomorrow?"

"Might be a good idea at that," he answered, mulling it over until he smiled a full smile that revealed his white teeth and formed long, narrow creases in his sun-reddened cheeks. "Once that judge gets a look at the boys and sees for himself how much they really care about each other, and how very much we care about them, he'll have to do what's right."

That settled it. Anna was to stop by the judge's office on her way home and request a ten o'clock appointment; then, at precisely ten o'clock the following morning, they would all march directly into the judge's office and, together, convince him to do the right thing.

* * *

It was fifteen minutes before ten when Harry volunteered to go to the door and ask for Anna. Knowing how painful it was for Mark to climb in and out of the buggy, he did not bother to wait for a response. He was far too eager to get on over to the judge's office and have his say. With hurried strides, he marched up to the door and knocked sharply.

While waiting for someone to answer, he pulled off his hat and pressed it against the front of his starched white shirt. He wanted to make a good impression should the reverend himself answer, having always thought it a good idea to stay on the good side of anyone who knew God directly.

"Hello, Reverend Cross. I'm here to pick up Miss Anna Thomas for that meeting we have with Judge Parish this morning. Is she ready?" he said in his most cordial voice.

"Is she ever!" the reverend responded with a cheerful laugh. "Why, she's been up and dressed since before sunup." He turned and called over his shoulder, "Anna, they're here."

There was a soft, rustling noise from behind the door, then Anna stepped into sight, dressed in a very demure dark gray woolen dress with matching tailored jacket. When her gaze met Harry's, she noticed that he looked every bit as frightened as she was.

"Ready?" she asked as she slipped the corded drawstring of her handbag over her wrist.

"As we'll ever be," Harry answered, his eyes wide and unblinking when he turned to offer his arm.

"Good luck," Reverend Cross called after them, watching while they hurriedly descended his front steps. "I'll be waiting to hear the outcome."

Anna ran her tongue over her lips, hoping the

outcome would be worth hearing. She took a deep, apprehensive breath when she glanced toward the street and saw Mark, Jamie, and Abel sitting quietly in a small four-seater carriage, all dressed in their finest. Her attention focused first on the boys. They looked as pale as little ghosts. Mark, too, looked a little pale, despite the dull pink of his sunburn. They all sat stiff as boards, with Mark and Jamie in the front seat and Abel in the back. Mark's expression was solemn. He looked as if his whole future was at stake. They all did, and, in a way, it was true. Everyone's future was about to be decided by a man they'd never even met.

Anna's heart went out to all of them, even Mark. In the few days she'd gotten to know him, her opinion of the man had changed dramatically. Though he continued to show occasional signs of obstinacy, especially where she was concerned, he was not the ogre she had originally thought. He might be a little hard to get along with at times, but clearly he loved those boys. She only hoped the judge would overlook his handicap and realize that, with Harry's help, he would be able to provide Jamie and Abel with a good home. She did not doubt they would be well cared for. And Anna planned to do all she could to point that out to the judge. It was her whole reason for wanting to be there.

"I sure hope that judge proves to be the understanding sort," she commented when she and Harry passed through the small gate in front of the reverend's house on their way to the carriage.

"Me, too," Harry responded in a low voice so no one else could hear. "I don't know what Mark will do if he doesn't get custody of at least one of the boys. He's really got his heart set on this. We both do."

"Well, all we can do is plead our case to the best of our ability and hope the man has a kind heart," she said, then smiled at Jamie, who had climbed down from the carriage to let her sit in the middle.

"My, don't you look nice," she commented as soon as she was close enough for the youngster to hear. Smiling, she lifted her skirts several inches so she could step up into the carriage, then quickly smoothed the material back into place. While Jamie hurriedly scampered onto the seat beside her, she glanced at Mark, who was dressed in a well-fitting three-piece suit. The dark color of the dress coat he had chosen looked a little warm for such a hot day, but made the dull pink of his sunburn seem less noticeable. "You *all* look very nice. I certainly hope the judge notices."

"Did you get that appointment set for ten?" Mark asked, feeling a little too awkward over such an unexpected compliment.

"Yes, I did. I also explained why we were coming," she told them, then turned in her seat to look at the boys again. Jamie sat to her right, his thigh touching her skirt, while Abel sat directly behind his brother, with Harry seated directly behind her. "The judge promised to listen to whatever we have to say with an open mind."

"That's good," Mark commented, then clicked the reins. "Let's hope he listens with an open heart as well."

For the next several minutes, nothing else was said. Everyone was too concerned with what was about to happen to think of anything to say. After they finally arrived in front of the courthouse, where the judge took care of whatever business he had

161

while he was in Pinefield, everyone climbed down, one at a time, Mark last. While Mark worked to steady his balance and smooth a rumpled trouser leg, Jamie reached into the back seat for his cane and quickly handed to him. Harry hurried to tether the horse to the hitching rail.

"Here goes," Mark said as he sucked in a deep breath. His tone revealed little of the turmoil he felt when he turned to face them, but his expression was that of a man waiting to be hanged.

"Do you want us to go in with you, or would you rather we waited out here until you've had a chance to speak with the judge alone?" Harry asked, placing a protective arm around each boy's shoulders.

"I don't know," Mark admitted, then glanced at Anna. "What do you think we should do? You know more about these things than we do."

Anna was pleased to be asked for her advice, aware it was a definite turning point in their relationship. Until then, Mark had shown very little interest in anything she had to say.

"I think it would be better if you and I went in first and gave the judge an overall idea of what you want to him to do, then bring the boys in so he can see for himself how much they want to live with you."

"Then, that's how we'll do it," Mark said with a sharp nod. "You three sit out there on those benches under the shade trees and wait for us to call you." Then, before turning back to face Anna, he took another long, self-sustaining breath. "I sure hope this turns out all right."

"It will," she said with far more confidence than she actually felt. Her heart went out to him when his lips compressed into a hard, determined white line. When he glanced back at the boys one last time, there was so much fear darkening his pale blue eyes that Anna wanted to slip her arms around him and comfort him.

"Let's go," he said, his voice barely above a whisper, then turned and headed up the small walkway that led to the front door. As she followed, Anna offered a short, silent prayer. She knew exactly what Mark was about to face, and it wouldn't be easy.

Chapter Nine

Anna sat in a small chair near the window, her hands clasped in her lap. Unblinking, for fear she would miss something, she studied the judge's facial expressions while he and Mark discussed the children. Mark had already explained the unusual circumstances that had allowed Jamie and Abel to enter his life, and he had also explained how very much he wanted to keep them in his life by making them both permanently a part of his family. He then began to detail all the work he'd accomplished to get his place ready for them.

Judge Parish listened quietly, nodding occasionally, which was his way of encouraging Mark to continue. Finally, with a hope radiating from the glimmering depths of his pale blue eyes, Mark explained that, by allowing the boys to live with him, he would be allowing them to stay together until adulthood — or longer, if they chose to stay on and help him run the farm. Mark finished his little speech by telling the judge that the boys were just outside, sitting in the benches out under the trees, waiting for their chance to talk with him.

Though Anna often thought of something she felt would be pertinent to mention, and had dearly wanted to interrupt the two men, she continued to sit quietly off to the side. She knew it was extremely important that Mark be the one to answer the judge's questions; therefore, it was best she wait until she was called upon to speak.

She felt certain that as soon as the judge had finished talking with Mark, he would have several questions for her. She just hoped she could think clearly enough to come up with appropriate answers. As nervous as she was at that moment, she was not certain she could answer any question intelligently.

"I must say, I am impressed with your sincerity, Mr. Gates, and with all the work you claim to have done since your decision to adopt the boys," the judge said, then glanced at Mark expectantly. "How old are you, Mr. Gates?"

Mark had been too nervous to sit and stood directly across from the judge's large desk, trying not to lean too heavily on his cane. He did not want the judge to place too much emphasis on the fact he had a bad leg.

"I'm thirty," Mark answered proudly, thinking that a good age to be.

The judge pursed his lips as he jotted down that bit of information. All during Mark's talk, he had continuously taken notes, glancing up occasionally to study Mark's expression.

Anna leaned forward, slowly rubbing her palms together. She wanted to catch a glimpse of those notes, but she could not see them from so far away. Worriedly, she watched the judge for any negative reaction to Mark's age, knowing that the majority of people who asked to take in an orphan were much younger. She prayed the judge would not hold his age against him and slowly released a trembling breath, one she had not realized she'd been holding.

"And how old is your wife?" Judge Parish then asked, glancing momentarily at Anna.

Mark's eyes widened. "My wife?"

Anna felt an sharp, foreboding pain twist deep in the pit of her stomach.

"Yes, your wife," the judge answered and nodded toward Anna. "How old is she?"

Mark glanced over his shoulder at Anna, then suddenly realized that in his eagerness to discuss the boys, he'd forgotten to introduce Anna to the judge. He felt a little embarrassed for having overlooked something like that. "I'm afraid there's been a misunderstanding. She's not my wife."

"She's not? Then who is she?" The judge looked at her with new interest. His thin, gray-spattered eyebrows arched high over dark brown eyes, causing the eyeglasses perched on his thin nose to slip downward half an inch.

Mark moved to Anna's side, leaning heavily on his cane for balance. When he turned to face the judge again, he gently rested his other hand on her shoulder. Instinctively she covered his hand with her own in a gentle display of support.

While she waited for Mark to continue, a slow, tingling warmth spread through her shoulder, downward, then along her arm with a spilling, languid ease. It was the first time they had actually touched, and for a brief moment Anna wanted

166

nothing more than to close her eyes and simply enjoy the feeling, but there was no time for that.

"I'm sorry, judge," Mark apologized, still wondering how he could have been so neglectful. "I really should have thought to introduce the two of you."

His only excuse for such inconsiderate behavior was that it had been over a year since he'd had any reason to introduce anyone and in that year's time he'd simply forgotten how. But telling the judge that would be admitting he'd closed himself off from the rest of the world for what now seemed like a ridiculously long time, and that could make the man view him as somewhat unstable. "I guess I was so eager to speak with you about those boys, I forgot to introduce you to Miss Anna Thomas, a very good friend of mine."

Anna glanced up into Mark's smiling face and her pulses quicken, causing light, fluttery sensations in her stomach. She liked the thought of being Mark's very good friend. What she liked even more than the thought of it was hearing him say it. She wondered if he truly felt that way about her, or if the pronouncement had been more for the judge's benefit. She wished she knew what Mark's true feelings were.

The judge pushed his eyeglasses back in place with the metal-capped end of his pencil while dividing his attention equally between Mark's and Anna's concerned expressions. "She's just a friend? I don't understand. If she's just a friend of yours, then why is she here? To give you moral support? Or perhaps she's here to vouch for your good character."

"Well, actually, she's here as more than just my

167

friend." Mark admitted. "She works for the Children's Aid Society—the charity group that brought the boys down here in the first place."

The judge leaned back in his chair. His forehead notched. "Then am I to understand that you are not married, Mr. Gates?"

Anna's stomach knotted with sudden apprehension when she noticed the accusing tone in the judge's voice. Far too often an adoption request was denied simply because there were not two adoptive parents involved.

"No, sir, I am not married," Mark answered honestly. His puzzled expression darted from Anna to the judge. "But just because I don't have a wife doesn't mean I can't provide a good home for those two boys. Why, I myself was raised by only one parent."

"That's regrettable, but I really don't see—" the judge started to say, but was interrupted in mid-sentence.

"After my mother died, which was only a few years after I was born, my father never remarried. He had no choice but to raise me alone. Despite all the obvious hardships, he did a very good job of it. For most of my life I had no mother, yet I was never lacking for love. And I can assure you that if you will see it in your heart to allow Jamie and Abel to come live with me as my sons, they will never be lacking for love either. I promise you, with God as my witness, that I'll be the very best father anyone can be."

"That very well may be true, but children that age need a mother, too," the judge said, already setting aside his pencil. "When they are as young as you say those two are, they need the special kind of care only a woman can provide."

Anna sucked in a sharp breath, then rushed to intervene, knowing that unless they did something to change the judge's mind soon, Mark was about to lose his chance to get those boys. "Oh, but there will be a woman taking care of them. Mr. Gates plans to hire a housekeeper immediately to help him take care of them, don't you, Mr. Gates?"

Mark looked at her, startled. Then, realizing what she was up to, he quickly agreed, "As soon as I can find someone I feel is qualified."

The judge stared at him for a long moment, then slowly shook his head. "I'm afraid that won't do. Housekeepers come and go. What those boys need is stability. They need a mother who will be there for them in all the trying years ahead. And Deborah Porterfield is just such a person. She and Richard have already spoken to me about adopting the older boy, and I believe they will make good, stable parents. I also believe that eventually the younger boy will find a good home, too. In fact, had I been told the boys had been found, I would have already signed the papers for the Porterfields. I'm sorry, but I really have to consider what's best for everyone."

"Then consider what's best for those boys!" Anna pleaded, her voice edged with anger as she lifted her hands, palms up. "What those boys need more than anything else is to be able to stay together. I know. I've been professionally acquainted with them for over a year now. I know how much they care for each other, how very much they *need* each other. Separating those two would virtually destroy

169

them—especially young Abel."

When the judge did not immediately comment, she dropped her hands back into her lap and tucked them beneath her handbag, where she curled them into tight, white-knuckled fists. Had the man no heart? "Don't you understand? That's why they ran away in the first place. If only you could see how dramatically Abel has already changed in the few days he and Jamie have been living with Mark! It is nothing short of astounding. Before knowing Mark, he'd been extremely withdrawn. He never talked. He never smiled. But, now, although he has yet to talk, he smiles all the time and he's even started to laugh right out loud."

The judge's expression remained unchanged, causing a cold wave of panic to wrap painfully around Anna's heart. She wondered what else she could say to convince him. "Call the children in here and talk to them. See for yourself how desperately the boys want to live with Mr. Gates."

Slowly the judge skidded his chair back from his desk and stood. "I'm sorry. But with no wife to help take care of them, I cannot allow Mr. Gates to adopt either of those boys. I'm afraid I'll have to make my judgment in favor of the Porterfields."

Anna's mind whirled in frantic search of a solution. Her heart ached with such strong, unadulterated fear, she did not think she could bear the pain another second. She had to do something to change the judge's mind—now. Jamie and Abel's happiness was at stake. Mark's, too.

"But, what if he is *engaged* to be married? What then?"

"Then I could consider his request with a clear conscience." The judge circled his desk, his expression suddenly hopeful when he turned to face Mark again. "Are you by any chance engaged to be married?"

Anna did not give Mark time to answer. She jumped up out of her chair, threw her arms around Mark's waist, and almost knocked him off balance when she answered emphatically, "Yes, he is."

When both men looked at her questioningly waiting for her to finish her statement, she eased her arms from around Mark's waist and shyly reached for his free hand.

"He's engaged to me."

Smiling, despite the painful hammering of her heart, she pressed the back of his hand to her cheek and looked adoringly into Mark's face. A comical expression of sheer disbelief widened his pale blue eyes. Her smile broadened. "We were not planning to be married until the end of summer, that's so my Aunt Nell from New York could be with us, but we can move that date forward if you think it would help. I'm sure my aunt would understand. I know Mark wouldn't mind, would you, sweetheart?"

Stunned by the dazzling smile she offered him, Mark opened his mouth to speak; but when no words ventured forth, he quickly clamped it shut again. Instead of commenting, he shook his head, indicating it would not matter to him in the least.

"Well, well, well," the judge said with a pleased smile. "This puts a whole new light on the matter."

Just as astonished as everyone else by what she

171

had done, Anna held her breath while the judge took a moment to consider this new bit of information. Had he believed her, or had Mark's startled expression given her away?

"Tell you what," Judge Parish finally said, narrowing one eye, still deep in thought. "I'll hold off making my final decision on this matter until Saturday. That will give you both two days to decide what you really want to do. If you two are indeed married by then and still feel as strongly about adopting those two boys as you do right now, then I'll consider it. Meanwhile, I'd like to have a little chat with the children—alone. And I'll also want to ride out to take a look at your house. I'd like to see for myself what sort of environment they'd be living in should I decide in your favor."

"That's fine. Come whenever you like," Mark said, finding his voice at last. He paused a second to allow his thoughts and his rapid heartbeat to settle a little before asking suddenly, "Exactly what are our chances of getting those boys?" He had to know. There was too much at stake not to.

"If you two are indeed serious about getting married right away, and if your farm is in fine order, as you claim it is, your chances are very good—because I happen to agree with you. Those boys should be allowed to stay together if at all possible. Now, will you please ask them to come in here?"

Mark opened the door and called to them, his voice noticeably strained with emotion.

Barely seconds later, Jamie, Abel, and Harry appeared in the doorway—all wide eyes and bobbing Adam's apples. Harry, who had shaved for the first

172

time in weeks and had donned his very best hat for their meeting with the judge, quickly slipped the hat off his head and pressed it firmly against his chest. Aware everyone was looking at him, he reached up to slick down the few hairs on top of his head with the flat of his palm and smiled tentatively at the judge.

"And who might you be?" Judge Parish asked, eyeing Harry speculatively, then looked to Mark who stood just inside the doorway, his hand still resting on the knob.

"That's our new grandpa," Jamie answered before anyone else had a chance to respond. "Grandpa Harry."

Harry grinned, pleased by the sound of it. Slowly, his shoulders relaxed and the grip on his hat brim loosened.

The judge stroked his chin thoughtfully while he continued to stare curiously at Harry. "Your new grandpa? Are you Mr. Gates' father?"

"No, sir, just a real close friend."

The judge stroked his chin thoughtfully. "I think I'd like to have a little chat with you, too." He then placed a hand at Anna's elbow, an obvious indication it was time for her and Mark to leave the room. "Would you and your fiancée please step outside. We won't be but a few minutes."

Harry blinked twice at the judge's casual use of the word fiancée, but he said nothing to indicate his surprise.

Anna saw the stunned reaction and tried not to laugh. The boys obviously had no idea what fiancée meant, for there was no indication they had found the judge's words at all startling. "Children, we'll wait for you out by the trees," she said with a reassuring smile. She glanced back and caught a quick glimpse of their worried expressions before she stepped outside to join Mark. Though she knew Harry would do all he could to help the children feel at ease, her heart went out to them.

Pulling at the inner edge of her lower lip with her front teeth, she followed Mark across the wide veranda and down the massive steps. Consciously she held her poise until she heard the metal click when the door closed behind them, then quickly dropped her shoulders and exhaled a heavy sigh of relief. Every muscle in her body felt suddenly limp, though her heart continued its rapid pounding when she turned to look at him. "I think it worked."

"Why did you do that?" he asked, shaking his head, bewildered by it all. He waited until they had reached the shade of the huge oak trees that dotted the wide courthouse lawn. "What happens when Saturday comes and he finds out we aren't married? I'll be right back where I started."

"By Saturday, we *will* be married," she assured him, then held her breath and waited for his reaction to that statement. Her gaze searched his concerned expression, her heart brimming with hope. At that moment, everyone's future lay in Mark's hands. Though the idea to marry him had come suddenly, it really was what she wanted to do. Then a frightening thought occurred to her. "That is, unless you have someone else in mind, someone who will agree to marry you in so short a time."

Mark shook his head. There was no one. No one would have him. Not anymore.

174

Anna shrugged, relieved. "Then it'll have to be me."

"Do you really realize what you're saying?" he asked. His forehead wrinkled with mounting concern; he was unable to believe she had thought this thing through. Without realizing his actions, he reached out to touch her cheek with the tips of his fingers.

A floodtide of vibrant sensations cascaded through her while she responded as much to his touch as his question. "Yes. Of course I do."

"No. I don't think that's true." Glancing away, he raked the same fingers that had lightly touched her cheek through his thick hair, then suddenly turned back to face her again. "If you go through with this, you'll have to give up your job with the Children's Aid Society and come live with us. That judge is not about to allow those boys to stay with me for very long if it turns out you are not actually living there with us. To make this idea of yours work, you'll have to give up whatever life you may have going for you in New York."

"I know," she said in a soft, reassuring voice. "And to tell you the truth, it doesn't matter. All that matters right now are those two boys. After everything they have been through, they deserve a chance to be happy. Don't you agree?"

"Of course I do." That was the one point he could not argue.

"Then it's settled."

"No it's not," he argued, tossing his hands up in a show of exasperation. "I can't allow you to do this. You haven't had time to think this through. You don't realize what you'll have to give up. Not just your job, but everything, and everyone. You'd have to turn your back on whatever men have become a part of your life. Don't you understand? By marrying me you'd be closing yourself off to any chance of ever sharing a *real* relationship with a man. You'd be destroying any opportunity you may have of ever marrying for love."

"There is no other man in my life, not anymore. And I *will* be marrying for love," she said. As soon as the words were spoken, she felt all bubbly and tingly inside, because it was the truth. But, when she noticed the startled expression that crossed Mark's face, she quickly added, so as not to frighten him with these new feelings of hers, "I happen to love those children as much as you do."

While studying the determined expression on her beautiful face, Mark felt a sharp stab of disappointment. There for a brief moment he had actually thought she'd meant that she loved him. But then, why should she? Why should *any* woman? He wasn't exactly what women looked for in a husband. But then again, she seemed sincere enough about wanting to marry him. Finally he sighed aloud with open resignation. "I sure wish there was some other way to help those boys—for your sake."

"But there's not." Her blood raced with the realization that he was about to agree. Though neither of them had officially proposed to the other, they were about to be married.

Smiling down at her with as much admiration as adoration, he reached out to touch her cheek again with the tips of his fingers. "You're quite a noble lady, you know that."

Tiny shivers of excitement cascaded down Anna's

spine, causing little bumps to form beneath the sensitive outer layer of her skin. She was delighted by his concern and amazed by his gentleness. It was hard to believe she had ever thought ill of him. "If that's true, I'm not the only noble one. If we do get married, you will also be closing yourself off to any real relationships. No decent woman would ever allow a married man to flirt with her." Even a man as handsome as you, she thought, but didn't dare say.

Mark closed his eyes briefly, as if unable to face whatever thought had flitted across his mind, then muttered in a voice so soft she almost didn't hear. "I did that long ago."

The muscles in his jaw hardened when he re-opened his eyes and looked at her again. He thought about the accident and how grotesquely it had disfigured his leg. The thought of what Anna's reaction would be if she were ever to see his leg unclothed made him physically ill.

He had to make sure that never happened. "So you don't worry about such things, I want you to know that I understand the only reason you have agreed to marry me is to help the boys. Although legally you would be my wife, and as my wife I promise to take care of you, I would not expect you to—fulfill any of—ah—shall we say, your *wifely duties.*"

Anna's eyebrows shot up. She hadn't even thought of that aspect of their marriage. "You what?"

Mark swallowed hard, finding the topic a difficult one to discuss but wanting to reassure her. "It is enough that you are willing to be a mother to

177

the boys. I'll expect nothing more from you. It will not be necessary for you to share my bedroom. You can have your pick of any of the bedrooms upstairs." Anything to avoid the repulsion on her face were she ever to catch a glimpse of his badly mangled leg.

Anna continued to stare at him, dumbfounded.

Still wanting to make this transition as easy as possible for her, Mark continued. "I also want you to know that after the boys are older, and no longer have to fear being separated from each other by the court, I will give you a divorce and enough money to restart your life in style. I realize you'll be in your mid-thirties by then, and that being a divorced woman won't make things easy for you, but as pretty as you are, you should still be able to find a man willing to offer you a real marriage, the sort that might allow you to have children of your own."

Anna was too surprised that he thought her pretty to be embarrassed by the topic of their conversation. "I'll agree to whatever you want," she said, though it disappointed her to know he was already looking forward to their divorce. Even though he was willing to marry her in order to obtain legal custody of the boys, he did not want the marriage to be a permanent arrangement. But then, she couldn't really blame him. It was not something either of them had planned, and it wasn't as if they were madly in love with one another.

"Good," Mark said, also feeling disappointed. "Then it's settled. We'll be married with the understanding that when the boys are of age, I will free you from the marriage and let you do whatever you want with the rest of your life."

"When? When can we be married?" After all, the judge had given them only two days.

"Why not right now? I suspect we could get Reverend Cross to marry us." He smiled and held his hand out to her. "How about it?"

Anna's insides spun crazily when she gently placed her hand in his and felt his fingers curl into a firm grasp. Tiny jolts of excitement shot through her. She really was going through with it. She really was going to marry Mark Gates and become mother to Jamie and Abel. *Mother.* Suddenly, the one thing she thought she would never have in life would be hers: children. One of the reasons she had enjoyed working for the Children's Aid Society was because she so deeply loved children, yet could never have any of her own. Not since the carriage accident several years ago. And now, as fate would have it, she was about to become the mother of two.

She was so thrilled by the thought that she wanted to laugh right out loud, especially when she thought of what Gordon's reaction would be when she calmly told him she would not be returning to New York with him. The poor man would have to take care of any other children himself. What a pity—for the children.

"Let's at least wait for Harry and the boys to finish talking with the judge," she said, her eyes glimmering like twin emeralds when she glanced up at her husband-to-be. "I want them with us."

"Of course," Mark agreed, although, now that the decision had been made, he was ready to get it

179

over with, before she had a chance to rethink the outcome.

As it turned out, the *little* chat the judge had claimed he wanted to have with the boys lasted for well over half an hour, giving Mark and Anna enough time to make a few plans for their future. By the time the door opened and Jamie and Abel ran out to greet them, any apprehension Mark or Anna had felt about their sudden decision to marry was gone. In its place was pure excitement. It felt like they were about to embark on some thrilling adventure, an adventure that they could all share.

The ceremony was short and sweet, ending with the traditional kiss—a kiss that sent Anna's senses reeling even harder than before. Too much was happening too quickly. She needed some time alone to sort through these many different feelings. But there wasn't any time for that. First she'd have to pack her things; then she'd have to unpack.

While Anna and the boys stayed at the Crosses' to take care of the packing, Mark, Harry, and the reverend went back to the judge's office to tell him the good news and to show him the marriage certificate. The judge was pleased to see it and agreed to allow the two-month trial period to begin as of that very afternoon. He warned them he would visit at least once before he left town, to be sure that everything was running smoothly; and if he found no problems, and none cropped up within the next sixty days, the boys could become theirs permanently. He also promised to explain his decision to Gordon Franklin as soon as he returned the following morning. That way, all Anna would have to do was tell Gordon she would not be returning to New York with him.

When the five of them left town barely an hour later, Mark, Anna, Jamie and Abel were a real family, with Harry an honorary member. The boys no longer had to worry about being separated from each other or from Mark and Harry. Anna felt good about that, but obviously not as good as Jamie felt.

Jamie was so excited by the judge's decision that he babbled incessantly about all the things he planned to do to show his appreciation to both the judge and to Mark. It wasn't until they had turned off the main road and had started down the narrow lane that cut through the woods toward Mark's house that he leaned forward in his seat so he could see up into Mark's face. Looking very pensive, he asked in a serious voice, "Now that you're to be our father, what do we call you?"

"I don't know," Mark answered, surprised by the question. "What do you want to call me?"

Jamie scratched his head while he thought about that. "I guess we could go on calling you Mark, but somehow that don't seem right no more." He twisted his face, lost deep in his own thoughts. "If we're going to be calling Harry Grandpa from now on, how about us calling you just plain Pa?"

Mark grinned. "Okay, just plain Pa it is. But what do you think we should call Anna? Just plain Ma?"

Jamie studied her with a wrinkled nose, obviously displeased with the suggestion. "No, I don't think so."

Anna felt a sharp stab of disappointment. Jamie

181

obviously had not yet adjusted to the fact she was to be a part of their family, too. Maybe he was against the idea.

Unaware of her sudden doubts, Jamie continued to stare at her thoughtfully for a long moment. "I think I'd rather call her Mama. She looks more like a Mama than she does a Ma."

Mark glanced at her for a moment. "I guess you're right. Mama, it is." Then, as if he suddenly realized she should have some say on the matter, he asked, "That is all right with you, isn't it, Mama?"

Anna appreciated the chance to voice her opinion. Smiling broadly, she said aloud, so all could hear, "Yes, Just-Plain-Pa, Mama is fine with me."

Jamie and Abel burst into a fit of giggles, while Harry and Mark tossed their heads back and laughed loud and long, too happy even to consider the problems that might lie ahead.

Chapter Ten

Knowing how difficult it would be for Mark to climb the stairs, especially as sore as he was from too much work, Harry volunteered to stay and help Anna settle into one of the bedrooms upstairs. After carrying her trunk inside, he showed her the three bedrooms still vacant as well as where she could find fresh linen for her bed and clean towels for her washstand.

Though Mark had been willing to stay downstairs and help Jamie and Abel put together a quick supper, he frequently returned to the foot of the staircase and called up to them to make sure they were finding everything they needed. Not having been upstairs since his accident, he was worried that many of the items she might need for her room would not be there, or would be in such poor condition that she could not use them. He was relieved to be told that everything was fine; but even so, he continued to seek reassurance every few minutes.

By six o'clock, Anna was unpacked and settled into her choice of the upstairs bedrooms. Her trunk had already been put away in the attic, and she took the time to give her new bedroom a thorough sweeping and then dusted the furniture and made the bed with fresh linen.

While she attended to a few last-minute changes in

the general arrangement of her bedroom, Harry quietly left the room so she could have a moment to collect her thoughts. He went back downstairs, eager to help the others get supper on the table.

Because of what had happened that day, he wanted to be sure that tonight's supper was special. After all, it was really a victory celebration of sorts, and they deserved the best. If, when he arrived downstairs, he discovered there was still enough time, he planned to make a quick panful of his cinnamon-glazed sweet rolls to go with those steaks he had insisted they buy while in town and the vegetables the boys were supposed to prepare.

Only moments after Harry had left, Anna decided to try out the elaborate hand-carved, high-backed rocking chair that sat near the side of her bed. As she settled into the fancy chair, she realized how very pleased she was with her new surroundings. Although the bedroom she had eventually chosen was not the largest of the three that had been available to her, it was much larger than the room she'd had back in New York, and it was directly across the hall from the boys' bedroom, which would allow her to be close by, should they need her in the middle of the night.

Besides, this was a very pretty room, decorated in bright yellows, with contrasting splashes of blue and green. Anna smiled, unable to resist the temptation to hug herself. It seemed odd; she'd come to Texas searching for homes for the orphans they had brought with them, yet somehow she'd managed to find one for herself in the process. *Home.* That had a good sound to it. Having been tossed back and forth between her two uncles' houses during the five painful years following her parents' death, she liked the thought of this place being home. And she liked the thought of Mark being her husband.

A tiny wave of excitement washed over her, making her feel vibrantly alive. That morning, she had awakened a single woman with no real ties other than the one to her job, and no overwhelming desire to make any changes in her life. Yet now, just hours later, she was a married woman. The proof lay in the hastily purchased band of gold at the base of her fourth finger.

She studied the ring's flawless beauty while she considered how remarkable it felt to be married. *Married.* Suddenly she had a husband and two children, all three waiting for her downstairs. It was so unbelievable. And it was all so thrilling. She could hardly wait to start her new life as wife and mother.

With those exciting and somewhat frightening thoughts in mind, Anna pushed herself out of the chair and hurried downstairs, eager to take over the supper preparations. As the new woman of the house, that was now *her* kitchen — and they might as well get used to the idea.

Having spent so much time at Mark's, helping put that first crop of his in the ground, Harry had a lot of catch-up work to do at his own place. Therefore, for the first few days following the wedding, he purposely stayed away from Mark's. Besides, he felt it would give the four of them a little time to get used to each other and start adjusting to their new life together.

It was Monday noon before he finally decided enough time had passed and he could safely return. Besides, he was too eager to see how they were getting along to stay away any longer. When he rode into the yard just a little before one o'clock, he spotted Jamie

185

and Abel out front, playing with one of Mark's chickens. He recognized Old Shirley right away and wondered what the rattle-headed old Banty thought of Mark's new family, then he chuckled. As dumb as Old Shirley was, she wouldn't know if she was being unduly harassed or not. In fact, the way she was prancing around, it looked to him like she was actually enjoying the attention. Stupid chicken. Never had been good for much. Even when she did remember how to lay an egg, it was never proper sized. Never had been. Not even in her younger years.

"Howdy," he called out in greeting, aware the boys had not heard his horse because of Shirley's loud, continuous squawking. Quickly he swung his leg over the saddle and dropped to the ground with a low grunt. "How's things been goin' around here?"

"Grandpa!" Jamie shouted, and immediately took off toward him, running as fast and as hard as his little legs would allow.

Harry grinned, opened his arms wide, and caught the boy in a big bear hug. Abel soon followed and Harry made room in his arms for him too. Kneeling so he could better see their faces, he asked, "How you been?"

"Great! We helped Pa plow up that back field so he can plant that new grass seed tomorrow."

"But I thought he was going to wait until the end of the week to plow that field so I could help."

Jamie shook his head apologetically. "I guess he was too eager to get started. Besides, he had us to help him." He patted his chest proudly.

Harry chuckled. "How much did you get done?"

"Most of it. Enough that he told us we'd be planting that seed some time tomorrow morning and in a few months we ought to be able to get our first cows. He plans to let me and Abel help pick them."

"I see," Harry said, laughing with sheer joy at the boy's enthusiasm and at how easily he had called Mark his "Pa." It was easy to see that the boys had already adjusted to having a whole new family. "And what has Anna been up to these past few days?"

"Mama? Oh, she's mostly been cleaning and rearranging things down in the cellar and in the kitchen pantry. You know how women can be about dirt and clutter. She's been busy tossing out things that are too broken to be fixed or have gotten too old to be useful, and she's been making a list of things she needs for Pa to buy when he goes to town. Right now, I think she's in the kitchen getting ready to make jelly out of the blackberries we picked for her this morning."

"Blackberries? Already?" Harry asked, then realized that Thursday would bring the first day of May. Where'd the days go?

"Yes, blackberries. They're just starting to turn color, but we found enough black ones to fill a whole bucket. Those woods are full of them." He pointed to the thicket of trees and bushes that blocked the main road from view.

"A whole bucket? My, but you two fellas must have been busy," Harry commented appreciatively, then glanced around. "Where is Mar—I mean, your pa?"

Jamie's eyes widened, as if he was hesitant to tell. Suddenly he seemed very interested in the scuffed tips of his brown leather shoes. "Oh, he's around somewhere."

Harry eyed him suspiciously. "Got any idea where?"

Jamie shrugged while he continued to study the rounded end of his shoes. "In the barn maybe."

"In the barn? Why?" Harry glanced toward the open door. "What's he doin' in there?"

Jamie lifted his gaze to the leafy green limbs of a nearby pecan tree. "Well, ah, he's, ah, sorta fixing something he sorta broke."

Harry's eyebrow arched while his suspicions mounted. "And just what is it he's fixin'?"

"A plow blade," Jamie admitted, then winced. *"Your* plow blade."

"My plow blade?" Harry shouted, pretending to be outraged as he hurried toward the barn to find out what had happened, and to see if he could help.

Thinking the situation far more serious than it was, Jamie ran to the house to find Mama. He wanted her to come outside and make sure there was no trouble. He didn't understand that Pa had been teasing when he had claimed that Harry would have his hide for having bent his new plow blade.

"Please. You've got to come," Jamie insisted, tugging frantically on Anna's arm when she did not head immediately for the back door. "You have to come outside and explain to Grandpa that it wasn't Pa's fault. He couldn't see that big rock, not even from where he sat. It was buried down in the dirt. Even me and Abel didn't see it, and we both walked that entire field before Pa ever started plowing."

Anna knew Harry would never harm Mark, but realized Jamie was not so sure. Finally, she set the bowl of freshly washed berries aside and followed him through the back door, across the narrow porch, and out into the yard. When they turned to face the barn, they saw Harry come out of the nearby tool shed with a heavy sledgehammer in his hand. He too was headed for the barn.

"Grandpa, don't!" Jamie shouted and flew across the yard to try and stop him.

"Don't what?" Harry asked, puzzled by the boy's

188

odd behavior. "Your pa asked me to go get the sledge-hammer so he could try to hammer out that blade." He glanced down at Jamie's firm grasp on his arm and puckered a frown, obviously confused. "You got some use for this hammer?"

"Pa sent you for that hammer?" Jamie's shoulders relaxed while he glanced back over his shoulder and looked at Anna sheepishly. "No, I got no use for it."

Anna chuckled then called out to Harry, "You're not planning to use that thing on Mark when you're through with the blade, are you?"

"Wasn't plannin' on it. But if you want me to, I'll sure consider it." Harry pulled off his hat and scratched the back of his head with the side of his little finger while he tried to figure out why she'd asked such a strange question.

Deciding the situation was hilariously funny, Abel let out a shrill laugh, then ran over to tug on Jamie's shirt sleeve.

"I'm going. I'm going," Jamie muttered, still feeling a little foolish for having thought the worst. "Where's Shirley? We'd better get her back in the pen before she gets caught up under the porch again."

The pen? Harry glanced toward the chicken coop and was surprised to see a new twelve-foot-high mesh-wire fence, forming a small scratching yard near the front. Harry's eyes widened with disbelief. Mark had even repaired the broken cock walk. Harry shook his head, amazed at how much his friend had accomplished in just three and a half days. Not only had he made several noticeable repairs to the outbuildings, he'd found the time to start plowing that back section of land. Mark had managed to do more to his place in just three and a half days than the two of them had done during that entire year. Someone had even swept the sideyard clean as a cabin floor and picked up all the clutter.

"Right nice lookin' chick'n pen. Looks like we won't have to worry any more about accidentally steppin' in no chicken-s—," he paused, catching himself before he said something he would surely regret, "—*stuff* whenever we go walkin' across the yard."

Glancing back at Anna, he grinned guiltily, then raised the hammer high and shook it. "You never said if you wanted me to use this on Mark or not."

Anna plucked a strand of hair that had fallen across her damp forehead and tucked it back, away from her face, then laughed at Harry's nonsense. "Only if he doesn't get on into town to make some of those purchases he's promised to make. He told me I'd have the sugar I need to make my jelly by tonight."

"You plannin' on cookin' jelly at night?" Harry thought that a mighty odd time to be worrying about such matters. Nighttime was for sitting and admiring the work done that day.

"It'll be cooler then," she said, fanning her face with her hand. Although she truly loved everything else about her new home, she could easily do without all the heat. Sometimes it became so hot in the kitchen that she felt physically faint. "Besides, I like keeping busy."

Harry looked at her for a minute, thinking she looked a little too tired to him, but extremely happy; then he shrugged his shoulders. "Whatever primes your pump." Turning back toward the barn, he shook his head questioningly. Keeping busy was one thing, but working oneself into the ground was quite another. But then, it wasn't none of his business.

Anna watched until Harry had disappeared through the door, then returned to the house to finish washing the blackberries, setting them aside with what sugar she had left.

Barely an hour later, while she sat at the kitchen table reattaching a button to one of Mark's work shirts, Harry and Mark clambered through the back door and announced that they had washed up and were ready to go into town for more grass seed and whatever it was she needed. When Mark asked her for her list, he was surprised to have three pages thrust into his hands.

"All this?" he asked, glancing over the first page with wide-eyed curiosity.

"Yes. As you can see, mostly I've listed things I'll need either in the kitchen or the laundry room, but there are a few items on there that we will eventually need for the house, too. You'll also find that I've written down a few sewing notions. I can't believe you've made do all these years with one needle and only two colors of thread. But then, judging by the condition of your shirts, you haven't been too concerned with how many buttons you have—or how many holes."

Tossing his chin out playfully, Mark pretended to be insulted by such a remark, but offered no biting response. "Are you sure this is everything? Remember, I don't plan to go back to town for at least a week."

Harry couldn't resist. "Heck fire, you buy up everything on that list and you won't be having to go back for a couple of *months*."

Aware they were teasing, Anna laughed good-naturedly while she lifted the corner of her apron and dabbed at the perspiration trickling down the side of her neck. "That's all I could come up with for now."

"All?" Mark asked, eyeing the list with a raised brow.

Dropping the apron and smoothing it down over

191

her heavy woolen skirts, she conceded, "I realize it might be too much for us to try to purchase at one time. Just pick out the things you think we'll need the most. I'm aware that some of the items on there, like the porcelain soap dishes and the new cuptowels, can easily wait. Those are just items I thought might help dress up the place a little. I'll trust you to use your better judgment in selecting what we really need."

Mark frowned, noticing how flushed Anna looked. Having spend the past three and a half days working outside from dawn until dusk, he had not realized just how hot she was during the day. Although he had come inside for lunch every day, he'd not paid that much attention to what now seemed very obvious. He felt guilty for having completely overlooked her discomfort. "Maybe while I'm in town I'll buy some lemons and ice, too, so we can have iced lemonade with our supper. You look like you could use a nice frosted glass of lemonade."

"Only if you return in time for me to prepare it," she cautioned with a playful smile, touched that he had thought of her comfort. More and more, he proved to be the exact opposite of that mean old ogre she had originally thought him to be. "But, the way you've been dawdling today, it'll probably be midnight or later before you ever get back."

"That's true. And judging by how many items you've written down on this list, it could be even later than that," he chuckled, knowing it always caught her off guard whenever he agreed with her. "We'll be lucky to get back by morning."

"Go!" she ordered, pointing toward the back door with the tip of Mark's only sewing needle.

"Yes, Ma'am," he said with a firm nod while he quickly folded the list and tucked it into his shirt pocket. Deep dimples sank into his cheeks.

Harry grinned, already headed for the door. "Don't it beat all how women get so darn pushy once you've gone and put a weddin' ring on their finger?"

"Hush!" Mark cautioned him with a quick wave of his hand. "Or I could be sent to bed without any supper tonight."

"Much less any lemonade," Harry said, nodding agreeably. "That's where the women have it over the men. They've got full control of the kitchen—and a man's *got* to eat."

Anna crossed her arms as if thoroughly enjoying this newly acquired power. "You two just keep that in mind when you find yourselves wanting to dawdle in town."

"Yes, ma'am," they both said in unison, then ducked their heads accordingly and hurried out the door, leaving only their laughter behind.

Chuckling along with them, Anna listened to their rapid footfalls as they tromped across the back porch, then out into the yard. She was still smiling to herself when she tugged at her collar, which she'd already unbuttoned at the back. Gently she fanned her skirts to admit a little cool air next to her hot, damp skin before finally returning her attention to her husband's missing buttons.

"You know what her problem is, don't you?" Mark asked after he and Harry had climbed down from the wagon and Harry had secured the tether strap to the hitching post. Because there had been too many wagons and carriages in front of the mercantile, they had been forced to leave their wagon across the street, in front of the town's only restaurant.

"Whose problem? You still talking about Anna?" Harry asked, glancing at him with a curious expression. It had been a good ten minutes since they had talked about Anna, yet Mark acted as if they had never stopped. Clearly, the woman stayed on his mind.

"Yes, I'm still talking about Anna. Do you know what her problem is?"

"You mean besides you?" Harry asked with wide-eyed innocence.

Mark's lips flattened with exasperation. "Yes, besides me."

Quietly, Harry studied his friend for a minute, wondering if the man yet realized how truly smitten he was with his pretty new wife, then shrugged as if not really interested in whatever it was he had to say. "Okay, I'll bite. What's her problem?"

"She's from up north," Mark stated matter-of-factly, tapping the end of his cane on the ground for emphasis.

"Yeah, I can see why that'd be a problem all right," Harry agreed with a nod, glancing at Mark with an arched eyebrow, as if he believed his friend might not have all his candles lit.

Mark sighed heavily, then leaned against his cane with both hands while he tried to explain so Harry would understand. "She's not used to all this heat."

Aware now where this conversation was headed, Harry tilted his head to one side then smiled that know-it-all smile of his. "And that concerns you, does it?"

"Of course it does. Didn't you see how she looked before we left? She looked like she was about to pass out from all the heat." He frowned when he pictured her damp face and flushed cheeks. "And it's all because of those stupid dresses she wears."

"Um-hum, and I suppose you'd prefer she not wear them," Harry commented with a wry grin and an understanding nod. "Yes, I can see how that would make things cooler for her, all right."

Mark ran his hand over his face, then shook the tip of his cane at Harry threateningly, though in truth he found the idea down right intriguing. "That's not what I was going to say."

"It's not?"

"No. I was thinking instead about buying her a new dress or two while I'm in town. Dresses specially made to wear in hot weather. Problem is, I don't know anything about buying ladies' dresses. Did you ever have to buy a dress for Lilly?"

"No, but I went with her to the dressmaker's a couple of times to help her carry some of her purchases," Harry admitted, though even that had been a long time ago. "Actually, there shouldn't be too much to it. Seems to me you'd just tell the dressmaker that you're lookin' to buy some lightweight dresses for your new wife and then you tell her about what size you figure Anna is and she should be able to take it from there."

Mark looked down the street toward the brightly painted entrance of Perry's Dress Shoppe and frowned. "Dressmaker, huh? I thought maybe I could buy dresses at the mercantile."

"You can, but the dresses at the mercantile aren't all gussied up the way the ladies really like 'em."

"Gussied up, huh?" he repeated, dampening his upper lip with the tip of his tongue. He didn't much like the thought of having to enter a store that had pink doors, but he did want Anna to have something cooler to wear. The hottest months were still to come. "Will

195

you go with me?"

"Long as you don't ask me to try nothin' on," Harry said with a loud guffaw. "I'm not much for modeling frilly dresses."

"Come on," Mark muttered, that look of total exasperation back. "We'll leave this list at the mercantile so they can fill it while we head on over to the dress shop and see if Miss Perry has anything that might fit Anna."

Barely ten minutes later, Mark and Harry had entered Perry's Dress Shoppe, their hats in hand and their necks pulled in as far as possible, eager to get the dresses bought so they both could get out of there.

To Mark's chagrin, buying a lady's dress turned out to be far more complicated than Harry had claimed it would be. Before they could even look at dresses, Mark had to try and guess exactly how tall and how big around Anna was—and in more places than just her waist and neck. Finally, feeling awkward at not being able to guess at Anna's measurements in exact inches, he spotted a woman walking down the sidewalk who appeared about the same size and pointed her out to the saleslady, relieved to hear the woman say that she had several dresses that should fit his wife. After that, he was promptly shown nine different summer dresses the woman thought would do nicely and was told to choose the ones he liked best.

While he watched, the proprietor quickly spouted the different attributes of each garment and draped them, one at a time, over a long metal rack so Mark could study them at length.

"Which ones you think?" he asked Harry, finding it hard to decide. They were all pretty in some way, but it was hard to judge what they would look like on Anna, though he was fairly sure they would all look pretty darned good.

Harry stroked his chin thoughtfully. "Well, I'm tired of seeing her in gray, so that there gray one is out, even though it is a lighter shade of gray than she tends to wear."

The saleslady immediately pulled the gray one off the rack and set it aside.

Mark pursed his lips into a studious frown while he studied the remaining eight. "And I'm not too partial to brown, so as far as I'm concerned, that brown and tan one is out."

The brown and tan one was removed from the rack in one swift motion.

"And that pink one on the end there has too many silly bows sewed to it," Harry decided, then when he realized the sales lady had taken offense to that, he pulled in his neck and meekly apologized.

Stiffening her back, the woman promptly snatched aside the pink dress with all the bows.

"Now what?" Mark asked, reaching out to touch the material of some of the remaining dresses, wondering which would feel best against Anna's skin. "I don't see anything wrong with these other six."

"Then buy them all," Harry said with a shrug. "The way I see it, you've got the money, and that little gal' deserves all the new dresses you can buy. Look what she was willin' to give up just so you could adopt those two boys and offer them a good home." Though, in truth, Harry suspected Anna had gained a lot more than she had given up. He had seen that telltale sparkle light up her eyes whenever Mark entered the room. It was the same sort of sparkle that now glittered in Mark's eyes at just the thought of surprising her with the dresses. The two might not know it yet, but they were already falling in love.

197

"You're right," Mark said with firm resolve, then turned to the saleswoman, who stood watching his every move. "I'll take all six of these, as long as I can bring them back for alterations if for some reason they don't fit."

"That will be fine," the woman said with a bright smile. All trace of injured pride at having been told her pink dress looked silly disappeared from her face the moment she realized exactly how large a sale she was about to make. "Now, might I interest you in some ladies' undergarments?"

Harry's eyes widened at the thought. "I don't know about him, but you could sure interest me in some." He chuckled, then licked his lips at the thought. "Yep, I'd be right pleased to see some ladies' undergarments."

Aware of the teasing undertone of Harry's voice, the woman turned to face him coolly. "Oh? And what size might you wear?"

Harry's cheeks flamed bright red while Mark tossed back his head and roared with laughter. It was not until he had that laughter under control he finally answered the saleslady's question. "Yes, ma'am, I really think I might better get her some new underthings, too. I'm not sure what all ladies wear up under their dresses these days, but whatever it is, get her three of everything. Just make sure they are made of something that will be cool to wear."

"I have just the thing," she said with a knowing wink and quickly turned her back to Harry while she hurried to the back of the shop, where the undergarments were kept in large white boxes. Lifting out a camisole made out of the sheerest silk with delicate satin straps and tiny eyelet ruffles across the top, she exclaimed in a soft, sultry voice, "I think this is what you probably

198

want for your new wife."

Mark's blue eyes widened when he looked at the flimsy material and thought of what Anna might look like wearing such a thing. Suddenly the room grew very hot. Finding he needed more room to swallow, he slipped his finger beneath his collar and pulled it away from his neck.

Showing no mercy at all, the saleswoman then lifted out a pair of matching bloomers and slid her hand inside to demonstrate just how sheer they really were. Mark could see the outline of her fingers, and suddenly it felt as if he was standing out in the hot August sun. The room was stifling. Sweat dampened his palms and beaded his forehead. "Y-yes, ma'am, those'll be fine . . . just fine."

By the time the saleslady was through making her suggestions, Mark and Harry walked away from that little dress shop carrying stacks of ribbon-tied boxes as high as their chins. Inside the different-sized packages were dresses, hats, ribbons, parasols, slippers, summer gloves, stockings, nightgowns, and a wide assortment of undergarments, which included several cotton underskirts and a small white corset, which had been bought at the saleslady's insistence because Mark really wasn't sure Anna needed one.

As soon as they had unloaded the boxes into the wagon, Harry glanced back at the new clock in the church tower to see what time it was and let out a long, low whistle. "Ooo-eee, are we ever going to get it. It's after five o'clock. By the time we get the things from the mercantile loaded up and then get back to your house, it'll be pert near dark."

Mark wrinkled his brow when he, too, looked at the town clock. "After five? How'd it ever get to be so late? Anna is going to skin us alive!"

199

"Us? Where'd you get this "us" business? I'm not going in that house, not as late as it's going to be when we finally do get back there."

"You'd make me face her alone?" he asked.

Harry nodded. "But then, maybe you'll get lucky, and when she sees what-all you brought her, she'll forgive you and let you keep your skin." He tapped his fingertip against his whiskered chin while he thought more about it. "But then, again, maybe she won't. Gawd, but you'd be an ugly thing without your skin. You're ugly enough with it."

The two men looked at each other briefly, each lost in thoughts of what Anna would have to say to them, then glanced back at the clock. Another minute had passed. Slowly they lowered their gaze to the mercantile across the street, then, almost as if someone snapped a whip high over their heads, they lit for the front door as fast as they could run, almost knocking over a customer in their haste.

Chapter Eleven

As far as Harry was concerned, the time had come for drastic measures. During the past week he'd tried his level best to make Mark see for himself how very much he'd come to care about Anna over the past couple of weeks—which Harry could tell was every bit as much as he cared for the boys, maybe more. Still, the young man obstinately refused even to consider the possibility that he had developed some pretty strong feelings for his new wife.

No matter what Harry did to try to trick Mark into realizing the truth about himself, his young friend remained adamant that whatever feelings he and Anna had developed for one another, they amounted to little more than close friendship. Mark had also claimed that the only reason he was always doing favors for her was because he was so very grateful to her for all she had done—for the sacrifice she'd been forced to make.

To Harry, it seemed like Mark was downright afraid of admitting the truth, even to himself, and Harry had put up with just about enough of that. It was obvious that Mark was in love with Anna, just as obvious as it was that she was in love with him. Why didn't they see that for themselves? Why did they continue to sleep in separate bedrooms on separate floors when the natural thing would be to admit their love and start sharing the same bed? Theirs was more than a marriage of convenience, much more. What was keeping them from seeing that?

Well, Harry was tired of waiting for them to discover what seemed so gall-derned obvious and had finally devised a plan to help hurry things along. What those two needed was a little prodding in the right direction . . . and a little time alone—time enough to let nature take her course—and he decided he was just the one to see to it they got just that.

Grinning at the different possibilities if his plan was to work out just right, Harry chuckled right out loud when he approached the boys with the first part of his scheme.

"What would you two say to goin' on a little campin' trip with your new grandpa?" he asked with a chipper smile. His kept his tone casual while he eased down beside Jamie and Abel in the new porch swing Mark had built just two days earlier.

"Camping?" Jamie asked, surprised. His face twisted into a quizzical expression when he looked up at Harry.

"Yes, campin'. You know, sleepin' out in the great outdoors with nothin' over your head but a blanket of stars and nothin' beneath your—uh, backside but a warm bedroll and the good solid earth," Harry answered, waving his arms with a flourish, hoping to make it sound a tad bit more exciting than it usually turned out to be.

Jamie cocked his head to one side for a moment while he thought over Harry's description, then shook his head as if he couldn't understand anyone wanting to sleep outside, stars or no stars. Jamie had always thought camping was something a person did as a last

202

resort, when there was no other choice. "Why would we want to do that?"

"For the adventure of it," Harry answered with enthusiasm, but when he saw yet more skepticism on the young boys' face, he shrugged. "If for nothin' else, to get away from chores for a while and do something different. While we're away together, I figure we could probably get in a little fishin' and maybe even a little huntin'. There's a pretty good-sized lake about two miles west of here where you can find catfish swimmin' around as big as my arm."

"Fishing?" Jamie's eyes lit instantly, and for the first time he appeared truly interested in this idea of Harry's. "We haven't ever been fishing before. Are fish hard to catch?"

"Never been fishin'?" Harry looked at them, stunned. "You mean to tell me your pa never took you fishin'? Why, I thought every boy your age had been fishin' before, least once." He wondered then what sort of man their real father had been. "Heck no, fishin' ain't hard a' tall, especially if you're fishin' for cat. Just takes knowin' what bait to put on your hook and how to pull 'em in so's you don't lose 'em once they've started to wigglin'."

"And you'll show us how to do all that?" Jamie asked eagerly, glancing at Abel to see his reaction.

Abel stared at him with wide-eyed excitement, intrigued with the idea of learning how to fish. Being on the opposite side of Jamie, he had to lean forward so his grandpa could see just how thrilled he was with this idea.

Assured of his brother's approval, Jamie then turned back to face Harry. "Can we take Pa with us? I'll bet he would sure enjoy going off camping with us."

Harry frowned while he considered his response. "Naw, I don't think so. Your pa's still got too much to do around here to be takin' time off like that. Besides, I was sorta hopin' the three of us could go alone. You know, a grandpa and his two grandsons, off together for a weekend."

"A whole weekend?" Suddenly Jamie appeared to have second thoughts, but Abel lost none of his bright-eyed enthusiasm.

Harry hurried to reclaim Jamie's earlier eagerness. "Sure, a whole weekend. If we're to get our camp set up and a good-sized cookin' fire goin' before dark, we'll need to leave out of here sometime this afternoon. That way we can get up early and spend all day tomorrow fishin' for cats, and maybe we could spend part of Sunday huntin' us up a squirrel or two."

"A squirrel?" Jamie asked. His eyes once again sparkled with interest. "If we find one, can we keep him here? Can I be the one to name him?"

Harry looked at him puzzled, aware the boy expected to make some sort of pet out of the animal. That wasn't exactly what he'd had in mind, but obviously the thought must not have occurred to Jamie that someone might actually want to *eat* a squirrel. Afraid it might come as a shock to the child to learn what the eventual outcome he'd had in mind for those squirrels, he nodded agreeably. "Sure, you can be the one to name him. And I'll build you a big, sturdy cage so he can have lots of room to move about."

Jamie glanced at Abel again, his face aglow with re-newed enthusiasm. "What do you say? Want to see if we can go with Grandpa on a camping trip?"

Having already made up his mind, Abel nodded so hard his dark curls bobbed; but barely a second later Jamie's expression fell and his shoulders sagged visibly. "We can't go. We are supposed to put fresh hay in the chicken coop tomorrow morning. We already promised."

"No reason you can't do that today. In fact, I'll help you," Harry said, and stood to do just that. "Come on, let's get the work done, then go see what your pa thinks about lettin' the three of us go campin'."

Though Mark resisted the idea at first, he eventually agreed to let the boys go with Harry and in the end volunteered to lend Jamie his own bedroll since Harry had only one extra. By three o'clock that afternoon, the trio had loaded all the things they might need into the back of Mark's wagon and were ready to head out.

Mark and Anna stopped work and joined them outside to see them off—and to remind the boys to be very careful. After watching them drive away, Mark turned to Anna, curious to see her reaction. It was then he suddenly realized that the two of them were alone—and would be for an entire weekend. Suddenly he felt a little awkward. In the two weeks since their unexpected marriage, he'd never truly been alone with her—not *totally* alone. The closest they had come to it were the few times he'd gone into the kitchen to get something to drink while she was there working.

"Sure am going to miss those two," he commented. He swallowed hard, wondering what Anna thought about this unexpected situation. "It will seem awfully quiet around here without them."

Anna, too, felt a sudden awkwardness and brushed absently at the bib of her apron with the side of her hand, as if smoothing out some unseen wrinkle. Her pulses raced wildly at the thought of being alone with Mark for the next two days. Whatever would they find to talk about?

Whenever Jamie was there, the child jabbered constantly, first at the supper table then later when they moved to the parlor. Conversation had never been any problem in the past, but with both boys gone for the entire weekend, she and Mark would have to find some way to fill the silence. Nervously she laced her fingers together and rested her hands on her hip, hoping to appear calm. It wouldn't do for him to know how frazzled she felt. He might suspect the reason. "I certainly hope you're hungry. I had no idea Harry was planning this trip with the boys. I'm afraid I've prepared far too much food for our supper tonight."

Mark apprehensively ran his thumb back and forth across the worn handle of his cane while he thought about it. The realization that he and Anna were now alone and would be for the next two days had taken away any desire he might have had for food. Besides, the way his stomach was flopping about, he'd never be able to keep much down anyway, at least not for very long. "That's okay, what we don't eat tonight we can hold over and have again tomorrow. Who knows? It could be you won't have to cook again until the boys return on Sunday."

"Wouldn't that be nice," she said with a nervous smile, wondering what she'd do with the additional time. She was used to spending several hours a day preparing their meals.

For a long moment, Mark and Anna stood barely a yard apart, staring silently at each other, until Mark finally thought of something to say. "I guess I'd better get on back to work. I still have a lot of chores that I need to finish before suppertime. Can't stand around talking the afternoon away." Having made his excuse to leave, he immediately started toward the barn.

"Neither can I. I have housework to do," Anna said

with a firm nod and turned to go back into the house, as eager to be out of his sight as he was hers.

But a minute later, when she finally reached the kitchen door, she could not resist a brief backward glance. She felt a perplexing leap of her senses when she discovered he'd done the same. Smiling awkwardly, she waved, then opened the wire mesh door and slipped carefully out of sight. Yet as soon as she was safely inside and no longer had to worry about his seeing her, she could not remember exactly what it was she'd planned to do with the rest of her afternoon. Surely there were things she should try to get done, but all she could think about at that moment was the evening ahead.

With supper already underway and nothing else really pressing, Anna hurried upstairs to change into one of the two new dresses she had yet to wear. Because the two had appeared to be a little nicer than the other dresses, she had decided to put them aside for special occasions and, though she wasn't quite sure why, tonight seemed like it might be the perfect time to wear one of them, but which?

After several minutes of careful consideration, she selected the pale-blue silk over the white cambric lawn. Both dresses were fashionably designed with moderately low necklines, narrow-fitted waists, and wide, flounced skirts, but the pale blue had one clear advantage: blue appeared to be Mark's favorite color.

Not having sufficient time to bother with heating an entire tub of water for a proper sit-down bath, Anna had to make do with a quick sponging. Once bathed, she powdered herself lightly with scented talcum before slipping on a fresh set of undergarments and styling her hair into a thick but simple array of curls. Though she realized that he would probably notice the trouble she'd taken to look especially nice for him, and might then place far more emphasis on the reasons why than she'd prefer, Anna did not let such nagging thoughts bother her for long.

By six-thirty she was downstairs, eagerly checking on the progress of the food she'd left simmering on the stove while watching through the narrow window near the back door for an indication that Mark was on his way in. Her insides twisted with nervous apprehension while she wondered what Mark's reaction would be when he saw her.

Having been upstairs most of the afternoon, since a few minutes after the boys had left, Anna had no way of knowing that Mark had decided to come inside a little earlier than usual, also wanting to make a few preparations for their first evening alone.

With the dining table already set and the food ready to serve, and thinking it far past time for Mark to come inside, Anna stood at the window beside the back door, tapping her slippered foot impatiently, when his voice suddenly sounded from somewhere behind her. Gasping aloud, she felt her hand fly instinctively to her throat when she spun about to face him.

"What are you doing here?" she asked, breathless from having been taken by complete surprise.

"I, uh, I —" His response died on his tongue, but his eyes widened the instant he caught sight of the beauty before him. Though Anna was always pretty — it would be impossible for her to be anything but — tonight she looked truly exquisite.

From the top of her head, where soft, shiny brown curls had been gathered and allowed to spiral past where her sleeves rested just off her creamy white shoulders, to the tips of her silk-clad toes, she was the most beautiful, most alluring woman he'd ever seen.

How he ached to snatch her into his arms and gently kiss the ivory softness of her skin. He wondered then what her response would be if he were to act on such a wild impulse. Then he remembered his earlier decision to keep his distance and pushed the thought aside. But, aware she still awaited an answer to her question, he blinked twice, then stammered, "I—I live here."

It was not one of his more witty responses, but it was all he could think to say.

"I'm aware of that," she said while she, too, quickly noted his appearance, instantly aware of how perfectly the dusty blue dress shirt and the dark blue trousers he'd chosen to wear fit him—maybe a little *too* perfectly. It made her just that much more aware of his narrow waist, his wide shoulders, and his long, lean legs. She hardly noticed the wooden brace strapped to his left leg.

"But what I wanted to know was why you were already in the house. I thought you were still outside."

Mark shifted nervously, wondering how he should answer that without letting her know the real reason. "I, uh, tore my shirt on a nail out in the barn and had to come in to change," he said, indicating his fresh clothing with a brief wave of his hand. "You weren't in when I came through. I guess you must have been upstairs."

"I probably was," she agreed, while she thought to come up with her own excuse for having changed clothes. *Any* excuse other than wanting to impress him. "I splattered grease on my other dress so I, too, had to change clothes."

She felt it silly that they both had resorted to such ridiculous tales when the truth was really quite obvious: they had both wanted to look their very best for

209

their first evening alone together. Why was that so hard to admit? Why did the thought of having to do so send a frenzied tingle through her bloodstream?

Despite the fact that their first evening alone together got off to such a clumsy start, supper itself went somewhat smoothly. Rather than set large serving bowls filled with everything she had prepared for their meal on the table, since there were only the two of them, Anna quickly filled their plates directly from the pots on the stove and then placed them on the table, directly across from one another. Though their dinner conversation lagged noticeably from time to time, all in all, they managed to keep each other pleasantly entertained, mostly by sharing humorous tales from their pasts. It was not until after they'd finished the meal that any true feelings of awkwardness returned.

Ordinarily, as soon as they had finished with supper, Mark and the boys would retire to the front parlor to play a few short games of checkers or cards while Anna cleaned up the kitchen. As soon as she had the dishes washed and put away, she usually joined them in the parlor until bedtime, often with a lapful of mending.

Tonight, though, there were no little boys to entice Mark into several games of checkers, and Anna had very little cleaning to do in the kitchen, and no mending awaited her in the parlor. When the two entered the parlor together later that evening, they were at a complete loss over what they might do to pass the remainder of the evening, since Anna didn't know how to play the games Mark played and Mark didn't know how to play the ones she knew.

As it turned out, they ended up seated on opposite ends of the same couch, facing each other while they discussed first the weather, then how oddly quiet the house seemed without the boys.

Finally Mark turned the conversation to a topic he'd been curious about for quite some time. While casually lifting his arm and resting it along the curved back of the small, rococo couch—his hand stretched outward to within inches of Anna's creamy white shoulder—he asked, "Tell me something: why is it that a beautiful woman like you has never bothered to get married?"

Having let her thoughts stray to the fact that Mark's fingertips now lay so very close to her shoulder, Anna glanced at him, surprised that he thought her beautiful. She stared at him for a long moment, carefully considering her answer, then forced a tiny smile, determined to ignore the dull, throbbing ache that the unexpected question had caused.

"Ah, but I *am* married," she responded lightly.

Mark refused to let her tease her way out of answering the question. It was something that had bothered him for days. As truly beautiful and intelligent as Anna was, she should have been snatched up to be some man's wife a long time ago. "You know what I mean. Before now. Before you came to Texas. Before you ever met me. Why is it you weren't married years ago? Or is that something I shouldn't ask?"

Anna considered how she should answer, not wanting to admit the truth, but at the same time, knowing Mark had a right to know more about her. After all, he was her husband. Even if it was not a permanent arrangement, they shouldn't keep secrets from one another. "I was engaged once but that was years ago."

"You were?" Though it was something he'd wanted to know, for some reason now that he did know, he didn't like it. He wondered why.

"Yes. At one time I was engaged to a man named

211

Charles Roark."

"Charles Roark?" Mark repeated, wrinkling his nose as if rolling the name off his tongue had been distasteful. "If you were engaged to this Charles Roark, whatever stopped you from marrying him? Didn't you love him?" he asked, then blinked when he felt a curious stab of pain which had resulted from the mere possibility that Anna may have been in love with this Roark character.

"Oh, I loved him, all right. Loved him very much," she admitted, then looked away. "Problem was, he didn't love me, at least not as much as he should have."

The man must be an utter fool, Mark thought while he watched several different emotions flicker across her face. Wanting to comfort her, he reached out to touch her cheek lightly, unaware of the fiery jolt that the simple action would send through him. He jerked his hand back, though only a few inches, and tried to get his suddenly pounding heartbeat back under control. "That must have been devastating."

Anna's reaction to Mark's unexpected touch was no less intense. Vigorous waves of tingling warmth skittered across the gentle curve of her cheek, then spread quickly through her entire body, making her toes curl in response. She wondered what sort of magic powers he possessed that would cause her to react as she had to something as simple as his touch. It made it hard for her to concentrate on an answer.

"Yes, it was devastating at the time, but I've long since gotten over it." That was not entirely true, and knowing that it wasn't, Anna had to stop and take in a deep, reassuring breath before continuing. "I'm just glad I found out that Charles's love was not what it should have been *before* we exchanged our wedding vows."

"You don't act very glad," he pointed out, studying the sadness that darkened her brown eyes.

"Oh, but I am. The only thing I really regret about that whole situation is the fact I will never—" She couldn't say it. She could not admit, even to Mark, that she was no longer a whole woman. He might turn away from her as Charles had and she could not bear that. Yet, in a way, he had right to know. Though theirs was never to be *that* sort of marriage, he *was* her husband.

In an attempt to build her courage, she curled her hands into tight fists in her lap, then turned to meet his gaze straight on. The best way was to come right out and say it. "A few weeks after Charles and I had formally announced our engagement, I was in a terrible carriage accident. In fact, I almost died as a result of my injuries."

Mark's forehead pulled into a puzzled frown. "But it seems pretty obvious you *didn't* die," he commented, not seeing how that could tie in with a broken engagement. "Was he so eager to be married that he could not wait long enough for your injuries to heal?"

Anna looked away again, focusing on the dim glow of a nearby table lamp, as if suddenly entranced by its soft yellow light. "In a way, a part of me did die. One of my injuries resulted in some very serious physical damage, the sort that can never heal." She pressed her lips closed, a result of the pain piercing her heart, unable to continue with her explanation for now.

Mark studied her tortured expression for a long moment before he realized exactly what sort of physical damage she'd meant.

"You can't have children, can you?" he asked, his tone soft and caring.

Anna closed her eyes against the sharp, twisting

213

pain his question had caused. "None of my own, no." When she looked at Mark then, tears clung precariously to her lower lashes. Her voice was strained with emotion. "That's why Jamie and Abel are so very important to me. Having those two little boys is as close to having my own children as I'll ever come."

Mark longed to comfort her, but didn't know how. And he was not sure if he should. He had vowed to keep his distance, as much for her sake as his own, and he knew that by comforting her, he might in some way bring them closer, make her believe there could be more to their relationship.

Again reminded of the excruciating pain and deep humiliation that had been hers for so long, Anna bent her head and stared down at her hands, unaware of the battle that raged inside Mark.

"You can't know how devastating it was for me to be told that I was no longer a complete woman, that because of one careless accident I could never hope to have children. I guess that's why my job with the Children's Aid Society was so very important to me. It gave me the opportunity to cherish someone else's children. And, in an odd way, I was able to make each one of those children my own — at least while they remained in my care." Her voice trembled when she lifted her head and looked back at Mark. "You can't imagine the heartache I've lived with, knowing I would never experience the miracle of giving birth, of giving life to a child of my very own. You can't imagine the pain."

"Yes, I can," Mark said softly. He glanced at the leg stretched out in front of him at an awkward angle and was suddenly reminded of his own physical inadequacies, inadequacies that had also resulted from an accident. In a way, their suffering was similar. Though he wasn't sure it was the best thing to do, he was unable to resist stretching his arm forward and touching her cheek again with the tips of his fingers. "Those boys certainly were lucky to have ended up in your care. Now I understand why you were so willing to do all you did for them, why you were willing to give up your job and whatever life you had established for yourself just so they could have a good home."

Anna tried to ignore the strange shimmering sensations that washed over her, causing tiny bumps of apprehension to spread across her neck and arms. What was it about Mark Gates's gentle touch that set her blood to racing? "In all honesty, I didn't do it for them nearly as much as I did it for myself," she admitted.

Somewhere deep inside, she yearned to tell him everything, including how she'd given up her job and married him for other reasons than providing the boys with a home. She'd done it as much for herself as for him.

She may not have been aware of that fact when she first suggested marriage, but she was well aware of it now. She cared about Mark Gates—cared about him deeply. Under that sometimes harsh exterior and beneath that wide, muscular chest beat a heart of true gold.

Mark tilted his head to one side. "So, now I guess you plan to convince me that your motives were purely selfish," he commented. A hint of a smile played at the outer corners of his mouth. "I really find it hard to believe that you have one selfish bone in your entire body, Anna Gates." Instinctively, he glanced down at that body and was reminded of how truly feminine she was. His smile grew wider.

Unaware of where his gaze had gone, Anna also smiled, pleased to hear her new name. *Anna Gates*. She had yet to adjust to it but it did have a nice sound. Anna Gates. It was a name to be proud of, because Mark was a man to be proud of. "Nor have you a selfish bone in your body, Mark Gates."

"Oh, yes I do. I'll have you know, I'm a very selfish person," he said, his tone playful. "I prefer having things my way. That's why I didn't try any harder to talk you out of your sudden decision to marry me." Unable to resist and almost without thinking, he ran his fingertip over the outer curve of her cheeks again. How soft she was.

"You wouldn't have been able to talk me out of it even if you had tried. My mind was made up, and like you, I like to have things my way, too."

Mark chuckled. "I dread the day we find ourselves at odds with each other over anything."

"Oh, I don't know. As truly stubborn and selfish as we both apparently are, it might be interesting to find out which of us ends up having her way." She looked at him with a raised brow.

"*Her* way?" Mark responded, having caught the use of the feminine pronoun in her last statement. He narrowed his gaze for a moment, as if he had some cutting retort, but in the end tilted his head back and laughed. "Yes, it would be interesting, all right. In fact, I have a feeling our entire marriage will prove interesting — very interesting indeed."

Anna tingled in response to the warmth in his laughter and felt the color rise in her cheeks. She wondered if he was as pleased with their marriage as he seemed. "Do you ever regret having married me?"

"Are you kidding?" Mark asked, bringing his laughter to an abrupt halt. "By having married you, I have brought myself nothing but happiness. The boys are a delight, and you —" He paused to consider how he wanted to say it. "And you, my dear wife, are a true joy. Why do you ask? You aren't having second thoughts about our marriage, are you?" The thought that she might made him ache inside.

"Of course not," she answered readily. "It was my idea, after all."

"And what a wonderful idea it was," he commented, fighting the desire to pull her into his arms and hold her close, at the same time aware of how wrong that would be. "It not only allowed the boys to stay together, it also gave me the chance to make them a permanent part of my life."

Anna was disappointed. He had not mentioned anything about her having become a permanent part of his life, too. It was a harsh reminder that he did not consider their marriage permanent, that as soon as the boys were old enough to have a legal say in their own futures, Mark would then ask her for that divorce. And she really could not blame him. Although they had married for honorable reasons, they had not married for love and Mark should one day be free to marry again, this time for love.

And so should she, but then she had a sneaking suspicion that she already had. She looked at him longingly and wondered for the first time if it would ever be possible for him to fall in love with her. Her heart twisted with unbearable pain when she realized it was something that would probably never happen. They were destined to be good friends and nothing more.

"Just so long as you don't regret it," she finally thought to say. "I'd hate to think I'd ruined your life in some way."

"Well you can certainly get that idea out of your head. I've already told you that our marriage has brought nothing but happiness for me. Truth is,

217

you've helped make life worth living again. If I hadn't gotten custody of those boys, I don't know what I'd have done." He paused to consider that. "Oh, yes I do. I'd have sat around here in that blasted wheelchair until I finally rotted. And that's what I really think I was trying to do, rot to death. I was so bitter about the fact that I had been maimed that I simply gave up caring about anything. In a way, I think God sent the boys to me for a reason—to straighten me out. And just to be sure I understood the message that it was time I got on with my life, he sent you right behind them."

Anna looked shyly away, feeling an uncharacteristic loss for words. She wasn't sure how to respond to his words.

"That's what I believe all right," Mark continued, pleased by the high color in her cheeks. "That you and the boys were all three gifts from God." The desire to pull her into his arms grew with incredible force, until he was afraid he might not be able to control himself much longer. Aware that it might prove disastrous to act upon the impulses he felt at that moment, he quickly pushed himself up off the couch and reached for his cane. It would be wrong to do anything that might make her believe they could ever share a real connubial relationship—not as repulsive as he was. He could never do that to her. He could never subject her to anything as vile as that.

No matter how badly he wanted her.

"It's getting late," he said in explanation to his sudden decision to move away from the couch. He twisted and stretched his back muscles as if weary of having sat for so long. "Better be getting on to bed. Got a long day ahead."

Anna glanced at the clock. It was only nine. Mark

did not usually go on to bed until nine-thirty or ten. But rather than question this sudden decision, she merely nodded and stood up. It seemed pretty obvious that he was uncomfortable being alone with her. She wondered about that.

"Yes, I guess we should get on to bed," she said in a cheerful tone, though disappointment weighed heavily inside her. "I'll see you in the morning."

With no further comment, she turned to leave. Without looking back, she entered the hallway and started up the stairs.

Having followed as far as the doorway, Mark felt a strange sort of emptiness while he watched her slowly disappear from his sight. Sadly, he walked toward the back of the house, to his own bedroom, wishing more than ever that Fate had not dealt him such a cruel blow.

Chapter Twelve

As soon as Mark had closed his bedroom door, he set his cane against the wall near his bed and immediately removed his leg brace. Tossing the awkward contraption aside, he then reached for the buttons of his shirt. When he had the shirt undone, he moved his hand to the two buttons that fastened the waistband of his trousers.

Though he did not feel much like sleeping, he couldn't see any reason not to go ahead and get undressed for bed. He stepped over the boot fork and slid the heel of his right boot in place. As soon as he had tugged out of both boots, he hooked his thumbs down under the opened waistband and slid his trousers down over his hips. Then, bending at the waist, he pushed down with his fingertips until the garment fell around his ankles. He freed his good leg first by lifting his foot until it pulled clear of the material, which turned the right pant leg inside out, then he worked to remove his lame leg.

Anchoring the material of his pants against the floor by standing on it with his good foot, he then gave his bad leg a sharp tug, which brought his foot about halfway through the pantleg. Repeating the process by repositioning his good foot higher on the excess material, he eventually freed his bad foot from the clothing.

It was a slow process, but because he could no longer bend his left leg, there was little he could do about it. Next he turned his attention to his stockings. The right stocking was no problem to remove. He balanced his weight against the dresser and bent his good leg at such an angle that he could easily grasp the top of the stocking in his hand and simply yank it off. He then used the toes of the bared foot to work the stocking off his lame foot.

Having accomplished that, he was just about to slip his shirt off his shoulders when he caught a glimpse of his maimed leg in the large dressing mirror across the room. Glancing away from the mirrored image and down at the leg itself, he scowled with anger, then grimaced with bitterness, aware of what a horrible sight that leg would seem to Anna. His stomach knotted when he considered the tormented expression that would fill her face, and he looked away.

Though Mark had viewed his mangled leg many times since the accident, he still was caught off guard by his own sickened reaction. He could well imagine how Anna would respond to the horrid sight.

Glumly, he forced himself to look again at the flat, rumpled plane that had once been his knee.

Because the heaviest part of the tree had landed squarely across the kneecap, his knee had been crushed beyond repair. Eventually, Doc Edison had realized the extent of the damage and had surgically inserted a series of metal pins to reinforce the crushed knee joint and allow him to support his weight. Though the small pieces of metal meant he could not bend his leg, it was better than never being able to use it at all. He would never walk again without limping, but at least he could walk.

Mark knew he should feel grateful for that much, but at the moment, while he stared down at his disfigurement, it was hard for him to feel anything but resentment — resentment for having been left less than the strong, whole man he had once been.

A frown pulled at the corners of his mouth while he stared at his affliction. The foot, though still useful for standing and balancing his weight, was discolored and twisted grotesquely off to the side. The bone in the lower part of that leg had been broken in four places. Though the doctor had done a remarkable job of repairing it, the lower sections of bone had not healed perfectly straight, and his foot pointed out at an awkward angle. The shape of the leg was irregular. Fact was, his left leg reminded him of the gnarled limb of a stunted mesquite tree.

Thinking it was a damned good time to feel sorry for himself, Mark plopped down in a nearby chair with his crippled leg stuck straight out in front of him, as always. The thought of Anna's reaction if she were ever to catch even a glimpse of it made the muscles around his stomach contract painfully and his blood run ice cold. He closed his eyes and waited for the anger and the bitter resentment to ease.

Tilting his head back against the padded top-board of the tufted armchair, Mark sank deeper into his misery. There were times he almost wished the doctor had decided to forget any attempt to save his leg and had gone ahead and cut the damn thing off. At least he would not have to look at it and be reminded of what a careless mistake he'd made. On the other hand, he knew he would have had a hard time walking again without a support for his weight and to keep his balance. He would have been forced to wear a wooden peg for the rest of his life, and that wouldn't look any better than his twisted leg.

"Damn," he sighed bitterly. Reopening his eyes, he stared absently at the intricate pattern carved into the white plaster ceiling.

His thoughts returned to the accident. Why hadn't he paid closer attention to what he was doing? Where had his head been? Why hadn't he at least noticed that the tree had started to list in time to get the hell out of the way? But then again, why had he been out there alone in the first place? He should have taken one of his men with him, someone to watch the trees while he cut. Going off to cut those trees without any help at all was a fool-headed thing to do.

Mark groaned aloud when he remembered hearing the crack and looking up in time to do nothing more than let out a terrifying cry for help. Since that fateful day just over a year ago, he had relived the accident many times—watching the images in his mind with bone-chilling horror while the huge tree slowly crashed down on top of him—over and over again.

Each time he replayed the incident, he felt the same overwhelming leap of heart-stopping fear that had shot through his body the moment he realized he did not have enough time to get out of harm's way. How he wished he could force the haunting images from his mind, but they stayed with him as if they had a determination of their own.

Suddenly, Mark was startled from the past by a crash. Leaning forward in his chair, he gasped. Anna's horrified scream told him that his vivid imaginings had not produced the ear-splitting sound. The crash had been real, and it had come from upstairs.

"Anna!"

His breath caught in his throat while he pushed himself out of the chair and onto his feet in one swift motion. He looked back up at the ceiling as if by doing so he might see right through it.

"Anna, answer me—what happened?"

He waited, unmoving, for a response.

When none came, a frightening chill skittered down his spine, sending him into immediate action. He headed for the hall door. In his panicked state, he overlooked the fact that all he had on was a pale blue unbuttoned dinner shirt and a pair of white pullstring underdrawers that covered him only from his waist to his knees. Nor did he think to grab his cane.

Fearing the worst, he moved toward the main stairs as quickly as his lame leg would allow while keeping his left hand against the wall for added balance. Concerned only with what might have caused the crash, he called out at the top of his frightened voice again and again.

"Anna? Are you all right?"

Still no answer.

Mark's blood could not pump rapidly enough to wash the panic out of his heart. Why didn't she respond to his calls? What had happened to her? It had sounded to Mark as if the whole ceiling had given way. Had the ceiling caved in? Was that why she hadn't responded? Was she lying crumpled on the floor below? Crossing the area from the hallway to the stairs, he called out again in a high, strangled voice.

"Anna! Anna, damn it, answer me!"

Straining harder to hurry, Mark felt his breath come in short, painful bursts while he fought his way up the stairs. Forced to drag the dead weight of his crippled leg behind him one step at a time, he thought he would never reach his destination.

By the time he finally reached the top of the stairs, a hard, throbbing ache pounded in the center of his chest, but he didn't know if it was from exertion or fear. Immediately he headed toward Anna's room, aware the door had been left open.

"Anna, answer me!" If she was at all conscious, she should have responded by now. *If she was conscious.* . . . Horrified by such a thought, he moved faster.

Though Anna heard Mark's frantic calls and dearly wanted to answer, she could not. The fall had knocked the breath out of her, so much so, she had felt a moment of panic before she finally managed to gasp for air. Relieved to know the scream that had escaped her lips during the fall was not going to be her last, she sucked in breath after needed breath. Having gone a full two minutes without oxygen, she took several long minutes to recover. When she thought she could, she tried to call to him, but a rasping wheeze was all that came out.

Finally, after the initial moment of panic had passed, Anna realized what had happened and started kicking at the sheets in an attempt to free herself, but she only managed to become more and more entangled. Frustrated, she gave up her efforts and lay perfectly still.

Aware by the sound of Mark's hurried footfalls and his loud cries of anguish that he was headed toward her bedroom, Anna tried again to call to him, wanting to reassure him she was all right. This time his named burst past her lips in a broken cry. "M-ark!"

Instantly, he appeared in her doorway, his blue eyes round with fear, his face pale as death. Although his brain registered what had happened and that Anna appeared to be uninjured, his aching heart sent him charging forward with maddening speed.

"Mark, the bed fell," Anna said in a bewildered voice, stating the obvious, for the two thick mattresses that had once rested upon a sturdy wooden bedframe now lay directly on the floor. The heavy wooden legs had broken off at odd angles.

"Are you all right?" he asked as he collapsed onto the mattress beside her and collected her into his arms. "When I heard the crash, I didn't know what had happened. Then, when I heard you scream, I was scared half to death." He laced his fingers into the soft thickness of her hair and held her all the closer, glad to find her unharmed.

"I'm all right. Just a little shaken," she assured him, reveling in the warmth of the strong male shoulder supporting her soft cheek. Enjoying the feel of his arms around her and of his hands in her hair, she felt her heartbeat continue to throb wildly inside of her, though her moment of fright was well over.

"Just a little shaken? Then why didn't you answer me?" he asked, pulling back to see her face. His expression grew dark with concern—and something else—while his gaze searched hers, eager for an answer. "I thought something terrible had happened when you failed to answer me."

"I tried, but when the bed collapsed, it knocked the breath out of me. I'm sorry." She looked then at the damaged bed and frowned. Her lower lip began to tremble. "I didn't mean to break your bed."

Mark, too, looked at the bed, then at the dismay on Anna's face. Dressed in one of the soft cotton nightgowns he'd bought her, with her long brown hair spilling down around her shoulders in casual disarray, she looked very much like a small child who had accidentally done something very wrong and now awaited punishment. For some reason, that struck him as funny. When he pulled her close again, this time drawing her firmly against his chest so he could press his cheek against the top of her head, he started to laugh. "I can repair the bed. I'm just glad you weren't hurt."

Anna was relieved to know that Mark was in no

way annoyed with her for having destroyed his bed. Though she didn't feel the accident was her fault, she had worried that Mark might think it was. Smiling happily, she snuggled into his embrace and closed her eyes, eager to enjoy the golden sound of his laughter and the wonderful feel of his arms around her, holding her close.

She sighed aloud her contentment. How warm and strong he felt. Then she became aware that the warm, solid surface she felt pressed against her cheek was Mark's skin, and that something feathery light touched the tip of her nose.

Bravely, she parted one eye to see what had tickled her nose and discovered Mark's shirt was unbuttoned, exposing most of his chest. In her earlier state of muddled shock and confusion, she had been aware only of Mark's presence, not of his appearance. Though she recalled glancing up when he entered her bedroom, she did not remember having noticed his opened shirt; but it must have been, even then.

For the moment, Anna did not move. Though a part of her told her she should pull away, the other more brazen part of her refused to obey, realizing the fascinating opportunity that his opened shirt provided.

Trying not to be obvious, she remained still while she allowed her gaze to rove over the strong, muscular shape of his chest and the soft, curling pattern of dark hair that covered so much of it. Then, ever so slowly, her eyes dipped lower to follow the narrowing path of body hair ever downward until she suddenly caught sight of what he had on—or in this case, what he *did not* have on.

228

"Mark?" she spoke his name calmly, though her first inclination had been to gasp aloud with shock. Just knowing that he was in her bedroom in only his shirt and underdrawers caused her heart to beat with a strong, relentless force. Then suddenly she remembered that all she had on was her nightgown, made of the sheerest cotton. Her heart beat with even more force, making her wonder if her chest could withstand the onslaught.

"Yes?" he responded, only vaguely aware she had spoken. He was too lost in the sweet scent that lingered in her hair to worry about conversation at the moment.

Mark's voice was so deep and so rich with emotion that it sent chills through Anna. "May I ask you something personal?"

She chewed nervously at the inner edge of her lower lip, wondering what his reaction would be when he realized that he had burst into her room not even half dressed. Her face drew into a perplexed frown while she wondered if she should tell him, or let him discover what he'd done on his own.

"A personal question? Sure, what is it you want to know?" he asked, still holding her close, so relieved to find her safe that he was unable to let go.

Anna snatched a quick breath, then asked, "Did you know that all you have on is your underwear and a shirt?"

Judging by the manner in which his arms stiffened, Anna concluded that he had not known, and despite his obvious consternation, she could not help grinning.

Startled, Mark gasped aloud, then pushed her

229

away, making an immediate grab for one of the bed sheets only to discover it was tangled around Anna's legs.

Anna knew she should turn away and give him a moment to collect his wits, but for some reason she could not. Brazenly, she peered downward, wanting to get a better look at him before he succeeded in covering himself. "You didn't realize you were in your underwear, did you?"

"I forgot," he admitted, his tone gruff and annoyed while he continued to jerk at the sheet again until it finally pulled free. Immediately, he tossed it over his lower torso, careful to see that his left leg was completely covered.

Anna couldn't help but laugh at such a grand show of modesty. After all, he was her husband. It was no great sin for her to see him in his underwear.

"Got something to hide?" she asked with an innocent look on her face.

"You know I do," he responded, his words edged with anger. The muscles in his jaw hardened.

Taken aback by his reaction, Anna glanced down at the sheet, bewildered. Then suddenly the reason for his anger dawned on her. "Mark, if you're trying to hide your injured leg from me, it's too late. I saw it."

Mark looked stricken. "When?"

"Just before you covered it with that sheet," she said, with a light shrug of her shoulders. Of course, the leg was badly disfigured, but she had expected that. After all, he'd nearly lost it. She lifted her gaze to meet his. "But I don't understand why you think you need to hide it from me."

230

Mark searched her face for some evidence of repulsion, but saw none. His forehead notched into a questioning frown. "Didn't it upset you to see it?"

"No," she answered, surprised.

"The bed falling upset me. And being unable to breathe upset me even more. But seeing your leg didn't upset me in the least. Why should it?"

Mark looked truly puzzled. "Because—because it looks so—so grotesque."

Stunned to discover that Mark was ashamed of his injured leg, Anna reached for the sheet and tried to pull it away. She wanted to show him that his apprehensions concerning his leg were totally unfounded. When he moved his hand to grip the sheet, she stopped tugging, then rested her hand on top of his reassuringly. "Let me prove to you that I'm not frightened of your leg in any way."

"No. I don't want you to have to look at it again." The mere thought of it cut deep into his gut.

Anna gazed into his eyes, so he could see how very much she wanted to prove to him that she was not at all bothered by it. "Mark, why won't you let me see the leg? Just because it bears ugly scars from that accident is no reason to hide it from me. A few scars are not going to make me think any less of you or cause me to change my opinion of you in any way. Let me prove that to you. Let me look at it. Let me show you that I'm not affected by it."

Mark studied her determined expression for a long moment before his grip loosened and she was able to pull the sheet away.

Anna did not look down right away, rather she

continued to gaze directly into his eyes. She wanted him to understand that his disfigurement was not important. "I think you should know, I formed my opinion of you weeks ago, and a badly injured leg isn't going to make me change my mind."

"Oh?"

He wondered if he dared ask what that opinion might be, considering that just a few weeks ago they hardly got along.

Slowly, Anna lowered her eyes to his leg, which lay straight out in front of him. Though her heart ached at the thought of all the pain he must have endured, the disfigured leg did not appall her in any way. How could it? It was a part of the man she loved. "See? I'm not turning away in fright." She returned her gaze to his. "I'm not turning away at all."

Mark had believed that a closer look at the leg would repulse her, and he found her calm reaction downright bewildering. He could not resist the urge to reach out and take her hand, as if to thank her in some way. "Are you sure? Are you sure you don't find the sight of my leg revolting?"

"The only thing I find revolting is knowing that you thought so little of me. Do you really believe I'm that shallow? That I'd be affected by something so trivial?"

Knowing that was indeed what he'd thought, Mark could no longer meet her gaze. He glanced down to where he held her hand between both of his. How could he have misjudged her so completely? "I—I didn't think you were shallow exactly. I just didn't think you would be able to—" He hesitated, not sure of how to say it without making it seem worse.

"Ah, there's the problem in a nutshell. You didn't think," she scolded playfully, preferring to concentrate on the gentle warmth of his touch than on the fact he had thought so little of her. How she wished he would take her into his arms again and hold her close. Her insides trembled at the thought.

"You're right. I didn't think. And I'm sorry."

As if able to read her thoughts, Mark let go of her hand, then lifted his arms to draw her near, pressing her soft cheek against the hard, curving planes of his chest. Suddenly, he felt like a complete fool for having thought she would rebel at the sight of his leg.

Delighted by the feel of her cheek lying firmly against his bare chest again, Anna felt her pulse jump to life, making her giddy.

"And you should be sorry," she continued to scold, though her voice showed no ill feeling. "I'm not the coward you obviously think I am."

Anna then felt his fingertip press beneath her chin. Reluctantly, she allowed him to lift her cheek away from his chest, away from the comforting warmth of his embrace. When their gazes met in that next second, their lips were only inches apart.

"No. You are not a coward," he said in a low, sultry voice. "Far from it. In fact, you are the most beautiful and most courageous woman I have ever known."

His compliments caught Anna by surprise, causing her to be at a temporary loss for words. But then again, words were no longer needed.

233

Slowly, Mark's mouth came toward hers, causing her heart to bound with eager anticipation. Mark planned to kiss her. Instinctively, she leaned forward to meet him halfway, eager to sample the taste of him.

The kiss that resulted was so tender, yet at the same moment so overwhelmingly powerful, that it left Anna momentarily breathless. Suddenly light-headed, Anna closed her eyes as a strange, all-consuming warmth slowly invaded her senses. When the kiss deepened, her heartbeat grew ever stronger. Her pulses throbbed with an alarming, yet thrilling intensity. Her lips parted beneath the gentle pressure of his tongue while her arms rose to encircle his strong shoulders. Never had she experienced a kiss so powerful, so deliciously demanding.

Overwhelmed by a sudden desire to be closer to him, she strengthened her embrace and met his kiss hungrily, eager to explore the passion that swelled unexpectedly inside her, pleased by the contented groan that rose from deep inside Mark's throat.

Taking full advantage of her parted lips, Mark's tongue gently teased the sensitive inner edges of her mouth, going ever deeper with each probing entry, until she could not help but respond. Entering his mouth shyly at first, Anna savored the tantalizing taste. It was like nothing she had ever experienced, to explore such intimate recesses and feel his lightly shuddering response.

Suddenly, she was struck with the desire to discover even more about him, to explore the secrets of his body. Eagerly, she brought her mouth harder against his, dipped her tongue deeper, and pressed her body closer, while wishing there was some way to bring them closer still.

Mark was delighted though somewhat surprised by her willingness. He was aware that Anna's passions had become ignited and now raged deep within her. He knew he could take her then, and that she would let him, but he chose to proceed with caution. If they were going to make love, he wanted it to be as enjoyable an experience for her as he knew it would be for him. Therefore, rather than hurrying things along for his own gratification, he let his lips linger on her sweetly demanding mouth while he slowly eased his hands down the curve of her back, then around to her rib cage.

Well aware that Anna's breathing had become more labored, Mark delighted in knowing that he had created such an intense response in her, that he was capable of giving her such true and basic pleasure. He fought to hold back his own growing response while he carried her from one new height of arousal to another. Aware they were about to make their marriage into something real at last, he wanted it to be an experience she would treasure always.

Unhurried, he moved his hand over the smooth surface of her gown, until he felt the soft undercurve of her breast. Cupping his fingers around the precious find, he gently played with the tip through the thin fabric until he felt it grow rigid with desire. He waited a few seconds more before undoing the four buttons that clasped the material between her breasts. Meanwhile, he allowed his hand to continue its hungry prowl on the outside

235

of the gown—ever seeking, ever searching, but never quite finding.

While Anna's body quickly absorbed the pleasures that came from his magical touch, her thoughts became instantly lost in a deep, swirling torrent. Unfamiliar emotions stirred to life inside of her like a rising tide, sending liquid fire through her veins and causing her arousal to spiral ever higher until it filled her entire being.

Every part of her yearned for more, though she was not sure she could survive it. Even so, she wanted to feel his touch on her naked skin. Suddenly, she wished she did not have on that burdensome gown and wanted him to remove it. Unable to bear the rapacious flames that burned deep within her, she considered taking off the garment herself, but could not find the courage to do it.

Finally Mark's hands began to work with the buttons. His fingers dipped inside the garment and brushed against the swelling curves of her breasts, which sent even more of the delicious, yet unfamiliar waves of ecstasy cascading through her body.

Trembling with expectation, Anna closed her eyes when he finished with the last button and parted the material. With mounting impatience, she waited for him to push the nightgown off her shoulders and uncover her body at last.

While his kiss continued to work its overwhelming magic, his hand slipped beneath the warm fabric to caress one of her straining breasts. He found great delight in the tiny moan that swelled inside her. Ready now to remove the gown, he gently tugged on the material, pushing it back over her ivory shoulders, while he continued to play with the sensitive peak of her breast. Anna gasped with pleasure and arched her back.

Gently, Mark reached behind her and lowered her onto the mattress, resting her head on one of the soft feather pillows. Hungrily, he continued to devour her kisses while he quickly worked the gown down past her hips, until she was unclothed at last. Eagerly, he broke away from her to remove his own clothing. When he returned to her side, he was as gloriously naked as she.

Trailing a finger lightly over the sensitive skin along the side of her breast, he gazed longingly at her exquisite body, unable to believe anyone could be so beautiful, so absolutely perfect. When he spoke, it was in a deep, raspy voice. "Anna, I want you. I want to make love to you."

Anna's eyelids drifted partially open, revealing the dark, unfulfilled passion that raged inside her. "I want that, too."

Mark growled in response when she lifted her arms to him. Lying on a broken bed, pressed against the side of her, he bent forward and claimed her lips once more. Gently, he allowed his hand to slide over her warm, bare skin, eagerly exploring every swell and every curve. It took more and more effort on his part to abide by his earlier decision to place her pleasure before his needs, especially when he knew he could take her at any moment and find complete fulfillment.

Basking in the warmth of Mark's touch, Anna moaned softly when his hand returned to her breast to tease and to taunt. Though his slow, circular motions came ever closer to the sensitive tip, Anna thought Mark was taking far too much time.

Unable to bear the gentle torture another moment, she arched her back, thrusting her breasts higher, wanting his hands to hurry and reach their destination.

When he broke off the kiss to gaze down at her writhing form, Anna moaned with protest. How could he bring her to such a state of madness and not do something to fulfill the strange, burning need inside her? Why was he torturing her like this? Moaning again, she reached out to bring his mouth down to hers, hoping that she might remind him of his intentions.

But Mark needed no reminders. Before her arms had encircled his neck, he was already returning, eager to oblige her with another long, lingering kiss. But barely seconds later, he brought his lips away again. But this time he left her mouth so he could trail light, feathery kisses across the high curve of her cheek, then down the gentle slope of her neck and beyond, until finally he arrived at one of her round, thrusting breasts.

Deftly, he teased the hardened tip with short, tantalizing strokes of his teeth and his tongue, nipping and pulling, until she cried aloud with pleasure. Then, when she thought she could bear the wondrous torture no longer, he moved to the other breast. Again he brought a cry of ecstasy from her lips.

Anna was not certain how long she could endure the continuous onslaught and grasped his shoulders to make him stop his tender torment. She wanted him to do whatever was needed to bring her body the release it so desperately needed. But Mark did not heed her urgent pulls at his shoulders. Instead, he allowed his mouth to continue with its pleasurable assault. She shuddered visibly from the delectable sensations developing deep within her until she felt certain she would burst. A delicious, throbbing ache centered low in her abdomen, and she craved immediate release from her sensual anguish.

"Mark," she called out his name, only vaguely aware she had spoken. She pulled again on his shoulders.

Aware the time had come, Mark suckled first one breast, then the other. Carefully, he eased through the barrier that proved he was her first true lover, and with smooth, lithe movements, brought their wildest longings, their deepest needs to the ultimate height. When release came for Anna, it was so wondrous, so deeply shattering that she gasped aloud with pleasure and awe. Only a moment later, the same shuddering release came from Mark.

With their passions spent and the bonds of their marriage forged, they lay together, perfectly still, atop the broken bed while quietly listening to the steady rhythm of each other's heartbeats. Bound in each other's arms, they sank slowly into the warm depths of marital satisfaction, both overwhelmed by what had happened between them.. It was like no other experience in their lives; nothing else even remotely compared.

Settled contentedly in the crook of Mark's arm, Anna marveled that this incredibly handsome man, this most exquisite of lovers, was her husband. Such happiness would be hers forever. But then, as suddenly as her joy had blossomed to life, it died. *No*, this astonishing happiness was *not* to be hers forever, for Mark had made it perfectly clear that their marriage was only temporary. One day he would ask for his divorce and she would have to give it to him.

The thought of that day was so painful that she cried.

Chapter Thirteen

At some point during the night, while lying in Mark's embrace and unable to sleep, Anna decided not to dwell on the day when Mark would ask her for that divorce. The only way she could possibly keep a grip on her sanity during these next several years was to live each day as it came and to accept whatever happiness fell her way.

Aware now how very much in love she was with the man she'd married—probably had been all along—Anna decided to enjoy having him as a part of her life while she could. Rather than worry over their inevitable parting, she would treasure each moment they did share together, and hold that precious time dear in her heart. She knew now that even after their marriage had been dissolved legally, at which time she would have no choice but to go somewhere else and start a new life, she would still have her memories to cling to, and cling to them she would—with no regrets.

By the following morning, her mind had become so set upon enjoying whatever time they had together that when Mark suggested she move her things downstairs into his bedroom—since her bed was still in a shambles anyway—Anna did not argue.

Rather than try to find reasons for not sharing his bedroom and his bed, as soon as she finished putting away the breakfast dishes, she started transferring her things downstairs, placing them into the drawers he had quickly cleared for her in one of his dressers.

While Anna attended to the pleasant task of moving, Mark went outside to the tool shed to gather the tools, nails, bolts, and wood he needed to repair the broken bed. After Anna had so readily agreed to move into his bedroom, he saw no reason to put off replacing the broken legs.

Pleased with the way things had suddenly worked out between them, Mark re-entered the house with a happy smile that turned dimple deep when he passed Anna on the stairs. She was on her way down with another armload of clothing, and that pleased him immensely. She had not changed her mind.

"Are you sure you don't need any help carrying some of that?" he asked, watching while she continued on down the stairs. His eyebrows arched appreciatively while he focused on the gentle way her hips swayed whenever she took a step. He caught himself remembering how well those hips had moved the evening before, and what pleasure he had derived from that movement. Who would have thought there was that much woman packed away in such a slender little body? He grinned when he remembered that he had had the same thoughts weeks ago, but then he had tried to push them aside and forget them.

"Yes, I'm quite sure I don't need any help. Besides, you have enough to do," she called out to him

242

in a mellow, singsong voice, just as happy, if not more so than he. Never had she felt such overwhelming joy or such childlike excitement. Although she knew that their lovemaking and his invitation to move into his bedroom were no guarantee against their marriage ending in divorce, she also was convinced it definitely would if they'd remained apart.

Even so, she also knew that the memories of their lovemaking would get her through the rest of her life. She remained determined not to dwell on the sad aspects of her situation, but focused on the good, like the wondrous way she felt when she was in Mark's loving arms. "I just hope you can repair that bed. Even though I may not be sleeping up there anymore, we will probably need the extra bed from time to time. You never know when we might have guests drop by."

The thought of guests intruding on his newly discovered happiness made Mark scowl. He did not like the idea of having to share even some of their time together with anyone else. Maybe, instead of repairing that bed, he should do something about destroying all the other unused beds in the house. It would be one way to make sure they had no guests. His scowl lifted into a devilish grin at such a clever but wicked thought, though he knew he'd have one hell of a time explaining such strange behavior to Anna or the boys once the deed was done.

"I don't think you should count on having too many guests," he called down to her. "We don't receive very many visitors out here."

"Still it is best to be prepared," she commented in the same singsong voice as before, glancing back at him for only a second.

243

Mark continued to stand near the top of the stairs, gazing down at her, watching until she had waltzed completely from his sight. Then, sighing heavily, he turned to do what he'd promised and repair that bed, mainly so Anna would quit feeling so guilty about having broken it in the first place.

Although Mark would never have suspected tampering, when he stripped the covers from the bed and examined the corners, where the legs had broken off, he discovered four flat nubs still firmly attached to the frame, about an inch long. Thinking that peculiar, he examined the legs and noticed all four had smooth, flat tops. It was apparent that all four legs had been carefully sawed—almost completely through, but not quite. Judging by the narrow, splintery edge found along one side of each leg, a scant quarter-inch of the wood had been left intact, probably so the bed would not collapse right away, giving Anna time to situate herself safely in the middle.

Mark narrowed his eyes. Someone had planned for that bed to fall, and he could well imagine who that someone was.

Late Sunday afternoon, when he finally confronted Harry with his suspicions, he discovered that he had guessed right. Rather than try to deny his guilt, Harry responded to Mark's accusing questions with a wry chuckle, then asked with open-eyed eagerness, "Well? Did it work?"

Having expected Harry to proclaim his innocence, Mark looked at him with surprise, then shook his head and laughed. "That's none of your business, old man."

Since Mark was the only person Harry allowed to get away with calling him old, Harry ignored the derogatory comment. Instead, he bent over and slapped his bony knee with obvious delight. "Hot damn, it did work, didn't it? I figgered it would."

"Oh, you did?"

"Yep. I may be gettin' on in years, but I sure ain't blind. I could see that there was somethin' a'sparkin between the two of you, but I just couldn't seem to get either one of you to see it. So I figgered all you two lovebirds really needed to get it through those thick skulls of yours just how much you'd come to care about each other was a little nudge."

He hooked his thumbs up under his suspenders and puffed his chest out like a strutting rooster. "So, tell me, did you go runnin' upstairs to the rescue when you heard that bed break? And was she then real eager to be comforted?" He lifted his hand to scratch the stubble on his jaw. "I don't suppose she ended up downstairs in your bedroom after havin' suffered such a frightenin' ordeal, did she?" His eyes brightened at the thought.

Mark cocked his head to one side and wondered how the old man could have known he would rush upstairs to her rescue the way he did, much less ask her to move her things into his bedroom after it was all over. Was he some sort of wizard? "That is none of your business either, old man."

"Hot damn. She did it. She moved right into your bedroom with you, didn't she?" he responded, his forehead wrinkled with delight. "And it's about time, I'd say. It just wasn't natural for the two of you to keep on sleepin' in separate bedrooms. You two is

245

man and wife. It just wasn't natural a'tall."

"I'll tell you what's not natural, and that's the way you go poking your nose into other people's business," Mark complained with a sharp wag of his finger, though his blue eyes sparkled with amusement. "You ought to be ashamed of yourself for interfering like that."

Harry ducked his head as he toed the rough planks on the back porch, where Mark had confronted him. Though he tried to look ashamed, his shoulders shook with delight and his eyes were bright with excitement. "Oh, I'm right sorry for what I done. Right sorry. It was downright wrong of me to go interferin' in your lives the way I done, downright wrong of me. I sure see that now. And you can rest assured that I'll probably never do anything like that again."

"Probably?" Mark quizzed, eyeing him suspiciously.

Harry frowned, as if to question what more Mark could possibly expect from him. "That's the best I can do. Take it or leave it." Then he grinned.

"I tell you what I'd like to take or leave," Mark grumbled, then turned to go back inside, aware Harry Munn wouldn't even know the meaning of the word sorry.

The next few weeks were happy ones for Anna, Mark, and the boys. After the one true barrier Mark had placed between himself and his new wife had been cast aside, there was no reason for them to avoid each other. Instead, they found more and more excuses to enjoy each other's company, as well as that of the boys.

By the time May had turned slowly into June and the days had grown increasingly longer, the four had become surprisingly close. With the arrival of summer upon them, which meant longer days, there was more spare time for them to spend with each other. Though Mark usually worked from sunup until suppertime, he soon developed the habit of spending his evenings and all day Sunday with his new family, getting to know them better.

Gradually, the four became as close as any blood family could ever hope to be. Anna was amazed at how quickly they had become an integral part of each other's lives. Though they had known one another only six weeks, it felt as if they had always been there for each other. Never had Anna known such contentment, and though Mark constantly questioned her sanity for having married him, she knew she had made the right choice. She could not have been happier.

Each day began and ended in Mark's arms, and in the hours between, they found ways to steal an extra moment or two alone. Usually it was Mark who sought Anna's company, pulling her into the pantry for a quick kiss, or catching her upstairs while she was making the boys' beds or gathering up their dirty clothes. If he was fortunate enough to find her in a bedroom, he usually rewarded himself by tossing her across the mattress and pretending that he intended to make wanton love to her. And occasionally, when their passions got the better of them, they went beyond pretending—though they were always careful to make certain the boys were occupied so they would have no unexpected surprises.

And in the short time that had passed, Mark's leg had become stronger. Soon he was able to work without the cumbersome leg brace and walked with only the cane for balance. As the days progressed, he felt stronger, more alive than he had in years.

To Anna, each day brought new joys, new rewards, making her believe that the future could hold nothing but more happiness for them, until late one Saturday afternoon, while Mark, Harry, and the boys were in town getting haircuts and a few supplies, a young woman dressed in a bright, emerald-green satin dress trimmed with bold strips of black lace appeared at their front door.

"May I help you?" Anna asked when she opened the door and discovered an unfamiliar woman standing on the front veranda, carefully surveying the house, the yard, and the surrounding fields. Glancing past her unexpected visitor, she noticed a small, empty buggy tethered to one of the hitching posts, and frowned. Whoever this woman was, she had come alone.

"I hope so," the woman said, responding to Anna's query, though she had yet to look at Anna. Instead, she continued to glance about, as if appraising everything she saw. "I'm looking for a Mr. Mark Gates."

"I'm sorry, but you just missed him," Anna said, though that was not exactly the truth. There was something about this woman that made her glad Mark was gone. Maybe it was the brazen cut of her garish clothing, and the voluptuous way she filled out every curve, or maybe it was the way she seemed to be busily placing a monetary value on

248

everything she saw. But whatever the reason, Anna hoped Mark and this woman would never meet—that is, if they hadn't already.

It then occurred to Anna that this woman might be from Mark's past. She appeared to be about the same age as Anna, maybe a year or two older, it was hard tell with so much face powder on her cheeks. At any rate, it was entirely possible she and Mark had shared some sort of relationship.

Anna shuddered at the thought, then quickly set it aside. Mark would have better taste than that. Although very pretty, she was obviously a woman of loose morals. No decent woman would pay call on a stranger dressed in such a getup.

"Maybe I can help you," Anna offered, sincerely hoping she could so this woman would be well on her way before Mark returned. It was then she realized she was jealous—and of a woman she knew nothing about. What a startling revelation that was. "I'm *Mrs*. Gates, Mark's wife."

Suddenly the woman turned and looked at her, her green eyes wide with surprise while she glanced down to take in the simple cut of Anna's pale pink and white cotton dress. "You're his wife? I figured you to be the housekeeper. Usually folks who live in houses as fine as this one don't go around answering their own doors."

Rather than answer her on that point, Anna stepped out onto the veranda and tried to hide her mounting concern. She kept her voice level when she asked, "What do you want with Mark?"

"I wanted to speak to him," the woman stated matter-of-factly, then glanced around as if searching for something in particular. "It's about my boys."

249

Anna felt an icy chill pass through her, making her more cautious than ever. "Your boys?"

The woman reached up to push a loose strand of hair back into the thick pile of black curls atop her head. "Yeah, I've traveled all the way from New York to find them."

The resulting stab of fear was so sharp, so intense, the pain sliced right through Anna's heart and into the core of her soul. "And what boys might those be?"

"Why, Jamie and Abel, of course," she answered with a slight shrug of her shoulder, as if that much should have been a foregone conclusion.

Anna's dark eyes narrowed with fearful suspicion as she thrust out her jaw. "Who are you?"

"Oh, I'm sorry," the woman said, as if suddenly aware of her neglect. "I forgot to introduce myself, didn't I? My name is Clara Wilkins, Mrs. Clara Wilkins. I'm Jamie and Abel's mother, and I've come a long, long way to find them."

Anna was too dumbfounded to speak. She simply stood, staring at the woman, searching her face for any similarity that would indicate she had spoken the truth. At the same time, she hoped she wouldn't discover any noticeable resemblance. Even so, the woman had an upturned nose much like Jamie's, and her eyes appeared to be a shade of green similar to Abel's. Still, those traits could be nothing more than coincidences. Or at least Anna hoped they were.

"Where are my boys?" Clara asked, unaffected by Anna's silence. Again, the young woman's gaze scanned the premises, as if hoping to catch sight of them.

"They aren't here," Anna answered simply. She swallowed hard, then glanced down at her hands, relieved to discover that they were not trembling visibly. Still, she couldn't help but wonder why the woman was even there. After all this time, what could she possibly want with Jamie and Abel? Surely she did not plan to take them away with her. Or did she?

"They aren't here? Then where are they?" The woman tilted her head to a foreboding angle and tapped her foot impatiently. Her shoulders tensed, as if preparing to do battle. "I was told they would be here. I was told your husband had temporary custody of them."

Temporary?

The word cut through Anna like a knife. It was true. At that moment, she and Mark had nothing more than temporary custody of the boys. Yet in two weeks if no problems had arisen, they would receive permanent custody. Until now, she had forseen no problems with obtaining the full guardianship. And once they had been granted the legal adoption, it would have taken a formal reversal through the courts before their legal rights as parents could be taken away.

If only this woman had waited another two weeks to come, their chances for keeping the boys would be a lot better. Once an adoption went through, it required a lot of legal red tape to reverse it. As it was, Anna was not sure what Mrs. Wilkins's rights might be. She was not aware that this had ever happened with any of the other children. But the woman must have signed a letter stating that she willingly gave up all parental rights to the children before the Children's Aid Society would have taken them in. That was really the only hope she and Mark had at the moment, so she clung to it fiercely.

"Mark does have custody of them," Anna responded, avoiding any repetition of the word temporary. "But I'm afraid you just missed them. The boys went with him into town just a little while ago." Anna realized it would serve no purpose to lie.

Clara's shoulders slowly relaxed while she let out a relieved sigh, as if she had worried there might be further complications. "Went into town? For a minute there, I thought you meant they had taken off someplace. How long until they return?"

"Hours yet," Anna answered honestly. Then, aware it would not be wise to do or say anything that could alienate this woman, at least not until she knew more about her reasons for being there, Anna smiled and gestured toward the front door. "I really don't expect them home until nearly dark. Why don't you come inside? Perhaps you would enjoy a nice glass of apple cider while you are waiting."

"Over ice?" Clara asked, lifting her skirts high above her black stockinged ankles before heading immediately for the door.

"I'm afraid we don't have any drinking ice. The only ice we have at the moment is what little is left of the big block in the cellar, and that has been covered with sawdust to make it last longer. But as it just so happens, ice is one of the items the men intend to bring back from town." Anna hurried inside, eager to lead Clara into the front parlor, where she hoped to keep her pleasantly occupied until Mark's return. She certainly did not care for the thought of this woman roaming about their house at will, and

252

she had a feeling that if left to herself, that is exactly what she would do.

"Men?" Clara asked, turning her head to Anna with sudden interest, while allowing herself to be escorted through the entrance hall toward the first open door to the right. "Who went with the boys?"

"Just Mark and Harry." Finding the woman's sudden show of interest a little odd, Anna glanced back over her shoulder with a curiously raised brow. Why would a married woman with two children be so concerned about other men? And for that matter, why would a married woman travel around dressed up like some saloon tart? Something was not right.

Then Anna realized that Mrs. Clara Wilkins might not be the person she pretended to be. But then, the boys would tell them if she was really their mother. Surely, if she was an impostor, she'd have thought of that. Anna then wondered why Mr. Wilkins was not with her. Didn't he want to see the boys, too?

"And who's Harry?" Clara asked, interrupting Anna's thoughts.

Aware Clara asked a lot of questions that were really none of her business, Anna chose to be as vague as possible with her answers. She did not like the thought of giving this woman too much information about them. At least not yet. "Harry Munn is a friend of ours. He lives near here."

"Does he have a place as nice as this one?" she wanted to know while she followed Anna into the large, ornately decorated room. Her eyes widened speculatively while she studied the obvious quality of the furnishings and ran a slippered foot over the expensive carpets that decorated the gleaming hard-

253

wood floor.

Though it bothered Anna that Clara showed more interest in knowing what Harry's house was like than in the health of her own boys, Anna answered honestly. "Yes, I suppose his place is as nice as ours, maybe not quite this large. But then, I've seen it only once, and that was about a week ago, when I volunteered to take the boys over there because Mark was too busy at the time."

"The boys go over there?"

Though Anna had indicated with a slight dip of her hand that they should sit in the pale blue rococo chairs nearest the open windows, where they might better enjoy the afternoon breeze, Clara ignored the gesture. Instead, she passed right by the chairs and continued to roam about the room, randomly touching things she had no business touching. "Tell me, do the boys work for this Mr. Munn often? How do they ever find the time to work two farms?"

Anna bristled at the non-too-subtle assumption that the boys were there strictly for labor purposes. True, they had their regular chores to do, but nothing more than most boys their age, which left them with plenty of time to play. "I think you have the wrong idea. Jamie and Abel don't work when they go over to Harry's; just the opposite. They usually end up fishing. Harry is sort of like a grandfather to them."

In addition to being a matchmaker for her and Mark, Anna added in her thoughts, knowing only too well that the weekly fishing excursions were also a way of allowing her and Mark to have a little time to themselves. She smiled at the thought, reminded just how very much she owed the dear man.

"Grandfather? Then this Mr. Munn is old," Clara responded with a puckered pout, clearly disappointed. "And I suppose he's married, too."

Seething inwardly, Anna wished Harry had been within earshot of that first comment. He'd have let her know in a hurry who was and wasn't old around there. As for his being married, that was really none of the woman's business. "I wouldn't say he's *old*, exactly."

Clara glanced up at her, obviously interested again. "Oh? And what *would* you say he is—*exactly?*"

"Spry," Anna concluded with a decisive nod, spouting aloud the second thought to have popped into her head, the first having been "cantankerous."

Again Clara's expression fell, and she resumed her quiet survey of the room, paying far more attention to one of the paintings on the north wall than to Anna. "It has always been my experience that people who are referred to as spry are usually old, too."

Growing more annoyed with Clara Wilkins's impertinence by the minute, Anna decided it would be worth the risk of leaving the woman alone in the parlor if it resulted in a few minutes away from her. "I'll go get the cider. It shouldn't take but a minute. While I'm gone, do make yourself at home."

No sooner had she spoken the words than she regretted them. She had a strong hunch that making herself at home was exactly what Clara Wilkins had in mind. Prickling bumps of icy apprehension sprang to life beneath the smooth surface of her sensitive skin, causing the tiny hairs along her nape to stand straight out.

Although earlier, Anna had hoped Mark would not have to meet this woman, now she wished he would hurry home. He'd know what to do to see that this woman was soon on her way. It was obvious she was there for a reason other than her desire to see the boys. After all, Clara had been there for nearly fifteen minutes and, though she had had a bundle of questions, she had yet to ask about the welfare of either child. Something was not right. Not right at all.

Judging by the woman's behavior, Clara Wilkins was apparently an opportunist, and Anna had a sickening feeling that Mark was in line to be her next victim. As she left the room, Anna shuddered and hoped she was wrong. Still it made her hurry.

Minutes later, she returned with the cider and a half dozen teacakes left over from a batch she'd made the day before. She was relieved to discover Clara had finally tired of prowling about the room and had sat down in one of the richly upholstered chairs.

"I thought you might be hungry as well as thirsty, so I brought something sweet to nibble on," she said as she placed the hand-carved wooden tray on the small claw-footed table between Clara's chair and her own. Originally, Anna had reached for one of Mark's elaborately designed silver serving trays for their cider, but at the last minute she'd decided not to give Clara any further indications of wealth. Since the woman just might be after money, she did not want her to think they were any better off than they actually were.

"Teacakes!" Clara responded with delight. Reaching forward, she took one of the napkins, shook out the folds, then quickly piled all six teacakes onto it, leaving nothing on the dish but a few crumbs. "This

256

ought to tide me over until supper," she said, breaking one of the teacakes in half and plopping the entire half into her mouth. Then, without waiting until her mouth was cleared, she turned her gaze on Anna, "You do plan to invite me to supper, don't you?"

In truth, Anna had already tried to figure out a way to avoid it. But rather than do something that might anger the woman before they found out what she wanted, Anna offered a pleasant smile while she leaned forward to lift the cut-glass decanter that held the cider. "Of course, you are invited to supper. I'm sure the boys will be delighted for the chance to visit with you."

Clara's eyebrows rose questioningly. "Visit? Is that what you think? That I'm here for a visit?"

"Aren't you?" Anna asked, holding her breath while she waited for the answer.

"No. This is far more than just a visit. I'm about to head out to make a new life for myself in California, and I plan to take the boys with me."

Chapter Fourteen

Anna glanced at the tall Jeffery clock on the mantle. Only five o'clock. Because Mark and the boys did not leave for Harry's until nearly two, it could be hours yet before they returned. In a way, that was good, because although she wanted to hurry and get everything over with, she also dreaded seeing what the boys' reactions would be when they came home and discovered their mother was waiting for them — to take them away.

If, upon seeing their mother again, they went running to her with open arms, Anna was certain her own heart would shatter into a thousand pieces. But even if that didn't happen and the boys rebelled or withdrew because of all the hurt and confusion they had suffered since they'd last seen their mother, that would also break Anna's heart. She hated the thought of those children having to suffer any more emotional upsets, especially if those upsets were caused by the very woman who had given birth to them.

Anna's blood ran cold and thin like icewater, but instead of dwelling on the boys' reactions, already knowing that she could deal with whatever they were, Anna decided to approach the situation in a far more practical way. First, she would find out as much about this woman as possible.

"So you're going to California," Anna commented casually. Her stomach turned to lead when she tried to calculate how many miles there must be between the infamous "gold state" and East Texas. "That's a pretty risky step to take, isn't it? I hope your husband has work waiting for him out there. I hear jobs are hard to come by."

"My husband died nearly two years ago," Clara responded, showing little remorse while she popped another oversized piece of day-old teacake into her mouth.

"He died nearly two years ago? Was he ill?" Anna then wondered if that might be the reason they had left the children with the Society in the first place. Did they know that Mr. Wilkins was dying and that they could no longer properly care for their boys? It was possible. If the man died nearly two years ago, that must have been only a few months after Jamie and Abel had been brought to the orphanage. Suddenly Anna felt ashamed for having automatically assumed the worst about Jamie and Abel's parents. She had passed judgment on them before knowing the entire story.

"No, he wasn't ill. Well, not exactly," Clara responded as soon as she could speak. With her finger, she reached up and dabbed at a few of the crumbs stuck on her lips and quickly tucked them inside her mouth. "Frank was poisoned."

Clara had said that so matter-of-factly that it caused an eerie feeling to creep along Anna's neck, raising tiny little bumps along her skin. This woman acted as if the death of her husband was no more important than an expected change in the weather.

259

The feelings of compassion that had been slowly gathering inside Anna quickly dissipated.

Because the reason for Clara's husband's untimely death was really none of her business, Anna decided not to pry further. Even so, she wondered if the death had been an accident, or whether someone had poisoned him on purpose. For a fleeting moment, she wondered if Clara herself had poisoned him.

"I imagine his death was very hard for you," she commented, watching Clara's expression closely.

There was still no indication of remorse, only a slight frown of petty annoyance when she licked her lips clean before she finally responded, "It certainly was hard for me. He left me without a penny."

Anna fell momentarily silent. She didn't know what to think. Should she feel sorry for the woman for having to face the world alone after her husband's death, or bothered that she displayed no real emotion?

"Is that why it took you nearly two years to come after the boys?" she finally asked, wondering why Clara was now attempting to locate them. "I guess you wanted to get back on a sound financial footing first."

Clara looked surprised by that statement. Her eyebrows arched as if she had considered something very profound for the first time. "Yeah—of course. I had to get myself back on a sound financial footing. I sure didn't want to come after the boys until I was able to support them better. That's what I did, all right. I waited until I had saved up enough money to come get them."

Anna could tell she was lying, and it took all the restraint she had to keep a civil tongue. "And do you think you will be able to support them now?"

Before Clara could formulate an appropriate answer to that question, the clattery sound of an approaching wagon caught her attention.

"Is that them?" She rose immediately from her seat and stepped to the nearest open window. Standing on tiptoe and leaning forward, she knotted her hands together in front of her while straining to see as much of the drive as she could from behind the wire mesh window covering.

Having misgivings about this woman's motives, Anna wondered if Clara's sudden display of nervous tension was more for show or because she was eager to see her sons again. Or was she suddenly afraid of what their reactions might be after two long years? Was it eagerness Anna witnessed, or fear? Or a little of both? Anna wished she knew, though for some reason, she doubted Clara's nervousness had much to do with eagerness. What galled her was that the woman had not inquired about either boy's health or happiness.

"I'll go outside to let them know you're here. Stay here and try to relax while I bring them to you," Anna said. Quickly she rose from her chair and headed for the door. She did not need to go to the window. She knew from the familiar clatter that it was their wagon.

Mark glanced curiously at the buggy and unfamiliar horse when they passed by on their way around to the back. He was disappointed to see they had visitors. Having been away from Anna for nearly four long, torturous hours, he had anticipated an affectionate return. During the endless ride from Harry's ranch, he'd thought of little more than catching his pretty little wife alone somewhere and stealing a long, lingering kiss, something passionate enough to whet his appetite for later that night. But now, as he brought the wagon to a halt in the shade of a large spreading pecan tree that stood barely a dozen yards from the back porch, he realized the kiss would have to wait. Frowning, he wondered who their visitors were and how late they intended to stay.

Quickly, he tethered the horse to a nearby post, then returned to the wagon, where he reached into the back and singled out the package containing the special purchase he'd made in town. While carefully balancing the brightly colored beribboned box on his denim-clad hip, he reached beneath the wagon seat for his cane, then started immediately for the house. Though the present could wait, he wondered mischievously what Anna would do if he greeted her with that long, passionate kiss anyway — right there in front of their visitors.

Mark's playful thoughts ended abruptly when he glanced toward the house and noticed Anna standing on the back porch near the step. He could tell by her grim expression that something was terribly wrong. His heart thumped hard. She looked to be very close to crying.

Glancing back over his shoulder to check on the boys, he was relieved to find that they hadn't left the wagon. They were still trying to decide which purchases they wanted to carry inside first. Seeing that he had a chance to talk with Anna alone, he hurried toward her, eager to discover what was wrong.

"We have company," Anna announced softly as soon as Mark was within earshot, but then hesitated to finish. How she dreaded being the one to tell him, knowing that Mark was as attached to those youngsters as she was, and would be as devastated over the thought of losing them.

"I know. I saw the buggy," Mark responded in a whisper. He glanced back over his shoulder again to see if either boy had started in their direction, but neither had. "Who's the company?"

Trying to find an easy way to tell him, Anna ran her hands over her arms as if to warm them, although it was a comfortable eighty-five degrees outside. Finally, she came out with it. "It's Jamie and Abel's mother."

Mark froze in mid-stride, still several feet away. His face paled and his blue eyes widened with alarm. "What's she doing here?"

Seeing his troubled expression, a knot of pure dread formed in the pit of Anna's stomach, making her own pain worse. She hoped she could tell him without bursting into tears. "She—ah—says she has come for Jamie and Abel. She claims she wants them back. She wants to take them to California with her." Anna flexed the muscles in her jaw to keep from crying.

Mark's expression hardened with stark disbelief and anger when he glanced back at the boys again. His lips pressed together into a firm, white line while he watched Jamie happily hand a few of the smaller packages down to Abel and carefully stack them in his arms.

Mark wondered how long those cheerful smiles would remain on their faces after they had learned their biological mother waited for them inside.

"Who do you think should tell them?" he asked, his voice so strained with emotion that even he'd had a hard time recognizing it.

"I think it would be better if we told them together," she said bravely, though she would really prefer not to be anywhere around when they found out. She doubted her own ability to handle the resulting pain.

"Very well," Mark said. His chest expanded when he took in a long, deep breath. Having forgotten all about the package under his arm as well as his eagerness for Anna to see what he had bought, Mark turned to face the wagon and called to the boys, "Jamie. Abel. Come here a minute."

When Abel headed toward them, his arms were so full of tiny packages, he could hardly see over them. Smiling, Mark quickly added, "You can put the packages down for the moment. We have something to tell you."

Shrugging, Abel dropped the packages carelessly onto the sideboard, then he and Jamie hurried from the wagon.

"What is it?" Jamie asked eagerly as they skidded to a quick halt in front of them, kicking up dust in their wake. The two boys glanced at each other then up at him, as if anticipating a fun surprise.

Mark groaned inwardly. He hated the thought of stripping away such happy, trusting expressions. "Seems you two boys have a visitor."

Jamie's smile slowly withered when he glanced back at Abel again, then at the house. Anna could tell by the way his eyebrows had pulled together into a worried frown that he already suspected trouble.

"Who is it?"

When Mark failed to answer right away, Anna realized he couldn't, so she took the initiative, knowing there was no reason to delay the inevitable any longer. Hoping to ease any fears the boy might have, she forced a pleasant smile and tried to sound as unconcerned as possible. "It's your mother."

264

Jamie's eyes grew round with disbelief as he reached immediately for Abel's hand. For the longest moment, the two boys stood perfectly still, hands locked. The only movement came when Jamie finally blinked.

Still trying not to reveal any of her own fear, Anna continued to put up a surprisingly brave front. "And she is very eager to see you."

"Why?" Jamie finally asked, his blue-green eyes narrowed with caution. "Why would she want to see us?" Tears glistened across his lower eyelid. His grip tightened protectively around Abel's. "What have we done wrong?"

Pure anguish seared Anna's heart. How could the child think he had done something wrong? Blinking back her own tears, she knelt, knowing they would go immediately into her arms.

"Nothing, Jamie. You've done nothing wrong." While she hugged them to her, she glanced at Mark questioningly. A tiny piece of her heart tore away when she saw that he'd pressed his eyes closed, just as deeply affected by their assumption of guilt as she was.

"If we didn't do anything wrong, then why is she here?" Jamie asked, struggling valiantly to keep his emotions out of his voice and doing a surprisingly good job of it for an eight-year-old. "Don't you want us no more?"

Anna, too, closed her eyes against the pain and was relieved when seconds later she felt Mark's arms come around the three of them in a warm, protective embrace. It gave her the strength she needed to answer. Opening her eyes and meeting Mark's gaze, she attempted to reassure Jamie, whose face remained buried against her. "Of course we still want you. We love you, both of you . . . you know that."

Jamie pulled away and looked into Anna's eyes. It was obvious by the arch of his eyebrows that he wanted to believe her. "If that's so, then why is she here?"

"We didn't send for her, if that's what you think," Mark inserted, wanting to make that clear right away.

Jamie turned in Anna's arms and, while keeping his arms firmly locked around Anna's neck, sought Mark's eyes as he asked his next question. "Then how did she find out where we were?"

Mark shook his head, then looked to Anna for the answer, for he had no idea.

Shrugging helplessly, Anna admitted, "I don't know. She didn't say." But what a good question that was. Why would the Society tell her of their whereabouts without first notifying them? Either she'd tricked the information out of them, or there had been a serious problem somewhere. "But we mustn't have all these tears. Your mother has come a long, long way to see you," Anna said soothingly, still smiling bravely. "You wouldn't want her to think you were unhappy here, would you?"

"No," Jamie admitted and reached up to wipe away some of the moisture clinging to his eyes with the back of his hand.

"Neither would we," she said, then let her gaze dart from place to place, as if searching for something.

"What are you doing?" Jamie asked.

"Looking around. We need to see if we can find that handsome smile that was on your face just a few minutes ago. It must have fallen off around here somewhere."

Though Jamie did not smile, he gave her silly comment enough consideration that it eased some of the harshness from his expression. Abel, on the other hand, had not revealed any emotion at all. Though he had followed the entire conversation with his eyes, his face had remained blank.

"There, now, don't you think that's better?" Anna asked, glad that Jamie was no longer on the verge of tears, but frowning at the way Abel refused to meet her gaze. How she wished she knew what was going through the younger boy's mind! "Are you two about ready to go in there and greet your mother?"

"*You're* my mother," Jamie muttered, and slowly pulled away and began to straighten his shirt.

Touched to the point of crying, Anna leaned forward and kissed his temple, for the first time aware of his haircut. "I agree. In my heart, I *am* your mother. But for the sake of argument, she's your mother, too."

Jamie decided not to comment further. Instead, he reached again for Abel's hand, then thrust his chin out bravely. "Let's go, if we're going."

Abel was reluctant to move at first, but after a couple of sharp tugs on his arm from Jamie, he allowed himself to be led toward the house. A few minutes later, walking in pairs with the boys in front, the four entered the front parlor, where they found Clara Wilkins restlessly pacing the floor, obviously annoyed by having been forced to wait so long.

"Here they are," Anna announced needlessly as she broke away from Mark and placed a hand on either boy's shoulders. Gently she encouraged them to move a few steps forward.

"Jamie! Abel!" Clara exclaimed, clasping her hands over her heart in what appeared to Anna an extremely melodramatic gesture.

Jamie's feet froze to the floor while he was still several yards away, but Clara seemed unperturbed by his reluctance to go to her.

Batting her eyes as if overcome with joy, she crooned, "My sons . . . my dear, dear sweet sons . . . I have found you at last." Spreading her skirt, she knelt down and threw her arms wide in a seemingly rehearsed gesture. "Come here. Come to your mother." She then closed her eyes as if preparing herself for the onslaught.

Jamie's only response was to narrow one eye.

When the boys failed to fill her arms, Clara reopened her eyes, wet her lips with the tip of her tongue, then tried again. "Jamie? Abel? Don't you recognize me? I'm your mother."

Though it pained her, Anna took her hands off the boys' shoulders and stepped back. She did not want either boy to feel pushed into this woman's arms, nor did she want them to feel held back. Whether they went to her or not, she wanted it to be of their own accord.

"Jamie? Darling . . . surely you recognize me," Clara continued, her voice honey-sweet. She clasped her hands to her breast again as if heartbroken by his response. "Surely you recognize your own mother."

Jamie's grip loosened from Abel's one finger at a time. His lower lip trembled when he slowly took his first tiny step forward.

"Mama?"

His voice had come out barely above a whisper.

"Yes, Jamie, it's your mama," Clara said reassuringly, and spread her arms wide again to receive him.

Still several feet away, Jamie took two more tentative steps toward her, swallowing hard after each, then suddenly he flung himself forward into her waiting arms. Burying his face into the soft flesh of her shoulder, he shook all over, overcome by his suppressed emotions. When he spoke again, it was in a choked, but almost reverent tone, "Mama."

Smiling victoriously, Clara patted his trembling shoulder rhythmically, then glanced at Abel, who had not moved a muscle. "Abel? Little darling. Don't you remember me, too?"

Abel scowled and shook his head that he did not.

"I guess that's understandable. You were still awfully young that day I was forced to give you up. As I recall, you weren't even four years old," she said, and for the first time since her arrival, sounded truly regretful. "But that doesn't change the fact that I am your mother. Won't you please come here and give me a hug?"

Abel's nostrils flared with such true hatred that it was frightening to behold, and again he shook his head, this time more adamantly.

Growing impatient, Clara narrowed her eyes, though slightly, while she repeated her request in a much firmer voice. "Please, Abel. Come here and give me a hug. I've come a very long way." Then, while patting Jamie on the shoulder with one hand, she reached her other arm out to encourage the younger child.

With eyes widened in panic, Abel took a small step back, then turned and fled the room.

The pain in Anna's chest was so profound that she was certain she could not bear the anguish much longer. She hurried to follow.

Mark watched her go, but then turned back to

gaze again at Clara and Jamie. He still could not get over the initial shock he'd felt when he'd first seen what their mother looked like. She was nothing like he'd expected.

In his mind, he'd pictured Jamie and Abel's mother as being a thin, sad-looking woman dressed in demure but tattered clothing, her shoulders bent from the torment of having been forced to give up her precious children. Yet the woman before him was nothing like that. He swallowed uncomfortably when she then glanced up at him with heavily lashed green eyes and smiled appreciatively at what she saw.

"I gather I finally have the pleasure of meeting Mark Gates." Pushing Jamie aside, she stood and quickly adjusted first her shiny green skirts, then her snuggly fitted bodice. "I must say, you are not at all what I had anticipated."

"And you are not what I had anticipated," he responded honestly, leaning heavily on his cane while he considered how true that was.

Taking his statement as a compliment, she smiled prettily and moved toward him, which left Jamie standing alone. Aware he'd been left behind, he pouted in confusion while he rushed to follow.

Clara paid no attention to the child. Her regard was focused on the extremely handsome man standing before her.

"I suspect you've already figured out that I'm Clara Wilkins, Jamie and Abel's widowed mother," she said, extending her hand for a formal greeting.

Mark did not miss the emphasis she had placed on the word *widow*, but chose to wait and ask Anna for the details about her husband's death. He did not want this woman to come to the false conclusion that he was at all interested in her marital state. He also had not missed how easily she had dismissed any desire to comfort Jamie. And judging by the confused look on the child's upturned face, little Jamie was still in need of more comfort.

Angered that the woman had so quickly cast the child aside, he purposely ignored her outstretched hand and bent low so he could speak with Jamie instead. "Jamie, I know you are probably looking forward to a long visit with your mother, but could you do me a small favor first?"

Jamie took his gaze off his mother and looked at Mark. "What sort of favor?"

"It'll be dark soon, and I still have all those supplies to unload. Would you help me carry everything inside? It shouldn't take but a few minutes to clear out the wagon if we both hurry."

Jamie looked back at his mother, as if hoping she might offer a reason for him to stay, but when she did not, his shoulders dropped and he nodded. "I'll help."

"Good," Mark said, then stood upright and looked at Clara, flattening his brow in a meaningful gesture. "Mrs. Wilkins, I *know* how anxious you are to spend some time getting reacquainted with your sons, but I do need to get that wagon unloaded before it gets too dark. You do understand, don't you?"

Clara's eyebrows notched, aware of the sarcasm in Mark's voice. "Of course I understand. And there's plenty of time for me to get reacquainted with the boys. I've been invited to stay for supper."

Mark felt his gut tighten at the unappetizing thought of having this woman sit at his table, pretending to care for the boys when it was obvious she could barely tolerate them. What he could not understand was why she had come for them if she wasn't interested in their welfare.

"We shouldn't be long." He turned to follow Jamie from the room, never bothering to look back.

Clara crossed her arms over her ample bosom and tapped her slippered foot impatiently, angered that he had dared refuse her proffered hand. Staring at the now empty doorway, she narrowed her green eyes perceptively while she wondered how a cripple like Mark Gates had ever developed such a high, almighty opinion of himself. True, he was a handsome devil, but what real use could a man who has to use a cane be to anyone? Then Clara's thoughts turned to Blake, and her angry scowl lifted into a wide, adoring smile. Now there was a man—a *whole* man. One who knew what it took to please a lady.

Suddenly, she was reminded of her reason for coming, and her smile slowly faded. She had two weeks.

Chapter Fifteen

All through supper, Anna managed to keep a civil tongue, though barely. While listening to Clara's idle chatter and noticing the way she hardly looked at the boys, even when Jamie spoke to her, Anna was reminded again and again of all the suffering Abel and Jamie had been forced to live with during the past two years. She also thought about all the suffering they would again face once they learned that their mother had not come to Pinefield merely to visit, but instead had come to take them far away.

The more Anna thought about it, the more her resentment escalated, and the more she wanted to tell the woman just what she thought of her. Still, she knew that would serve no purpose, other than to relieve some of the anger growing inside her. It remained in everyone's best interest for her to continue to be courteous toward their uninvited guest. She did not want to do or say anything that might provoke this woman into doing something hasty in retaliation. She and Mark needed time to think this thing through, to figure out what their rights might be in this unfortunate situation. Until then, she had to behave as cordially as possible.

It was not until Anna had started to clear the table that her firm resolve to hold her tongue at all costs finally snapped. Because Mark and the boys had decided to take a short trip out to the barn to check on their new colt, which had been born two days earlier, it left the two women alone again for the first time since the boys' return from town.

As expected, Clara did not offer to help clear the dishes. Instead, she continued to lounge at the table, helping herself to more of the wine she had asked to have—wine Mark and Anna had been saving for an occasion far more special than this. That alone had caused Anna's blood to boil, because she had envisioned sharing that wine with Mark during a romantic evening alone. She clattered the dishes together loudly, hoping her anger would be evident.

"I certainly am glad I was able to find my sons as quick as I did," Clara said, as a way of starting a conversation. She seemed oblivious to Anna's pent-up emotions. "And I'm grateful to you and Mark for having taken such good care of them during these past few weeks; but I especially want to thank you for having helped take care of them for the entire two years I had to be separated from them. Jamie told me that you used to work for the Children's Aid Society."

"I did. And Mark and I don't expect any gratitude. We did what we did because we happen to love the boys." Anna glanced up from the platter she'd scraped the leftover food onto to let Clara see the sincerity in her expression.

"Still, it was generous for you two to provide them with such a nice temporary home."

There was that word *temporary* again. Anna's stomach muscles clenched into a hard, painful knot, making it that much harder for her to control her anger. It was annoying enough that this woman considered herself to be on a first-name basis with them, but it infuriated her more to hear the way she kept using that word *temporary*. It was as if the woman knew how painfully it hurt her and used the word on purpose to injure her again and again.

"Mrs. Wilkins, I'm afraid you have the wrong idea about why the boys are here," Anna said, the muscles in her jaw rock hard, although she tried to sound calm.

"Oh?"

"Mark and I did not ask to take Jamie and Abel in just to give them a temporary home. We took them in because we wanted to give them a *permanent* home, one filled with lots of love and compassion—something those two desperately needed and now have. I think you would be making a grave mistake by taking them away from us. They have all the love and the stability of a real family here. If they go with you, they will find themselves lost in an unsettled world again, and I'm not sure they could cope with that."

"But I *am* their real family," Clara responded tersely, flinging her head back in a grand show of defiance. "I happen to be the one who gave birth to them."

"I realize that, but you've been out of their lives for over two years now," Anna ventured. Her arms and shoulders moved with stiff, jerky movements while she made one last effort to remain civil.

"By no fault of mine," Clara put in, slamming her fist down on the table so hard it rattled the dishes Anna had carefully stacked nearby. "Leaving those

275

boys at that orphanage was my husband's idea, not mine. I had nothing to do with it. I never wanted to give them up. It's been pure torment for me, living all this time without once seeing my own precious children." Blinking profusely, she reached for her napkin and dabbed at the corner of a suspiciously dry eye.

Anna took in a long, protracted breath before continuing. "If that's true, if you missed them so very much, then why did it take you this long to come after them?"

"I told you . . . I didn't have enough money to take care of them." Clara eyes narrowed, as if daring Anna to dispute her word.

Anna paused in her work, turned, and again met Clara's angry green eyes. "You could have at least written to them. If that was really the situation, if you were really trying to put together enough money to come after them, you could have at least written to them and told them that in a letter. You could have let them know what your situation was and that you planned to come after them as soon as you could. You also could have written to the Children's Aid Society, to let them know that you planned to reclaim the children."

Clara's gaze darted about the room, as if she hoped to find the perfect retort hidden somewhere in her surroundings. "I thought about writing. And I almost did write to them. But I—I didn't want to get their hopes up in case I was never able to get enough money together."

Anna knew she was lying, and it made her angrier still. She wanted to take the water left in the glass she'd just picked up and throw it in Clara's face. "Even so, you could have written to the Children's Aid Society, and explained your plans to return for the boys so they would not continue with their efforts to place them. Why didn't you at least do that? It would had saved a lot of hurt feelings."

"I told you, leaving the boys there was not my idea in the first place," she snapped in an obvious effort to change the direction their conversation had taken. "It was my husband who decided to leave Jamie and Abel at that place. I was against it from the start."

Anna thought about that for a moment. "I worked with The Children's Aid Society long enough to know they never would have taken Jamie and Abel in without first having obtained some form of a release document signed by both parents stating in no uncertain terms that you both gave up all parental rights to the boys."

"I never signed anything," Clara insisted, rising from her chair. Leaning toward Anna, she curled her hands into tight fists and placed them on her ample hips. "And I don't like the way you keep insinuating that I had something to do with giving up my own children. I think maybe the boys and I should go ahead and leave right now."

The muscles in Anna's chest tightened painfully around her heart. "You can't take them with you."

"And why not? I'm their mother."

"Because Mark and I are still responsible for them. We have papers signed by the local judge that clearly state we are their legal guardians," Anna said with a determined lift of her chin. But she was not at all sure which would win out in court, their custodial papers, which stated that as long as no problems had arisen within their two-month trial period they would be granted permanent custody, or Clara's rights as the biological mother. If it was true that Clara had never signed any papers agreeing to give up all parental rights, their own chances of keeping the boys were practically nonexistent.

Clara grunted heavily to show how unimportant she considered those papers. "So you have a few pieces of paper that say you have legal custody of Jamie and Abel. That doesn't change the fact that I'm their real mother. And when I leave here, I have every intention of taking the boys with me."

Neither Anna nor Clara had noticed Mark when he reentered the room a few moments earlier, nor had they seen how angry he had become on overhearing their conversation. They both jumped when he suddenly spoke out.

"There's no purpose in arguing about any of this. This is something a judge will have to decide. And until he does, those boys are staying right here."

He spoke with such finality that Clara wisely decided not to argue the point further. "That's fine with me. We'll go see the judge first thing Monday morning." The sooner the better.

"Can't," Mark informed her, his grip tightening on the handle of his cane. "The judge won't be back in Pinefield until Thursday—the twelfth."

"But that's five days from now," Clara complained, having done a little quick arithmetic in her head. "Where am I going to stay until then?"

"For now, you can stay right here with us," Mark said, meeting Anna's startled gaze across the room. "We have plenty of room upstairs."

A slow smile spread across Clara's face while she considered the offer. Why not enjoy a few days of leisurely rest before taking off? Blake wasn't expected to arrive at their meetingplace until the latter part of the week anyway, and he had told her she could have as much as two weeks.

"All right," she finally agreed. "I'll wait until the twelfth before leaving here with my sons. I'd much rather go with the court's blessing than worry about someone coming after us, forcing us to return to Pinefield to clear up any unresolved legal matters. But I want it clear that as soon as that judge has given me permission to take my boys, I plan to leave for California that same afternoon. And I also think it is time to tell them exactly what's going on so they will be ready to leave when the time comes."

"Why put them through anymore heartache?" Mark wanted to know. "They have suffered enough uncertainty in their short lives."

"That may be true, but they have every right to know what's happening," Clara said, spinning about, already heading for the door. "And I also think they should be allowed to have some say in their own futures."

Knowing she was right, though wishing there was some way the boys could be spared the pain and confusion of having their worlds turned upside down again, Mark followed.

"I want to be there when you tell them," he called out to her, his voice filled with warning. He paused in the doorway long enough to extend his hand to Anna. This was something they should all face together.

That night Mark could not sleep. He was too tormented by the pain and utter confusion he'd seen in Jamie's eyes and the anger that had flashed across

279

Abel's face after they'd been told about Clara's decision to take them with her to California. Though he had wanted to comfort them somehow, to try in some way to reassure them, they had refused anyone's comfort. They had also refused to listen to any reasons why this was happening.

Instead, they had run upstairs and shut themselves in their bedroom, refusing to open the door. When Mark tried to convince them to open the door so they could talk about what had happened, his efforts had been met with angry shouts to go away and leave them alone, which eventually everyone did. Even Clara, who had become a little impatient with their refusal to talk with her, eventually gave up and went across the hall to bed.

Yet even though being alone was what the boys wanted, Mark had found it painfully hard to walk away from that closed door and go on to bed. Knowing how terribly upset they were, and knowing he was unable to do anything about it made him ache deep inside. Then, having seen the tears in Anna's eyes when she, too, finally turned away from the door, he thought he would die from the pain and helplessness he felt. Why did Clara Wilkins have to show up now, of all times—why *now*, when everything was going so well for them?

Tightening his arm around Anna, who lay pressed against his side wearing the satin-and-lace nightgown he'd bought her earlier that afternoon, he wondered what would happen to them if for some reason the judge decided in Clara's favor. The thought of losing their sons hurt beyond anything, but the thought of losing Anna too was nothing short of devastating.

If Clara somehow managed to convince Judge Parish that she should have her sons back, then Anna would have no reason to stay married to him. It was for the boys' well-being that she'd agreed to the marriage in the first place.

The thought of life without her was unthinkable. Tears spilled down his cheeks.

"Anna?" he whispered softly, not wanting to waken her if she'd been fortunate enough to fall asleep.

"Yes?" she responded, her voice as hushed as his when she raised up on one elbow and gazed down at him. Though she could not see his face because of the dark shadows that fell across his pillow, it made her heart flutter with appreciation, knowing he was there for her. "What is it?"

Mark stared up at her for a long moment. Moonlight filtered through the bedroom window, allowing him to see the shape of her face. Even in such undefined light, Anna was the most beautiful woman he'd ever known. Blinking to clear his tears, he reached his hand to stroke her cheek. "I can't bear the thought of losing the boys."

"Neither can I," she said, her voice trembling. Nor could she stand the thought of losing him. Having been plagued by thoughts very similar to his, she was beside herself with worry. She was afraid of losing everything that had made her happy these past several weeks.

"I'm going to ask Clara Wilkins to live with us," he stated so matter-of-factly that Anna was not sure she'd heard him right.

"You're what?"

"You know as well as I do that if the woman never signed any papers giving away her rights to her sons, we don't have a chance in hell of keeping them. I'm going to ask her to live here with us. It's the only way we can possibly hold on to Jamie and Abel, because if I can convince her to live here with us, then the boys can go on living here, too. They won't have to be uprooted to California after all."

Though the thought of having Clara Wilkins around indefinitely made Anna's stomach knot with revulsion, she saw the practicality of the solution. Still, she wanted with all her heart to hold onto the way things were before. "But what if she did sign something that gave up all her rights to the boys? What if she's lying about that?"

Mark was silent for a moment. "Can you send a telegram Monday, asking the Society to search their files?"

"I'd already planned to do just that," she admitted, smiling because they had shared the same idea.

"How long should it take to get a response?"

"Depends on how quickly they can get on it. Maybe if I explain in the telegram that it is an emergency, they will be willing to get the information to me in a few days."

"Before the judge arrives in Pinefield?" Mark asked, wondering if that was possible.

"I hope so," Anna answered, then swallowed back her apprehension. "I truly hope so."

While he considered the possibility of obtaining the necessary information before they ever talked to the judge, Mark continued to trail his fingertips lightly over the soft curve of Anna's cheek. Unable to bear being this close to her and without kissing her, he slid his hand into the thick darkness of her hair and cupped the back of her head with his fingers, then slowly brought her lips down to his.

Anna was as eager for his kiss as he was for hers, and her mouth parted while his other arm came around to encircle her, pressing her body firmly against his. With a passion spawned from the knowledge that they might soon lose each other, he slipped his tongue into the warm recesses of her mouth, eager to sample her sweetness while tugging frantically at the uncooperative straps of her new summer nightgown, so eager to make love to her that he eventually tore the gown in his haste.

Aware he'd damaged the garment, but not caring in the least, Anna moaned softly when he finally removed it. Knowing he slept naked meant they could now press their bodies together, flesh against flesh.

Wanting to make love as desperately as he did, she trembled with expectation when he slid his hand between them and quickly claimed her breast. Eagerly, she arched her shoulders, allowing him easier access to the aching globe.

Mark burned with a need to be closer and pulled her higher atop him so he could taste the other breast first with the tip of his tongue, then with the whole of his mouth. Hungrily, greedily, he lifted his head off the bed to devour her.

Anna closed her eyes against the sensual onslaught that wracked her body. The result was a pleasure so unbearable, she wanted to cry aloud. Tossing her head back, her hair streaming riotously over them, she bit her lower lip to keep from vocalizing the wild, driving need Mark had magically awakened inside her.

While he continued to tug hungrily at her breast, his hand roamed eagerly over the rest of her body, re-exploring every sensual curve, every delicate contour; he was overcome with his need for her. Though it

283

would have been impossible to imagine it, Mark wanted Anna more at that moment than he had ever wanted her. His body ached with his need for fulfillment.

Unable to control his raging desire, Mark took no more time for teasing or taunting, and Anna was relieved, because now there was an urgency inside both of them that had to be answered. He rolled them as one until he was on top of her, then dipped to place a fiery kiss at her throat while he carefully positioned himself.

The passion that had burst to life inside Anna was so intense it was almost frightening, yet she was in no way afraid. Restlessly, she tossed her head from side to side, then, thinking he was taking entirely too much time, she rose to meet him halfway. He entered her easily, and she found the reward to be so wondrous she whimpered aloud her joy. How glorious it felt for him to be a part of her. How glorious, and how right. How very, very right.

She met each of his long, lithe movements with upward thrusts of her own, until that mounting ache that only Mark could create inside her finally burst in a magnificent explosion, wracking her body with one glorious spasm after another. Barely seconds later, Mark's body shook and he softly cried her name.

Sinking into the warm depths of satisfaction, Mark rolled to lie beside her, then while holding her naked body against his own, he felt a sudden urge to weep.

The thought of life without Anna was just too painful. He had to do something to make sure he did not lose her. He had to do something to keep both her and the boys. Despite what Clara Wilkins had said, the four of them were a family, a real family, and he would do everything within his power to see that was what they remained. He then thought of Harry, aware that losing the boys and Anna would destroy the old man nearly as much as it would him. Something had to be done. But what?

Mark had never felt more like striking a woman than he did that following morning, when Clara refused even to consider living there with them.

"I'll stay only until we've seen that judge on Thursday, and not a moment longer," she stated, tossing her head with contempt while she met his gaze straight on. "Because just as soon as we have left that judge's office, I'm taking my sons and heading straight for California, as I said I would."

Mark leaned back in his chair and glanced at the kitchen door, wondering if Anna overheard any of their conversation, and hoping she hadn't for her own sake as much as for his. She had suffered enough. "But what if the judge refuses to give you custody after all?"

"Oh, come now," Clara responded, pushing her chair away from the table and standing to look down at him with righteous indignation. "I happen to be their mother. What judge is going to refuse a mother custody of her own sons?"

Mark wasted no time in standing. He tried to think of a good, convincing argument that might make her change her mind and stay, aware if he didn't, he could very well lose everything he held dear.

Unaware that the boys had entered the dining room from the main hall, Clara and Mark both turned in surprise when they heard Jamie ask, "But what if we don't want to go with you? What if we want to stay here instead?"

Clara's eyes narrowed briefly, but then widened again when she set her napkin aside and moved toward them. "Why would you want to stay here? I'm your mother. Don't you want to be with me? Don't you want to go to California and live in that big house I told you about?"

Jamie's face twisted with painful confusion. "I don't know what I want. I know you are our mother, but I don't remember you much. And I don't understand why you left us."

"I thought I explained that to you," Clara said with only a hint of irritation in her voice. "I had nothing to do with the decision to leave you at that orphanage. That was your father's idea, not mine. But you have to try and understand; we were very poor at the time, and your father was afraid you two might starve to death right there in the streets if we didn't do something drastic to get food and medicine for you."

"Medicine?" Jamie looked back at Abel, who stood in the doorway just behind him.

"Yes, Abel was very sick when we took you to that orphanage. He'd fallen down some metal stairs and hurt himself, and was badly in need of a doctor's care. We were afraid he would never get any better without someone's help. That's why your father finally had to do what he did. But I want you to know that I never agreed to it. I wanted to try to keep you two, if only a little while longer; but Frank didn't care much what I wanted. He didn't even tell me what he'd done until he'd already done it."

Mark thought about what she'd said and realized something did not quite ring true, though he could

286

not put his finger on it. Just then his mind was in too much turmoil.

Instantly, Jamie's eyes filled with tears. "Then why didn't you come back for us after he died?"

Clara knelt beside the boy and pulled him into her arms, pressing his head against her shoulder, careful not to wrinkle the bright blue material. "Because deep down inside, I knew he was right. I couldn't afford to feed or to clothe you properly, and I had no place to live. You were better off in that orphanage, where you could at least have a clean bed to sleep in and food to eat."

Mark studied her face for any indication that she might be telling the truth for once, but was not terribly surprised to find none. Angered that she could continue to lie to her own child like that, he felt like confronting her, in front of both boys, but realized he had no real proof that she had lied. All he really had was his own gut feeling, and that was not enough.

"Jamie, dear, try to understand how hard it was for me, too," Clara said in her very best honey-sweet voice, continuing to hold the boy's head against her shoulder while she patted him rhythmically across the back. As she continued to say reassuring words to the older boy, her gaze fell on Abel, who stood several feet away, glaring at her.

"What about you?" she asked of her younger son. "Do you resent me too?"

Abel stood stone still, his jaw rigid, his eyes dark with hatred.

Heaving an impatient sigh, she tried again. "Abel, I'm growing tired of your impertinence. I asked you a question. You can at least show enough courtesy to answer me. Do you resent me, too?"

Abel's piercing gaze narrowed while nodding that he did.

"That's not an answer," she said, more annoyed with the child than ever. "Answer me, yes or no . . . Do you resent me even after I've explained to you that our leaving you at that orphanage was not my idea?"

Abel's face reddened with rage while he thrust his chin forward and continued to stare angrily at her.

Aware of the problem, Jamie pulled away and looked back at his younger brother. "Abel can't talk."

"Quit protecting him. I happen to know he *can* talk," she said, setting Jamie away from her and inching her way closer to where Abel stared contemptuously at her. "And he is going to answer my question."

"Jamie is telling you the truth," Mark intervened. Stepping over, Mark dropped his cane and collected the smaller child in his arms. "Abel cannot, or at least he *does not* speak. To the best of my knowledge, he hasn't muttered a word since that day he was brought to the orphanage."

"He hasn't?" she asked, and for the first time she seemed truly concerned. "Why not? What happened to him?"

"No one seems to know," Mark answered, looking at Abel, who continued to stare at Clara with fury-darkened features.

"Oh, the poor dear," she crooned, then reached out to touch his cheek only to have the boy jerk his head back to avoid her hand. Frowning, she drew her hand away and studied him cautiously from a distance. It had been two years . . . Abel was not even four at the time. Could he possibly remember events from that far back? Clara wondered.

Of the two children, Clara had thought Abel would

288

be more likely to have forgotten, when instead it appeared Jamie was the one to have pushed aside the most memories of the past. Though it worried her that Abel might actually remember what his life had been like before they had finally gotten rid of them, she was relieved to learn that he refused to talk. That stubborn refusal to speak might keep him from being any real threat to her, aware that if he did suddenly decide to speak out before she'd seen that judge, he could end up ruining everything. She then wondered if she should bother getting the judge's permission after all. Maybe she should just pack them up and leave that night. After all, kidnapping the boys in the dark of night was what Blake had wanted her to do right from the beginning.

Chapter Sixteen

For the rest of the morning and for several hours that afternoon, Clara wondered what she should do. Should she stay in Pinefield until the judge arrived on Thursday, which meant taking the very real risk of Abel finally finding his voice in the meantime and telling someone about her before she could obtain legal permission to take the children? Or should she kidnap the boys as she had planned all along, and risk Mark and Anna trying to find her?

The main problem with kidnapping was that she would be forced to keep the children hidden away until Blake finally arrived at their meeting place sometime Friday and she would have to put up with both those boys all alone, and for several days. She did not like the thought of that either. She would much rather stay right there and have someone else cook her meals and do her laundry. It was the sort of life she wanted because as soon as they reached California, she and Blake would be able to get the money they needed for that brand new start Blake had promised.

Before making any final decisions, Clara decided to try to catch Abel alone and test his refusal to speak. If after talking with him, she felt fairly confident that the child would indeed continue to keep his little mouth shut, she would stay and play on that circuit judge's sympathies, as she had planned. Otherwise, she would have to go through with the kidnapping.

Of the two choices, waiting around to see the judge was really the simpler — and the least expensive.

Anna worried about Abel. Shortly after two o'clock, he had suddenly taken to his room again, refusing to come out for any reason, or let anyone else inside, except for Jamie.

Though there was no way she could prove it, she suspected that his sudden need for seclusion had something to do with Clara's attempt to talk with him right after lunch.

Anna had been furious to discover the two of them in the front parlor, with Abel backed against the far wall, cornered by his own questioning mother. Why couldn't that woman accept the fact that Abel was not going to talk to her or anyone, no matter how hard she tried to make him? Why did she make matters worse by trying to force the child to talk to her? Had the woman no compassion? Mother or not, the thought of one day having to hand those two precious little boys over to someone like Clara Wilkins made Anna's stomach crawl. She could hardly wait until morning, when she could drive into town and send that telegram to New York.

Their only hope of keeping Jamie and Abel was if they could get a reply by Thursday that in some way confirmed Clara Wilkins had indeed signed away her parental rights to the children. If that proved to be the case, then it would be up to Judge Parish to decide which of them could provide a better home life, and remembering how wise and noble-hearted the judge could be, she felt confident he would give the matter his careful and thorough consideration before making a choice.

It really was their only hope.

Although Judge Parish did not arrive in Pinefield until almost three o'clock Thursday afternoon and normally would have waited until the following morning before consenting to see anyone about legal matters, he agreed to meet with Mark, Anna, and Clara in the courthouse at five.

Though Harry had wanted to come, too, so that he could give his very strong opinions on the matter, the judge had limited the meeting to the three most directly involved, in an effort to keep everything as uncomplicated as possible. And once he'd heard what the three had to say, he was very glad he had kept the meeting closed to others. The problem was more complex than he had at first thought.

"So, what it really amounts to is this," he said after having heard both sides. He looked first at Mark, then at Anna, noticing how concerned they were. "You two are still just as eager to adopt the boys as you've always been, and you want me to go through with signing the papers that will allow you to receive permanent custody."

He stroked his chin and thought more about it. "I must admit, had this new situation not arisen, and had a visit to your farm revealed further improvements, I had full intention of granting you the adoptions despite the fact it's only been six weeks instead of eight." He then glanced at Clara, who stood at the opposite corner of his desk, and tilted his head to one side to study her. "Yet now this woman has come here claiming to be the boys' biological mother and wants permission to take them with her."

"Yes, sir," Clara put in, then looked beseechingly at the judge. "I'm very eager to be on my way. I would have already left Pinefield with my boys, but I decided it would be better for everyone concerned if I stayed to get your blessing before I went."

"My blessing? Madam, I'm not a preacher. I'm a judge," he said, smiling slightly. "And I try to be a fair judge."

"Yes, sir," she said again, then quickly returned his smile. "I could tell that about you right off."

Sitting back in his chair, he folded his hands together over his waist and arched his brows, all the while studying her carefully. "Then you will understand when I tell you that I do not plan to make my decision today. I feel compelled to know what the Children's Aid Society has to say first. And since Mrs. Gates was thoughtful enough to have already sent a telegram asking them for the information I need, it shouldn't be but a few days before I can make a proper decision."

"But I've already waited five days," Clara complained. Her green eyes widened with concern. "Why make me wait any longer? I promise you, I *am* Jamie and Abel's real mother. I am the woman who gave birth to them."

"No one is disputing that fact," the judge assured

her. "But one of the things I'll have to know before I can make a final decision on this matter is whether or not your signature appears on any of the release forms. If it's not there, if you never signed anything relinquishing your rights, then there is nothing I can do but grant you permission to take those children. But if it does turn out that you signed away your parental rights, I'll have to make my decision by trying to determine which of you can provide the best home for the children. Their happiness is what's important here."

Without giving her further opportunity to protest, he turned to face Mark again. "While we are waiting for the reply from New York, I'll ask that the boys remain in your care and that you continue to offer Mrs. Wilkins a place to stay so she can be near them. I'll also want to proceed with my original plans, which include taking a short trip out to your farm to see if you have indeed completed all those improvements you claimed you'd have finished before my next visit. And then too, I'll want to have a talk with the boys while I'm there. I think they should have some say in what happens to them."

"Of course," Mark agreed.

His voice had revealed none of the churning turmoil he felt inside. If it were not for the way his grip had tightened on the handle of his cane, Anna would have thought him amazingly calm. Instead, she believed him amazingly strong.

"Then you won't have any real objections to my stopping by tomorrow afternoon?" The judge bent forward to make a quick notation in his appointment book.

"Not at all," Mark assured him. "Come whenever

you like."

"And the boys will be available to chat with me then?"

"I'll see that they are," Mark said, then ran his tongue across his upper lip before adding, "I want to do whatever I can to help."

"Fine. Then you should expect to see me there about two, or a little after." He then smiled at Anna, who had said very little. "And I wouldn't consider it a bribe of any sort if you were to offer me something cool to drink after I arrived. As hot as it has been here lately, I'd consider it a common courtesy."

Anna smiled for the first time since entering his chambers. "Is lemonade all right?"

"Lemonade will do just fine."

Clara's gaze narrowed when she too smiled, then rushed to insert, "I'll see to it that there are a few teacakes to go with that lemonade."

Anna glanced at her, stunned. That had been the first offer Clara had made to do anything at all since her arrival five days ago. Wondering over the woman's sudden generosity, Anna felt compelled to ask her if she even knew how to make teacakes, but then realized Clara had not offered to make any, just to see that there were some. So rather than chance sounding waspish when she needed to make the very best impression possible, she smiled sweetly and responded in a sugary voice, "Yes, Clara, I think it is a marvelous idea for you to bake teacakes for the judge. After that long ride out, I'm sure he'll be as hungry as he is thirsty. Since we'll probably finish the rest of the ones I made yesterday morning, you can get started on a fresh batch as soon as we get back."

"I look forward to sampling them," Judge Parish said as he glanced from one woman to the other. Quickly, he lifted his hand to hide the telltale twitch at the outer corner of his lips, knowing that if he decided to play the situation to his best advantage, he would probably end up with a complete steak dinner followed by a wide selection of desserts.

When Mark, Anna, and Clara returned to the house barely an hour later, they found Harry and Jamie sitting on the back porch trying to teach Old Shirley to dance to a lively tune Harry was playing on his harmonica. Though the scraggly chicken refused to shuffle her feet when they called out their encouraging commands, she did oblige them by flapping her wings wildly and tossing her head back and forth, which pleased Harry and Jamie immensely and earned her several tiny pieces from one of Harry's day-old biscuits.

"She might not be much use when it comes to layin' eggs," Harry called out to them when he noticed the carriage enter the yard, as if he felt it was necessary to offer some sort of explanation for what they were doing, "but we've proved one thing — the old girl's still got some life left in her."

Not wanting to know more about this odd undertaking of theirs, Anna shook her head while she climbed down from the buggy. "Where's Abel?" she asked. Because those had been the first words she'd spoken since having left the judge's chambers an hour earlier, they had come out scratchy sounding.

"Up in his room." Jamie said, then frowned and looked off in the general direction of their bedroom.

"We tried to get him to come down and see what we've taught Old Shirley to do, but he's only come out of that room once all day long, and that was to go to the privy. Then he grabbed up a couple of peaches on his way back upstairs." Jamie looked back at her and shook his head apologetically, as if he felt he was partly at fault.

"Then he *did* eat something?" Anna asked, relieved. Just before they had left for town, she had gone upstairs to tell him good-bye and noticed that the tray she'd carried up to him had gone untouched. Rather than leave the food up there to spoil, she had taken the tray away, hoping he would have a better appetite by supper.

"I *guess* he ate them." Jamie shrugged. "I didn't see him take a bite or anything like that, but I can't figure any other reason for him to snatch them up, other than that he was hungry."

By that time, Mark and Clara had also descended from the buggy and joined the others near the back porch. Although they had walked side by side, neither had given any indication that the other was there. Both had stared angrily straight ahead.

"How'd it go?" Harry asked, unable to wait a moment longer to find out what the judge's decision had been. Though he'd searched all three faces for some indication of who had come away the victor, still he had no clue.

His whiskered face twisted into a perplexed frown when no one answered his question. He tried again. "So, what did the judge have to say?"

Finally Mark responded. "He wants to wait until we've received the reply from the Children's Aid Society before he makes any decisions."

Because Mark and Anna's backs were to Clara, only Harry noticed the way her green eyes darkened and her arms stiffened across her chest. Clearly, the woman was not pleased with the delay.

"Makes sense to me," Harry said, watching while tiny lines of anger formed at the outer corners of Clara's eyes. Oo-wee, was she ever furious! He fought a sudden urge to chuckle. "Well, supper's about ready. Maybe one of you should go up and see if you can persuade Abel into comin' down and eatin' with the rest of us."

"I'll go," Clara volunteered, heading immediately for the door.

"I'll go, too," Anna said and hurried to follow, not wanting to give her a chance to be alone with him.

Harry waited until both women were well inside before he scratched his whiskers, then suggested to Jamie, "Might be better to go put Old Shirley back in her pen. It's about time for us to be puttin' that supper we cooked on the table."

As soon as Jamie had gathered the squawking hen in his arms and was well on his way to the coop, Harry turned his full attention back to Mark. "So, tell me, what do you think your chances are? Did the judge give you any indication at all?"

Mark shook his head and shrugged, his gaze focused off in the distance, though on nothing in particular. "Hard to say. If it turns out that Clara's signature is indeed on those permission papers, then I think Anna and I might have as good a chance as Clara, if not better, of getting the boys. But if her signature is not there, if there's no evidence that she participated in leaving her sons at that orphanage, then there's not much we can do. The judge says he will have to allow her to take them."

Harry's ragged eyebrows arched high into his weathered forehead, an indication he had not given up hope. "At least he's willing to wait and see what those orphan people have to say about all this. I was afraid he might want to go on and get this whole matter over with by making some sort of snap decision — in favor of *her*." Harry had refused to refer to Clara by name right from the beginning.

"Well, he didn't," Mark said, also finding solace in the fact that the judge was willing to take every precaution before making a decision. "He's coming out here sometime tomorrow afternoon to look over all the improvements I've completed since he was here about six weeks ago. He also wants to talk to the boys and find out what their feelings are."

Harry heaved a relieved sigh and shoved his battered hat to the back of his head. He rubbed his forehead with the flat of his palm as if trying to soothe his own frayed nerves. His pale green eyes searched Mark's face for an indication of his thoughts. Then he asked, "That's got to be a good sign, don't you think? He wouldn't bother comin' all the way out here to check on everything unless he was still pretty darned serious about choosin' you two to be Jamie and Abel's parents."

"All we can do at this point is hope," Mark said, reaching out to pat his friend's shoulder reassuringly. "Hope that the judge continues to take his time and then makes the right choice for the boys."

Because Jamie returned at that moment, ready to help Harry with the last of the supper preparations, Mark left. He went upstairs to change out of the three-piece summer suit he had put on, hoping to impress the judge. But now that he was back home, he wanted to change into a pair of comfortable denims and a shirt that wasn't as stiff as wood from all the starch.

Meanwhile, Harry could not stop thinking about everything Mark had told him, and about the judge's decision to visit with the boys the following afternoon. While he ladled thick beef stew out of the kettle into a large serving bowl, he wondered what Jamie's thoughts were about going off to California with his mother. The boy had never really said much to him about it. Was he for it, or did he prefer the idea of staying right there with Mark and Anna? Rather than predict, he decided to find out.

"I hear Californy is a right wild and adventurous place," he said, as a way of leading into the subject. "Just the sort of place a boy your age would want to go to."

"I suppose," Jamie said, while snatching the biscuits Harry had just taken out of the oven off the pan and dropping them onto a large plate.

"And I hear that mother of yours has a big house just waitin' for her out there," Harry continued, glancing over at the boy out of the corner of his eye.

Jamie's head came up, his expression confused. "I thought Anna was my mother now." The napkin he'd been using like a hot pad slipped out of his hand and fell unnoticed to the floor.

When Harry saw the stark pain that flickered across the boy's face, he wished he'd kept his big mouth shut. He hadn't meant to worry Jamie. He'd just been curious to know where he stood. Setting the ladle aside, he turned to face the boy squarely.

"As far as I'm concerned, Anna is your mother. But I'm afraid my opinion doesn't really matter too much. The final decision is still up to that judge."

Jamie shoved the plate across the counter hard enough that it should have broken when it hit the wall. He then looked at the back door as if planning to bolt from the room, but in the end, he picked the plate up and resumed tossing biscuits onto it, this time using his bare hands. It was several minutes before he spoke again. "If the judge decides that our first mother is still our real mother, then we'll have to go off with her, won't we?"

Harry tugged at the towel he'd been using as an apron, jerking it out of his waistband, then set it aside as he hurried to put his arms around Jamie.

"I'm afraid so," he said, kneeling so he could hold the child close. "But we're goin' to do all we can to see that that don't happen. And tomorrow you're goin' to get a chance to tell the judge yourself exactly how you feel about everything. He's comin' out here just so he can talk with you about it."

Mark's eyes widened with renewed hope. "He is? Do you think, if I tell him how me and Abel want to stay here, he'll let us?"

Harry closed his eyes and hugged the boy closer. "Only if it turns out your mother is lyin' about never havin' signed nothin'. But I'm afraid, if she's tellin' the truth about that, the judge might have no other choice than to let her take you with her."

"No!" Jamie wailed, then buried his face deep in the wrinkled folds of Harry's cotton shirt. "I want to stay here. So does Abel. We both want to stay here."

Tears filled Harry's eyes while he continued to hold the boy close. Sadly, he tilted his head forward, resting his whiskered cheek on Jamie's head. Fighting the pain that filled his chest, he spoke in a low, husky voice. "And we want you to stay here, too. We all do . . . we want that more than anything else on this earth."

It was several minutes before either one attempted to pull away, and then it was only when Harry felt certain his tears were no longer noticeable.

"Well, I reckon we'd better get a move on with this here supper," he said, tryin to get their thoughts off a situation they were powerless to change. "I imagine everyone's gettin' pretty hungry by now."

"I reckon so," Jamie said with a sniff, then hurried to put the last two biscuits on the serving plate, trying his very best to be brave. "They're probably ready to shoot us by now."

But as it turned out, no one seemed to have much of an appetite, and most of the stew went uneaten, as did the biscuits. Conversation was at a minimum, and what was said came out sounding awkward and forced.

Mark, wanting to spend every minute possible with the boys before they had to go off to bed, did not linger long at the supper table. As soon as Harry and Anna had started to clear the table, he and Jamie went upstairs to see if they could persuade Abel to leave his room and go with them to the barn to check on the new colt and feed Jamie's pet squirrel. It was at Jamie's insistence that Abel finally agreed. Minutes later, the three of them left the house.

Though they were gone for over half an hour, to Mark it had seemed like only a few minutes. Aware the telegraph from New York could come through at any time and had the power to alter every aspect of his life, he savored their time together, feasting his eyes upon every little detail about the boys.

His heart felt like a heavy weight inside his chest while he tried to memorize every tiny freckle on Jamie's nose and each shaggy little curl on Abel's dark head. Often, he had to turn away and fight a very real urge to cover his face and cry. How he hated the possibility of losing the boys, of no longer being allowed to gaze down into their bright, smiling faces or hear their high-pitched, little-boy laughter. The resulting pain was so severe, so all consuming, that he was not sure he could bear it much longer. Then, when he thought of losing Anna, too, he knew he needed time alone—time to shed some of these painful emotions in private.

Reluctantly, he returned the boys to the house so Anna could help them prepare for bed. As soon as they had disappeared from his sight, he walked straight through the house and stepped out onto the front veranda. Alone at last, he saw no reason to hold back his tears. Leaning heavily against the nearest porch column, he bent his head and wept quietly. When he had regained control and lifted his head he realized he was not alone. Someone or something had moved in the darkness at the far end of the veranda.

Turning toward the movement, he hoped to find his old yellow cat perched along his favorite windowsill, but noticed instead that a large black shape rested in one of the lounge chairs at the furthermost end of the veranda. "Harry, is that you?"

"No. Mr. Munn left about fifteen minutes ago," came the soft-voiced reply.

Mark's stomach compressed into a hard lump of anguish when he realized the black shape was Clara. He hated that she had witnessed his tears.

"What are you doing out here?" he asked, striving to control the emotion in his voice.

"Obviously the same thing you are. I wanted some time alone to do a little thinking," she said, then slowly rose from the chair and came toward him.

"I'm sorry I interrupted," Mark said, already heading for the door, wanting no further confrontation with her. "I'll go back inside so you may have your privacy."

"No, please—wait. I want to talk to you."

There was something about her voice, some unexplainable urgency, that made him turn back to hear her out. "What is it? The boys?"

"Yes."

Although no one had made an effort to light one of the outdoor lanterns, nor were any of the front windows aglow with indoor light, Mark's eyes had adjusted well enough to see that Clara had nodded. He wished he could make out her expression, but it was too dark. "What is it you want to say?"

There was a long, heavy silence before she answered. "I'll be quick about it. What I have in mind boils down to this: for fifteen thousand dollars, I'd be willing to leave here and never come back. You would then be free to adopt the boys. I'd even agree to sign a paper telling the judge that I have changed my mind and that I give my full consent to the adoption."

Mark stood dumbfounded, unable to believe he'd heard her right. "You mean to tell me that you would be willing to sell me those two boys for fifteen thousand dollars?"

"I wouldn't be selling them to you, exactly," she replied, her tone bordering on indignant. "It's just that I don't want to have to wait around here any longer. I'm very eager to be on my way to California, and I fear it might be weeks yet before the judge gets any information from that orphanage."

"It would still be selling the boys to me," Mark pointed out, angry that she could even consider such a thing.

"To me, it would be more like an exchange of gifts," she retorted angrily. "My gift to you would be the boys. Your gift to me would be to help pay some of my traveling expenses."

"Fifteen thousand dollars? Those must be some traveling expenses," he muttered, shaking his head to let her know he was not that stupid.

"I like to travel in style," she snapped angrily, but then turned her voice silky smooth. "Think about it, Mark. All you'd have to do is give me that money tonight and I'd write that letter and be gone from here by morning. The boys would be yours."

"Do you honestly think I keep that sort of money laying around?" he asked. His voice rose with anger. "I happen to be a man who believes in keeping his money in a bank, but I don't happen to have that kind of money, even in the bank. I've sunk most of my money into getting this place back in shape so the judge will see how eager I am to provide the boys with a proper home. Just last week I paid Jake Simmons two thousand dollars to buy two hundred head of cattle for me while he was in Fort Worth. And I sent an extra three hundred to defray any shipping costs getting them here."

305

"And there's no way you can get your hands on fifteen thousand dollars?" Clara asked, clearly unconvinced. "Not even from your friend Harry?"

"Harry is not a rich man either. Between the two of us, I doubt we could come up with a full thousand."

"That's too bad," Clara said with a haughty shake of her head. "Because when the judge gets that telegram from New York verifying that my signature is nowhere to be found, I'll be free to leave here with my sons and there won't be anything you can do to stop me. But if you could somehow get me that money by, say, tomorrow noon, you wouldn't have to worry about any more trouble from me. I'd be on my way to California within the hour."

The muscles in Mark's jaw tensed while he thought more about it. The only way he could get that much money would be to sell his ranch, but in doing that he would also be selling his livelihood, which would probably cause the adoption to fall through anyway. But then again, if she would be willing to bargain with him, he could try to pay her something. He'd do anything to keep the boys—and Anna.

"What if I were to give you three thousand now, and sign a note promising to send you a thousand a year for the next twelve years?"

"I thought you couldn't come up with even a thousand dollars," she pointed out, her tone accusing.

"I could probably get a loan from the bank for that much," he explained. Clenching his jaw, he spoke his next words through his teeth. "Well, what do you think? Would you agree to three thousand now, followed by a thousand a year for the next twelve years?"

"No," she said with finality. "Either you promise to come up with all fifteen thousand by tomorrow noon, or you can forget it. I'd rather have the boys anyway."

Mark's boot tapped impatiently on the planked floor. "What if I could come up with five thousand dollars by noon tomorrow and agreed to pay you the rest at a thousand a year?"

"No. Either you hand me the entire fifteen thousand, or it is no deal."

"There's no way I can come up with that kind of money by tomorrow noon, even if I wanted to."

"Then it looks like there's no deal," she said with an indignant toss of her head. "The boys will go with me to California." She then spun about and marched into the house, her arms swinging stiffly at her sides.

Chapter Seventeen

Anna was so furious when she later learned of Clara's offer to sell the children that Mark had to restrain her physically to keep her from charging out of their bedroom, right up the stairs, and telling that woman exactly what she thought of her.

"Let me go," Anna insisted, squirming in an effort to free herself from the hard, muscular arms wrapped around her waist. It was frustrating to know she had gotten within a foot of the door when he caught up with her. Even now, if she stretched forward far enough, she could probably touch the brass door handle with her fingers; but as tight as he held her, it would do her no good.

Obviously, she was not going anywhere until he decided to let go, and no amount of squirming would free her. If they hadn't already begun preparing for bed, she would still have on her boots, and could try a backward kick to his shins, but in her stockinged feet, she doubted the action would have much effect. She was trapped. It seemed ironic that the very arms that had become her haven now held her prisoner.

"I'm not letting go until you've calmed down," Mark stated, arching his neck to keep from being butted under the chin with the top of her bobbing head. Yet, despite the immediate danger to his jaw, he refused to loosen his hold. "Anna, it won't do anyone a bit of good for you to go storming upstairs to start an argument with Clara."

"Yes it would. It would make me feel a lot better," she muttered, though she slowly gave up her struggle for freedom. She knew he was right. Telling the woman off, no matter how deserving she was, would do more harm than good. Finally, she stopped fighting him completely and relaxed in his arms, defeated.

When he felt the weight of her body lean back against him, he loosened his grip so she could turn around to face him, yet still be held securely in his arms.

Anna's face changed from pouting with defeat to pure, opened-eyed confusion when she asked, "But how could she do such a thing? What kind of a person is she?"

"I've asked myself that exact same question," he admitted with a slow, questioning shake of his head. He gazed down into Anna's pale green eyes, perplexed by it all. "What sort of woman would attempt to sell her own children like that?"

There was a long pause when neither could come up with an answer.

Suddenly in need of Mark's comfort, Anna parted his already unbuttoned shirt and laid her cheek against the warm, solid muscles across his chest. His chest hair felt springy and soft against her face, making her want to close her eyes and enjoy the feeling.

Although she knew she shouldn't, because she knew Mark would not always be there for her, she had started to rely more on his strength and less on her own. "What happens if Judge Parish decides Jamie and Abel belong with her? How can we let them leave with Clara, knowing the kind of woman she really is?"

"What we have to do is make the judge see her for what she is," Mark answered. "For starters, I plan to tell Judge Parish all about my conversation with Clara tonight. I realize that if he decides to question her about the incident, it will end up being her word against mine; but I really think he should be told. Even if it does little more than put a nagging doubt in his mind, he needs to know."

Anna opened her eyes and stared absently at the dark hair that ran in soft, smooth patterns across his chest. "But what if he decides you made up the whole thing hoping to make Clara look bad?"

"I still think I should tell him," Mark said, then lifted her cheek away from his chest. "If I don't tell him, and Clara Wilkins ends up with Jamie and Abel, I will probably regret having kept silent for the rest of my life."

"There's no probably to it. I *know* you will," Anna agreed, smiling as she gazed up into the concerned depths of his pale blue eyes. Her heart gave a tiny jump. How she adored him! "And I agree. Judge Parrish should be told. I just hope that when you do tell him about her, he believes you."

"Well, we'll know tomorrow whether he believes me or not. If I can catch him alone, I plan to tell him then."

"I'll try to keep Clara away," she volunteered, and continued to gaze longingly into the crystal depths of his blue eyes. How she wished he would kiss her. Couldn't he see that? Was he so concerned with the boys that he did not realize how desperately she needed the comfort of his lovemaking? Did she dare ask for it?

As if suddenly able to read her thoughts, Mark smiled briefly, then slowly lowered his head, touching his lips lightly to hers, as if he wanted to do nothing more than sample her sweetness. But when his lips came down for a second kiss, it was with the passion of a man possessed. He was rewarded with an appreciative moan.

Still aware that each night they shared could be their last, because at any moment that telegram from New York could arrive and destroy everything he'd fought so hard to gain, Mark opened his mouth and dipped his tongue past her lips, wanting nothing less than to devour her, body and soul.

Filled with the hunger of a starving man soon to be denied his one true source of food, Mark pulled her closer, molding her soft curves against the hard, muscular planes of his body. How desperately he loved her. Although he knew he would suffer traumatically should he lose the boys, he could eventually recover from that loss, but his life would be worthless without Anna. He could not bear the thought of losing her too.

Anna felt the same about Mark. Wondering how she could ever endure life without him, she lifted her arms to circle his neck. She tilted her head farther to one side to kiss him. The thought that each time they made love could very well be the last time was devastating. It made every encounter between them, each sharing of their passion for one another, a treasured experience.

Overwhelmed by her own needs, Anna wrapped her arms tighter around him, drawing him closer, wishing there was some way to pull him right inside her. Hungrily, she met his kisses with a passion equal to his, dipping the tip of her tongue into his mouth at every opportunity. Closing her eyes to enjoy the pleasure she found in his arms, she leaned heavily against him and allowed herself to be swept away by the raging tidal wave that had risen to claim her body.

In a continued effort to draw him into her, Anna's fingernails bit through his soft cotton shirt and with each ravishing kiss, with each new place his hands touched, her trembling need became more demanding.

Quickly, Mark undressed her while she struggled to free him of his clothes. Never had they encountered such contrary garments. Clothing fell in all directions until they finally stood in each other's arms, totally and gloriously naked, husband against wife.

For several minutes they enjoyed the feel of pressing their bodies intimately together while they resumed the hungry assault of each other's mouth. But their need for more became too great too quickly. Soon Mark nudged her toward the bed and she went willingly.

On the soft feather mattress, in frantic exploration, their hands roamed freely over each other's body. They delighted in the feel of every curve and every flat surface, each wondering if it would be the last time they would share such pleasure.

Willingly, Anna lost herself to the tumultuous sea of sensations that Mark always aroused in her. She became further intoxicated by the sweet taste and the spicy scent that assailed her senses, and felt as if she was drifting aimlessly without anchor. Her heart raced at amazing speed and her pulse pounded with incredible force while she yielded to his every touch.

Responding to the splendid furor that had risen inside her, Anna reached first for his shoulders, then for his waist, then finally his hips, pulling at him, trying to make him aware that she could wait no longer. She needed the sort of fulfillment only Mark could provide.

Obligingly, he rose above her, then down, until finally he became a part of her. Caught up in her resplendent need, Anna moved with him, matching him thrust for thrust. Her breath became short and strained while desire rose ever higher inside her, until finally pure-white ecstasy exploded within her and stole her breath from her.

Within seconds, a similar, deeply shuddering explosion wracked Mark's body, causing him to gasp aloud. Though it seemed impossible, their lovemaking grew more potent each time.

Mark fell back into the softness of the pillows beside her, so astounded by the incredible power of their lovemaking that at first he could not speak. Silently, he lay with her at his side, unwilling to release her from his embrace.

It was several minutes before he found the strength to speak. "Anna, there's something I think you should know."

"What?" she asked, turning in his arms and raising an elbow so she could look into his face. Her heart ached with cold dread when she saw the seriousness in his expression. Was he about to remind her of that promise to give him a divorce should they lose the boys? Please, no . . . not yet. Fighting her tears, she lowered her head to his shoulder and steeled herself for the worst.

Mark arched his neck so he could continue to look at her. He wanted to see her reaction. "I'm not sure exactly when it happened, and I know I should have tried harder not to let it happen, but it is something I couldn't help."

"What?" Her body tensed in preparation for his answer.

"Anna, I think you should know — I've fallen deeply in love with you."

Anna's head came off his shoulder with a start. She was not at all sure she'd heard him correctly. "You *what?*"

Mark studied her wide-eyed expression for a long moment, wishing he had the ability to read her thoughts, then took a deep breath before repeating his message. "I've fallen in love with you."

When she opened her mouth to speak, he stopped her by placing his fingertips gently against her lips. "I know. I have agreed to give you a divorce if and when the boys no longer needed you here for them. And if it turns out Clara does get custody of Jamie and Abel, I'm not going to go back on my word. I just wanted you to know how I feel. The thought of losing you is ripping me apart."

For several seconds, Anna was too overwhelmed with disbelief and joy to say anything. All she could do was stare at him in amazement while she blinked back a sudden rush of tears. When she finally did find her voice, it was so strained with happiness, her words sounded strangled. "Oh, Mark . . . is it really? Is the thought of losing me really ripping you apart? Do you really love me?"

Mark nodded then swallowed to remove the sudden constriction blocking his throat. "I couldn't help it."

"Oh, Mark!" she cried, half-sobbing, half-laughing. "Don't you know that I love you, too? The thought of leaving here was breaking my heart, too."

Mark took a minute to let her words sink in. "Then you'll stay? No matter what the outcome with the boys, you'll stay here with me? As my wife?"

"Until death us do part," she said, repeating the vows she'd spoken not two months earlier. Unable to contain the joy bubbling inside her, she squealed with delight when Mark pulled her down on top of him, his arms hugging her so tightly she could hardly breathe.

"Why didn't you tell me you'd fallen in love with me, woman?" Mark demanded playfully. "Why did you let me suffer like that?"

"I didn't know—" she began only to have the explanation cut short by a wildly passionate kiss, which was immediately followed by another, and another, until they were again soaring to that pinnacle of passion they'd both come to know so well.

After having found fulfillment a second time that night, Mark thought for certain he'd be able to fall asleep, but although he did doze from time to time, it was almost morning before he finally slipped into a deep, restless sleep.

When the bright summer sunlight that slanted in through the window near his bed reached his face, he awoke with such a start, it made Anna cry out in alarm.

"What's wrong?" she asked, looking around.

Mark blinked several times, trying to shed his muddled thoughts. What had happened? Lifting his head off the pillow, he stared curiously at the sunlight streaming across his chest. "What time is it?"

Anna rolled over and glanced at the clock on the

mantle, surprised at the time. "Why, it's after nine o'clock. How'd we ever sleep so late?"

Instantly alarmed, Mark sat up and cocked his head at a slight angle. "Listen."

Anna fell silent and tried her best to hear whatever it was he wanted her to hear. "To what? I don't hear anything."

"That's just it. I don't either. Why aren't the boys up? Why haven't they come to our door, clamoring for breakfast?"

"Maybe they overslept, too," Anna suggested, though the tightened muscles in her stomach told her differently.

"Something's wrong. I can feel it in my bones," Mark said, already throwing the covers back and reaching for his underdrawers, then his trousers, which had been carelessly flung over the arm of a chair.

Anna also hurried to dress, but when she saw that all Mark intended to do was put on a pair of pants and a shirt, she realized she did not have time to bother with getting dressed. Snatching her robe out of the wardrobe, she barely had time to secure the sash before Mark bolted from the room, leaving both his cane and her behind.

"Mark, wait," she called after him, but despite his immobile leg, Mark was already halfway up the stairs by the time she had stepped out into the hallway.

Running as quickly as her bare feet would allow, Anna arrived outside the boys' room only a few seconds behind Mark. But by the time she entered the door, he was already on his way out.

"They aren't there," he informed her, his voice filled with panic. "Neither are their clothes."

A quick glance around the room revealed he was right. Their wardrobe stood against the far wall with both doors open. Nothing remained inside. Several drawers lay on the floor empty, and the bedsheets were twisted and tangled and lay more on the floor than not. It looked as if there had been a struggle. The pillow from Jamie's bed was on the floor, but without any pillowcase, and the pillow that had been on Abel's bed was missing altogether.

Turning, Anna followed Mark across the hall, to the bedroom Clara had been using. She clasped her hands over her chest as if to protect herself from any more pain. The fear that already engulfed her was so powerful, it threatened each throbbing beat of her heart. "Where are they?"

"I don't know," Mark answered just before he leaned into Clara's bedroom and found a similar mess. "But I sure intend to find out." He then turned and stormed back toward the stairs.

"Where are you going?" she wanted to know, afraid of what he might do.

"To the barn. To see if they took either the buggy or the wagon. I doubt they went on horseback. Abel won't get on a horse. And if they are on foot, there's a very good chance I can still catch them. But, if Clara knows enough about hitching up a horse to have taken one of the vehicles, then I'll need to get right into town and round up some help. They could be halfway to anywhere by now." He had already started down the stairs.

"Aren't you going to finish getting dressed first?" she asked.

"No time," he shouted back, already out of her sight. "But I'll grab up my boots on the way out."

"Don't forget your cane," she shouted, worried that

as hurried as he was, he might fall without it; but she knew the reminder had come too late when barely a second later, she heard the back door slam. He was already on his way to the barn.

Anna didn't know whether to follow Mark or to heed her own advice and take the time to get dressed. Finally, she decided it would be wiser to have clothes on. By the time she finished dressing, Mark would have returned to the house with a full report on what he'd discovered out in the barn.

Because the clothing strewn about the bedroom floor was the handiest, Anna quickly dressed in the same clothing she had worn the day before. The only change she made was in her stockings, but only because she could not find the ones she'd had on the night before.

When Mark failed to return to the house by the time she had finished dressing, she decided to go out to the barn to see what was keeping him. Worried that he'd left without her, she called out as soon as she had stepped outside. "Mark? Where are you?"

"In here," came his immediate response.

Relieved to know he was still in the barn, Anna lifted her skirts and hurried across the yard, wondering again what had kept him. When she stepped inside, she was surprised to find that he'd already saddled one horse and was busily harnessing a second horse to the wagon.

"She took that buggy and horse she'd rented from the livery in town. We've got no time to waste. I want you to climb into this wagon and ride over to Harry's as soon as I finish getting her hitched. Tell Harry what happened. Tell him to saddle up and meet me in town," he stated, having guessed some of her questions even before she asked. "Meanwhile, I'll ride on into Pinefield and try to get as much help as I can. Tell Harry to go straight to the sheriff's office. If I'm not there when he arrives, tell him I soon will be."

Anna did not question any of his decisions. Instead, she returned immediately to the house for a sunbonnet and Mark's pistol. Though she had no real reason to believe Clara was a violent person, she felt it would be a good idea to carry along some protection. After all, the woman was capable of selling her own children. There was no telling what else she might do.

By the time Anna had snatched up a sunbonnet, located the pistol, checked to be sure it was loaded, and then returned to the barn, Mark had already left. Quickly, she tucked the pistol into one of the small wooden compartments built under the seat and made a mental note to try to remember to give it to Mark as soon as she reached town.

She waited until she had settled onto the wooden seat and had prodded the horse into a fast trot before pulling the sunbonnet over her head and tying it into place. Though summer had not yet officially begun, for it was only the second week of June, the sun was hot and she'd discovered how easily she could sunburn that first day Mark had taken her horseback riding.

When Anna drove within view of Harry's house, she saw him standing outside in the corral beside his favorite horse. He was busy currying the animal's sleek black coat when he first glanced up and noticed that she was traveling unusually fast. He wasted little time climbing over the wooden fence before crossing the yard to greet her.

"What's up?" he asked, pushing his battered work

hat back on his head so he could see her face.

"Clara has taken the boys."

All color drained from Harry's face, leaving him pale and drawn. "She what?"

"She took the boys, sometime during the night. Mark has gone into town to report it to the sheriff and see if he can talk some of the people in town into helping us find them. He wants you to meet him at the sheriff's office."

Before Anna had finished, Harry was already on his way back to the corral. With the agility of a man half his age, he scampered back over the planked fence and entered the barn. Seconds later, he came back out with a saddle in his arms and a leather bridle draped around his neck.

"I'm going on," Anna called to him, aware the bulky wagon would slow her down. "I'll see you at the sheriff's office."

The only indication that Harry had heard her was a brisk wave of his hand. Aware he was probably too overcome with emotion to speak, Anna gave the reins a sharp flick and started on her way into town.

As expected, Harry passed her several minutes later. He slowed down to reaffirm that Mark wanted him to go directly to the sheriff's office, then forced his horse into a fast gallop. Within seconds, he was around the next bend and out of Anna's sight.

Frustrated that the horse could not pull the wagon any faster than a trot, Anna dearly wished Mark had saddled the animal instead. True, she did not have a lot of experience when it came to riding horseback, but she'd had enough practice during the last few weeks to be able to direct the animal and stay in the saddle. But then again, saddling her a horse would have cost them precious time. She would've had to go back inside and change into one of her split skirts. Mark had probably realized how long that would take, and time had been far too important at that moment. Every second counted.

Biting her lower lip, she flicked the reins harder, but the horse was already traveling at top speed. It had been trained to go at a trot when in harness and refused to go against that training. All Anna could do was hang on to the bouncing wooden seat as best she could, and pray she did not arrive in Pinefield too late. She was not quite sure Mark would wait for her if she was too long in getting there.

By the time Mark finally reached town, he realized what had bothered him about that conversation Clara had had with Jamie and Abel the other afternoon. Originally, she had used the word *we* when she mentioned having left the boys at the orphanage. But then, only minutes later, she had declared she was never aware of what her husband had in mind until he'd already done it. How could both be true? Either she *was* with her husband when the boys were left at the orphanage, or he had indeed taken them there behind her back and then told her later.

The woman had to be lying which was why she had stolen the boys in the middle of the night. She was afraid of what the telegram from New York might reveal. In fact, Mark now felt absolutely certain that Clara Wilkins's signature would indeed be found at the bottom of those permission papers. That would also explain why she had been suddenly so eager to bargain the boys off. She knew exactly how slim her chances would be once that telegram arrived and wanted to salvage *something* out of the situation. But the most important question was why did she want her sons back enough to steal them, especially since she was willing to sell them?

Overcome with anger, Mark rode directly to the sheriff's office, relieved to discover the man already outside, standing on the boardwalk, talking with Reverend Cross.

"I've got trouble," he called out as he brought his horse to a halt only a few feet away. Then he swung his leg over the saddle and dropped agilely to the bricked street.

"What sort of trouble?" the sheriff asked. He turned to watch while Mark looped his reins loosely around the hitching rail. The reverend, too, turned to face him.

"Clara Wilkins has kidnapped Jamie and Abel. She took them right out of their beds sometime last night."

The sheriff's eyes widened when he met Mark's frantic gaze. "Who is this Clara Wilkins? Why would she want to kidnap your boys?"

"She's their mother," Mark answered, his words coming in a rush. "Their natural mother. Last Saturday she suddenly showed up at my place, wanting Jamie and Abel back. Of course we weren't about to give up the boys so we decided to let the court handle it. In fact, are still waiting for the judge to decide. But evidently, she didn't want to wait for that. She was probably afraid of what we would find out. Afraid the judge would then refuse to let her have them. So she took them."

"Slow down," the sheriff said, pushing his hat back on his head, while he tried to sort out what Mark was trying to tell him, "Now give that to me one more time. You say this Clara Wilkins is actually their mother?"

"Maybe."

"Maybe? You don't know for sure? Did the boys seem to think she is?" The sheriff could not have looked more puzzled.

"Oh, she was their mother, all right, but that was before the boys were left at that New York orphanage. But she swears she had nothing to do with that. I think she did. At any rate, the judge was looking into the matter for us, but hadn't gotten the response yet."

"From whom?" The sheriff looked more confused by the minute. He glanced at the reverend to see if he was comprehending any of this.

Mark sighed impatiently. "From the Children's Aid Society. Judge Parish is expecting a telegram from them any day."

"But as far as you know, this Clara Wilkins is their real mother?" the sheriff asked.

"If you mean, did she give birth to them, yes," Mark replied, frustrated that the sheriff had not grasped the situation.

"Then I'm afraid there's not much I can do. It's just not considered kidnapping if a mother takes her own children."

"But there's a very good chance she may have given up all of her parental rights to the boys when they were left at the orphanage two years ago. We won't really know until that telegram arrives."

"Still, I'm not sure I have a legal right to help you chase this woman down until then." He scratched his head and studied the very real panic on Mark's face. "Tell you what. Let's go over and have us a quick talk with the judge. He'll know if I have any legal right to get involved in this."

Irritated over the time that would waste, Mark heaved out a frustrated breath, then turned and headed toward the courthouse, his hands balled into fists at his sides.

"Not that way," the reverend called to him. "I saw Judge Parish just a few minutes ago. He was entering the hotel, and it looked like he was carrying a yellow piece of paper that just might be that telegram you mentioned."

Mark's heart leaped with sudden anticipation when he spun around and followed Sheriff Weathers and Reverend Cross toward the hotel several blocks away. Anxious to know if the judge had indeed gotten the telegram, he had soon rounded the two men and was rapidly putting distance between himself and them.

When he entered the hotel lobby, he was further frustrated to discover the judge not among the usual loiterers. Frowning, he stepped over to a pair of older men bent over a game of dominoes. "Has either of you seen Judge Parish?"

Without ever looking up from the table, they both pointed toward the door that led into a small restaurant owned by the same couple who had just recently bought the hotel.

Having caught up with Mark by then, the sheriff and reverend entered the restaurant right behind him. Because of the late morning hour, there were only four men inside and none of them was the judge.

Recognizing Jeff Wells among the four, Mark asked his friend if he had seen the judge.

The young man looked surprised to see him, but did not question his reason for being there or the fact that he was now walking. "Sure I've seen him. He just left here with a cup of coffee in his hand.

Probably headed back to the courthouse."

Angered more, because that had been his original destination, Mark stormed outside and headed down the street toward the judge's chambers. When he arrived inside the building seconds before the sheriff and a minute before the reverend, he felt like screaming with rage. The judge was not there. No one was. He felt as if he was living a nightmare.

"Well?" he asked, turning to face the two men who had stood quietly behind him. "Where do you suggest we look now?"

The sheriff shrugged and glanced at Reverend Cross, as if hoping for an answer.

"It's Friday. Maybe he stopped by the *Gazette* to get a newspaper."

No sooner had he spoken the words than Mark was on his way.

Chapter Eighteen

When Anna arrived in town, Harry was already seated on one of the narrow benches that sat out in front of the sheriff's office, impatiently tapping his foot, causing a hollow sound against the boardwalk. With arms crossed and a scowl deeply etched in his face, he continuously looked both ways, obviously still waiting for Mark.

There were three horses tied to the hitching rail out front. The two blacks Anna recognized as Mark's and Harry's. The other, a large bay with a white splash across his chest, no doubt belonged to the sheriff. At least they had not left without her.

When Anna brought the wagon to an abrupt halt in front of the alleyway that divided the sheriff's office from the feed store, Harry jumped to his feet and hurried to talk with her.

"H'ain't seen hide nor narry a hair of Mark since I got here. Sheriff ain't been here either. Are you sure Mark said for me to meet him here?"

"Yes. He said to meet him at the sheriff's office. He also said that if he wasn't here when you first arrived, he soon would be."

"Well, I've been here a good ten minutes already, and I haven't seen neither one of them," Harry muttered impatiently while rubbing his hand over his whiskered jaw, as if that might help him to figure out why he'd been kept waiting so long.

"Maybe they walked over to see the judge," Anna suggested, though she wasn't sure why they would. Judge Parish did not seem like the type to climb up onto a horse and join a search. Still, it was the first thought to have come to her mind. "Why don't I go over to the courthouse and see if they are there?"

Harry nodded that he thought that might be a good idea and stepped away from the wagon.

Flicking the reins, Anna focused her gaze on the courthouse lawn several blocks ahead. She was barely halfway there when she heard someone call her name. The voice had come from somewhere behind her. She turned in time to see the judge hurry out of the livery, headed in her direction. Quickly she pulled on the reins and brought the horse to a stop.

"Mrs. Gates. I was just hiring a rig so I could ride out to your place. I got the telegram." When he came to a halt just a few feet from the wagon, he patted the front of his summer coat to indicate he had tucked the telegram into one of the inside pockets.

She could tell by his expression that he was deeply concerned with whatever the telegram had revealed. "And? Did she ever sign any papers relinquishing her parental rights?"

"No," Judge Parish answered between rushed gasps for air. Having had to run to catch up with her, he was momentarily short of breath.

Anna's heart collapsed with pain and disappointment. Clara had told the truth, at least about that. The Children's Aid Society had offered the boys for adoption without ever obtaining the legal authorization. But how could that be? They were usually so careful about such matters. She closed her eyes against the tears.

Pressing his hand to his chest, Judge Parish rushed to explain, "She didn't have to sign anything. The boys were taken away from her by order of the court."

"What?" Anna's eyes opened wide as she too pressed her hand to her chest.

The judge reached into his pocket and came out with two rumpled sheets of yellow paper. Stepping forward, he offered them to her. "See for yourself. The children were removed from her and her husband's care because either she or her husband not only abused them both terribly, but had tried to trade them to a childless couple for two horses and a large overland wagon."

Anna looked down at the paper, but her mind was in too much of a whirl to concentrate on the message. While she listened to the judge, her fear for the children grew tenfold.

With the back of his finger, the judge tapped the paper she held to emphasize what he had to say. "That telegram tells us we are not to let either parent near those children. Seems those two boys were covered with hundreds of suspicious-looking cuts, bruises, and scars when the police brought them in. In fact, the younger brother was near death."

Anna's hand flew from her aching chest to her mouth. She had seen the scars, but had believed Jamie when he explained they had been the result of an accident. Although he had admitted he did not really remember the accident, he did remember someone telling him about it later. It had all been a blur in his mind at the time. Anna shuddered to think that the someone who had told him he'd been in an accident was probably one of his own parents, hoping to drum the accident story into his head, so he would then convince everyone else of the lie. Or maybe he had remembered at first, but found the memory too painful and had eventually cast it aside in favor of the lie.

The judge crossed his arms, satisfied with the outcome. "And, if that's the case, then I have no other recourse. I feel obligated to grant you and Mr. Gates permanent custody of the children like I had originally planned," the judge said with a bright, beaming smile. But when Anna did not smile in return, his forehead wrinkled and he peered quizzically at her. "What's wrong? Aren't you pleased?"

Anna felt so weak, she could hardly answer. "Clara kidnapped the boys last night. And we don't know where she's taken them."

"Oh, my word, no! What are you doing about it?"

Anna wished she knew. "Mark's trying to gather a few volunteers to help us look for her."

"Anna! Judge Parish!" Mark shouted from a block away, effectively interrupting the two. "Wait up. Don't move."

He immediately broke into a dead run, followed closely by the sheriff. Half a block behind, Reverend Cross continued at a brisk walk.

"Mark? Have you heard?" Anna asked, so bound by her painful emotions, her voice had sounded like that of a little girl.

"Heard what?"

Trembling too hard to say more, Anna thrust the two-page telegram at him. She broke into rasping sobs when she spoke. "Read this."

Glancing curiously at her, then at the paper, he was torn between the desire to jump up into the wagon to comfort her and his need to read what was obviously the telegram they had all been waiting for. Taking the paper, but not actually reading it, he then reached for her hand. Turning to the judge, he took a deep breath, then asked, "What does it say?"

"It says that Clara Wilkins has no legal rights to the children. It claims that in the guise of parental discipline, Clara and Frank Wilkins nearly beat their own children to death." His thin face grew rock hard. "Discipline is one thing. Physical torture is quite another."

"Then you think it's safe for me to round up a few men and start out after this woman?" the sheriff asked, trying not to look at Anna, who was making every effort to stop crying, but couldn't.

"Yes, quite safe," the judge assured him. "In fact, the sooner you go after this woman, the better. Those children could be in serious danger."

Anna closed her eyes against the resulting pain and willed herself to remain strong—for the children.

Within fifteen minutes, six men had agreed to help with the search. At the sheriff's request, they gathered in front of his office for last-minute instructions, which he quickly supplied. When it soon became apparent to Anna that she was not to be included, she stepped forward and demanded to know why.

"Well, I'd think that should be pretty obvious," the sheriff answered, looking down at her as if she had suddenly grown a third ear. "You're a woman."

Mark winced, aware that answer was not about to set well with Anna. Having come from up north, where women seemed to get away with far more than their counterparts from the south, Anna would not consider her gender a hindrance. Rather than let the sheriff take a brisk tongue-lashing in front of all these men, he hurried to intervene.

"Besides, Anna, you don't have a horse. And there's no way you can keep up with us in that wagon. Clara

330

has anywhere from a three- to six-hour head start on us. We'll have to move fast and ride as hard as we possibly can." Thinking he had come up with a far more acceptable excuse to leave her behind, he relaxed and turned to await further instructions from the sheriff.

"I can leave the wagon here and hire a fresh horse from the livery," Anna said, to everyone's surprise.

Frowning at her refusal to give up, Mark looked at her, his eyebrows arched with silent warning. "But you are not dressed for riding a saddle." He cast a meaningful glance at her ruffled skirt. "If you tried to sit on a saddle in that, you would end up showing off your legs to everyone in Pinefield. Granted, they are a beautiful sight to see, but I'd rather the entire town not be given that privilege."

Several sets of eyebrows shot up at the mention of Anna's legs.

Anna refused to be talked out of going, and she tossed her head back defiantly before meeting his gaze head on. "While a horse is being saddled for me, I can go over to the mercantile and buy a riding skirt to wear. It shouldn't take but a few minutes to put it on."

Mark's eyes narrowed, but when he opened his mouth to give his response, Anna never gave him a chance. Meeting his dark, angry gaze with one of her own, she calmly stated, "Whether I have your permission or not, I am going to help search for the boys. I will not be left behind."

Aware she meant every word, Mark finally shook his head with resignation, then glanced at the sheriff. "She can ride with Harry and me."

The sheriff appeared disgruntled by that decision, but did not argue. Instead, he turned to the others and continued with his instructions. As soon as each of the four groups had been assigned a specific direction to take, they all mounted and rode out, except for Mark and Harry, who had to wait for Anna.

While Mark went over to the livery to have a horse prepared, Anna hurried down the street to the mercantile. By the time she'd changed into the hastily purchased divided skirt and riding boots and had returned to the livery, her horse was ready and Mark and Harry had already mounted. Quickly she returned to the wagon and removed the pistol from the hidden compartment, then placed it in her saddlebag.

"Where did you get that?" Mark wanted to know, having looked up in time to see what she had done.

"The pistol? I got it from your desk. I thought we might need it."

Mark heaved an impatient sigh and stuck out his hand. "Give it to me. You don't know the first thing about shooting a firearm."

Not wanting to press her luck, and knowing he'd spoken the truth, she quickly reached inside the saddlebag and handed the pistol to him. "I was planning to give it to you anyway."

"Let's go," he said, unwilling to acknowledge her statement. When he then bent back to tuck the weapon into his own saddlebag, he wished she had thought to grab up his holster, too. "We are supposed to head out on the road that leads north toward Pleasant Grove."

"What if we don't find her?" Anna asked, wrapping her reins around the saddle horn to get them out of her way while she mounted.

"As soon as we reach Pleasant Grove, we're to ask around. Find out if anyone saw her. Then we're to check at the telegraph office to find out if any messages have come in from any of the other groups. If, by chance, we find any evidence that indicates we are

332

the ones on her trail, we're to wire that information back here before heading out after her. That way we can keep each other informed."

He watched with considerable interest while she swung herself up into the saddle and with even more interest when he noticed how nicely the divided skirt molded to her legs and hips after she had settled into the seat. Reminded again of how very much a woman she was, he wondered at what point during the day she would decide to drop out. Although he didn't think she could endure the kind of riding they would have to do for very long, he had a feeling it would be late afternoon before she finally gave in.

"Where's Harry?" she asked with a quick smile, aware of where his gaze had gone. It pleased her to know she affected him like that.

"He's waiting for us at the edge of town," Mark answered, then forced his gaze back to her face, which he decided was every bit as inviting as the shape of her bottom.

"Then why are we still here?" She gathered the reins into her right hand just before she gave the horse a sharp nudge with her heels. The animal responded with an immediate forward leap, but Anna managed to grab hold of the saddle horn to keep from being thrown right out of the saddle. The horse from the livery was far more powerful than any she was used to riding. Suddenly, she wasn't so sure that going with them had been such a good idea. But the thought of staying behind and not knowing what, if any, progress had been made was unthinkable.

In her effort to keep up with Harry and Mark, Anna concentrated on the constant, loping movement of the horse, as determined to stay in the saddle as the animal seemed to be to lose her. Sometimes trotting the horses, but usually galloping at full speed, they quickly covered the twelve miles to Pleasant Grove.

Although Pleasant Grove was half the size of Pinefield, it had both a sheriff and a telegraph office. Both were in the same building, and Mark headed there first.

Not certain her legs would hold her if she were to climb down, Anna remained on her horse while Mark and Harry hurried inside to see if the sheriff might have seen Clara and the boys. If he had not, they wanted him to spread the word. They wanted as many people as possible keeping an eye out for them, and they wanted them to report any possible sightings to Sheriff Weathers in Pinefield.

While she waited for the men to return, Anna glanced around at the different buildings that surrounded her. When she did, she noticed a small boy who looked about Jamie's age standing in the shadows near the front of what appeared to be a hardware store. Thinking he might have noticed if other children his age had passed through the town, she called to him. Reluctantly, he stepped forward.

"Hello there. My name is Anna Gates," she said. "May I ask your name?"

"Yes'm," he said with a heavy Texas accent, then cut his gaze back toward the hardware store, as if he wasn't exactly sure he should be talking to her. "My name's Londell. Londell Duffy."

"Pleased to meet you, Londell. Would you mind telling me how long you've been standing over there?"

"I don't know," he said, then shrugged awkwardly. "Awhile, I guess."

Aware the child was probably only eight or nine years old and obviously had no concept of time, she asked, "Have you been keeping a close eye on the

334

people who ride through town?"

He shrugged again and shoved his hands in his pockets, his shoulders slumped. "I guess so."

"You didn't happen to see a buggy pass through here, did you, a buggy carrying a woman and two small boys? One of the boys is about the same age as you."

His face lit in response and his shoulders straightened. "Did she have on a bright red dress and did she wear a funny-looking hat with a big black feather in it?"

That certainly sounded like Clara. Anna drew in a long, slow breath to help calm her excitement. "I think so. She likes bright colors. Did you happen to notice which way they went?"

"Sure did," he said with an eager bob of his head. Stepping forward, he pointed toward a place just outside of town where the road forked. "She went off that away."

"To the right?" she asked, then chewed on the edge of her bottom lip for a moment. If only the child knew more about telling time. "How long ago do you suppose that was?"

Suddenly the boy's shoulders drooped again, and he took a tiny step back. "I don't know. It's been awhile I guess."

"Over an hour?" she prodded, hoping the boy knew how long an hour was.

"I don't know. I guess. Maybe. It was this mornin'. Not real long after my ma opened up the store."

"Are you sure about that?"

Londell nodded that he was.

Excited about the little information she now had, Anna forgot her earlier reluctance to climb down from her horse. Swinging her leg over with ease, she

335

dropped to the ground with an aching thud, then hurried into the sheriff's office to find Mark.

"Anna? What is it?" Mark asked the moment he had glanced back and saw her flushed cheeks.

"They came this way," she answered, her face alive with animation. "They headed out the road to the northeast. They came through early this morning."

"How do you know that?" he asked, perplexed that she suddenly had so much information. "The sheriff said no one with two little boys has passed through here today."

"Oh, but she did. One of the little boys outside told me. He saw them."

"Which little boy is that?" the sheriff asked, stepping over to his window and scanning the sidewalk.

Anna joined him at the window and pointed to Londell, who had crossed the street and now stood in front of the leather shop, peering quizzically at the sheriff's office. "That little boy there. He saw them come through shortly after his mother opened her store, which I would guess to be about seven or eight o'clock this morning."

Rolling his eyes heavenward, the sheriff shook his head and turned his back to the window. "That's little Londell Duffy, Louise's boy. You can't believe half of what that child tells you. He's always telling tall tales. It's his way of getting attention."

"But this time he isn't telling tall tales," Anna insisted. "He's telling the truth. I know he is. He even went as far as to describe Clara's dress, and it sounded like something she would wear."

"Then what are we waiting for?" Harry asked, already turning to head outside. Anna was right behind him.

Mark followed, but then paused at the door. "Sheriff, would you mind sending a telegraph to Pinefield for me? Leave a message for Sheriff Weathers explaining that we've picked up her trail right here in Pleasant Grove. Tell him she's probably headed for Copperville."

"I'll send it, if that's what you want. But I really don't think you should set too much store in what little Londell Duffy has to say."

"If Anna believes he's telling the truth, then I have to assume he is. She's a darned good judge of character."

Then he hurried outside to remount. By the time he sat square in the saddle and had his reins in hand, Anna and Harry were already on their way. Riding hard, they took the right fork in the road headed straight for Copperville.

It was three o'clock when they rode into the small town, which amounted to little more than a dozen buildings strewn along a wide dirt street. By the time they realized there was no sheriff, Anna's legs had started to feel a little numb, but her adrenalin remained too high for her to care. While Mark and Harry went into the general store to see what they could find out there, she glanced around for another small child, convinced now that children were far more observant than adults could ever hope to be.

"Hello there," she called out when she finally spotted a little girl playing with a rag doll in the shade of an elm tree.

The child glanced up at her curiously. "Do I know you?" She watched while Anna climbed down from her horse and looped her horse's reins around the hitching post.

"No, but I have a very important question to ask you."

The girl's eyes widened when she mentioned the word *important*. "What sort of question?"

"May I ask your name?"

"That's an important question?" she wanted to know, and notched her forehead as if she believed Anna did not have all her candles burning. "My name is Charlotte. Charlotte Tinsfield."

"Well, Charlotte, my name is Anna Gates," she said hoping to allay any fears the child might have. "And, no, that is not my important question. I happen to be looking for a friend of mine. She may have traveled through Copperville earlier today and I thought, as bright and observant as you are, that you might have seen her."

The girl smiled at such open praise. "Who's your friend?"

"You wouldn't know her, but you might have noticed her because she was wearing a bright red dress and would've had two young boys with her."

"Oh, I remember them," she said, frowning while she thought back. "We passed them on our way into town. Real fancy dress she had on. It was as red as a ripe strawberry. But I only saw one boy with her."

Anna's heart froze. "Only one?" Had Londell been mistaken? Or was this little girl in error? "Are you sure?"

"That's all I saw," she said with an unconcerned toss of her long brown curls. "He was sorta cute, too. But I think he was probably too young for me."

"Why? How old did he look?"

"Maybe eight, or maybe he was nine. But, you see, I just turned ten, and my mother says I'm not to go giving the eye to any boys who look younger than I am."

If it weren't for the seriousness of the situation,

Anna might have found the statement ludicrous, having come from a ten-year-old. As it was, she was terrified. Either they were chasing the wrong buggy, or something dreadful had happened to Abel. Her heart hammered furiously inside her chest.

"Did you happen to notice what the boy was wearing?"

"Not really. I think it may have been a white shirt, but I'm not sure. It could have been gray." She twisted her mouth to one side and considered it further. "Or it may have been brown."

That certainly didn't help. "Did you get a good look at the woman?"

"No. I was too busy looking at the boy. I did notice her red dress, though."

"Who was with you at the time?"

"Mother was. But she turned the other way. She doesn't take to women dressed in fancy clothes. Not since Father ran off with that painted lady who worked at the saloon."

Anna felt that was understandable. "Can you remember which way she was headed?"

"Toward our house."

"Which is—" she prompted.

"That way," Charlotte answered, and pointed off toward the north.

"And when was this?"

"About ten, because we left the house a little after nine-thirty."

Ten? That meant Clara had at least a five-hour lead. That is, if Anna was trailing the right buggy.

Aware that was probably all the information the girl would be able to give her, Anna thanked her for her help, then turned to find Mark. She spotted him coming out of the general store, headed for the building

339

across the street. Harry followed a few feet behind.

"What did you find out?" she asked as soon as she had joined them. Though she wanted to share her information, she was just as eager to find out what they knew.

"Nothing much," Mark answered. "One woman said she thought she saw them on the road toward Cedar Hill, but wasn't sure."

Anna wondered if that might have been Charlotte's mother. "And which direction is Cedar Hill?"

Mark looked at her suspiciously. "North, why?"

"Because that's the direction Charlotte told me they were headed."

Mark looked at Harry with a flat expression, aware Anna had outdone them again. "And who is Charlotte?"

Rather than explain, she merely pointed.

"You sure got a way with children," Harry muttered with a shake of his grizzled head. "Now, if I was to go over there and try to ask that little girl a question or two, she'd go running for her mother. A mother, who no doubt would be six-foot-two and weigh about two-hundred and fifty pounds, and be totally against any strangers talkin' to her daughter."

Mark chuckled as he cast him a meaningful look. "I'd run, too, if an ugly old reprobate like you suddenly came at me."

"Which I've a notion to do right now," Harry shot back. His tousled eyebrows lowered with warning, though his mouth twisted into a wry grin.

Then, suddenly reminded they had no time for such nonsense, Mark shifted his attention back to Anna. "What did your Miss Charlotte have to say?"

"She saw a woman, dressed in bright red, driving a buggy along the road north. Problem is, Charlotte saw only one boy with her."

"One?" Harry and Mark said in unison, then Mark added, "Was she sure about that?"

"She seemed to be. And that boy sounded a lot like Jamie."

"Then where's Abel?" Harry wanted to know, his hands drawing into gnarled fists. He seemed about to reach his emotional limit for one day.

"I don't know. Maybe he was there, only lying down in the seat for some reason, out of sight."

"Are you still sure we're chasing after the right people?" Mark wanted to know, his face twisted with fresh concern.

Anna had to be honest. "No, I'm not. But it's the only possibility we have right now. I think we should follow through with it."

"Okay," Mark said, not ready to argue the point. "Then mount up. I'll send a telegraph telling the others that we are now headed toward Cedar Hill. We should be there before dark."

While Mark went into the building that served as both barbershop and telegraph office, Harry and Anna returned to the horses. They both let out deep groans when they remounted, but made no comment while waiting impatiently for Mark to return.

Two minutes later, Mark stormed out of the building, wanting to know if either of them had any money. He'd run off and left his wallet at the house, and the telegraph operator was demanding three cents before he'd send the message.

"Well, damnation," Harry blurted, thinking it the final blow. Angrily, he shoved his hand into his pocket and came out with a small gray coin purse. "Here, give him a whole damn nickel. Let's get out of here."

Anna watched the muscles in the side of Harry's jaw

341

tighten while Mark returned to pay for the telegram. She wondered how much more stress and aggravation he could take. He looked terribly pale.

"Harry? Are you feeling all right?"

"Hell, no. I don't feel all right and I won't until we finally find those boys," he muttered, then narrowed his gaze until they were nothing more than two angry slits of gray-green. "I tell you one thing . . . if it turns out that woman has harmed either of those boys in any way, I'll take her apart with my own bare hands."

And as angry as he looked at that moment, Anna had no doubt he would do just that.

Chapter Nineteen

Cedar Hill was little more than a ghost town. Although a dozen or so buildings lined both sides of the main street and ventured out along two narrow side streets, very few appeared occupied. Only a general store, a blacksmith, and, of all things, a dress shop looked as if they might still be in business. The remaining buildings were boarded shut and, in places, weeds and bushes grew high enough to hide the windows.

Entering the south part of town, Harry was first to slow his horse to a walk. "It's gettin' pert near dark, and I don't see no place to eat," he commented. "And I don't see no livery, neither. I tell you one thing. Not only do *I* need a good hot meal and somethin' cool and wet to soothe my parched throat, my horse could also use a long draw of fresh water and a big bucket of oats."

Mark twisted in his saddle, frowning when he saw no one on the street. Both the dress shop and the general store were already closed for the day, but it appeared the blacksmith was still open. He nudged his horse in that direction.

This time, both Anna and Harry chose to remain mounted, and to wait until Mark returned with a full report. Neither was accustomed to spending an entire day in the saddle—especially Anna—and the exertion had clearly taken its toll on both of them. Their drooping shoulders and tired, dust-streaked faces confirmed it. They were both near exhaustion, but too determined to find the children even to consider the possibility of quitting.

For several minutes, neither had the strength to speak, until Harry finally broke the heavy silence. "Heck, even if they did come through here, I doubt anyone was around to notice," he commented, then puckered his lips at an angle, clearly irritated, while he slowly scanned the deserted buildings a second time.

Anna, too, gave the town a second look, wondering what had happened to cause the town to fail. Considering the number and the size of the abandoned buildings, Cedar Hill had once been a flourishing community. But now . . . .

"Look," she gasped, pointing to a small door high in the top of the blacksmith's shed. "There's a little girl."

Harry glanced up, puzzled by her excitement. He notched his forehead, but nodded agreeably when he saw a small, dirt-smudged child dressed like a boy, but with long brown braids dangling from both sides of her head. "Yep. That's a girl all right. It's that hair that gives her away."

"I'll be right back."

Suddenly Anna had the strength to climb down from her saddle and tether her horse. Within seconds she had limped inside, leaving Harry to wonder not only about her sanity, but about her rapid rate of recovery.

Pulling his hat off and scratching his head, he

peered back at the door to the loft and blinked with surprise. The child was gone and the door was shut, yet he hadn't heard a sound, not the creak of a hinge nor the thud of wood closing against wood.

If Anna hadn't also seen her, he'd worry about his eyesight. After all, everything else on his tired old body felt like it was about gone — except for his butt. He could damn sure acknowledge that his butt was still there. In fact, if he didn't know better, he'd think Mark had caught him when he wasn't payin' attention and gave him a good swift kick. But Harry knew it was old age that had snuck up on him and given him that cruel kick in the butt.

He snorted with disgust, wishing Mark and Anna would hurry. He wanted to get on to the next town, where they'd have a better chance of finding something to eat. He couldn't remember ever feeling as hungry as he did at that moment. He was already starting to get the shakes.

Finally, Mark did come out, and when he walked over to where he'd left his horse, he glanced momentarily at Anna's empty saddle, then looked at Harry questioningly.

"Where's Anna?"

"Didn't you see her?"

"No. Where is she?"

"Off playin' in the loft, I reckon," Harry muttered and shook his head, then motioned to the blacksmith shop with his hand.

"She's what?"

"I don't rightly know. I suppose she's hopin' that little girl we saw up there might be able to tell us somethin' about the boys. Come to think of it, Anna's been havin' pretty good luck with the younguns all day

345

long." He scratched his jaw and thought about that. "You know, she's been havin' far better luck than we have. She just might be onto somethin'."

And she was. When Anna returned, she carried a weary smile. "Clara's still headed north."

"Then the little girl did see her?" Harry asked, raising in his eyebrows in surprise.

Anna's smile widened. "Saw her and *both* of the boys riding with her."

"Both?" Harry's eyes glistened with renewed hope.

"Yes, both. From Kim's vantage point, she was able to see right down into the buggy, and it looks like I was right. Abel was lying on the seat asleep."

"He slept that long?" Harry asked, not sure he liked that. "Must have been plum' tuckered out. But, then, I can understand that. I'm plum' tuckered out myself."

"Well, *we're* sure not going to be getting sleep any time soon," Mark commented quickly, showing a renewed burst of energy. "Let's get moving. The blacksmith told me it was almost seven miles to the next town."

"I hope the next one has a livery," Harry grumbled. When he leaned forward in the saddle to pat his horse's neck, he winced from the pain that shot through his lower hip. "Ruby here can't go much longer without something to eat. Neither can I, for that matter."

To Harry's relief, the next town did indeed have a livery and not one, but two restaurants that were still open. After leaving their horses at the livery to be fed, watered, and rubbed down, they headed straight for the nearest establishment that served food. Anna breathed deeply the delicious aroma that had drifted out into the street, so tantalized by the smell, it left her weak.

Even though they were rumpled and covered with sweat and road dust, the owner of the small restaurant did not turn them away. Instead, she led them to a table near an open window and hurried to get them water.

Harry rubbed his hands together and smacked his lips loudly in anticipation of food at last. Eagerly, he pulled out one of the four chairs at the table and plopped down, blinking hard at the resulting pain. He frowned when he considered how stiff and sore he would be by morning, but pushed that thought aside so he could concentrate on what he would eat.

"I don't know about you two, but I'm goin' to order me up the thickest, juiciest steak they got in this place, with heapin' mounds of mashed potatoes and buttered carrots on *both* sides of the plate. Then I think I'll top that off with a huge slab of whatever pie they got and wash it all down with a tall, cool glass of buttermilk." He smiled wide at the thought of all that food.

"Not unless they have that steak already cooked. We don't have time to order anything that will take too long to prepare," Mark cautioned, pulling his chair out while he glanced around at the few patrons who remained at such a late hour. Suddenly reminded of the time, he pushed his chair back toward the table. He had not yet bothered to sit. "We need to order whatever they can get out on the table quickest. And whatever that is, order one for me. Just be sure you can afford it, because you're the only one with any money."

"Where are you going?" Anna wanted to know, hoping it was to ask about any "facilities" that might be available. Although they had stopped twice that day,

347

she again needed a privy.

"To see if I can find the sheriff," Mark told her. "I figured while we were waiting for our food to cook I might as well find out if the local sheriff happened to notice anyone drive through this town wearing a bright red dress, accompanied by two little boys."

Harry cocked his head at an angle. "If you think about it, it really was downright considerate of that woman to wear such notable clothin' for her get away," he commented drolly, in a much better mood now that he was finally going to get something to eat.

"Wasn't it, though," Mark agreed. "I just hope she doesn't stop off somewhere to catch a few hours of sleep. She might not want to put that same outfit back on come morning."

"I hope she does stop somewhere for some sleep," Harry retorted and pushed his lips into a wrinkled scowl. "Then maybe we can catch up with her." His eyebrows lifted. "Who knows, she may have decided to stop somewhere right here in Daingerfield hopin' to catch herself a little shut-eye. If you stop and think about it, that foolish woman's been travelin' full speed even longer than we have. She's bound to be purdy worn out by now."

"But then again, it was probably about five o'clock when she arrived here," Anna was quick to point out. "I imagine she'd choose to keep right on traveling for as long as she had daylight."

Harry arched one eyebrow while lowering the other. "You're just a regular little Mary Sunshine, ain't ya?"

Mark chuckled. "I'll stop by the hotel and ask, just in case."

"You do that," Harry agreed. "Meanwhile, I'll order us up three of the quickest cooked steaks in town." He waited until Mark had left the restaurant before he turned to Anna and winked. "You know, if it wasn't so danged late, you could sure save that man a heap of time and trouble."

"How's that?" she asked, puzzled by such a remark.

"Why, it's after nine o'clock," he answered with a wide upward sweep of his hands, as if that should tell it all. When it didn't, he leaned forward and rested one arm on' the table in front of him. "All the children are bound to be in bed by now. We got no one reliable to ask." He chuckled at his own wit.

Anna would have laughed, too, if it were not for the fact she had to get to a privy. If the waitress did not return to their table soon to take their order so she could ask where the nearest public facility was Anna was certain she would burst. Pressing her knees together, she tried to concentrate on something else.

When the woman failed to reappear during the next few minutes, Anna decided she had better not wait any longer.

"Excuse me," she said politely to Harry, then lifted her napkin out of her lap and set it neatly on the table.

Having become engrossed with watching some of the other patrons eat, Harry glanced at her with surprise. "What's the matter? Did you spot a kid somewhere?"

"No."

"You mad cause they haven't taken our order yet? Goin' to go raise some Cain about that?"

"No."

"Then what is it?"

When she looked at him with a purposely raised eyebrow, he blinked hard, then blushed. "Oh. Well.

349

Go right ahead. If the waitress comes while you're gone, I'll order for you."

When Anna returned from the hotel across the street, where the only public privy was located, she was surprised to discover their food already on the table. She looked at Harry questioningly, and he shrugged in response, hurrying to chew the food he'd just shoved into his mouth so he could speak.

"Seems they only have two meals on the menu here. Meat loaf or roast beef. I picked the roast beef. Got an order for all of us. It was already cooked, so they brought it right out."

"Mark hasn't returned?" she asked after she'd sat back down and returned her napkin to her lap. She wondered if that should worry her, but decided Mark was quite capable of taking care of himself.

"Not yet. I guess he's either still over at the sheriff's, or else he's at the hotel."

"He's not at the hotel," she informed him, glancing up while she lifted her fork off the table, eager to sample the roast before it turned cold.

Harry looked at her as if he was about to ask how she knew that but thought better of it. *Clearly,* he worried the answer might have something to do with the reason she had left.

"Then he must still be at the sheriff's," he concluded, returning his attention to his plate. "He'd sure better hurry, though. As hungry as I am, I just might eat my supper and his too."

It was fifteen minutes before Mark finally returned, and true to his word, Harry had both finished his meal and had to pick at the food on Mark's plate. By the time Mark had sat down and pulled his chair up to the table, most of his peas and potatoes were gone and his roll had completely disappeared.

"Find out anything?" Harry asked, hoping to avoid any confrontation about the missing food.

"That I did. She's been here, all right," Mark said, at the same time reaching for his water glass.

"You are absolutely sure it was her?" Anna wanted to know, wondering why he seemed so confident.

Mark waited until he had drained the contents of his glass and set it back down before answering. "I am indeed. She stopped to trade horses at the livery down the street."

"The one we just left?" Anna asked, wondering why he had gone back there.

"No, a different one. There are two."

"And you are *certain* it was her?" She studied his confident expression, wishing he would explain himself.

"The man at the other livery distinctly remembers that a lady dressed in a fancy-cut red dress came by to trade horses with him. He remembers hers was so near exhaustion that he made her pay a difference of two dollars before he would agree to any trade. But the clincher is that he also remembers hearing her call one of the little boys 'Jamie.' Also, the man said something about the younger child being too shy to speak."

Anna's eyes widened with disbelief. "He definitely remembers hearing her call Jamie by name?"

"That he does. I never mentioned either boy's name, yet he remembered the name Jamie. He said she used it at least twice. He also said something about her asking him to hurry with the horse because she wanted to be in Union Hill before dark."

"She's headed for Union Hill?" Harry asked, glad to know the destination. Suddenly he didn't feel as sore,

351

or as tired. "Then why are you dawdlin' like that? Eat up, so we can get back on the road. We still have to see if we can buy a couple of lanterns off that man at the livery so we can see where we're goin'. Hurry, I said. We don't have all night."

"Well, it shouldn't take me too long to eat this," Mark commented with a lift of his brow as he pulled his plate closer, then picked up his fork. Quickly he stabbed an oversized piece of roast and lifted it to his mouth, where he held it suspended half an inch from his lips. "Looks to me like there's only about half a meal here anyway. Maybe I should complain to the owner for such undersized proportions."

"Don't have time for that," Harry reasoned quickly, then, eager to change the subject, he asked, "How much a head start you figure she got on us this time? Did the man say?"

Having just put the large chunk of meat into his mouth, all Mark could do was nod. He waited until he had swallowed the food before answering. "According to the man at the livery, she left about three hours ago."

"Hot damn, we're gaining on her," Harry said, before he could stop himself. He looked apologetically at Anna, knowing how ladies didn't cotton much to foul language. He felt bad enough for some of the things he'd let slip earlier. Tired or not, he should watch his mouth when there was a lady present.

Mark nodded, his blue eyes sparkling with amusement. "Sure looks that way. She used a little extra time to take care of some shopping. While the man was busy changing horses for her, she took the boys down the street to the mercantile, where she later came back with a box of food, including a lot of canned goods."

352

Mark grinned. "Seems she was in such a hurry to leave this morning, she forgot to pack herself a picnic lunch."

"You mean those boys went all day without any food?" Harry asked. Suddenly he was very angry again.

Anna was, too. And concerned. "Did the man at the livery say anything to you about the boys' appearance? Did they look like she may have harmed them in any way?" Though she had tried not to think about it, she was worried Clara had hurt them. If it turned out their mother was the abusive parent mentioned in that telegram, there was a very real chance she might revert to violent behavior.

Mark reached out to take her hand, aware of what worried her. "He said they were a little dirty is all."

Anna closed her eyes and let some of the tension leave her body. How good it felt to have Mark touch her. "Then they didn't look as if they might have been beaten?"

"Not according to Mr. Pyle at the livery. His only comment was that they were both badly in need of a bath and looked like a couple of frightened rabbits. He figured they were afraid of him because he's so tall."

Knowing the real reason for their fearful expressions, Anna bit back the yelp that sprang to her lips. "Those boys have every reason to be frightened . . . *very* frightened."

Even more frightened than she was, and at the moment, she was terrified.

Because Union Hill was only six miles from

Daingerfield, they arrived within the hour. But at ten-thirty on a Friday night, the only places open were the two saloons, and they were doing a brisk business.

Though Harry had not accompanied Mark into any of the buildings to ask questions during either of the last two stops, he was quick to volunteer to take on one of the two saloons.

Anna suspected from the way he'd smacked his lips when he dismounted that this sudden renewed interest in helping to gather information had something to do with what he might be able to purchase inside. Something cool and wet would be how he would describe it.

Since respectable women were not allowed in saloons, Anna did not even bother climbing down. Instead, she volunteered to wait with the horses, down the street, where Mark felt she'd be less likely to have to contend with wayward drunks. She figured it shouldn't take them long.

Until now, they had managed to gather their information within a very few minutes, but this time it took much longer. After fifteen minutes had passed, Anna started to grow impatient. When twenty minutes went by and neither man had yet to reappear, she decided to ride by and see if she could peer in over the cut-down doors. She was curious to know exactly what was keeping them. Surely they realized they were wasting precious time.

Tying the other two horses to a hitching post, she climbed back onto her horse and was about to make the first pass by the two saloons when Mark appeared.

He hurried in her direction, his expression distant.

"What did you find out?" she asked, though her first inclination had been to comment on how long he had been in that saloon.

354

He did not answer right away. Instead, he looked curiously at the reins when he bent to untie his horse, making no comment that when he'd left, she had been holding them in her hand. "Clara was through here all right. But she didn't stop. The men I talked to said she and the boys went straight on through, then took the road toward Mount Pleasant." He then looked around. "Where's Harry?"

"Still in the other saloon."

"If there are as many men inside his saloon as were inside mine, we could be here another half hour before he's questioned them all. I'd better go get him." He quickly relooped his reins around the post, but by the time he'd stepped back up on the boardwalk, Harry sashayed out of the other saloon, his shoulders arched back as if he were a peacock.

Mark's forehead wrinkled with amusement while he watched Harry strut out into the street, then turn in their direction.

"Hurry up, we need to get going again," he called to him. "Clara didn't stop here after all, but I found out where she's headed."

"So did I," he said, waving his head proudly.

Then when he came closer, Mark and Anna exchanged startled glances when they saw the bright red imprint on Harry's cheek. The mark was shaped suspiciously like lips.

"And just where did you get your information?" Mark wanted to know, starting to grin.

"From very reliable sources," Harry assured him. "They told me she came through just as it was turnin' dark. They also told me that she took the road toward Pittsburg, headed west. So there."

"Pittsburg?" Mark looked at him, puzzled. "Are you

355

sure they said Pittsburg?"

"Of course I'm sure. I only had one drink while I was in there, and it was a little one. She said Pittsburg just as clear as can be."

"Wonderful," Mark muttered, wondering now what to believe. "The men I talked with seemed pretty certain she was headed for Mount Pleasant."

The three of them fell silent for several minutes while they thought over their predicament. Finally Anna offered the only logical solution. "We'll have to split up. Harry and I will take the road to Pittsburg while you go on to Mount Pleasant. How far away are these towns?"

"They are both about fifteen miles from here," Mark told her with a defeated shake of his head. "It'll be at least one or two in the morning before we reach either one. I doubt there'll be anyone around to question at that hour."

"Then maybe it would be better to stay here and get a little sleep," Harry suggested, already eyeing the hotel across the street. "We'd probably function better with a little rest."

"That's true, but not here. I think we should wait until we've reached our separate destinations. That way we can start asking around as soon as those towns start stirring."

Harry's shoulders slumped. "But what if this Pittsburg don't have a hotel? Or what if it does, but the manager don't like being disturbed at two in the mornin'? I sure don't cotton to the idea of sleepin' on the ground. Not as sore as my—" he hesitated a moment. "Not as sore as my behind is right now."

"Okay, okay," Mark agreed, as eager to get some rest as they were. "We'll see if we can get a couple of rooms. Then we'll get up early tomorrow morning and take off."

Harry was the only one with any money. Mark knew that if he wanted a real bed, he'd be wise to be as agreeable as possible. At least this way, he would be able to share that bed with Anna, and if the truth were to be known, he was too used to having her next to him to be able to fall sleep without her.

The sky was turning a dull, murky gray when the three climbed back into their saddles the next morning. Although Anna had fallen asleep almost immediately, and had slept like a child until Mark had aroused her shortly before dawn, she was still tired and twice as stiff as she had been the day before. While attempting to flex her sore, aching muscles, she wondered if it had been such a good idea to stop for a few hours' rest after all. But when she remembered the feel of Mark's arms around her when she'd drifted off to sleep, she knew it had been worth it. Quite worth it.

Only now she wished she had chosen to ride with Mark instead of Harry. She hated the thought of being separated from her husband, even if for a little while. But she also hated the thought of Harry riding alone. Even after several hours of sleep, Harry did not look very well. His face was pale, and his eyes looked dull. She wondered how much longer he could hold out and hoped they would catch up with Clara soon. She also wondered why Sheriff Weathers and his men had not caught up with them yet. If they could increase their manpower, they could hope to catch her that much sooner.

After agreeing to send reports to each other, by way of telegraph, as soon as either of them had found out anything worthwhile, they rode off. Mark headed northwest to Mount Pleasant, while Harry and Anna rode directly west to Pittsburg.

Anna continued to glance back until Mark had completely disappeared from sight. When he did, her heart felt like a heavy weight inside her . . . not just because she was having to be apart from Mark, but because they had yet to find Clara and the boys. She hoped that someone in either Pittsburg or Mount Pleasant would remember seeing them. As late as it had to have been when they arrived at either town, it could be they had never been seen driving through.

Trying not to be so pessimistic, she turned her thoughts to the possibility that Clara may have decided to stop for the night at one of the two towns. Then she might still be there when they arrived. They would have her at last. They might even catch her while she was still asleep, which would make taking the boys from her that much easier.

As it turned out, the distance was not quite fifteen miles from Union Hill to Pittsburg, and Anna and Harry arrived there shortly after nine o'clock. Never having heard of the place before, Anna was surprised to see how large it was. It was twice the size of Pinefield, and it had a train station. She wondered why the Orphan Train had never stopped there.

"You go find a likely kid to question, and I'll see if I can locate the sheriff," Harry suggested, interrupting her thoughts while he quickly scanned the town, trying to familiarize himself with his new surroundings.

Anna glanced at him to see if he was teasing about finding a kid, but when she saw no smile, she realized

358

it had been an honest suggestion. She started searching the streets for a child who appeared to be the type to notice what went on around him.

"Then I guess the next logical thing for us to do is to check with the hotels," Harry continued. "See if a lady dressed in red stayed the night anywhere."

At that moment, Anna noticed a little boy with hair so red it looked orange and a face packed with freckles sitting high in a large oak tree. Though she was still half a block away, he had already given her the once-over and had then turned his attention to Harry.

"I think I've found the child I want to question," she said, and immediately turned her horse in that direction. Though the tree had been planted in the corner of the courtyard, it was close enough to the side that the limb the boy had chosen for his seat draped over the street.

She waited until she was only a few yards away before looking at him again. "Hello up there."

Because the boy's gaze had followed Harry on down the street, the child jumped with surprise at hearing a voice so nearby.

"You talking to me?" he asked, pressing his small hand to his chest.

"Of course I am," she said, smiling. "What a clever place to sit. I wager you can see everything that goes on around here and yet still be out of everyone's way. How long have you been up there?"

"A while, I guess."

Anna closed her eyes briefly, wondering if this child was in any way related to Londell Duffy, the little boy she had questioned in Pleasant Grove. "Do you sit up there very often?"

"I guess so. It's a lot cooler up here."

Aware this boy had no qualms about talking with strangers, she did not bother to introduce herself. Instead she got right to the point. "You didn't happened to notice a woman drive by in a buggy, wearing a bright red dress, with two young boys at her side, did you?"

The boy scratched his unruly curls while he thought back. "No, can't say that I have. When d'you figure she came by?"

"I really don't know. Could have been late last night or very early this morning." But she hoped it would prove to be early that morning. A boy this young would have been in bed by the time Clara and the boys arrived in Pittsburg.

"Sorry. I haven't seen a lady dressed in red ride by at all. Saw one done up all in orange, though."

"Did she have two little boys with her?" she asked, thinking Clara may have changed clothes.

"Nope. Just her."

"Did she have black hair?"

"Nope. It was yellow."

"Then that couldn't have been her," Anna said, disappointed.

"Didn't figure it was," the boy admitted. "I just thought I'd mention it. The woman in orange looked a little silly if you ask me. Even her gloves were orange. Why would anyone want to wear orange gloves?"

Anna heaved a short sigh before trying again, "Do you happen to remember seeing any woman with black hair driving a buggy with two little boys at her side?"

"Just Mrs. Roberts. She had Rebel and Cole with her. But I reckon that doesn't help you much either."

"Thanks just the same," Anna said then prodded her

horse forward, already looking around for another likely child. Her heart pounded painfully in her chest when she considered the very real possibility that they might have lost Clara's trail.

She next noticed a little girl dressed in a frilly pink dress, with perfectly shaped blonde curls springing down on either side of her head. Though the child sat ramrod straight, with an awful scowl wrinkling her face, it was apparent that nothing slipped her notice. Anna decided to try her next, especially since the child sat in front of a hotel. If she did not have answers to any of Anna's questions, then Anna could at least go inside and see if Clara and the boys had stopped there for the night.

Quickly, she dismounted and took the chair directly beside the little girl, then waited until she had turned to look at her before asking, "Been here long?"

Before the girl had time to respond, a woman also dressed in pink came out of the hotel and grabbed the child by her arm, leading her immediately away from Anna. Judging by the disdainful look the woman had given her, Anna had not met with her approval. Glancing down at her dust-covered riding skirt and scuffed boots, she could easily understand why.

Anna frowned wearily while she watched the mother drag the little girl down the sidewalk. Finally she pushed herself out of the chair and went inside to talk with the clerk at the main desk. To her further frustration, no one at the hotel remembered seeing a woman dressed in red either. But she did learn that there were two other hotels in town, and Clara could have stayed in either one.

When she returned to untie her horse, she noticed Harry standing out in the middle of the street, talking to a stocky woman who was waving her arms frantically about, as if terribly upset about something. Anna wondered what Harry had said to upset her and decided she had better go to his rescue. Leaving the horse tethered to the post, she hurried to intervene.

"What seems to be the problem?" she asked, when she was close enough to be heard over the noise in the street. Now that she was closer, she could tell by Harry's stern expression that he was as upset as the woman.

When he turned to look at her, there was so much hatred in his eyes that it caused Anna a moment of true concern.

"She was here all right," he said, then sucked in a breath between clenched teeth before continuing, "So were the boys."

Fear mounted in Anna's throat while she studied his hostile reaction. "What has she done to them?"

Harry took in another deep breath, as if that was the only way he could stay in control. "She had them begging in the streets this morning."

"She what?" Anna was so overwhelmed with rage that she, too, found it hard to breathe.

"She had them begging in the streets. Mrs. Beebe here claims the older boy was doing all the talking while the younger boy held out his hand and tried to look pitiful. She says their clothing was dirty and ragged and they looked half starved."

"Where are they now?" When Harry did not answer, she looked to the woman for a response.

Mrs. Beebe let out an indignant huff, then spoke. "We don't allow such things in Pittsburg. In fact, we have a town ordinance against it. So I told them that if they didn't leave immediately I was going to go get the sheriff and have them arrested."

"And they left?"

"Yes. And that's when I got a look at their mother. Imagine, a mother dressed the way she was!"

"And how was that? In a red dress?"

Mrs. Beebe's nostrils flared with righteous indignation. "What there was of it!"

Harry shook his head, abhorred by what they'd learned. "We need to get going. According to Mrs. Beebe here, they left only about half an hour ago. Headed north again."

"North? Toward Mount Pleasant?"

"I suppose," Mrs. Beebe answered. "That road forks about five miles out. She could be headed to Mount Pleasant, or she could be headed for Cypress Bend."

Harry looked at Anna for a decision. "Should we split up and take both roads?"

"It's our only choice," Anna said, dearly hoping that whichever road she chose would be the right one. She so wanted to be the one to find them. As much as she wanted to rescue those boys, she wanted a chance to confront Clara face to face. She wanted to tell that evil woman exactly what she thought of her.

Chapter Twenty

After giving the matter some thought, Anna concluded that had Clara's destination been Mount Pleasant, she would have taken the same road Mark had taken out of Union Hill. It made far more sense to believe Clara was headed for Cypress Bend. As a result, Anna volunteered to take the left fork in the road leading north out of Pittsburg, leaving Harry to take the right.

Having already sent a wire to Mark, warning him that Clara might be coming in on the road south of there, Harry expected either to catch up with Clara himself, or to cross paths with his friend at some point along the way. Where depended on how much time passed before Mark stopped by the telegraph office to check for a message.

"Remember, if you don't find Clara but you do meet Mark along the road, and he also has not crossed paths with Clara, you both are to head straight for Cypress Bend. Even though there is no sheriff there, as small as Mrs. Beebe claimed the place to be, you should have no trouble finding me or finding out where I've gone," Anna said to Harry, wanting to be sure they understood what they were to do.

To Anna's way of thinking, the sooner they reunited, the better. Even though she honestly felt she could handle Clara alone, she knew she would feel better about any confrontation if she had the two men's support. At this point, she wanted to take no chances with the boys' safety. "Likewise, if when I reach Cypress Bend, I discover she was never there, I will then turn right around and proceed directly to Mount Pleasant. Leave any messages for me at the sheriff's. I'll go there first."

"Just you also remember that if you do happen across that woman somewhere between here and there, you are not to do anything foolish, not till we get there," Harry warned with a firm wag of his finger.

Anna tilted her head to one side, struggling to keep a solemn expression. "Then what you are saying is that as long as one of you is with me, it's perfectly all right for me to do something foolish."

"You know what I mean," he grumbled, tugging his hat low over his forehead. "You just remember to be careful. I don't want you to go and get yourself hurt. Mark would never forgive me."

Anna arched a delicate eyebrow. "I really think you should be more worried about Clara being hurt rather than me. As angry as I am right now, I think that's a far more likely possibility."

"Well, if anyone does get hurt, I sure rather it be her," Harry commented with a wry grin.

"You don't fool me any, Harry Munn. The only reason you don't want me to do anything until you get there is because you don't want to miss out on the capture. And if anyone should have to cause her any real pain, you want that someone to be you."

Harry grinned, revealing the gap at the side of his

mouth as he prodded his horse into action. "I wouldn't mind havin' that privilege," he shouted back over his shoulder. "I wouldn't mind that a' tall."

The hot, mid-June sun had risen high in a cloudless blue sky by the time Anna finally arrived in Cypress Bend. Even so, as long as her horse had kept moving, she had not really noticed the heat. But when she slowed her horse to let it walk the last quarter mile, the ninety-degree heat became suddenly oppressive.

Perspiration blended with the dust that had coated her skin to streak muddy trails down her face and neck, which she eventually wiped away with her sleeve. Unfortunately she had not thought to buy a hairbrush when she had made her purchases in Pinefield, and had lost most of her hairpins during the day and a half she'd spent in the saddle. So her hair had fallen from the simple bun she'd molded earlier that morning and now streamed in unkempt waves down her back, quickly trapping her own body heat against her neck and shoulders.

While studying the small town ahead, Anna looped the reins loosely around the saddle horn. The horse continued to walk as she reached up to try and restructure her hair into a small twist atop her head. She had only three hairpins left, and as thick as her hair was, that was not nearly enough. But she had to do something to make her look more presentable before she entered town and started asking questions. What she really needed was a long, hot bath and a set of clean clothes, but those were luxuries she would not be soon afforded. They had to rescue Jamie and Abel first.

As she'd been told to expect, Cypress Bend was a very small community situated along the north side of the winding Cypress Creek River, near one of the few bridges in that area wide enough to accommodate carriages and wagons. Although the water was usually shallow enough to cross safely on horseback, during the rainy months of late spring, early summer, and early fall, the depth sometimes rose to ten to twelve feet and the water traveled at twice its normal rate.

During those times, like now, the only crossings were made at the bridges, which is why Cypress Bend was such a thriving community, especially during the spring and summer months. There were nearly a dozen buildings, including two large cotton warehouses, yet oddly enough, there was no sheriff's office, nor was there a telegraph.

Still, it didn't take Anna very long to determine that Clara and the boys had not been there. Though she'd found no curious children playing in town, because most were down by the water either fishing or wading or playing in the mud, she did come across an old man seated in a rocker near the front of a warehouse. When she approached him with questions about Clara, he readily admitted that it was rare for anyone to cross the bridge without his knowledge. He was confident that no woman, dressed in red or not, had driven a buggy across the bridge that day, nor the day before.

Disappointed, but needing to be absolutely certain, Anna stopped in at the largest mercantile to let her horse drink from their water trough and asked if anyone there had seen Clara. The three women inside agreed with the old man. No strangers had been through in several days, especially no one dressed in bright red accompanied by two young boys in tattered clothing. A trio like that would surely have been not only noticed, but thoroughly discussed.

Heartsick to have chosen the wrong road after all, Anna headed back the way she'd come. She waved at the old gent in front of the warehouse when she crossed the bridge. Having learned that there was no shorter route, she realized she would have to retrace her route all the way back to the main fork in the road between Pittsburg and Mount Pleasant, then turn left.

It would be nearly three o'clock before she arrived at her new destination, and it would probably take another ten or fifteen minutes to locate Mark and Harry. By that time, they would have already captured Clara and freed the boys. Though that was exactly what she wanted, she was disappointed to think she might miss her only chance to tell that vile, wicked woman exactly what she thought of her. But then, even if they did have her already locked away in the local jail, there was nothing to prevent her from paying Clara Wilkins a short, unfriendly visit. She would have her say yet.

Anna then became lost in her thoughts, planning exactly what she would say to that horrible woman— so lost, she did not at first recognize the approaching riders. But then, she hadn't expected to. She was at least sixty miles from Pinefield by now. Every face she'd seen since leaving the Pinefield area had been that of a stranger.

It was not until the two riders were almost upon her that she realized it was Mark and Harry, but when she did, her mind whirled, as if she doubted her own eyesight. Mark and Harry were supposed to be in Mount Pleasant taking care of the boys and waiting for her. *The boys?* Just where *were* the boys? Her heart felt sheathed in a heavy cloak of ice while her brain did a few quick calculations. There had not been enough time for Mark and Harry to have captured Clara, turned her over to the nearest authorities, filed their complaints, found someone to watch the boys, and still have ridden more than half the distance to Cypress Bend. Something had gone wrong. Her stomach knotted with dread.

"Where you headed?" Harry asked, calling out to her. The notch that had formed between his eyes revealed he was as confused and worried as she. "I thought you were going to wait for us at Cypress Bend. Where are the boys?"

"I'd hoped they were with you," she answered. Her heart ached with sudden fear when she swallowed back the bitter lump at the base of her throat.

Harry's worried expression deepened. "Why would they be with us? Didn't you catch up with them?"

"Clara never passed through Cypress Bend. And there is no other road near there that she could have taken without being seen." She looked at Mark's stricken face, wishing he would say something. She wanted to know what his thoughts were. Did he think she had failed him in some way? Had they failed her? How could they have lost her so easily?

But Mark did not speak. He did not move. He simply stared at her, working the information through his mind.

"If she didn't go to Cypress Bend and she didn't go to Mount Pleasant, then where in the Sam Hill did she go?" Harry asked, turning to Mark for an answer. "Where else is there?"

Mark had pulled his horse to a stop right beside Anna's horse, still facing the opposite direction, and at a direct angle to Harry's horse. His blue eyes bore into hers as if wanting to gauge every word that passed her lips. "Are you absolutely certain she did not go through Cypress Bend?"

"Positive. There's only one way to get to Cypress Bend, and that is over a bridge. And it just so happens there's an old man who has taken it upon himself to be the town's watchdog. He keeps up with everyone who crosses over, either into or from town. He was certain that no woman driving a buggy had passed over that bridge in well over two days."

"Then she's turned off the main road somewhere," Mark concluded, rubbing his thumb along the side of his reins restlessly while his eyes narrowed with thought. "But where? I've been watching for fresh buggy tracks leading off the main road and I haven't seen any—not any." Twisting in his saddle, he glanced back over his shoulder, as if to convince himself he'd done as reliable a job as he thought.

"But I haven't," Anna admitted. It had never occurred to her that Clara would have any reason to leave the main road. And why would she? *Unless she suspected she was being followed.*

Anna felt a sudden leap of her pulse. What if Clara had pulled off the main road and hidden from sight, possibly to rest the horse, and at the same time had watched to see if anyone she recognized passed by? If that were the case, Clara would know without a doubt she was being followed. And if she knew that, she would not risk going on toward Cypress Bend. But where would she go?

Mark twisted his face in thought, carefully rethinking the situation as it now stood. "Since I'm pretty sure I have not passed any fresh tracks that may have veered off the main road, I think we should backtrack to Cypress Bend first, carefully watching for any indication someone left the main road. If we

370

don't find any fresh tracks leaving the road by the time we reach that bridge, then I guess we'd better backtrack all the way to Mount Pleasant," Mark concluded, already flicking his reins. "The only reason I know that she might leave the main road would be to try to shake anyone who might be following her. And if she suspects we're behind her, I don't think she'd chance returning to Pittsburg for fear we'd have left instructions with the local sheriff to keep an eye out for her when we passed through."

"Speaking of sheriffs, I wish that Pinefield sheriff and some of those men he recruited would hurry and catch up with us," Harry muttered as he too put his horse into motion. "We could sure use the extra men about now. Surely, they got our messages. After all, we've sent telegrams from perty near every town we passed through and left word with the local law whenever there was one."

"I'm afraid they aren't coming," Mark said, his expression grim as he prodded his horse into a fast walk. "Seems that sheriff in Pleasant Grove did not send that telegraph right away and it was nearly three that afternoon before anyone in Pinefield knew where we were. By that time we'd put a good twenty miles between us and them and Sheriff Weathers figured by the sound of our messages, we'd have caught Clara long before he could ever reach us. When I wired him this morning, letting him know I was in Mount Pleasant and headed for Cypress Bend, his response was that he thought we'd be on our way back by then, but he wished us good luck and suggested we ask the Mount Pleasant Sheriff for help."

"So why isn't he here?" Harry asked, wondering why Mark had not mentioned this before.

"He claimed he had far more pressing matters to

371

take care of right there in town than to be chasing off after a woman and two children. I don't think he really understood the danger those boys are in."

For a long moment no one spoke. But rather than dwell on the fact that they were facing the problem alone, they tried to turn their thoughts to why Clara might have wanted to leave the main road. They tried to figure out why a woman as determined to go to California as Clara was would want to do so without the money she'd obviously need to get there. Was it her plan to have those children beg their way west?

"Or maybe she does have the money, but is saving it to buy the tickets for the trip west," Anna suggested, trying to decide why Clara had sent the boys out onto the street to beg.

"But if that's the case, why hasn't she already stopped somewhere and bought those train tickets west?" Harry wanted to know. "Surely she doesn't plan to drive that buggy across the desert, not in the middle of summer. They'd fry their brains."

"I don't know what she plans," Mark answered, clearly puzzled by the woman's behavior. "She's been through two different towns that had train depots. She could have bought tickets at either one. If she has the money, why hasn't she bought them? Just what is she waiting for?"

Anna's thoughts bounced back and forth between the two possibilities. Did Clara plan to go to California by train, or was she really that foolish to try to drive the buggy across the desert during the hottest part of the summer? And even if they *did* make it through the desert alive, would they reach the mountains before winter set in? And if they didn't, would she be so stubborn as to try to cross over during the dangerous winter months?

Though Anna remained lost to such tormenting thoughts, her gaze continued to scan the roadside for departing tracks. She was shaken from her painful reverie when Mark suddenly shouted, "Look—over there! Tracks. Fresh tracks!"

Startled, Anna glanced first at Mark to see where he pointed, then ahead to the tracks themselves. "But there isn't even a road there," she commented, wondering why Clara would do such an odd thing. There wasn't evidence of so much as a horse trail or footpath. It was just a wide, open field that appeared to end at the base of a sparsely wooded hill in the distance.

"There may not be a road, but those have to be her tracks," Mark commented, already turning his horse.

"But what if they aren't?" Harry asked, following closely behind, squinting while he studied the two parallel strips where the tall grass had been laid flat by the wheels of either a wagon or a buggy. "What if someone else made those tracks? What if there are other tracks further down the road?"

Mark slowed his horse to a near stop and glanced back at his cautious friend. "I guess it might be a good idea for you to continue following that road to Cypress Bend, to be sure. Meanwhile, Anna and I will follow these tracks. Catch up with us when you know something."

Harry agreed and within minutes was gone.

Meanwhile, Anna and Mark followed the tracks across the wide, grassy field, then into a large wooded area. Though the tracks were not as easy to detect after they rode into the thick layer of pine straw that covered much of the ground, Mark seemed to have little problem following Clara's trail

373

and occasionally pointed out a bent branch or a flattened berry vine to reassure Anna they were on the right track.

"Why do you suppose she'd want to come this way?" Anna asked as she dodged one low limb after another. The woods had become thicker the further up the hill they climbed, making her wonder at Clara's buggy skills. Surely, she would come to a place she could not squeeze the conveyance through and they would have her at last. "Why would anyone want to come this way?"

"I've been wondering the same thing. But then, why would she'd take off across country at all? She can't be very familiar with the territory. Why would she take the chance of getting lost?"

"I still think she knows we're following her and she's willing to do anything she has to to keep us from catching her." It seemed to be the only logical answer.

"She must know," he finally agreed, though reluctantly. "Or surely she would have turned back by now."

"I wonder how far ahead she is."

"Can't be too far. Traveling through terrain like this in a buggy, she can't be making very good time."

"I hope not," Anna said, worried more than ever for the boys' safety, because if Clara was traveling through these woods at breakneck speed, she was endangering everyone's lives. But rather than voice her growing concern, she fell silent again. Mark had enough of his own worries without her adding to them.

To their surprise, a few yards after they crested the small hill and were headed down the other side, the tracks came out onto another road, but because the smaller road was less traveled, there were only a few sets of tracks.

Turning in the direction the buggy had turned, they followed the road until a set of tracks again branched off into the woods. This time the tracks seemed to be following an overgrown path that eventually led them to a large, brushy clearing. On the far side stood a dilapidated wooden shack. Outside it, near the back door, sat Clara's buggy, the horse still in harness. But there were no belongings inside. No valises, boxes of food—nothing.

Coming to a stop behind a clump of bushes at the edge of the woods, Mark motioned for Anna to do the same. When Anna looked at him questioningly, he leaned toward her and spoke in a hushed voice. "I don't want them to know we are here. Not just yet."

Anna did not question his decision, but watched while he parted the bushes and carefully studied the house.

"Looks like an old sharecropper's house," he commented softly, never taking his gaze off the building.

"One that hasn't been used in quite some time," Anna agreed. "What do we do now? Storm the place and take the boys from her?"

Mark's face pulled into a cautious frown while he carefully surveyed every foot of that clearing. "No. I don't think she's alone in there."

"You don't?" Anna asked, surprised. "Why not?"

"For one thing, she seemed to know where she was going, she followed a pretty straight path. Also, this is not the sort of place someone just happens across. This is the sort of place someone uses to meet secretly with someone else."

"But there are no other horses . . . just Clara's buggy," Anna pointed out, eager to confront the woman now that they had caught up with her.

Because they were on a small rise that allowed them to view the house and the only two outbuildings from a downward angle, there was very little they could not see.

"There may not be a horse, but there's a boat," Mark pointed out, looking beyond the house to where a small winding river served as the northern boundary only a few hundred feet from the house.

Anna scanned the gently sloping riverbank and saw that he was right. There was a small wooden boat, half in and half out of the water. It was her guess that it was used to travel to and from Pinefield, since the river would provide the most direct route.

"What should we do?" she asked, bewildered.

"I don't know. I don't even know if that boat has been used recently. And even if it has, there couldn't have been more than two people in anything that small. But then again, we have no way to be sure there are no horses hidden inside one of those sheds. For all we know, there could be half a dozen people holed up in that shack."

"So what do we do?" she repeated, starting to feel the first strains of panic. Though she found it comforting to know Mark had a pistol, she was reluctant to mention it. At this point, she didn't want him to attempt anything rash.

"Well, we can either wait for Harry to trace us here and then send him back to Pittsburg for help, or—" He was just about to ask Anna if she thought she could find her way back to the main road when he noticed the back door open.

"Look, there's Abel," he said and pointed toward the house.

Anna opened her mouth, wanting to call to the

child, to reassure him that they were there; but she stopped herself in time. "He's carrying a bucket. I wonder what he's up to."

"He's probably been sent to get water," Mark commented. Slowly he swung his right leg over the saddle and dropped quietly to the ground. He watched the little boy until he had crossed the yard to what appeared to be a small well house. Quietly, he secured his horse to a nearby tree limb, then without speaking, he motioned for Anna to climb down.

When she did, he leaned close to her ear. "Tether the horse, but stay here. I'm going to try to get a little closer."

Knowing it was no time to argue, Anna did exactly as he said, watching with a trepid heart while Mark quietly maneuvered his way through the woods toward the river. She was amazed at how quickly he moved without making any noise, especially when he had such limited use of his left leg. But she suddenly realized, he had moved during the past few days as if he weren't lame.

While he quickly ducked from tree to tree, she lost sight of him, then glanced back to where Abel busily used both hands to turn the wooden crank that would eventually draw the bucket up out of the well. While she watched, she wondered how Mark's getting a little closer would help. The well was out in the open. Though weeds and brush had taken over the yard, both Abel and the well were clearly visible from the back windows of the house. Mark could not get to Abel without taking the risk of giving himself away. Suddenly, she wished he'd taken the pistol with him.

Soon Abel had raised the bucket high enough to reach the handle with his hands, and he immediately set it on the well housing, right next to his own bucket. He tiptoed to peer inside, then frowned as he shoved the bucket back into the well. He waited until the rope had reached its end before snatching up the original bucket and turning toward the river.

Aware the child must have come up with mud and now sought to get his water from the river, Anna's pulse raced with anticipation. She glanced off to her left to find Mark and saw that he was still headed toward the river. Unable to stop herself, she spun about and moved as quietly as she could through the shadows, also heading for the river.

"What's keeping that kid?" Blake muttered, glancing toward the back window with a dark scowl. "Didn't he hear me tell him to hurry?"

Reluctantly, Clara pushed herself up out of his lap and crossed the room. Using only the tips of her thumb and forefinger, she parted the dust-coated burlap curtains and looked out into the backyard. "He's not at the well. He must have had to go to the river after all. That's pretty far for him to have to carry a bucket full of water. Maybe I should go help him."

She then turned to look at Blake again, her lips curling into a sensual smile when she noticed that his gaze followed her every movement. She took a teasing step toward him and ran her fingertip across the opening of her blouse, where three buttons had already been undone. "After all, the sooner I get that water, the sooner I can have my bath, and the sooner I'll feel like . . ." She let that last statement go unfinished, aware that Jamie was still in the room. She nodded toward the only inside door, knowing it led to a small bedroom.

378

In the seven hours Blake had been there, he had not bothered to clean away any of the filth that coated the rough wooden floors and most of what furniture had been left behind. Yet he had shaken all the dust off one of the sheets he'd found draped over the table in the kitchen so she would not have to lie directly on such a badly stained mattress. Her heart soared—how considerate he could be at times! Far more considerate than Frank ever thought of being.

She scowled when she thought of her deceased husband, glad now Blake had wanted her enough to kill him, though at the time it had terrified her. Then she smiled again when she remembered the way Blake had openly declared his desire for her and then had taken her to bed that very night. Oh, what a lover he was. He knew how to make her want to do things she'd never thought of doing.

"What about us?" Jamie asked, startling his mother from her private thoughts.

The boy had been so quiet for so long, she had a tendency to forget he was even there. "What about you?" she asked, crossing her arms impatiently.

Jamie took a fearful step back while he gestured to his filthy clothing. "When do Abel and I get to wash up and put on some clean clothes?"

"You can use the water after I get through with it, if that's what you want," she said, annoyed that the child had worried her with such trivial matters. "Then, after you're bathed and changed, you can use whatever water is left to clean this place a little. We won't be leaving here until morning. Might as well do what we can to make it livable."

"You did remember to bring food, didn't you?" Blake interrupted, taking his gaze off Clara's inviting cleavage to glance at the pile of belongings near the

379

door. Beside his own two trunks sat two bulging valises, two stuffed pillowcases tied closed with yellow string, a large box, and a smaller lady's trunk.

"Yes. The food is in the box. I bought enough to last us several days. I'd have bought more, but the man at that livery wanted a lot more money than we'd anticipated."

"We'll stop for supplies after we cross over into Oklahoma," Blake assured her, then rose from the small ladder-backed chair and crossed the room. Lifting the right side of his mouth into an off-centered smile, he pulled Clara into his arms and bent to kiss first her neck, then the flesh that appeared through the opening between her breasts. "Right now, I'm hungry for something a little more sustaining than food. I do wish that kid would hurry with that water."

Turning so that her back was to Jamie, Clara lolled her head back and enjoyed the feel of Blake's hungry lips on her flesh. She moaned softly as she laced her fingers into his thick blond hair.

"Maybe I don't need that bath after all," she murmured, her breath coming in short, ragged gasps. "Maybe I'll wait until I've had a little nap." Then she gestured toward the bedroom door with a slight nod and a sultry smile. "You look like you could use a little nap yourself."

"Just as soon as that kid gets back in here," Blake assured her, his gray eyes dark with passion. He then lifted his lips to her ear so only she could hear his next words. Although he knew the younger child had no choice but to keep whatever secrets he overheard, the older one would be able to repeat everything. And they didn't dare take any chances until they were well on their way. "I want to relock that door so your boys can't escape," he whispered, patting his

380

shirt pocket where he kept the key he'd found. "We won't be able to afford that big fancy house in San Francisco, much less that saloon I want, if we don't have any kids to sell when we get there."

"Then maybe I should go help Abel with the water," Clara suggested again, eager to be alone with Blake. It had been almost a month since they'd lain together, and a month was an awfully, awfully long time.

Blake growled as he dropped his head to her breasts again. "You aren't going anywhere, woman. He'll be back just as soon as he gets that water. After all, we've still got his brother. And that little one isn't about to run off without him. You said that yourself."

"Still," Clara said, letting her eyes droop shut while the desire to be loved filled her being, "I wish he would hurry."

"Abel!" Mark called, his voice so close to a whisper that it had sounded more like a growl.

Startled, Abel dropped his bucket and prepared to run.

"Abel, it's me. Mark."

Careful to keep the trunk of the tree between himself and the house, he waved so the boy would easily spot him in the nearby brush. He'd gotten as close to the clearing as he dared. "Pick up your bucket and come closer to get your water. I don't want Clara to know I'm here."

With eyes as round as saucers, Abel glanced back at the house, then bent to pick up the bucket he'd dropped. Swallowing hard, he walked closer to Mark before stooping to dip the bucket into the water. While the water slowly spilled into the wooden pail, he turned to look at Mark again, as if he could not quite believe he was really there.

"Don't look at me," he cautioned, leaning out from behind the tree to see if anyone else was coming. When he saw no one headed their way, he let out a relieved breath, then continued. "Abel, I'm here to rescue you. But I need to ask a few questions first so I can know exactly what I'm up against in there. What I want you to do is nod your head once for a yes answer or shake it once if the answer is no," Mark instructed him, keeping his voice low. "Do you understand?"

Looking down at the bucket again, Abel nodded once.

"Good. First thing I want to know is if Jamie is in the house and if he is all right."

Abel cut his gray-green gaze at Mark again, clearly perplexed.

"Okay, okay," Mark said reassuringly. "I'll ask them one at a time. Is Jamie in the house?"

Abel nodded that he was.

Mark had expected that. "Is he all right?"

Abel hesitated, as if considering his response, then slowly nodded yes.

Mark let out another relieved sigh and leaned against the tree for support. He had worried about the older boy when Abel had been the one sent outside to get the water, and with a bucket almost as big as he was. He had feared that Jamie had been hurt in some way. "Is there someone else in the house besides Clara and Jamie?"

Again, Abel nodded, indicating there was.

"How many? One?"

Again Abel nodded, this time cutting his gaze back to the house, as if he had suddenly been reminded of something terrible.

"Is it a man?"

Abel's lower lip trembled when he looked at Mark again. Huge tears formed in his eyes. He then glanced into the woods behind Mark before pressing his eyes shut. His quivering lips pursed together as if he wanted to speak, wanted to form the words to tell him what had happened, but couldn't.

"Does the man have a gun?"

Abel's eyes flew open again and he nodded hard. Again his lips pursed as if he wanted to talk.

Having come close enough to hear what was being said, Anna asked the next question. "How many guns?"

Mark had not heard her approach and let out a strangled gasp when he spun around to face her. He threw his hand to his chest in an attempt to still his hammering heart while he tried to recapture his breath. When he finally did, he pressed his lips against his teeth and demanded to know why she was there. "I thought I told you to stay with the horses."

Also using a large tree trunk for a protective shield, Anna met his angry gaze with one of her own. "I tried, but I had to know what was going on."

The muscles in Mark's jaw continued to pulse in and out until finally he realized he would have done the same thing had he been in her place. Eventually, he acknowledged his understanding by nodding, but with it came a sharp warning, "Just don't go sneaking up on me like that again. You almost frightened the very life out of me."

Having temporarily forgotten Abel, he was surprised to hear a low whimpering sound behind him. When he turned back around, he found that the boy was still trying to form words with his mouth.

"What is it?" he asked, aware that whatever the boy wanted to say was of grave importance. "Does it have to do with the man?"

Abel nodded, then suddenly the words burst from his lips. "Two guns."

Anna was so astounded that he had spoken that for a moment all she felt was numb. She wanted to rejoice and break down in tears all at the same time, but knew the situation was far too serious to allow for either. They could rejoice for Abel later. First, they needed to get him and his brother to safety.

"He has two guns?" Mark asked, having recovered from the shock much sooner than Anna. He wanted the number of weapons verified so he'd have a better idea of what he was up against.

Abel nodded, his face contorted with fear. Anna and Mark both wanted to rush out and comfort him, but knew that was impossible.

"H-he w-w-was already h-h-here—" Abel said, stuttering violently, but able to make himself understood.

"He was? He was already here when you arrived?" Mark asked.

Abel nodded. "He t-told her h-h-he—" Abel swallowed, to clear his throat of his rising emotions.

"He told her what?" Anna prompted, afraid he was about to leave it at that.

"He s-said how he wants to s-s-sell us. To a sh-ship captain."

"He told you that?" Mark asked. The muscles in his face turned rock hard as he pressed his weight harder against the tree, waiting for Abel to answer.

"H-h-he said it to h-her."

When Mark turned to see Anna's reaction, he found that all color had drained from her face. She stood leaning against the tree, slightly bent, with her arms crossed over her stomach and her hands curled into fists. Angry beyond belief, he mustered all the restraint he possessed to keep from charging the house unarmed.

But he knew he had to keep his wits about him. He waited until he had drawn a deep, steadying breath, then returned his attention to Abel. "You'd better get on back to the house. We don't want them to suspect that we are out here."

Using both hands, Abel pulled the bucket up out of the water and stood. Setting the heavy bucket down in the grass beside his feet, he turned to face Mark and Anna one last time. "H-he wears one p-pistol on his s-side. The other is on a sh-shelf up high."

"Is it where you or Jamie could get to it?"

Abel shook his head no. "I-it's too high."

"Do you know when they plan to leave here?"

"T-tomorrow."

Tomorrow? Mark exhaled sharply. That certainly did not give them much time.

"Then we'll have to rescue you tonight. Get on back to the house for now. And if you get a chance to talk to Jamie without anyone else hearing you, warn him that we are out here. Tell him not to go to sleep if he can help it. Tell him I will rescue both of you, but it will be sometime after dark."

"P-Promise?"

Abel looked up at him with such hope that it made Mark want to cry. "I promise. We both do. Now you get on back to that house and act as if nothing unusual happened out here."

"And don't let them know you can talk," Anna cautioned, aware they might think it odd that he went out to fill a bucket with water and returned suddenly able to speak again.

Abel nodded that he understood, then bent to retrieve the heavy bucket. Straining from the heavy load, he slowly made his way toward the house.

Unable to resist, Mark peered cautiously from behind the tree, watching while the boy paused again and again to set the bucket down and rest his weary arms. He pressed his lips into a firm line, wondering how in hell he was going to keep the promise he had just made. The man inside that house had two guns to his one, and no doubt he also had two sturdy legs. Whether it came down to open gunplay, or a physical hand-to-hand struggle, the other man had the definite advantage. The odds were not at all in their favor.

At least it would be dark soon.

Chapter Twenty-one

"Harry should have been here by now," Mark said with an impatient huff, then shifted his weight so the ground did not feel quite so uncomfortable. "All I can figure is that he either found another set of tracks and decided to trace them, or somehow got lost trying to locate us."

Because they both expected Harry to try to follow their tracks even in the dark, using one of the lanterns they had purchased in Daingerfield the night before, Mark and Anna had moved well away from the house to wait for him. They wanted to intercept him before the light from his lantern could be seen. But it had been over four hours since the three had parted company, and as of yet, Harry had not appeared.

"You're right. Harry may be lost. But knowing him, he'll keep looking for us until he finally finds us," Anna said, merely stating the facts as she saw them. Then she turned her thoughts to what lay ahead for her if Harry did not return. While concentrating on the different aspects of what could go wrong in the next few hours, she fingered the rounded point of a broken twig she'd absently picked up off the ground beside her. The danger they faced was very real to her, but would be worth the risks they'd be taking.

"I know he will," Mark agreed, then leaned his head back against the tree he'd chosen to use as a back support. He shifted his weight again. His leg ached from his having sat in one position too long. "I just hope he doesn't suddenly show up after we've already set everything in motion. It scares me to think he could come riding up about the time we've begun to approach the house."

Reminded again of all that could go wrong with Mark's scheme, Anna asked, "Should I check to see if the lights are out yet?"

"Might as well," Mark answered, though he was not all that eager to make their move. He loathed the whole idea of Anna having to participate in such a dangerous rescue; but with Harry still missing, he had no other choice. He couldn't do it alone . . . not when there were two adults in that house and a gun for each. No, he needed someone to distract them, and at the moment Anna was his only choice.

Wishing there was some other way, he watched while Anna slipped quietly through the woods, truly amazed at her level of endurance. She had just gone through two days of hard riding with only one meal to speak of, yet she had not complained once. Her only concern was for the boys. It was hard to believe a city woman could be so tough. It was hard to believe *any* woman could be so tough. He swelled with pride while he watched her hurry back to report her find.

"There's only one light now," she whispered as soon as she'd settled back down. The only indication that she was in any pain at all was in the awkward way she had lowered her weight to the ground.

Thinking of how very much he loved her, Mark wished he could think of some way to rescue the boys without having to put her in any danger. "Does that one light look like it's coming through all four windows, or does it appear to be coming from only one or two?"

"If you are trying to decide if there are separate rooms in that shack, it's my guess there are two. The light is only in one section, along the far side, but it takes up nearly a third of the building."

Mark grinned, pleased by how perceptive she was. Good looks and brains, too. What more could a man ask for? "I wonder if they are all four in the lighted room, or if the boys have been separated from the adults." He wished there was some way they could know for certain.

"I guess that would depend on who the man is. If he is a boyfriend of some sort, then I'd think the boys would be in a separate room. But if he's just a friend, then they might prefer to keep the boys close at hand, to make sure they don't try to escape."

"But Clara and her friend have a key, they could keep the boys from escaping easily enough," Mark commented. "All they would have to do is lock the door from the inside, hide the key, then jam the windows so the boys couldn't lift them. Are the windows still closed?"

"As far as I can tell. But I don't see how they can stand it in that house with the windows closed on a night as warm as this."

"You'd be amazed what you can endure for safety's sake. And I'm sure they closed those windows as a precautionary measure to keep the boys from bolting. I think it's a pretty safe bet that Clara and her friend have jammed those windows with tiny wedges of some sort so the boys can't open them and climb out in the middle of the night."

"But if the boys can't open them even from the in-

389

side, then how can I hope to?" Anna asked, concerned that the rescue might go awry before it ever got under way.

"That's true," Mark agreed, nodding thoughtfully, wondering why that had not occurred to him before now. "Forget what I said about it trying to raise the window without anyone hearing. Anyway, the whole idea is for you to distract their attention long enough for me to get the drop on them. Might as well carry a rock or a stick and bust that window open. I'd say to use the pistol, but the way our luck has been, the impact would shatter the gun but leave the window intact. Just remember to be careful if you have to climb in and help. I don't want you to cut yourself on broken glass."

"I know to be careful," she commented, pleased that he was so concerned. "But I still don't see why I'm carrying the pistol. I barely know how to shoot."

"With any luck, you won't have to shoot except once," he explained.

"Still, I think you should carry it."

"I'll need both hands free to try to wrestle the man's gun away from him. I feel pretty sure he'll make a quick grab for his weapon the minute he hears all the noise, even before anyone bothers to light a lamp. Therefore, if I'm successful, I'll be armed quickly enough — with his gun." Having said it aloud made Mark feel a little better about the inner workings of his plan. "Go see if they've turned out that light yet."

It was another twenty minutes before the light went out and another hour before Mark decided it was time to put his plan into action. He wanted to be sure the adults had had plenty of time to fall asleep before attempting anything so dangerous. The only real advantage they had in his scheme was the element of

390

surprise . . . and as long as Abel had done nothing to give their presence away, he should be able to get inside and make his attack before either Clara or her friend realized what was happening.

Praying that Harry would not blunder in after they'd set everything in motion, and hoping that Abel had managed to keep their secret, Mark finally agreed the time had come to move.

Approaching from opposite directions, he and Anna crept slowly toward the house. As planned, with only a sliver of moon offering any light, they both kept to the taller grass and lightly tested the ground with the tips of their boots before putting down any weight. That way they would be less likely to break any twigs or scatter any loose rocks.

Mark reached the back porch first, but waited, motionless in the shadows next to the house until he saw Anna in position beside the bedroom window.

Although they were now only a few yards away from one another to Mark, that distance may as well have been a mile. He could not call to her or reach out and touch her. Suddenly, he wished he had taken the time to give her a good-luck kiss, aware that if something went wrong in the next few minutes, that good-luck kiss would likely have been their last. The thought of that was momentarily devastating, but he pushed it aside. They had a dangerous rescue ahead of them, and that demanded his full attention.

Backing away from the door give himself a running start, Mark glanced toward Anna one last time, to making out little more than her silhouette in the pale moonlight. Then, when he felt certain she was looking at him, he gave the signal. The time had come.

With the pistol in one hand and a large rock poised ready to strike the window in the other, Anna watched while Mark propelled himself toward the door. The very second his shoulder slammed into the wood, causing the door to splinter open, she broke the glass, then lifted the pistol and fired once, at an upward angle, into what they hoped would prove to be the bedroom. Plaster shattered from the ceiling at the same time a scream pierced the night.

"What the hell?" a male voice sputtered from somewhere inside the window.

Anna guessed he was only a few feet away. Quickly she ducked out of sight. The idea was to distract him, not make herself a target.

"Blake, what's happening?"

Anna recognized Clara's voice immediately.

"I don't know. But I sure as hell intend to find out."

When Anna then heard a door open, her heart froze. She wondered if it was because the man had chosen to leave the bedroom or because Mark had entered as planned. She debated peeking inside the window in hopes of finding out, but decided it would be best to follow Mark's instructions to the letter. He'd ordered her to count slowly to twelve before she did anything to help, and she was determined to do just that.

But when she heard what was obviously a struggle inside, and another piercing scream from Clara, Anna lost count. Rather than start again, she returned to the window and with the butt of Mark's pistol began chipping away the rest of the glass.

Enter only as a last resort, he had cautioned her. But at that moment she was too eager to help to take time to reason whether this was what he considered a "last resort." He obviously did not have the man's gun. The element of surprise had not worked like he had planned. She had to help him.

With that thought in mind, she boosted herself into the window and listened to the thuds, grunts, and groans penetrating the darkness. She heard what sounded like a chair or table toppling over.

Turning to face the sounds, she saw a movement, but it was too dark to determine what the movement was or who had the upper hand in the struggle for the gun. Eager to find out if Clara was involved, not wanting Mark to face the odds of two against one, she lowered her foot to the floor and stood cautiously in the broken glass. Wanting to get closer to the crashing sounds coming from across the room, she took a tiny step into the darkness, but was stopped short when something hard and narrow jabbed into her lower back.

"I've got a gun in your wife's back, Mr. Gates," Clara called out. The angry voice had come from inches behind Anna's head.

Suddenly the sounds of struggle stopped, replaced by the rapid gasps of heavy breathing, then the sound of an unfamiliar male voice.

"Gates? How'd you know the man's name is Gates?" Blake asked, clearly perplexed by Clara's keen perception. "It's pitch black in here. You got cat eyes or something?"

"Who else would it be?" she responded, then grabbed Anna by the hair, jerking it loose from its twist. "I am right; it is you, Mark, isn't it? And this is your wife I have over here."

"It is" came the bitter response from across the darkened room.

"I thought so," Clara retorted. "Blake, light a lamp so we can see to tie them up. We need to get out of here."

Knowing Blake was the man Abel had told Mark

393

and Anna about earlier, Anna listened carefully to a faint rustling movement, then the definite striking of a match.

Soon the room was revealed and Anna saw Mark lying on the floor next to a broken table, his face battered, his expression frozen with fear. His blue eyes were trained on the place in her back where Clara pressed the gun.

Anna wanted to cry. It was all her fault. If she had stayed outside as he'd wanted her to, he might have been able to wrestle that pistol out of Blake's hands and it would all be over by now.

When she turned to look at Blake standing beside another small table near the door, she noticed he didn't even have a pistol. All he held in his hand was a smoking match. Mark had attacked the wrong person. Clara was the only one with a weapon. And at that moment, it was pressed painfully into her lower back. Worried the pistol could go off at any moment, Anna did not move. She barely breathed.

"Hurry up and get their hands tied," Clara commanded, her voice starting to reveal her irritation as she let go of Anna's hair and quickly snatched Mark's pistol out of her hand.

When the pressure of the pistol in Anna's back lessened, she decided to try reasoning with her. Moving very slowly so as not to alarm anyone, Anna turned her head to look Clara in the face, surprised to find her standing there stark naked. She did not even have the decency to try and cover her nakedness with her other arm. Frowning, Anna wondered why Clara would be completely naked when Blake had on a pair of unbuttoned trousers and stockings; then she realized she and Mark must have broken in on the two while they were in the throes of passion.

Anna hoped Clara would prove more forgiving of something like that than she would be. "Clara, I think you should know that the judge has indeed received that telegram he was waiting for. He knows you no longer have any legal claim to your sons. What's more, the Pinefield sheriff now knows it, too. If you try to take the boys with you, you will be guilty of kidnapping. You could go to jail."

"How can I be guilty of kidnapping my own sons?" she snapped, then returned her attention to Blake. "Hurry up and find something to tie them with. And get something to gag this one. I don't want to hear any more of her talk."

Instead of obeying Clara's angry commands, Blake quickly crossed the room, slid his hand beneath a rumpled pillow on the bed, then brought out the second gun. At the same time, he shouted to the boys in the other room, "Jamie, Abel, get in here."

Instantly, two wide-eyed little boys dressed in oversized nightshirts appeared in the doorway. "Jamie, go outside and get the rope that's lying in the bottom of my boat, then bring it back here."

Jamie and Abel both stared at him, unblinking, unmoving.

Blake stared at Jamie in disbelief, then took a menacing step toward him. "I told you to go get that rope, and you'd damn well better do it."

When Mark tensed, prepared to leap up and defend them from Blake's attack, Blake noticed the movement. Turning abruptly, he pointed his pistol at Mark's head and narrowed his gaze in clear warning. Though he continued to glare threateningly at Mark, the next words out of his mouth were directed at Jamie. "I told you to go get that rope, and I meant it. Go right now, or I'll splatter this man's head while you stand there watching."

Jamie let out a whimper. "But the door is locked. I can't get outside."

"Climb out the window," he said, motioning to the broken window with a quick wave of his head. "And hurry. Your mother is right . . . we have to get out of here and fast."

Oblivious to the shards of glass scattered across the dirt-encrusted floor, Jamie scampered barefoot across the room, hurled himself over the windowsill, then dropped out of sight.

"You, there. Abel," Blake called, having already turned his attention to the younger boy. "Fetch me my boots. Then take your mother her dressing gown so she can cover herself."

Abel jutted his chin proudly, but did what he'd been told. Meanwhile, Blake's pistol remained pointed at Mark's head and Clara's stayed pressed into Anna's lower back.

"I can't put this on," Clara complained when Abel brought her the bright green dressing gown she had laid across a table near the window. "It has glass all over it."

"Well, you'd damn sure better put something on," Blake warned, his expression harsh. Clearly, he was no more pleased with the way she was parading around than Anna was.

At that moment, Jamie returned with the rope. Whatever argument that may have begun to brew between Blake and Clara was quickly forgotten. As soon as Jamie was inside, Clara withdrew the pistol from Anna's back, but kept it pointed in her direction while she slowly backed toward the bed, careful not to step on any broken glass.

"I guess I might as well get dressed," she commented

aloud, as if it were her own decision, then slowly began to gather her clothes. "We're going to have to get on out of here as soon as we can."

"But for your own sakes, leave the boys with us," Anna tried again. "You'll just end up in a lot more trouble if you try to take them with you."

Blake snorted at that remark. "Honey, you don't know the first thing about trouble."

Clara nodded while she held up her bloomers in preparation for putting them on. "You'll soon find out that Blake's middle name is trouble." Then she chuckled. "Blake thrives on it."

Thinking he had been forgotten, though Blake's pistol was still pointed in his general direction, Mark slowly started to scoot toward the door, then stopped. He was not about to try to escape, not without Anna and both boys. No telling what a man like Blake would do to the others in retaliation.

Having seen the movement from the corner of his eye, Blake turned to face him again. His gray eyes darkened and his nostrils flared in anger as he slowly pulled the hammer back on his pistol, as if planning to shoot. But then, before moving his finger to the trigger, he shook his head and let the hammer back down. "Jamie, tie him up."

Jamie stood frozen to the spot, near the window, only a few feet from Anna. He looked beseechingly at Mark, who promptly closed his eyes in response.

Blake grew impatient. "I said tie him up. You do know how to tie a knot, don't you?"

Jamie nodded, still looking helplessly at Mark.

When Mark reopened his eyes, he met Jamie's with calm reassurance. "It's okay. Tie me up." He then stretched his arms out in front of him and crossed them at the wrists to facilitate the task.

"Not like that. *Behind* his back," Blake commanded, narrowing his eyes with warning. "Tie his hands behind his back then tie his feet in front of him."

Jamie moved slowly toward Mark, his eyes filled with tears. "I don't want to do this," he admitted as he knelt beside Mark and stretched out a length of rope.

"You're going to have to cut the rope into at least four pieces," Blake said, shaking his head as his impatience became laced with disgust. "Can't you think for yourself? Here, bring that rope over here to me."

Within seconds, Blake had drawn a small folding knife out of his pocket and cut the rope into four similar lengths. "Now tie him up right."

Mark was furious over the hateful way the man treated Jamie, but he realized there was nothing he could do about it, not as long as the man held a gun on him. Still, he seethed, wanting to tear Blake's throat right out of his body.

Aware all eyes were on him, Jamie knelt behind Mark and slowly looped the rope around his wrists several times, then bent his head while he concentrated on tying the ends together in a knot.

Blake stood watching until he was sure Jamie intended to follow his orders, then took several steps back so he could sit down in the only chair and tug on his boots. He set the pistol on the table beside him, within easy reach.

While Blake hurried to get dressed, Jamie shifted his weight, leaning toward Mark, then spoke in an almost inaudible voice. "The gun in Mama's hands isn't loaded."

Mark's eyes widened with this bit of information.

"I got the bullets right here." Jamie then patted his nightshirt about where his upper thigh would be, making Mark aware the boy still had on his trousers.

"But the other gun is still loaded. I never could get to it."

"Hey, not so tight," Mark complained loudly, so Blake would not become suspicious of any whispered conversation. "Tying me up is one thing. But cutting off my circulation is another."

"Shut up," Blake shouted, then grinned when he looked at Jamie's startled face. "Don't worry about anything he says. Tie him up as tight as you can."

Mark could tell by the loose tension in the rope that his arms had not been securely tied, but he pretended to struggle against the restraints as if he desperately wished he could break them and free himself. Finally he pretended to give up his struggle and sat glowering at Blake.

When Jamie knelt at Mark's feet and began to tie Mark's legs together, Blake turned his attention to Clara, who had hurriedly turned her stockings right side out and prepared to slip them on.

Mark waited until Jamie glanced up, then offered him a wry wink. But then he scowled angrily and snapped, "Be careful. That leg's been broken before."

Blake looked at him with surprise. "Oh, so *that's* who you are. You're that cripple who's been trying so hard to adopt these boys."

The word *cripple* struck Mark like a sharp blow to the stomach. In the past couple of months, having finally come to accept his limitations, he had quit thinking of himself as a cripple. He had hoped other people had too, but obviously Clara had seen him for what he really was. And it must be true because he had been unable to overpower Blake, even with the element of surprise working in his favor. Part of his problem had been that he'd been unable to get a firm foothold with his lame leg. Whenever he used it to support his weight, it had kept slipping out of place.

Blake's forehead furrowed when he glanced around, as if suddenly searching for something. "But if you're the cripple, where's your cane?"

"I don't have to rely on my cane as much as I used to," Mark said, lifting his chin proudly. "I've pretty well learned to get along without it."

Blake curled his lip to show how unimpressed he was. "Well, if I was you, I'd be real careful not to do or say anything to make me any more angry than I already was so I wouldn't feel obliged to break that leg of yours again." He then gave a cocky shake of his head, but frowned when he noticed Jamie had yet to finish binding Mark's ankles. "Don't pay any attention to his complaints, boy. Hurry up, and get him tied. We still have to get that woman tied up, too. And then we need to get everything loaded in the buggy."

Abel watched his brother with concern, his forehead notched, as if worried Jamie had turned traitor and had done something to hurt Mark.

Mark tried to catch his attention to offer him a wink, too, so he would not worry, but Abel's gaze was locked on his brother.

Meanwhile, Clara had finished dressing and immediately turned her attention to Anna.

"As soon as you're finished with him, bring me those other two ropes," she said to Jamie, then reached for the pistol beside her. "I personally want to tie the ropes on this one."

Slowly she rose from the bed and took several steps until she stood directly in front of Anna, glowering at her. Then without warning she gave Anna a hard shove that sent her sprawling into the broken glass. Abel rushed to help her, but Clara grabbed him by his shoulder and flung him aside, causing him to fall into the broken glass, too. "Leave her be. If she wants to get up, she can damn well do it without any help from you."

Having been challenged, Anna watched her opponent warily while she slowly got back to her feet. Anger filled her to her very soul when she glanced at Abel and saw that his hand was bleeding, but the anger was not enough to make her do anything foolish. While Clara pranced back and forth, waving the pistol in front of her, Anna did nothing to further enrage the woman. Instead, she merely stood there, picking tiny pieces of glass out of her own hands.

"You think you are so good," Clara said, wrinkling her nose with disgust while she flipped a lock of Anna's hair aside with the barrel of the pistol. "Miss Hoity-Toity from New York. Well, I hate to tell you this, Miss Hoity-Toity, but you aren't half the woman I am."

Anna wondered what had brought on this sudden display of animosity, but she refused to say anything in defense of herself. If the woman was this deranged when unprovoked, no telling what she'd do if Anna said something disparaging.

"I said bring me that rope," Clara shouted, having glanced back and discovered that Jamie had finished with Mark but had not complied with her earlier orders.

Reluctantly, Jamie carried the two remaining pieces of rope to her. The hardened muscles in his face revealed the depth of his anger when he held them up to her.

Snatching one of the ropes out of his hands, Clara then turned back to Anna and jerked Anna's arms around behind her, one at a time. She then tucked the pistol under her arm while she stretched the rope out to its full length. "You two boys tie her feet with that other rope while I tie her hands."

Though Abel stood beside them, he refused to help; but Jamie wisely grabbed him by the shoulder and made him squat down and at least look as if he was helping.

"There, now," Clara said with satisfaction when she gave the rope around Anna's wrists a sharp tug. "Let's see you get out of that."

Anna said nothing. She merely stood glaring at her.

"Hurry up, you two," Clara said, annoyed when she discovered that the boys had not finished tying Anna's feet. "Here, give me that rope."

Jamie and Abel backed away while Clara knelt to finish the task. "You two can't do anything right."

All the while Clara was carrying on about the boys' failure to accomplish such a simple task, Blake continued to divide his attention between the commotion across the room and buttoning his shirt. Only occasionally did he bother to glance at Mark, secure in the believe that Mark was firmly tied and no longer a threat.

Pleased by Blake's neglect, Mark kept his attention on everyone else in the room, making sure he was not being watched while he quickly worked to free himself from the rope that held his wrists. As soon as he'd wriggled his hands free, he let the rope fall to the floor. He then bent forward to untie the rope around his ankles, impressed with the way the knot practically fell apart in his hands. Jamie was pretty clever for an eight-year-old.

Blake had not yet noticed him as he slowly rolled over to the broken table and used it as leverage to get to his feet. At the very moment he started toward Blake, Blake glanced up and discovered that his captive was again free. Reaching immediately for the pistol beside him, he discovered he did not have time to take aim before Mark was on top of him.

Having heard the noise, Clara turned in time to see the chair break apart and both men tumble to the floor, the pistol wedged between them. Instantly, she grabbed her own pistol out from beneath her arm and aimed it at the tangled pair. She tried to single out Mark, but was having a hard time distinguishing which was which because of the way they kept twisting around on the floor.

"Stop right now or I'll shoot," she warned, then pulled the hammer back with both thumbs, still trying to aim at Mark.

"I swear, I'll shoot."

Unaware the pistol was unloaded, Anna's felt her heart leap in panic. Instinctively, she toppled forward on top of Clara, hoping to delay the inevitable. Though there was not much else she could do with both her hands and her feet tied, she struggled to keep Clara from getting back up.

"Get off me," Clara shouted, shoving Anna aside. Rising quickly, she stepped far enough away from Anna that she no longer posed a threat, then turned her attention to Blake and Mark.

Anna strained against the ropes in an effort to free herself, and did manage to free her feet — but not soon enough.

Chapter Twenty-two

Lifting the pistol a second time, using both hands, Clara again issued her warning for Mark to stop. When he did not, she waited until he was on top, his body arched high over Blake's in an attempt to wrench the gun from his hands, before she slowly and carefully pulled the trigger. She stared in amazement when nothing happened. Glancing curiously at the silent weapon, she tried to fire it again, and again there was no response, other than a tiny metallic click. Angrily, she flung the useless weapon aside and lunged forward to help Blake.

Anna had managed to struggle to her feet, but realized there was little she could do without the use of her hands. Still, she had to try.

At that moment, both boys burst past her, immediately attacking Clara from behind, knocking her face forward to the floor. Instantly, they were on top of her, wild with their determination to stop her.

By the time Mark had managed to wrestle the pistol away from Blake, Anna had freed her hands and was on her way across the room to help the boys. Although she was as eager as anyone to get her hands on the woman, she realized the boys already had matters well in hand and allowed them to finish taking care of her in their own way. Soon they had Clara pinned to the floor facedown, unable to move. When they looked up at Anna, they smiled triumphantly.

"Got her!"

"That you did," Anna said, glancing down at Clara's prone figure. When she did, she noticed blood on Clara's cheek and arms, and more blood spattered across the floor. Gasping, she wondered just how brutal the boys had been, but then realized the blood had come from the tiny cuts on Abel's hands and Jamie's feet. They, too, were splotched with blood.

She wanted to get a look at those cuts, to see how serious they were; but Jamie wanted no part of it.

"Bring me that rope," he commanded, eager to take charge. He pointed to the rope that Anna had shed from her arms. "We better get these two tied up."

Laughing as much with relief as she laughed at the comical way Jamie then hitched up his trousers through his nightshirt, Anna turned and did exactly what she had been told. She handed Jamie the two ropes Clara had used earlier on her. This time, he accepted the ropes willingly and tied two firm, secure knots, first at Clara's wrists, then at her ankles.

Meanwhile, Mark kept his attention centered on Blake. Because he now had possession of Blake's pistol, Blake sat on the floor, watching his every movement with quiet reserve. Though Blake appeared submissive, Mark knew he was waiting to make a break for it, so he kept the pistol pointed at Blake's chest. Without taking his gaze off his target, he then instructed Abel to bring him the pistol that still lay on the bed—his pistol—and the one Clara had slung across the floor. Abel hurried to do Mark's bidding.

As soon as Clara was securely bound, Jamie crossed the room to retrieve the ropes he had been forced to use on Mark, then headed for Blake, his intention clear.

"Wait," Mark called to him, stopping him. "Don't get too close to him. I don't trust him."

Jamie looked at Mark curiously. "Don't you want me to tie him up?"

"No. I don't want to give him the chance to make a grab for you. With you for a shield, he could make an easy getaway. I think we'd better keep our distance from this one until we can get help."

"But how do we get help way out here?" Jamie wanted to know.

"Can you shoot a pistol?"

"I don't know, I never tried," he admitted, his eyes wide at the thought. "But I *think* I can. I was able to get those bullets out without anyone showing me how. I imagine I can figure out how to pull a trigger the same way."

"Well, there's no time like the present to find out," Mark commented, then gestured to Abel. "Abel, give the unloaded pistol to your brother. He has the bullets for it. You take the loaded one. The three of us will keep a close watch on these two while Anna goes for help."

Now it was Anna's eyes that widened. "I can't find my way out of here in the dark. I wouldn't be able to see where the tracks were. I'd get lost."

Mark frowned, but then his face slowly relaxed. "You can paddle a boat, can't you?"

"I suppose," she said, already guessing what Mark had in mind. "But Cypress Bend doesn't have a sheriff. Is there another town I should try?"

"No. Cypress Bend is the closest. But you should

find someone willing to ride over to Pittsburg and bring back their sheriff. By the time he arrives in Cypress Bend, finds you a horse, and then the two of you reach the spot where Clara's tracks left the road, it should be nearly daylight. With your help, the sheriff should have no problem following the tracks here."

"Will you be safe until then?" she asked, not exactly pleased with the idea of leaving them there.

"As long as we have the guns and they don't, we shouldn't have any trouble," Mark said with a teasing grin. "Now go on . . . it'll take you at least an hour to paddle your way to Cypress Bend. Best get started."

Reluctantly, Anna left, promising to return as quickly as she could with help. Although Cypress Bend was only a few miles upstream, it was almost two hours before she reached the landing near the bridge. To her surprise, the first person she saw when she climbed the narrow embankment toward town was Harry. He had been about to lead his horse down to the water for a drink and was as shocked to see her as she was to see him; but he asked few questions before heading for Pittsburg to get that sheriff.

Harry had little trouble rousing the sheriff from a sound sleep, and Anna borrowed a horse, then met them halfway. But it was daylight before the three reached the spot where Clara's tracks had left the road. By the time they arrived at the second road, the sun was already well on its way into a bright blue summer sky.

Knowing that it had been almost nine hours since she'd last seen Mark or the boys, Anna began to panic. She had not expected it to take so long to get help. What if something had gone wrong in all that

407

time? Mark had had a total of only six hours of sleep over the past three days, and that worried her. He might not be able to stay alert too much longer. She spurred her horse into a fast trot, despite the dense underbrush that tore at her hair and clothing.

The closer she rode toward the house, the harder her heart pounded. She desperately needed to see Mark, needed to see the boys—to reassure herself that they were all safe. But as soon as she had the house in sight, she knew something was wrong, terribly wrong. Popping her reins hard, she forced her horse into a dead run.

"What's wrong?" Harry wanted to know, slapping his own reins hard in an attempt to keep up.

Anna did not explain until she had pulled the horse to a halt and had already climbed down. "The buggy is gone. It was right here when I left, but now it's gone."

Harry's face paled as he too quickly climbed down.

Having overheard Anna's comment, the sheriff reached for his rifle before he, too, dropped down from his horse and turned to face the house.

"Is that the window you were telling me about?" he asked, already headed in that direction.

"Yes, but be careful." Though it hurt to say it, she felt he should be warned. "It's possible that Blake and Clara somehow overpowered Mark and the boys. If that's so, then they could now be armed with three pistols."

"It's my guess that if they somehow managed to do that, they'd have left immediately. Which could be why that buggy is missing."

Anna closed her eyes while the sharp edge of fear pierced deeper into her heart. What if that was true? What if Blake and Clara had overpowered Mark and the boys. What if they had then escaped in the buggy? Would they have bothered to take the boys with them, or had they decided the boys weren't worth the trouble? Tears scaled her eyes. Would she find her family still alive? She didn't dare think about it.

The sheriff waited until he was almost to the window before raising his rifle and shouting at the top of his voice, "Is there anyone in there? This is Sheriff McAck."

There was no response to the sheriff's call. Anna felt as if the air had been sucked out of her. Her stomach clenched with fear.

Sheriff McAck stepped closer. "I said, this is Sheriff McAck. Is anyone in that house?"

"Huh?" came the startled response. "Oh, the sheriff. Yes. We're in the bedroom."

Anna was so overwhelmed with relief that her legs felt suddenly weak. The word *we* indicated they were *all* safe.

Then just as quickly, the feeling was replaced by pure, unadulterated anger. Why hadn't he answered the first time? Was he deliberately trying to frighten her to death? What was he trying to prove?

But when Mark stuck his head out the window only seconds later, she knew the answer to her questions. Mark's hair was tousled and his usually bright blue eyes appeared bleary and drooped.

She knew that look well. Mark had been asleep! While she was out there traipsing across the country, half out of her mind with worry, he had been asleep! Why hadn't he tried to follow Blake and Clara? Just because they had obviously left the boys behind did not mean they should be allowed to get away.

"Where are Blake and Clara?" she wanted to know,

planting her fists on her hips as she glared up at him, undecided whether she should slug him once across the jaw or throw her arms around him and kiss him.

"They're still here," he said, stretching his face and blinking hard, as if still trying to clear his muddled thoughts. "All tied up, nice and neat."

"Then you decided to chance getting close enough to Blake to put a rope around him," she surmised, smiling with relief.

"Nope. I decided to let him tie himself up," Mark said with a dimple-deep grin.

"Tie himself up?" she asked, her eyebrow arched with clear doubt. "How could he do that?"

"It's amazing what a person can accomplish when he has three pistols pointed at his head." Mark then leaned forward and handed her the key. "Here, let yourself in and I'll tell you all about it."

Anna was eager to know what had happened to the buggy and to hear how Mark had managed to talk Blake into tying himself up. However, Harry and the sheriff both wanted to hear the story from the very beginning and made them start with the part about having followed Clara's tracks to the clearing. Then Mark told how they had then decided to wait until dark before approaching the house. When Harry then heard the part about Abel talking, he immediately held up his hands to stop him.

"Wait a minute. Hold everything," he said, turning to look at Abel with a raised brow. "You say *Abel* told you all about this fella Blake being in the house. Don't you mean *Jamie* told you?"

"No, it was Abel," Mark said proudly. "And it was his information that made it possible for us to rescue them."

"You're not funnin' me about this, are you?" He then walked over to where the two boys stood near the front door and knelt down so he could look Abel directly in the eye. "Are they tellin' me the truth? Did you really talk?"

Abel nodded that indeed he did.

Harry cocked his head to one side, as if he still wasn't quite sure he believed that. "Prove it. Say somethin' to me."

Abel's smiled dimple deep then threw his arms around Harry's neck. "Grandpa!" he shouted as clear as could be.

Harry was so overwhelmed that he fell backward, bringing the boy down on top of him. "What did you say?"

"I said *Grandpa!* Y-you *are* still my Grandpa, aren't y-ya?"

"You bet I am," Harry responded, wrapping his arms around the boy. Blinking hard, he buried his face in Abel's dark curls, then repeated in an emotionally strained voice, "You can just bet I am."

There was a long moment of silence before the sheriff finally spoke. "I hate to break up this fine reunion, but I really need to get you all back into town so I can get all this straightened out." He pointed to Clara, who sat near the table with her hands still tied behind her back. "This woman claims to be the boys' mother, but you two claim you are their legal parents."

"We are," Mark said, hoping to reassure him.

"That very well may be, but I'd feel a lot better about all this after I've had that fact verified by someone in Pinefield."

"Of course, we understand," Mark said then glanced at Jamie. "Why don't you go get the horses?"

411

Suddenly Anna was reminded of the missing buggy and demanded to know what had happened to it.

"Nothing. The horse got a little tired of being tied up to the blame thing and decided to express his opinion in the middle of the night. Since Blake and Clara were both tied to the bed by that time, I decided the only way I was going to get any sleep at all was to let the animal have a bit of freedom. While I was out, I not only unhitched Clara's horse, but then fetched our horses out of the woods and unsaddled them, too. You'll find all three of the animals staked out by the river, where they can get plenty of grass and water."

"Where?" Anna wanted to know. "I didn't see them."

"Were you looking for them?" he asked, chuckling at her puzzled expression.

"Well, no, but you'd think I'd at least have noticed them," she muttered, feeling a little foolish for having overreacted as she had. Then, cocking her head to one side, she looked at him with renewed suspicion. "If that's so, where'd you put the buggy? Surely I didn't overlook that too." If he told her it was also right outside, she was going to the doctor and have her eyes examined.

"I put the buggy in the shed along with both saddles," he said, then laughed at the relief in her expression. "Want to see for yourself?"

"No, I believe you," she commented, frowning because she felt foolish again.

"Well, I don't know about you two," Harry put in, ready to take some of the attention off Anna. "But I'm ready to get on out of here. Come on, Sheriff, I'll help you get these two desperadoes outside." He ges-

412

tured toward Blake and Clara with a cocky toss of his head, then turned to Mark. "Want me to rehitch that buggy for you? I'd be more than glad to drive it on out of here."

Knowing how long Harry had been in the saddle, and having noticed the way he'd started to walk with a slight hitch, Mark had no doubt that his friend would be absolutely delighted to drive the buggy rather than climb back into his saddle. "That would be fine. That way, you and Abel could take the prisoners in the buggy while Jamie rides your horse."

Harry motioned for Abel to follow him outside. They paused near the door and turned to wait for the sheriff to escort his two prisoners outside.

Before stepping through the door, Blake turned to face Mark with a look of pure hatred. "I can't believe I let a damn cripple get the best of me."

Mark's shoulders stiffened, but he made no comment while he watched the sheriff grab him by the arm and push him on outside. Harry and Abel exchanged glances, then followed the pair.

As soon as everyone had left, Mark turned to Anna and shrugged. "Imagine that," he said, gazing down into Anna's worried face with a look of pure disbelief. "That man thinks I'm a cripple." Then his look of disbelief gave way to a wide, teasing smile. "I wonder where he ever got an idea like that?"

Anna searched his eyes for any hint of pain, for she knew how badly the word *cripple* had tormented him in the past. When she saw none evident either in his eyes or in his playful expression, she responded cautiously. "I don't know where he could have gotten an idea like that. Probably just a nasty rumor he'd heard somewhere. You know how rumors can be."

Mark chuckled and took a tiny step in her direction. "Yes, I do. I heard a good one the other day. I heard that old Mark Gates went and got himself married."

"Oh, he did?" she answered, relieved to know he was so unaffected by the nature of their earlier conversation. "I hear he's a real ogre. I wonder who would ever marry someone like him."

"Probably some mindless little twit," he answered, his blue eyes sparkling with amusement. "But the way I hear it, she's as pretty as they come."

"Mindless twit?" she responded, then lifted her chin with righteous indignation. "I'll have you know she's a lot smarter than he deserves."

"I agree," Mark said, ready to give up the game before it got out of hand. "Come here." He then opened his arms to her and enveloped her in a warm but tired embrace. "I've gone way too long without holding you."

"And I've gone too long without being held," she said, pressing her cheek against his chest, reveling in the feel of his arms around her. "I'm so glad to know you and the boys are safe. You don't know how frightened I was when I noticed the buggy gone and thought Blake and Clara had gotten away. I was so afraid they had hurt you."

"You don't have much confidence in me, do you?" he asked, his tone still playful.

"Oh, I have plenty of confidence in you. I just know how little sleep you've had these past few days."

"I've had more sleep than you have," he pointed out.

Remembering that he'd been asleep when they arrived, she nodded. "That's true. And to tell you the truth, I feel about ready to drop. In fact, I'd do just about anything for a long, hot bath and a nice, soft bed."

"Anything?" he asked, his eyebrows arching with sudden interest while he lifted her chin so he could see into her beautiful green eyes.

"Anything," she murmured in a soft, sultry voice, then brought her gaze up to meet his as she ran the tip of her tongue over her lower lip in a most beguiling manner.

"I'll get the water."

Contemporary Fiction From
Robin St. Thomas

Fortune's Sisters
(2616, $3.95)

It was Pia's destiny to be a Hollywood star. She had complete self-confidence, breathtaking beauty, and the help of her domineering mother. But her younger sister Jeanne began to steal the spotlight meant for Pia, diverting attention away from the ruthlessly ambitious star. When her mother Mathilde started to return the advances of dashing director Wes Guest, Pia's jealousy surfaced. Her passion for Guest and desire to be the brightest star in Hollywood pitted Pia against her own family — sister against sister, mother against daughter. Pia was determined to be the only survivor in the arenas of love and fame. But neither Mathilde nor Jeanne would surrender without a fight. . . .

Lover's Masquerade
(2886, $4.50)

New Orleans. A city of secrets, shrouded in mystery and magic. A city where dreams become obsessions and memories once again become reality. A city where even one trip, like a stop on Claudia Gage's book promotion tour, can lead to a perilous fall. For New Orleans is also the home of Armand Dantine, who knows the secrets that Claudia would conceal and the past she cannot remember. And he will stop at nothing to make her love him, and will not let her go again . . .